Praise for Lulu Taylor

'Utterly compelling. A really excellent winter's story'
Lucy Diamond

'Taylor is at the top of the chick-lit tree with her
beautifully written, emotionally compelling stories,
and this is perfectly timed for Christmas'
Daily Mail

'[This] engrossing romantic saga is a
hugely enjoyable, escapist treat'
Sunday Mirror

'Pure indulgence and perfect reading
for a dull January evening'
Sun

'Wonderfully written . . . this indulgent read
is totally irresistible'
Closer

'A creepy story of obsession and deception.
Very chilling'
Irish Sunday Mirror

THE
SNOW
ROSE

Lulu Taylor moved around the world as a child before her family settled in the Oxfordshire countryside. She studied English Literature at university and had a successful career in publishing before she became a writer. Her first novel, *Heiresses*, was published in 2007 and nominated for the RNA Readers' Choice award. It was followed by *Midnight Girls*, *Beautiful Creatures*, *Outrageous Fortune*, *The Winter Folly*, *The Snow Angel* and *The Winter Children*. She lives in Dorset with her husband and two children.

By Lulu Taylor

THE
SNOW
ROSE

LULU TAYLOR

PAN BOOKS

First published 2016 by Pan Books
an imprint of Pan Macmillan
20 New Wharf Road, London N1 9RR
Associated companies throughout the world
www.panmacmillan.com

ISBN 978-1-4472-9098-8

5 7 9 8 6 4

A CIP catalogue record for this book is available from the British Library.

Typeset by Ellipsis Digital Limited, Glasgow
Printed and bound by CPI Group (UK) Ltd, Croydon, CR0 4YY

Visit www.panmacmillan.com to read more about all our books
and to buy them. You will also find features, author interviews and
news of any author events, and you can sign up for e-newsletters
so that you're always first to hear about our new releases.

To all the Taylor girls out there

PART ONE

Chapter One

Heather is behind me in the car. I can see her as I drive. Sometimes she's gazing out of the window, and at other times she's humming or talking quietly to herself, expressions flitting over her face like bright little shadows. I wonder what's going on in that head of hers. She's always been full of whimsy and imagination. She's been quieter and more serious lately, but that's hardly surprising.

She never asks me where we are going.

Occasionally I catch a glimpse of myself in the rear-view mirror – just the glint of peroxide-white hair, or the frame of my sunglasses – and I wonder who on earth I'm looking at. I feel a jolt of fear, a rush of panic that makes my palms prickle and the ends of my fingers tingle, and have to fight the urge to press down on the accelerator and escape. Then I remember that this stranger is me.

Peroxide-white hair. What was I thinking?

I'm supposed to be anonymous. And here I am, with a platinum bob and a smear of scarlet lipstick on my mouth, looking like something from a science-fiction movie or a spy thriller. I'm even wearing a black trench coat, and my boots have a heel of almost an inch. My theory is reverse psychology: surely everyone will expect me to fade into the background, not draw attention to myself. They might suspect I'll change my appearance, but not to this.

Rory once gave me a hat – a big brown fedora sort of thing, the kind with a countryside look about it. I used to wear it out shopping because, I discovered, it concealed me. People I knew would walk by me in the street. The hat was all they noticed, and their innate desire not to be seen to stare prevented them from dropping their gaze to my face.

That was in my mind when I bought the box of peroxide. By looking extreme, I hope, I will automatically deflect the looks I most want to avoid: the searching gaze at my eyes, the frown as they realise I look familiar. Instead they will look at the bright white hair and that will draw them away from the things that mark me out as me. The things I cannot change.

I had planned to disguise Heather too. I bought gingery-red hair dye for her, and I was going to face-paint freckles on her nose and cheeks. Then I found I couldn't bring myself to do it. So I decided I would cut her hair; the feathery blonde tresses would have to go. I'd give her something totally different, a tomboy cut, perhaps even dress her as a boy. But I couldn't. I picked up the scissors and I couldn't alter her. So she looks now just as she always has: large china-blue eyes, thick, straight lashes, the chin that has a little round bump with a dimple in it – inherited from her father. And the fair hair rippling over her shoulders.

'Are we nearly there yet?' Heather asks from the back.

She has taken everything in her stride. All the huge changes in her young life. Everything that has happened between Rory and me. The departure from her home. The strange days we've spent together since then, before I discovered our new place. Our hideout.

I say cheerfully, 'Not long now, sweetheart. Maybe an hour or so. Not too much longer.'

Heather goes back to staring out of the window. Where did she learn this patience of hers? She's always been so self-sufficient, so able to retreat into herself and find everything she needs there.

'Do you want a story?' I ask. 'I can put a CD on for you.'

'*Winnie the Pooh*?' she says eagerly. We had it earlier, but I don't mind if she wants it again. I can shut out the narrator's voice and think. An entire CD can play and I won't hear a word of it.

'Yes,' I say, and push the button to start up the story. The music begins and Heather smiles. I watch the road, mile after mile disappearing under my wheels, hoping that where we're going is far enough.

I'm in a hire car. I didn't use my own because I know that every car on the motorway is recorded on camera and that there's an automatic number plate recognition system that means anyone using a major road can easily be tracked. I don't have a satellite navigation system for fear that I can be traced by it, so the journey takes an age because I follow the minor roads through countryside and small towns and villages. Not only that, but I've taken a strange, circular route, miles out of my way, in order to confuse anyone who might be on my trail. Every now and then I have to stop in a lay-by and learn the next bit of the route. I can't hold the whole thing in my mind in one go. That's something else that's happened recently: my short-term memory is kaput and things fall out of it swiftly and completely. As we near our destination after a long day driving, the route becomes more complicated and I have to stop more frequently. Heather has dozed off in the back of the car, her head lolling against the side of her safety seat. I'm glad. The journey has been tedious, the breaks at service stations limited to refilling petrol and quick loo visits, and the starts and stops only make it worse. I'm muttering to myself – road names, the order of right and left turns, the exits of roundabouts. We're in a part of the country I do not know well at all, and I feel almost as if we have gone abroad.

Perhaps that's what they will think. That's where they'll be looking.

I laid as many clues as I could to give the idea that we were leaving Britain. I emailed for information on accommodation in France, Italy and Spain. I bought tickets for planes, trains and ferries, creating a trail that led away in many different directions, hoping it would all cause enough confusion to buy me some time. But it probably won't fool anyone. There won't be a record of us going anywhere. Our car won't actually roll onto the Channel ferry, or our luggage be put in the hold of an aeroplane while we take our seats in the cabin. There won't be any CCTV footage of us, a white-haired woman in sunglasses holding hands with a small girl, as we walk through a terminal or pass through security. Our passports, scanned and checked, would surely be logged somehow to show that we'd crossed the border. Isn't that what happens? Don't they keep tabs on us all?

The problem is that I don't really know. But I've absorbed, somehow, the impression that we cannot hide, not these days. The speed of communication, the networks that surround us, the cameras filming us, the satellites tracking our movements, our electronic footprints – it all means that we can't go unnoticed for long. And when there is a child involved, there is no doubt that all those glassy, electric eyes will swivel after us, the virtual hounds on our trail, sniffing for our scent, waiting for us to flag our presence with one inadvertent touch of a button.

Which is why I needed an accomplice.

'You have to help me,' I said urgently, commandingly. I'd never spoken to Caz like that before and she gazed at me, afraid, cowed by me. There must have been something in my expression that told her that things were different now. I'd been ministering to her for years, while she got over what happened with Philip. I was always there, ready to talk, sympathetic, focusing on her troubles. But that was over. Now she would do what I wanted.

'But . . . how? What can I do?' She looked confused. It's strange, how people press their help on you, offer to do whatever it takes – right up until you say, 'All right then. You can help,' when suddenly it's not so possible after all. But I wasn't going to let Caz wiggle out of anything.

'I'll need money. I can't use the cashpoints. And I need some new ID details, so I want to use your address because it's not linked to me.'

'Use my address?'

'Pretend I live there. Don't worry, you won't even get any post because I'll put a redirection on it. It's just for their systems. It won't make any difference to you, I promise.'

Caz blinked at me, suddenly weak and helpless in the face of my strength and determination. 'You shouldn't do this, Kate,' she said in a small voice. 'It's the wrong thing, I promise you. You're going to regret it.'

'You don't know what I'm doing,' I said briefly.

'You're leaving. You're going away. I know you won't tell me where. It's not right, Kate. I'm telling you, you shouldn't do it.'

'You don't understand. It's all I can do,' I said. 'I don't have a choice.'

And I was right. It was only this that was giving me the strength to carry on. I was drawing my life force from the need to escape. The urgency of planning, the lists of what had to be done, all of this prevented me from falling into the black abyss that yawned – that yawns every day – below me. That, and Heather.

So Caz said yes, as I knew she had to. She helped me, letting me use her address and keeping quiet about what she suspected. Even so, I made sure that she knew as little as possible. I created a new email account and only accessed it from the public computers in the library, securing it with passwords unlike anything I'd used before. I applied for a credit card in my fake name and it duly arrived, redirected from Caz's house. Do these people ever check anything? Once I began to immerse myself in the plans, I even began to relish the game. What strategies could I think of to get around the people who might or might not be watching me? How could I trick them? I felt as though I was tapping into some primal desire to outwit the enemy, or like I was the leader of some small band of rebels working out how to escape a greater, more powerful foe. Robin Hood against the Sheriff. Boudicca against the Roman Empire.

And all the time I had to keep Rory from guessing what I intended to do. When we spoke on the telephone, which I tried to avoid, he'd always ask me, 'You're not planning on doing anything stupid, are you?'

'Of course not.' *As if I would tell you . . .*

'You sound . . . different,' he said just a few days before I planned to go. He'd called in the evening and I'd scooped up the phone and answered it automatically, before realising it was just the time he'd ring me.

'Really?' I tried at once to sound normal.

'Yes.'

'How?'

'Quivery . . . I don't know. Pent-up. Are you okay?'

I said nothing for a moment. I honestly had no idea how to answer that question. As I thought about it, hot rage flooded through me, twisting through my stomach and pounding at my brain. *What the hell do you expect? Okay? Okay? Nothing will ever be okay again!*

The line between us was heavy with silence. I could hear

only the faint whisper of Rory's breathing. I knew it was hopeless waiting for him to fill it. Rory was the master of silence. He could tolerate pauses so long I had to bite my tongue not to scream at him to say something, bloody *anything*, just something to fill the emptiness. It would not have been so bad if I hadn't known that his head was full of talk, he just refused to bring it out into the open. He'd only speak once he'd processed everything to his satisfaction, while I used talking as a way of understanding my own thoughts, something he could find incredibly tedious. So we each made the other suffer in our own way.

'I'm fine,' I said at last. The familiar bad taste was in my mouth again. Bitterness.

'Can I come and see you?'

'No,' I said instantly.

'Okay. That's absolutely fine.' The tone of mollification in his voice made me bristle. After a pause, he said, 'Have you seen the counsellor?'

'It's pointless,' I said briefly.

'It might help,' he said gently. 'I wish you'd give it a go.'

'Maybe. Maybe soon.' The idea that an hour of chat with a stranger might go any way to beginning to solve our mess seemed ludicrous. Like tackling a mountain of dirt with a spoon. There's too much, it's all too gargantuan. 'But not yet.'

'When? Next week?'

It was on the tip of my tongue to tell him that by next week, I'd be far away, out of his reach. I'd have escaped. I knew his plan was to take Heather away from me, even though he pretended it wasn't. I couldn't risk that happening, not now she is all I have.

'Yes, maybe next week,' I said, happy to throw him a bone. I'd managed to escape him, though he didn't yet know it.

'Shall I book the session for you? I'll pay for it,' he said, a hopeful eagerness in his voice. 'What time would suit you? Wednesday? I know there's a slot on Wednesday.'

'Yes. All right then. Wednesday. Text me the time. I'll be there.'

'That's great,' he said, his relief audible. 'It's the first step, Kate. The first step.'

'Yeah.' I shrugged. 'You're right. The first step.'

'You could . . . could talk about Ady, perhaps.'

That was too much. 'No!' I shouted. The shaking took hold of me instantly. I could feel my head trembling on my neck as though I was a badly handled marionette; my fingers were thrumming, my knees horribly light with the juddering nerves inside. 'Don't even say it, Rory!'

'Okay, okay, I'm sorry, I'm sorry. Calm down. No one will make you talk about anything you don't want to.'

You're right, buster. No one will. 'You know how I feel,' I managed to say. The trembling had reached my voice, my mouth and lips. I could barely get a word out. My shoulders jerked with the force of my shaking. 'I c-c-c-can't.'

'I'm sorry, Kate. Really. I shouldn't have said anything. Look, I have to go. But I'll book the session. We'll go from there.'

'Fine. Goodbye.'

I clicked the phone off, put it down and closed my eyes. I

knew exactly what he was trying to do. The counselling would be the first step in his relentless attempt to take Heather away from me. And there was just no way that was going to happen. I had to make a choice, and I knew exactly what I would choose.

'Kate?'

I jumped. It was two days before I planned to go and I was fuelled by adrenaline and nerves.

'What on earth are you doing here?' It was Sandy, my boss, gazing at me with a worried expression as I sat there at my desk.

'I'm . . . I really wanted to catch up on some things,' I said. Even though she couldn't see my screen, I swiftly changed to the homepage while drawing her gaze by patting the pile of papers next to me. I'd got them out just in case. The truth was that I was surfing the internet, having logged on as my old assistant, whose details were still live on the system. I'd notified IT ages ago that she'd left but they had not got round to deactivating her profile. It was lying there, unused, a safe little passageway onto the web. I'd stopped feeling comfortable at the library. As I huddled at my screen, I kept imagining people looking curiously over my shoulder, or the staff beginning to notice me and my visits to the computer terminals. Of course, there was no reason why I shouldn't be like all the other regulars. I'd begun to recognise them: the little crew of users. Job seekers, probably, mostly young people who plugged in headphones and bobbed in time to tinny music as they tapped away at the keyboard or moved the mouse, staring at the screen with complete absorption. I wondered if I stood out among them, and had lain awake at night thinking about it, wondering how I could get round the problem of not wanting to use the library. I needed the net. It was only once I'd thought about how I might operate without it that I realised how deeply it was now woven into the thread of my life. It provided the information and communication I needed, particularly if I wanted to move at speed. I suppose some people are still content to write a letter by hand, post it and wait for the reply that might or might not come, but I was no longer one of them. I wanted answers today. This afternoon. Within the next hour. Now. Now. Now. There was no time to lose. And that's when I had the idea of coming into work. Immediately, I wondered why I hadn't thought of this solution before. I'd fallen asleep, newly relaxed, almost at once.

Now, as Sandy stood in front of me, concern all over her face, and a certain wariness in her gaze, I realised why this was not going to be as simple as I'd hoped.

Why is nothing easy? Why can't I just do what I want?

She said slowly, 'That's really admirable, Kate. But honestly, you don't need to. We are perfectly able to cope without you while you take the time you need. Lindsey is doing a great job at covering for you.'

I took a deep breath. Time for some more obfuscation. 'Well, I know, but actually, I'm feeling a lot better and I just need to . . . I just need to . . . do something.' I smiled at her, my expression, I hoped, winsome, and perhaps a touch pleading. 'I'm going crazy at the house with nothing to do. I just felt the urge to come in and tidy up some loose ends. I thought about emailing Lindsey, and then I thought what the hell, I'll just come in and do it myself . . . and I did.'

Sandy smiled back at me. It was all there in her eyes. I could read what they'd been saying about me, what they were thinking – lots of sympathy, lots of interest, lots of 'there but for the grace of God' stuff. They're good people, but they're people all the same. We all, in the end, look at others and wonder if they really feel or think or understand things the way we do. Or we mull on someone's circumstances for a while, then go back to the confines of our own existence with all its multifarious problems and pleasures.

At the moment, no one wants to be where I am, and the reality doesn't bear too much thinking about. They close it out and go back to worrying about all the little things that take up so much space until one day the big thing comes that makes everything else look like so much pointless trivia and you long for the time when a shit day was one where the boiler broke down, or the car got dented, or you overstayed in the supermarket car park and they gave you a fine. All the meaningless irritants that can't really touch you.

I had come into the office as early as possible to avoid the stares and glances, and the swooping of concerned colleagues. When I had arrived, the night security guard was still on duty at the reception desk. He watched blank-eyed as I flashed my badge at him, and said nothing, clearly not recognising me, and the fourth floor was empty and silent but for the low hum of the photocopiers and hard drives. I forgot that Sandy likes to get in to the office extra early on the days when her nanny leaves at four. She must have seen me when she came out to get some coffee from the kitchenette.

'Kate,' she said softly, 'there's really no need. Everything is taken care of. I don't mean your job has vanished. It hasn't. We'll wait until you're in the right place and then we'll be delighted to have you back. But I don't think you should rush it. It hasn't been very long . . .'

'All right, all right,' I said, and my eyes flicked to the screen. I would log out now. It was obvious I had to leave. 'I know. I really do. But . . .' I smiled again. 'It's weird the way things can play on your mind. I feel better now I've sorted it out.'

I hadn't. I hadn't done anything. But it didn't really matter. Lindsey would have done it, she's so efficient.

'I'm glad you feel better. But I don't think this is the right place for you at the moment.'

I bristled at her words, though I hid it. She might mean to be sympathetic, kind and constructive but for an instant I heard her telling me that I was bringing something awful with me into the workplace. I was tainting it. They didn't want me bringing in my turmoil. I was someone leprous now, unclean. Should I be ringing a little bell to warn of my approach so that the whole and healthy could get out of my way before I infected them and their happy, comfortable little worlds? I couldn't speak as these thoughts raced wildly through my mind. Sandy put out a hand towards me, her expression sorrowful.

'Kate. We're all so sorry.'

'Yes. Thank you. I got the flowers.' I managed a smile.

'If it would ever help to talk, I'm here for you.'

'Thank you.' I shut down my computer and got to my feet. 'That's kind of you. Really.'

'Let's be in touch about when you'll be ready to return. We'd like you back. When you're up to it.'

'Yes, yes . . .' I grabbed my coat from the back of my chair. 'That's great. I'll be sure to let you know. Bye, Sandy. And thanks again.'

I headed out before she could say more. I didn't want pity and sympathy, I just wanted to be able to get on with things. There was so much to do. I was in a rush. I had to get away. There wasn't time to think about everything.

Rory called me that evening. I knew it was him. One glance at the clock and it was obvious. It was eight o'clock and I was busy clearing up after putting Heather to bed. Her supper things were still on the table, her bowl too full of abandoned macaroni cheese for my liking. She'd never been a hearty eater, usually eating so slowly that she managed to kill her appetite before she'd really had enough to constitute a meal, but some dishes, the ones she loved, disappeared extra fast. Lately she'd been eating less and less, and although I was cooking up her favourites as often as possible, I couldn't seem to get enough into her. I was scraping most of what I cooked into the compost bin.

I'll feed her up tomorrow, I promised myself, and then wondered what I would eat. I didn't much like macaroni cheese but my appetite for everything had diminished. I couldn't seem to taste anything anymore. The bitterness in my mouth was too strong for food to overcome, and without the

16

pleasure of taste, food became a boring necessity. More often than not, I put some bits of cheese on some crackers and ate that. Sometimes I remembered to pick up a pot of mackerel pâté, or something I could grill quickly and easily. I noticed in a vague way that I was losing weight, but it didn't matter to me a bit. Once I would have gloried in the way I had to pull my belt to the very last hole, and then make a new hole, or revelled in the feeling of my clothes falling away from my skin, the bagginess at the back of my jeans. Now I couldn't care less. My only concern was that I had to stay well, for Heather's sake. She needed me.

When the phone rang, the irritation surged through me. Couldn't he leave me alone? Why keep pestering me like this? It wasn't going to make any difference.

'What do you want, Rory?'

'Just to talk to you for a bit. See how you are.'

'I'm fine.'

'Can I come over?'

I glanced around at the mess still waiting to be dealt with: dirty saucepans, the colander, spoons, the sauce-spattered worktop, the yellow strands of grated cheese that had fallen about. 'No. I'm busy.'

'What are you doing?'

'Rory . . .'

'What?'

'It's none of your business what I'm doing.'

'I think it is. I care about you. You're my wife.'

'For now,' I said briefly. I didn't care what he made of that.

I didn't care about hurting him. After all, what could really hurt us now?

'Kate.' His voice was heavy with sadness. 'This doesn't have to happen to us. We can get through it.'

'I don't think so.' I meant it. I really didn't think it was possible. I could vaguely remember that we were happy once. He made me laugh so much. He cherished me and protected me, and we built a life together. Then he spoiled everything. He drove us apart. And no matter what he thought, I was sure it could never be put back together.

'I wish you'd let me see you, so we can talk.'

'What will we talk about?' Immediately after I said it, I wished I hadn't. I couldn't open the way to that. 'Listen, you can't come round. I'm sorry. We'll talk another time.' I put the phone down and stared at it for a moment. I supposed Rory and I would divorce at some point, when I'd got the time to think about it and the strength to tackle the dreary admin it would involve. The business of the house. The division of money and belongings, such as we had left. What would happen to Heather. The other unspoken things.

He's not taking her away from me. It's what he wants. It's what they all want.

Now here we are, in this grand but deserted old place. Just the two of us. *Safe at last.* I know they think I shouldn't keep her. My mother thinks it. That's why I won't see her either, or my sister. They're in cahoots with Rory, all of them scheming how to get her away from me. That's why I have escaped them while I can, while I still have the opportunity.

*

I'm outside the bedroom, looking through the crack in the door. The lights inside are off. I can make out the dark shapes of the bed and the man sitting on the edge of it. I hear the small voice asking, 'Daddy, are you going to die? Will Mummy die? Will Heather die?'

The answer is gentle. Firm, but absolute. 'Yes. We'll all die.'

'When? Will we die soon?'

'We might. No one knows.'

I can hear Rory's resolute emphasis on honesty. We always said we won't lie to the children. We'll tell them the truth about everything. About how they were born (no gooseberry bushes or storks), about what they can expect from life, about how transient it is, with no promise of God or afterlife or anything like that. We won't fudge, or patronise, or condescend. We'll tell the truth.

The boy's voice is anxious. 'Tomorrow? Will you die tomorrow, Daddy?'

'I might. We could all die at any time.'

'Don't go out tomorrow, Daddy!' The fear vibrates through his voice. I can almost see him clutching hard at his father's hand. 'Stay at home where it's safe.'

'C'mon now, buddy. It's not that likely. I'm sure it will all be fine. The chances are that I'll make it through tomorrow.'

'And the day after?'

'Probably.'

'But . . .'

'One day we'll all die. It's horrible, but that's the way it is. Now, shall we talk about something else?'

But the boy can't talk about anything else. He only wants to talk about death until at last he is persuaded to sleep.

'For God's sake,' I say later, when we're in front of the fire, glasses of wine on the table before us, 'just tell him you won't die!'

'But I can't guarantee it.' Rory sighs. I can tell he hates the thought of causing pain but that he's made a decision and feels he should stick to it.

'Can't you see you're scaring him? Is that really the best way?'

'I won't lie to him. Didn't we always say we'd tell them the truth?'

I look over at Rory, his brown eyes so full of sincerity and so well meaning. I already know he's lying to me, every day. He's been lying for months. And I can't help thinking we don't know the truth. We don't know anything.

Chapter Two

It's dark when we finally arrive at our destination, which lies behind a long, high wall some way from the nearest village. There is a pair of vast iron gates at the roadside, and I have to get out to open them. They are padlocked, but there is a key-safe box on the brick gate pillar, openable with the code they sent me via email. I tap in the series of numbers and it clicks open obediently, flooding me with relief.

See? It's all going to work. You just need to know what you're doing, and everything comes right.

A bunch of keys lies inside the metal locker, limp on the end of a worn leather keyring. There are several on the ring, and I have to try a few before I find the one that undoes the padlock. Then I push the heavy gates open and get back into the car to drive through, before jumping out again to close and lock the gates. I like the feeling of snapping the padlock shut and letting the chain drop against the railings. As far as I know, no one has seen us drive in. And now I've locked the rest of the world out. As I get back in the car, I see that Heather is awake.

'Are we there?' she asks, straining at the belt of her seat. Her wide blue eyes stare through the car window at the murky shadows beyond. The driveway is edged with high, overgrown shrubbery.

'Yes, we're here.' I sound jolly, reassuring. *Everything is all right. There's nothing to be afraid of.*

The headlights pick out a huge shape ahead of us as the car crunches up the gravel drive. It's hard to make out much. I've seen pictures, of course, the photos on the website, but the place is blanketed by darkness.

'We're at the house I told you about,' I say cheerfully. 'Isn't it amazing? It's like our very own castle!'

I gaze at the vast building in front of us, only a small portion of it illuminated by the car's headlights. It's brick built, and the pattern looks crazed, improbable, in this light, a herringbone madness of red blocks and black lines. We've stopped in the forecourt, a gravelled rectangle in front of the house, and there's nothing to show that there's any life within. The house is so large that it retreats into the shadows, a great mass of a thing. It's so much bigger than I expected. I wonder if it is as beautiful as it looked in the photographs, with its elegant lines and large windows, three storeys under gabled roofs ornamented with high chimneys.

'Is this our new home?' Heather sounds tired, and I can tell she just wants to be asleep somewhere warm and safe, that isn't moving. But when I glance in the rear-view mirror, I also notice how overwhelmed and intimidated she looks. Her blue eyes are wide and questioning, a little afraid.

'For now,' I say with determination, and undo my seat belt.

'It's going to be fine. I promise. The first night in a new place is always hard.'

There it is again, that bitterness in my mouth. My promises so far have proved to be hollow; why should she believe me now? She must have guessed that things are not the way they seem. Children are so trusting, so sure that they are meant to be here, so excited by the world and what it holds for them. How do we tell them the bitter truth? That things can't always be safe and normal and secure. Mummy and Daddy can't always make the bad things go away. *We'll always tell them the truth. Won't we?* But how can I? Why would I? Why not let them live in sweetness for as long as they can?

'Okay,' she says in a little voice. She's had to accept so much lately and she's tried so hard. My heart swells with love for her, my beautiful girl.

'Wait here a moment, sweetie, while I get the door open. I'll have us sorted out in no time.'

After all, we're bound to be happy in a place called Paradise House.

I use the torch on my phone to shine a beam of light onto the front door. I examine the keyring. Which one is for this lock? And what, besides the gate padlock, do the others open, for goodness' sake? I fumble with the ring of keys, trying them one by one in the lock, quickly losing track of which ones I've already tested. Panic starts to flutter inside me.

This is a disaster! We're going to be locked out all night, until I can call the people in the morning. Oh God, I knew it was all going to fail . . .

Then suddenly, unexpectedly, a key slides into the tight little lock and turns. Relief drenches me again. It's going to be all right after all.

I don't know how much more of this I can take. The see-sawing of extreme emotions is exhausting.

I step into the pitch-black interior and start patting at the wall just inside the door, feeling for a light switch. It's not until I relight the torch on my phone that I find them: a bank of old-fashioned round dolly switches in dark brown Bakelite mounted on a wooden board. I click one on and a bare bulb glows dimly over my head, the light weak and orange and sickly. Without waiting to look around, I head back to the car. I'm not leaving Heather alone for a moment longer than I have to.

She's waiting patiently in her car seat, not sleeping but showing dark blue circles under her eyes.

'Ready?' I ask.

She nods, and I unclip the seat belt. She scrambles out on her own – at six years old, she's almost too old for a child seat now – and slips awkwardly to the ground, stiff after hours of sitting.

'Shall I carry you?'

She shakes her head. She hasn't let me carry her since that night. Instead she slips her hand into mine and I click the car locked. It chirrups, its side lights flashing as it folds its wing mirrors in neatly. The descending locks make a chunky sound as the car closes down, its interior lights fading to nothing. Heather gazes straight ahead as we go towards the light, the bulb inside now glowing more brightly, adding just a little more cheer to the bleakness of our destination.

'Bed soon, darling,' I say with more certainty than I feel as I lead her inside, my free hand fumbling for the room plan I'm carrying. I know that there's a bed in a room towards the back of the house. All I have to do is find it, get the bedding from the car, make it up and settle Heather. Then, at last, we'll be able to rest.

Rory and I are lying together in bed. I'm on my back, staring up at the blackness of the ceiling, my eyes still adjusting now that the bedside light has been switched off. He rolls over, kisses my shoulder and squeezes me. 'Night, darling,' he says.

'Night.' I intended to say nothing, not yet, but I can't stop myself. 'Oh . . . how was your day? I didn't ask earlier. How are things at work?'

'Oh,' he says vaguely. 'Fine. Busy.' He yawns. 'I'm absolutely zonked. Do you mind if I go straight off to sleep? We can talk tomorrow if you like.'

'Of course not. You're tired.' I'm rigid with tension and make an effort to relax. I don't know how long I can keep all this going. 'But . . . your day . . . was fine?'

'Yes, you know. Same old. Train was packed. I got collared by Andy at lunchtime, had to go to the pub with him. The usual meetings in the afternoon – budgets.' He sighs. 'That's why I'm so knackered.' He kisses me again. 'See you in the morning.'

'Okay.' I say. Within minutes he's asleep, his body twitching

as it relaxes into slumber. I can't sleep, though. Not now I know.

I wake in Paradise House the next morning with the first red tinges of dawn that find their way through the thin curtain at the window. Our surroundings are grey but visible. The room we're in is huge but extremely bare. I don't think it can have been a bedroom originally, but now it has a cast-iron double bed with an old striped mattress which I covered with our bedlinen last night. A naked bulb hangs from a greying flex in the middle of the ceiling and the walls are whitewashed, speckled with holes and with faded grey outlines where pictures once hung. A fireplace has been painted white as well. It's almost like a stage set, or a location for the kind of ultra-chic interior shoot that makes a virtue of stripped-back shabbiness. There is an old pine wardrobe with a mirror set in the door, though the glass is smeary with dust, and a battered antique button-back armchair. Cobwebs festoon the corners of the room and feathery dust balls sit along the skirting. My nose tingles and I fight the urge to sneeze.

Heather is still asleep and I make sure not to disturb her as I slip out from under the duvet. The bare floor is cold under my feet and I shiver in my pyjamas. My slippers are in a bag somewhere, probably still in the car. I brought in only our essentials last night – my case and Heather's. Hers is a small purple sit-on thing that all the children have and it's open, her clothes neatly folded inside. I put her pyjamas on the top so that I could get at them easily when we arrived, along with the small pink oilcloth toilet bag with her toothbrush and strawberry toothpaste inside. I tiptoe to my suitcase, pick up a jumper and pull it on over my pyjamas. Instantly warmer, I decide to look for the kitchen and see what's there. In the car is a box of supplies but I might be in luck – there might be the tools for a cup of tea or coffee. I let myself quietly out of the bedroom and into the corridor beyond. As I walk down it in the gloom, I wonder at my ability to have found the bedroom last night when we were so exhausted. Somehow, with only the basic room plan provided by the company, I managed to get there on the first attempt. The lights I switched on are still glowing dustily, the low-wattage bulbs only just providing enough illumination. This place both is and isn't what I expected when I looked at the pictures. It's bigger and shabbier – I can see places along the walls where the plaster is blown and the picture rails that line the walls are black with dirt – but it has the kind of dignity I expected from an old building like this.

And now it's my job to look after it. How long has it been empty? Why did the previous owners go?

And, of course, who wants it now, and why?

I look down at the floor plan, which I scooped up as I tiptoed out of the bedroom. The ground floor spreads out from the large reception rooms at the centre to what look like dozens of smaller ones. Our bedroom must once have been something else – a small sitting room, perhaps, or a study. I work out where I am – somewhere on the eastern side of the house – and soon I've navigated my way back to the entrance hall where we came in last night. It's large and impressive, with a chequered black and white stone floor and a landing high above it. In the far left-hand corner, a staircase, oak and rather Gothic, climbs up towards it. A sturdy door opposite the way I have come leads to the western side, and I go through it and enter a new corridor lined by closed doors. One is ajar, and I peek inside to a large dining room with windows giving out onto the front driveway. The walls are an intense turquoise colour, the plasterwork white, and the wood floor scuffed and faded. In the middle is a huge old table, its surface dull with dust, and about sixteen old chairs are tucked under it. I wonder how long it has been since anyone sat around and ate a meal at that table.

This place feels so deserted.

I know so little about the house. The company hasn't told me much more than it's been empty for a while now. Not that it's falling down. It's just dirty and faded with that musty smell that settles on an empty house. No wonder they want someone in here. It's squatters' heaven with all this room. I look at the table.

It's strange what gets left behind. I wonder why they took everything else, but left the table and chairs? And who picked this colour for the walls? It's extraordinary.

I'm about to leave when something catches my eye. On either side of the fireplace, which is surrounded by a big grey marble chimney piece and a mottled mirror above, are arched alcoves with shelves built into them. In the alcove nearest the window, on one of the high shelves, is a small object. Curious, I walk into the room, and circle the huge table until I'm standing directly opposite the alcove. I can see it now, though it's too high to reach and tucked back almost out of sight. It's a marble bust, only about twelve centimetres high, of a beautiful little girl, her head cocked to one side, her eyes closed, her carved hair pulled back into a bun. Her lips are curved into a sweet half-smile, and on her shoulder sits a bird, its wings open as it looks up at her. I can almost hear the high lilt of birdsong as I look at it, and the small sigh of rapture from the girl as she listens. But . . . those closed eyes and the white cheeks and its unutterable stillness suddenly repel me and I turn and run out of the room, pulling the door to behind me, my heart racing and my breath coming short and sharp.

Don't be silly, I tell myself firmly, as I stand in the corridor outside. I mustn't let myself get spooked. The last thing I want is to start getting frightened of this place, when there's only the two of us here.

It's just a house. An empty house. Anything else you bring to it is only in your imagination.

Breathing deeply to calm myself down, I consult my plan and set off towards the kitchen.

The kitchen, like the rest of the house, is thick with dust and dirt, and has evidently never been modernised beyond the installation of an old gas stove, the kind with an open grill at eye height. It sits in the chimney breast, from where a much bigger range was probably removed, looking rather too small for its home. Next to it, a small fridge has been tucked in, its cord winding out and round to the nearest plug up on the worktop. The floor has been covered in patterned vinyl, probably to hide the original stone floor, but the real charm lies in the open wooden shelves that run along the sides of the room in an L shape, and the tall windows on the far side which look out over a mass of green beyond. The shelves are old-fashioned, and are no doubt where pots and pans and mixing bowls and all the rest of the paraphernalia once resided. On the far side, they are topped with a thick wooden worktop, worn with much scrubbing, and on the return they have a marble top. The shelves are almost empty now, apart from a small stack of mismatched china – some plates and bowls and cups and saucers, in a variety of floral patterns. The huge chipped double Belfast sink is surmounted by an ancient heater with a rusty tap for hot water.

Hmm. Not exactly overprovided with stuff. Still, let's see what there is . . .

As I wander about, I find more in the kitchen than I suspected: a drawer of mismatched old cutlery – a carving knife and fork with handles made of antlers; a stained plastic spatula. Then I spot a doorway that leads into a large larder cupboard, and that yields a small treasure: an old tin with three teabags lying in dark brown dust at the bottom, a jar of instant coffee, a box of ancient, concrete-hard sugar cubes, a tin of cocoa that looks to be at least a decade out of date. There's a glass jar of what might be table salt, though I don't feel inspired to taste it, some mustard powder and some empty tins. There's also an old-fashioned kettle, the type that whistles on the boil.

Then I can have a cup of coffee. Black, yes, but at least it means I don't have to go outside yet. Does instant coffee go off?

I take the kettle back into the kitchen and fill it at the sink.

Cold water gushes out, fast and strong, and the gas stovetop lights with no problem, so the utilities are all intact. Then I spoon some of the old coffee into one of the flowery cups and wait for the kettle to start hissing.

As I stand, leaning against the worktop in the huge room, I remember Rory making coffee in the mornings. Our kitchen was new, Shaker style, with dark blue units below and cream above, all wooden and dovetailed joints, granite worktops, a vast range cooker in baby blue, and shiny appliances tucked away behind tall cupboard doors. Only Rory's Gaggia was allowed to sit on the surface, and every morning he went carefully about the ritual of making our coffee: thick, dark, rich espresso with steamed frothy milk, exactly as I liked it. As we both liked it. We'd grown to share each other's tastes without trying. At weekends, we'd drink our strong coffees slowly over breakfast – muesli, toast and marmalade for him; something with fashionable seeds, berries, nuts and oat milk for me. But that's how life used to be: full of ease that I took for granted. There was our comfortable house, always warm and well lit, clean and pretty. It had taken years to get it as we wanted – with careful planning and budgeting, every year undertaking a project that brought us a little closer to our final vision. But all the while we thought we were making do, putting up with less than perfection, we were actually happy. Everything was fine. It was lovely. I can see our old house now: cheerful red brick behind thick green hedges, the path up to the dark-blue front door, the lamp glowing in the sitting room window. I remember stepping into the hall, throwing my keys into the china pot on the table, the cat blinking at me from her favourite spot by the hall radiator as she soaked up the warmth of the hot water pipes. I'm slipping off my coat, calling out, 'Hello? Where is everyone? I'm home.'

The china cup clatters onto the wooden worktop and coffee spills out in a black puddle as I'm caught by a horrible pang of pain and regret and overwhelming loss that weakens my fingers, bends me and makes me gasp sharply, shaking me with the fierce jerk of an electric current. It's too much to bear and if I let it go on for too long, I know it will start to destroy me so I summon all my strength and dispel it by an act of will.

I will not. I will NOT think of it. It's gone. It's over. I've made my choice.

I'm not in that oasis of calm and comfort and happiness anymore. I'm here in this strange place, where no one knows me. No one knows where I am.

And there's Heather. Her face comes into focus in my mind, and I imagine her waking alone in that room, wondering where she is, where I've gone. It's enough to make the pain release me. I take a deep breath and shake my head. I've got to get back to her. There are only the two of us now, and we have to look to the future.

Chapter Three

Heather and I wander about, looking at our new home. It's the time of year I used to hate the most – early February, cold, murky and grey, with the promise of something brighter if we can just wait a little longer – and the empty rooms are gloomy with winter. Despite their dormancy, they seem to be calling out for buckets of hot soapy water, cloths, dusters and mops. The light shows that the windowpanes are laced with patterns of dirt and strewn with cobweb strands, and I can't prevent a surge of desire to clean it all away.

'No wonder they couldn't find anyone else to take this place on,' I say out loud to myself. I was warned that it hadn't been cleaned in a while. It's been empty for some time and the new owners only took possession of the place a few months ago. I wonder if they've even been here. I suppose they wanted to save money by not having it cleaned before they put people in it and that was probably why it was cheap. But it means I'll be busy with the mop and bucket for a while. *So much for paradise.*

'What do you think of it, Heather?' I ask, as we open doors

and inspect the rooms beyond. At first we take our time, but after a while we start just peeping in to see more of the same: empty space, wooden floors, fireplaces, dirty windows and little else.

'It's big,' she pronounces. 'Where are all the people?'

'There aren't any other people, just us.'

She frowns. 'But why do we need all this to live in? There's no furniture!'

'We're looking after it. We're staying here for a while, until the owners need it.'

'Will other people come?'

'Maybe.' I don't know why I say that when there's no one coming, and immediately regret it when Heather looks interested.

'Who are they? Will there be children?'

'Oh,' I say vaguely, 'I don't think so. They're not coming for a long time, anyway. That's why they need us.'

She seems happy enough with this, and we resume our wandering through the ground floor, ending up back at our bedroom. This is certainly the best room for us, I think, not least because it's the only one with a bed. Heather seems tired so I settle her on the bed with a picture book, and sit down with the file of papers I've brought with me. It's the information about the property supplied by the owners, and I want to find out what I can about the way it all works, and how I'll switch the heating on. There are ancient radiators in every room, each one stone cold. The bathroom at the end of our corridor has a huge old iron bath and taps that ran icy and never warmed up. We'll need hot water before too long.

Despite going through the papers several times, I can't seem to locate what I need.

'Dammit!' I say crossly at last, and fling the papers down in frustration. It's like this all the time now. I can't take in information the way I used to. I'll just have a wander around and see what I can find.

Heather is looking over at me, concerned. 'Are you all right, Mummy?'

'Yes, yes.' I smile at her. 'I'm fine. Let's go and get all our things from the car. Then we can make it nice and cosy.'

She comes out with me and we spend the rest of the morning emptying the car of stuff: food and supplies; simple cooking equipment; more clothes, towels and linens; toys, books and games for Heather; a radio; cleaning things. Heather trots along beside me most of the time, not really helping much even when I suggest that she carries something for me. She gasps with delight when she sees some of her favourite books and in the end, I leave her sitting on the floor of the hallway, occupying herself with them, while I continue unloading.

After I've given the bedroom a good clean and made it more homely, with Heather's stuffed puffin on the pillow, it's time for lunch – tinned soup and ham rolls – and then I make a start on the kitchen, this time with Heather helping me when she's not distracted by playing around in the shelves and the larder. She starts 'cooking', mixing up the old powders she finds in tins and jars in a crackled china bowl, and adding water to turn it into what she says is a delicious soup, until she changes her mind and decides it's a magic potion.

'What does it do?' I ask, shaking damp hair out of my eyes. I've worked up a sweat cleaning out the old fridge.

'It can take us wherever we want to go,' she replies, stirring it hard.

'Where will it take you?' I ask, thinking she'll say 'Disney-land' or something made up.

'Home, of course,' she says at once.

There's a pause. I swallow, feeling a lump in my throat. I open my mouth to say something, anything, that might distract her from her impossible wish, but she speaks again before I can think of anything.

'Can I eat a sugar cube, please, Mummy?'

'Of course,' I say, relieved she's let it go so easily. 'Just be careful to suck it. You'll break your teeth on it otherwise, it must be hard as concrete.'

After I've finished as much of the kitchen as needs doing, I'm exhausted, and relieved to be able to make a decent cup of coffee with fresh milk, now stowed away in the clean fridge.

That's it for cleaning today. I'm bushed.

But then I find, a few doors down the corridor from the kitchen towards the middle of the house, a room that must once have been a morning room or small sitting room. It's cosier than most of the downstairs rooms, with windows and a pair of filthy French doors overlooking the tangle of garden at the back of the house. Its comfortable air comes partly from the fact that it still has some furniture: a round mahogany table with a few mismatched chairs around it, an armchair and an old sofa – a softly curving thing covered with scuffed and threadbare velvet in a mustardy yellow colour. The walls are papered with a delicate chinoiserie wallpaper in shades of silver and pale green, with pink, grey and blue birds perched among slender branches and blossom. It's the prettiest room I've yet come across, although, like everywhere else, it's neglected and dirty.

'We'll make this room much nicer,' I say, looking about. This will be our sitting room. There's a blocked-up fireplace and I wonder if I could possibly unblock it and if I would dare use it if I did. I try the French doors but of course they're locked and there's no sign of the keys. It doesn't matter. It's too cold to go out and, anyway, the state of the garden is a bit too much to take on right now. The inside is more manageable by comparison. *A bit of work and this room could be lovely.* I don't mind the work. I've enjoyed what I've done today, losing myself in the task of cleaning. It's good to have something simple to do – plain, physical labour that helps me relax. It's all I want. Simplicity. Quiet. Peace. Just me and Heather.

Even though I'm bushed, I bring in my little vacuum cleaner and give the sofa a good going over, until I feel it's possible to sit on it, then dust the entire room and hoover again. This is definitely going to be our HQ and I'm eager to bring in some books and make it more homely. While I work, the afternoon sun disappearing quickly into gloom, Heather mooches about, plays with her miniature animal families and reads quietly in the hall. I glance at her every time I go past.

She's kneeling, leaning forward on her elbows, her chin on her hands, rocking back and forth as she turns the pages. It reminds me of when she was a baby, and I'd come into her room to see her asleep in her cot, her bottom up in the air, her legs tucked under her, her flushed cheek pressed against the sheet. I remember how Rory and I used to stand together at the door, peering in and marvelling at how beautiful she was, how perfect.

Rory.

I wonder, in a flash, if he's realised yet that we've gone. If he has, what does he think and feel about it? He's going to be desperate, surely, wondering where we are, trying to find us. I ought to feel sorry for him, but I can't. I haven't got room for how he feels anymore. I only have an overwhelming urge to stay hidden, far from everyone, where it's safe.

Later, when it's dark outside and the hall is too gloomy for reading, we settle in the sitting room and I plug in the small electric fan heater, grateful I packed it just in case. Then I put some cartoons on the tablet for Heather; I brought one without internet access but loaded it up with plenty of films and programmes and music and stories to keep Heather occupied when it's not possible to play outside, or when she's tired. While she's lying on the sofa watching it, I put on my glasses and sit at the table to go through the paperwork from the company. Their logo is at the top: a centaur holding a stretched bow and arrow, like the emblem for the Sagittarius star sign. Below are three letters: ARK. I read the letter again.

Welcome, guardian!

We like to think of you as our guardian angels –
people who are providing vital protective care to our
properties. Thank you for joining our band. ARK has
properties throughout the country and we need them to
be occupied, so that we can prevent the decay and
degeneration of our assets and guard against the dangers
of squatters. Your role is absolutely vital to our work.

Inside, you'll find all the information you need in
order to look after your chosen property and the
necessary contact details for reaching us. You'll already
have been through our vetting procedure and we now
consider you part of our family. Settle into your new
home and enjoy it. We'll be in touch very soon to make
sure that you're completely happy – but don't hesitate to
call if you need any help.

There's more but I stop reading, struck by the thought that
I am part of this family, the ARK family, whatever that is and
whatever they do. Before I left, I looked them up on the internet and found a slick and well-presented site that was full of
the right kind of jargon about building for the future and
preserving heritage, but that actually told me very little about
them and why they have these properties. There were only
details for this place, probably because they were looking for
a guardian for it.

And they think they know all about me.

I feel a little rush of satisfaction that I've managed to

deceive them. I applied in a false name, using Caz's address. I wondered if they'd be able to tell that I hadn't lived there for long (in fact, not at all) but even though I prepared in case there were queries, they seemed happy with my application form.

After all, here I am.

I was sure there must be lots of applicants to guard a place like this, but they got back to me quickly and arranged an interview over the internet. A pleasant woman called Alison, businesslike in a dark suit, white shirt and black-rimmed glasses and with glossy pulled-back hair, asked me some fairly straightforward questions but on the whole I got the impression that she was trying to sell the place to me, rather than the other way around. I had to remember to reply to my new name, and not to be startled when she called me Rachel. That was me now. My new other self. *Rachel Capshaw.* I picked the name easily by opening a magazine at random and taking the first fore and surnames I saw. Once put together, they seemed immediately to form a whole other person, someone I could try my hand at being. Rachel Capshaw sounds normal, respectable and dependable. She could be any age, from any background. The Rachel Capshaw I've created is a peroxide blonde with a small daughter and a blue car, free and independent, keen to take on a vast and empty property in the middle of nowhere, 'so I can paint,' I'd said gravely to Alison, her eyes fixed on me through the computer screen and never flicking up to the smaller image of herself that must be in the corner of her screen.

'Oh, you're an artist?' she'd said smoothly, one well-tended eyebrow raising.

'That's right.'

Rachel Capshaw. Artist. I liked the way it sounded. And artists need peace and quiet, and solitude. Don't they?

'What sort of painting?'

'Oh. Well . . .' I stumbled a little, not expecting the question. 'Um . . .'

'I make pottery myself – just a hobby to help me relax.' Alison's dark gaze fixed me through the screen. 'Nothing professional.'

'Well . . . I paint abstracts.' I flushed just a little and hoped it didn't show. 'Oils and . . . acrylics.' It was true I'd painted a bit at school, but I'd done nothing since bar helping out on school projects or on rainy afternoons when there was nothing to do. 'And I'm not professional either . . . yet. Perhaps one day.'

'I'm sure that your stay at Paradise House will help that.' Alison smiled. 'Plenty of room for painting there. And your income doesn't seem to be a problem.'

'No.' I smiled back, open and candid. 'My divorce settlement.'

Alison looked uncomfortable just for a moment, then said easily, 'Well, as you'll be on your own, you'll have plenty of time to paint.'

'Yes.' I hadn't mentioned Heather. It would only complicate things. I knew they didn't allow children in their properties, and I wasn't going to risk losing this opportunity.

Alison tapped some papers on her desk and said, 'Well, it's

all in order as far we're concerned. If you're happy, I'll be in touch via email with more details and send you the paperwork.'

'Great, that's wonderful. Thank you.'

I breathed out when her face vanished from my screen. 'Rachel Capshaw, you're on your way.'

When the contract arrived, I had no hesitation in signing it with my new name, writing it out in a scribble as unlike my own as I could manage. And in the back of the car is a portable easel, a pack of paints and brushes, canvas and paper, just in case Alison comes calling.

When I go back through the information pack slowly and carefully, I find what I need to know about the heating and hot water system. There's a vast old boiler in the basement but I decide not to go down there tonight. Otherwise there are the water heaters and I manage to light the gas flame in the kitchen and in the bathroom nearest our bedroom. Once there is hot water, I clean the room thoroughly, scrubbing out the cast-iron bath until the enamel is almost white again, bar the rust marks and scratches. Even though I work up a sweat cleaning, it's still freezing cold in there. The chilly tiled floor and walls reflect the cold back at me, and there isn't even a radiator to warm it up, only an electric bar heater high up on the wall. I switch it on and it soon glows a radiant orange, but the heat remains in a discrete cloud around it, unable to penetrate the cold of the rest of the room.

I don't like to think of Heather in here, in this dank, cold room with its hard surfaces. She shouldn't be in a place like this. But what choice do I have?

I'm tired. Today, I've moved us into Paradise House, cleaned our bedroom, the kitchen and bathroom, and sorted out the sitting room. As I start to prepare supper on the old cooker in the kitchen, I sigh with fatigue but also with a sense of a job done. We've got away. No one knows where we are. They might know that Rachel Capshaw has arrived at this huge old place to find her artistic self, but they don't know that I'm here and that Heather is with me.

Heather drifts around the kitchen as I cook, singing to herself. She's been so good. No questions, no complaints. She seems quite happy to be here, apart from her one mention of home. Perhaps she thinks we're on holiday. She hasn't asked for Rory. *Not yet. But we've barely been here a day.*

What is she singing?

She wanders by me. Under one arm she's clutching her favourite stuffed doll, one that Caz gave her when she was only about four. It's an old-fashioned rag doll, with bright orange wool for hair and floppy pale legs and arms protruding from a colourful pinafore dress. Her face is stitched on: two black buttons for eyes, a red upturned semi-circle for a smile, two pink circles on her cheeks. Heather called her Sparkleknee. I frown as Heather goes by me on another circuit of the room, still singing.

I don't remember bringing Sparkleknee.

In fact, I don't remember seeing her for a while. I thought she'd gone, with everything else. But here she is, tucked under Heather's arm.

I shrug and turn back to the cooking pot, where I'm stir-ring onions as they fry gently.

Heather sings on, Sparkleknee smiling up from under her arm.

Chapter Four

The next day I go down to the basement and get the boiler going so I can turn on some radiators. As soon as they're heating up, the sun comes out of course, so we go out to explore the garden. The front, with its gravelled forecourt and drive, isn't in such bad shape, even if the rhododendron bushes at the edges have grown huge and straggly and the flower beds are bare except for rugged weeds and leggy bushes. But the back, broad and stretching away into the distance, has not been cared for in a very long time. It's a jungle of bare branches, the skeletons of shrubs, great thatches of evergreens, and long, wet, dead grass, but Heather seems enchanted by it. I keep my eyes open for any dangers – hidden ponds or smashed greenhouses – but I can't see how she might come to harm. She takes a fancy to a clump of barrel-shaped bay trees, and starts to make a den in the hollow underneath them. We play together for a while, and she arranges things as she wants them, making a little kitchen area, with stones for dishes and a fireplace, and a sleeping area. She's collecting bracken to make into a bed when my telephone beeps in my pocket.

I jump violently. The electronic riff I chose as the ringtone is still alien to me, and at first I can't work out what it is. Then I remember the phone and pull it out. I bought a pay-as-you-go one, but I haven't yet switched on its internet capacity, even though I'm sure I can't be traced if I use my fake email account. I stare at the screen. There is no name, just a number; but then, I've added only one contact – Alison at ARK – and this isn't her. The only mobile number I know off by heart is Rory's, and it's not his. I stare at it as it chirps away in my hand, not sure what to do. My pulse is racing and my breathing quickens. I crawl out from under the bay trees and stand there. Then on a wild impulse, I answer, my voice breathless.

'Hello?'

'Kate?'

'Who's this?' I'm horribly afraid all of a sudden. *They've found me. I knew they would.*

'It's me. Caz. Who did you think? Have you given anyone else this number?'

I exhale with relief. Of course. Who else could it be? Caz is the only person I've given this number to, other than Alison. 'No, no, I haven't. Why are you calling?'

'I'm worried about you, of course. I want to make sure you're okay.'

Irritation prickles through me. 'I told you not to ring unless it was absolutely necessary. An emergency. You're not to call to pass the time of day, don't you understand that?'

Caz sounds plaintive. 'But I have no idea if you're safe or not! You haven't let me know anything.'

'It's better if you don't, I explained that.'

'Yes, but . . .' Caz's voice fades away. She knows it's pointless to argue with me. I'm insistent. Obdurate. More firm now than I've ever been in my life. I think she's still getting used to this new me, the one who orders her about and refuses to negotiate with her.

'And,' I say strictly, 'you forgot to use the code.'

'Oh yes,' Caz says. 'The code.'

She's supposed to text a message to alert me before she makes any call, using agreed code words so that I know in advance that it's safe to answer. After all, it might be her number, but is that any guarantee that she's on the other end? The first time I told her what I wanted her to do, she laughed and said, 'Isn't that a bit over the top?' But one glance at my expression shut her up.

'Sorry, Kate,' she says humbly. 'I'll remember next time.'

'But only call if you absolutely have to,' I remind her. There's a pause and I soften. She's helping me. I need to rely on her. I say, 'Listen, it's good of you to worry but everything is fine. I'm at a good location, a safe house. It's all okay, I promise. It's just what I wanted.' I glance around at the wet, muted garden and the walls of the great house towering over us. There is a splendid view of its beauty from here. The red and black bricks are laid in patterns, with Gothic windows on the upper floor, and little stone balconies under them. On the attic level are small gabled dormer windows beneath Jacobean-style chimneys in herringbone-patterned bricks. It's a glorious Victorian pastiche. I already feel as though, somehow, it partly belongs to me.

'Where are you?'

I pause. 'I'm not telling you that, Caz. Sorry. It's better if you don't know. In case anyone asks you.'

'Okay . . . It's very strange not knowing where you might be. I don't know where to picture you!' She waits, as though hoping I might give her a clue of some kind, but I say nothing so she ploughs on. 'How long will you stay?'

'I don't know exactly. A few weeks probably.' I hesitate, then ask, 'How's Rory? Have you heard anything?'

'Not yet. I guess it won't be until he starts to get anxious. In a day or two, when you don't make contact with him. He probably thinks you've just gone off on a short trip somewhere.'

'Yes.' I feel a blanket of safety enfold me. No one is looking for me. Not yet, at least. 'Okay, then. Is that everything?'

'Yes.' There's a pause and then she says, 'Kate, it's not too late to come back. You don't have to run like this.'

'Sorry, Caz.' I hear Heather calling for me from under the bay trees. 'I've got to go now. Bye.' I flick the call off and get down onto the cold soil so that I can peer under the branches. 'Coming, darling. What are you doing now?'

'Who was on the phone?' Heather asks, turning her big blue eyes on me as I crawl towards her.

'Aunty Caz. She wanted to say hello.'

Heather looks pleased. 'Is she coming to visit us?'

'Not for a while. We're quite far away from her at the moment. It's too far to visit right now.'

'I'd like to see Aunty Caz,' she says, a touch of wistfulness in her voice. Caz is her godmother and mother of Heather's best friends. She's been a presence all of Heather's life. 'I'd like to play with Leia and Mika.'

'Maybe one day. When they come and see us. But it's a long way.'

Heather nods; she understands that we're far from home. I wait for her to ask about Daddy. Surely she's going to mention Rory soon, and wonder when she's going to see him, or speak on the phone. I've got my reply ready. But she turns back to the stones and leaves that she's been pretending are the food and says, 'Now, Mummy, it's time for lunch. I think you should have salad. I've got some ready here.'

'How delicious! Yes, please,' I say, grateful that she has given me another reprieve.

By the afternoon, we're back in the sitting room and Heather is watching cartoons at the table while I read on the sofa. Some of the pressure I've been under lately seems to have lifted. Last night I slept properly and without nightmares. It occurs to me that my plan has worked: I've found the escape I needed. But how long can it last? I know it can't go on indefinitely; at some point Rory is bound to realise what's happened. He'll start searching, and he'll have the weight of the world behind him. They'll all be out to get me. But until then, I'm going to enjoy my respite, and the breathing space I've craved so badly.

The words I'm reading dance in front of my eyes. My lids

grow heavy and my head lolls, and I sink into drowsiness and then sleep.

I wake with a gasp to the sound of banging on the French windows. Shocked and dazed, I spring to my feet, my book tumbling to the ground. I look instantly over at Heather, but she isn't there. The tablet is propped up on the table, playing a cartoon, but her seat is empty.

I turn to the awful racketing sound of the banging on the window and the dark shape that stands there. I can't make out more than a silhouette against the low afternoon sun.

'Who is it? What do you want?' I shout, the adrenaline of panic surging through me. The figure outside is pressing itself hard against the glass, peering in. Thank God Heather has taken herself off somewhere: not only would it terrify her, but she would easily have been seen.

The banging stops and a muffled voice calls through the glass.

'I can't open this door,' I yell, and point towards the front of the house. 'Come to the front. The front!'

I hurry out of the sitting room towards the hall, calling for Heather as I go. I hear a faint reply from near our bedroom.

'Stay in the bedroom, darling, till I come and get you!' I call. 'It's very important. Stay where you are!'

Approaching the front door, I see some of Heather's toys on the hall floor and quickly gather them up, open the door of the nearest room – a huge, bay-windowed empty space – toss them in and close the door. I scan to see if there's anything else that might give us away, and spot Heather's abandoned shoes so I drop my coat over them. Then I go to the big front door and open it, my heart beating wildly. Have we been discovered already?

There's no one there. I step out onto the stone steps and look about. Apart from my hire car, the driveway is deserted and all is quiet. The air is still and cold with the faintest whiff of bonfires. I try to calm my breathing, but I'm shaky with fear. Someone was there; I didn't imagine it. And they're close by. The next moment I hear the faint crunching of gravel as someone walks slowly along the side of the house and my pulse goes wild again.

Calm, you've got to be calm! Remember, you're Rachel Capshaw. You're alone. You've every right to be here. Whoever it is is the trespasser, not you . . .

Even so, I'm tense with anticipation as the footsteps come closer. And then, moving very slowly, a wide figure in a dark overcoat appears from around the side of the house. There's a mess of grey hair, then a face, and I realise it's an elderly woman. At once I relax just a little. She doesn't look like someone who'd be in hot pursuit of me and Heather. Under her coat, she's wearing an old flowery dress, and on her feet, a pair of rough boots are unlaced, showing thick socks beneath.

'Hello?' I say, sounding as normal as I can. 'Can I help you?'

'Afternoon,' she replies. 'Well, that all depends, don't it.'

She's got a strange accent I can't identify. It doesn't sound like any regional dialect I know, but then again, it's not colourless, placeless RP either.

She comes to a halt at the bottom of the steps, stuffs her hands into her pockets and looks up at me with an expression that's almost defiant. Then she smiles suddenly, revealing brownish teeth, and says, 'You the new owner?'

'Not exactly.'

'Oh?' She looks wary but interested. 'Squatter?'

'No. I've got permission to be here.'

'Ah.' She frowns. Her skin is lined with countless soft crisscrosses that deepen or disappear as her face moves. Wiry grey strands poke crazily upwards from her thick steel-coloured hair which is mostly tucked up at the back into a wild bundle. Her eyes are brown, the centres very black and with thin rings of iris around them. She turns her face to look at me sideways, almost like a bird, and I notice she does have a beaky nose, thin and curving. 'But you're not anything to do with the owner? No relation?'

'No. I'm the guardian. Appointed by the people who own the house.' We are wary of one another, observing each other carefully, answering slowly, not wanting to be the one to give anything away. 'Who are you? Do you live around here?'

Her black-brown gaze lingers as she seems to appraise me. Then she says, 'I live in the cottage over the way. Through the bushes.'

My heart sinks. A neighbour. No one said anything about other people being close by. 'What are you doing here? This is private property, you know.'

'I know that. But it's been empty a good while. We've been waiting for the new owner. But that's not you, you say.'

'That's right.'

52

She fixes me with a beady look from those dark eyes of hers. 'What do you know of the owner?'

'Nothing, I'm afraid. It's a private company, that's all I know.'

She stares at me as if waiting for more. I'm not going to tell her anything else. Not that I know much more anyway.

'Are you staying long?' she asks at last.

'I've no idea,' I say, trying not to sound annoyed at her inquisitiveness. 'A few weeks at least. It all depends. How did you know I was here?'

She turns and gestures at the car, parked on the drive. *Of course. What a stupid mistake. I'd forgotten all about that.* She looks at me again. 'And I heard you talking today. In the garden.'

'I was talking on my mobile phone,' I say quickly, hoping that's all she heard. I feel a rush of anger that our haven has been invaded. It's not safe after all. *Isn't there anywhere I can go to be left alone?* 'You must be very close, to hear that.'

The old woman shrugs and says, 'Not so close. But I went down the bottom of the garden to see to the compost and I heard talking. So now I've come to see what's going on. In case of squatters or vandals, you understand,' she adds. 'We've a duty to report anything we see. They've tried to get in before but we've always stopped them. We're used to it.'

I don't really believe her altruistic motives. Surely it was just curiosity that impelled her along to spy on us. I hope Heather stays where she is. The last thing I want is for her to be spotted by a busybody like this. I expect she's just the kind of person to register us and then make connections.

There is a bit of comfort in what the woman says, though. She only heard us by chance; she must have seen the car afterwards. Her cottage is not cheek by jowl to the house.

'I see. Well, I appreciate your concern but you don't have to worry about the house now that we're . . . I'm here to look after it.' I smile in what I hope is a cheerful manner. 'Thanks for being alert, I'm sure the owners are grateful. But there's really no need. In fact, I'd prefer it if you didn't come over unless invited. I'm working and need absolute quiet with as few disturbances as possible. Is that all right?'

She looks back at me, a frown creasing her forehead. 'You alone?' she asks, ignoring me.

'Yes, that's right,' I reply smoothly. 'Now if you—'

'All by yourself in there?'

'Yes.' I'm very firm about that.

'You might need me,' she says. 'If you do, you can call on me anytime, I'm always there. I'm over that way' – she lifts a hand from a pocket and waves towards the bushes on the right-hand side of the drive – 'in Nursery Cottage. Me and my sister, Sissy. I'm Matty, by the way.'

'Hello, Matty,' I say automatically, taking in the fact that there are two near neighbours. Then I refocus quickly. 'I'm Rachel. And I'm going to be absolutely fine. Really. There's no need to worry.'

'Hmm.' She stares at me and I feel an unpleasant prickle crawl down my back. 'We'll see about that. Well, I can tell you want to be left in peace. You don't have to worry about us disturbing you. We shan't come over unless there's a reason.' Then she adds, 'By the way, you might tell your lot that they made a racket to wake the dead last time they were here. They should keep it down next time.'

She turns on her heel and crunches back over the gravel the way she came. I watch her go and when she's out of sight, I hurry back inside to find Heather and make sure she's all right.

I'm nervous after the encounter with the old woman, and even though I don't think she'll come back in a hurry, I keep us inside.

'Can't I go outside to play?' Heather asks plaintively.

'Not today, sweetheart. Why don't you run around inside instead? You can play in the downstairs rooms, if you like.'

'But I want to go to my den!' she moans, casting a yearning glance outside where there is still a little sunshine remaining.

'No. It's getting cold. Inside today.' I'm firm and she knows I won't give in, so she trots off and soon I hear her in the hall, playing with her dolls and animals. She's turned the chequered black and white tiled floor into a game for them.

I want to settle down and relax, as I was just before I was disturbed, but Matty's arrival has made that impossible.

What did she mean by 'your lot'? There hasn't been anyone here for ages, has there? Maybe it was the people who stripped this place out.

Meeting Matty has turned my mind to interactions with the outside world. Although I brought a good supply of stores with me, they won't last forever and we'll need fresh food. I go through everything in the larder and the small fridge, and realise that I'll have to go out before too long; we can't live off tinned soup and pasta forever. We'll need vegetables and fresh bread. I think wistfully of the van that used to pull up outside my house once or twice a week and disgorge crate-loads of necessities, all just a tap and a click away. But, no doubt, all on record too: my ordering habits and preferences, and the location of the deliveries. All there for anyone who cares to look. Now I'll have to shop without being noticed. Before we left, I researched the nearest supermarket, which lies just outside the town to the west. It's going to be riddled with CCTV but if no one suspects my being here, and I keep my sunglasses on, I should be able to get away with it, especially if we haven't been reported missing yet. That's one good thing about Caz's call: knowing I'm still at liberty.

It would be better if I can do it all in bulk somehow. If I could freeze what I need. But how? The fridge doesn't even have an icebox.

A picture floats into my mind. It's the basement, where I went this morning to take a look at the boiler and get it firing. I think I saw a big chest freezer down there, but I was focus-ing on the boiler and didn't give it much attention. Leaving the kitchen, I hurry to the back stairs that lead down into the vast basement beneath the house. It's the workhouse of the property down there: huge boards of electrical fuses and connections, the gurgling hot water system and rows of industrial-sized copper pipes running along the ceiling. An old washing machine sits not far from the boiler, by rows of metal dustbins. I switch on the light; the fluorescent strip waits, then flickers into life, and, yes, there it is. Over on the far side of the main chamber is a closed door, and next to that is a large chest freezer.

I go over to it. It's surprisingly new-looking, considering the state of everything else. I expected it to be coated in a thick layer of cellar dust but there's only a light covering. I lift the lid with an effort, the inner vacuum keeping it firm, then I blink in surprise at the contents. I don't know what I expected, if anything, but I find myself looking at a stack of frozen food, carefully arranged into categories. There's bread, meat, fish and vegetables: packets of peas, sweetcorn, spinach, broccoli, and much more. There's even some fresh milk and cartons of juice. I stare, astonished. There are dozens of loaves in there and I pull at the label of one on top, turning it around until I can see its best-before date. It's faded in the icy interior but it's possible to make out a date of several months ago – assuming it's not years old. I pull out a box of frozen breaded chicken pieces and check the date on that. It's for later this year. So the freezer can only have been stocked within the last few months. I frown, puzzled.

Who put all this here?

I was told that the property had been empty for some time. So . . . I shrug, mystified but pleased. *Well, it's all going spare as far as I can tell.* Then I laugh out loud. What a result. I won't have to go shopping after all. If we're careful with our other supplies, we've got enough here to keep us going for quite some time. I'll keep a log of what we use and if the owners kick up a fuss, I'll just replace it. Simple.

I pick a few things out of the freezer, then shut it up. The closed door next to the freezer flickers with reflected light and

I notice that it is a shiny steel door, unlike any other I've seen in the house. I regard it for a moment, then tuck the food under my arm and turn the handle. It doesn't move. It is locked and there's no sign of a key. Then, to my surprise, I think I can see the flash of a light under the slim gap between the door and the floor. I frown, staring hard. Then I see it again – a quick flash of light, not white. Blue or green or red. A colour. But it's too fast to be sure.

I'm instantly on alert. 'Hello?' I call. 'Is anyone there?'

There's no answer. I stare hard at the gap under the steel door, listening for the sound of any movement, watching for more flashes, but there's nothing.

After a while, the frozen food begins to burn cold through my top. I head back upstairs.

Chapter Five

Matty makes her way back through the undergrowth and along the path to the cottage. The day is closing in now, but she notes that the sun has lingered a little longer today. The winter is releasing them from its dark grip, bit by bit.

This is the dankest part of the year, as spring wrestles to win over the days and set everything buzzing and burring with life, to bring back colour, light and warmth. Matty has watched it come to this place year after year. She's never known another.

She stomps through the long wet grasses, her hands deep in her pockets, frowning as she thinks over the arrival of the woman in the house. She goes up the path of a small, white-painted cottage with a thatched roof, trudges around the side of it and lets herself in through the back door. Pulling off her overcoat, she makes her way along the chilly hall, with its flagged floor and piles of possessions stacked along the sides, and hurries into the warmth of the kitchen.

Sissy is there, not in her usual spot in the rocking chair, but at the table where she is slowly polishing a mound of silver cutlery: carefully selecting a piece, dabbing her rag with polish, and anointing the silver before she rubs it all over to a gleaming shine. There is a mountain of it, left over from the days when there were many mouths to feed.

'Why are you doing that?' Matty asks, a touch of irritation in her voice.

'Why not?' Sissy replies, turning her face towards her sister. She is the younger but it would be hard to tell: they look so similar, with their salt-and-pepper hair, softly lined faces and beaky noses. 'It needs doing.'

'It does not. There's no one to use it now.'

'We can use it.'

'We could use a different knife and fork every day for a year and still not need to wash a set.'

'You like to exaggerate, Matty,' her sister says mildly. 'There's not that much. No harm in keeping things nice.'

'You shouldn't tempt fate. You don't want it all to start up again, do you?' Matty mutters with a note of accusation in her voice. She goes to the range and lifts the kettle to see how much water is in it, then goes to refill it at the sink. 'That chapter is closed, now the place has been sold.'

'I don't think it's beyond the realms of possibility,' replies Sissy, picking up a fork and starting her little ritual again: dab with polish, rub, move the cloth to a clean, dry spot and rub again all over.

'You shouldn't even think it. It's better that it's finished, isn't it? Aren't we free at last?' Matty shakes her head and mutters again, her words drowned in the gush of water so that Sissy can't hear. 'We're the last – and it's better that way.'

She turns off the tap with a sharp twist and says loudly, 'Anyway, I wouldn't get your hopes up. There's only a woman there. She says she's the guardian, whatever that is. She's a caretaker, if you ask me. I asked if she was anything to do with the owner but she said she didn't know much about it.'

Sissy frowns, polishing away, feeling the tines of the fork with the tip of her finger. 'Do you believe her?'

'I think so. All she wanted was for me to clear off and leave her to it. She seemed . . . absorbed. That's how I'd put it. She was half in another world, it seemed to me.'

'How many are there?' Sissy asks.

'Oh, just her. On her own. She was clear about that.'

Sissy stops polishing and goes quite still. 'Oh no,' she says. 'That's not right. She's not on her own.'

'What do you know, Sissy?' her sister asks, putting the kettle on the range and turning round to look at her. 'What have you found out?'

Sissy starts polishing again. 'Enough to know she's not on her own.'

Matty sighs. Sissy is enigmatic and often refuses to be drawn on what she discerns. But it always comes out in the end, and she's seldom wrong.

'Well, I didn't see anyone else,' Matty says. 'Or any sign, either.'

'You will,' Sissy says. 'When you go back.'

'She doesn't want me back. But I told her to be in touch if she ever needs us. If she is on her own over there, there's no telling when she might need our help.'

'Did you give her our telephone number?'

Matty clicks her tongue. 'No. Silly of me. I should have.'

'Drop it in,' suggests Sissy. 'I think we need to keep wary, that's all. I think we need to keep our eyes on that lady. Did she tell you her name?'

'Rachel.'

'Rachel,' Sissy says, as if testing it out. She frowns, puts down the fork on the pile of finished cutlery and picks up a spoon. 'Rachel.'

Matty turns back to check the kettle for warmth, but she listens to Sissy and she tells herself to remember to give the number to their new neighbour. Just in case.

Chapter Six

I'm glad I found the stored food downstairs because the next day the weather turns filthy. Heavy grey clouds descend, blocking out the weak wintery light and bringing an endless deluge of rain. I discover water coming in at the bay window in the front reception room and have to hunt around for a bucket to catch it. I dread to think what might be happening upstairs. I suppose it's my job to go up and look around but I can't quite bring myself to do it yet.

It must have rained before now and the place is still standing. One more rainstorm isn't going to make any difference.

We are trapped inside now, and Heather spends long minutes by the French windows in the sitting room, staring out into the rain-soaked garden beyond, watching as fat drops fall from the leaves of the trees and bushes.

I try to make things more amusing, offering to bake with her, but that doesn't seem to interest her much. A game of snakes and ladders lifts her spirits and she laughs merrily while we make up new rules and send each other spiralling up snakes and plummeting down ladders, but when it's over she sinks back into her languor. While I'm playing with her, she's alive and vibrant. When I stop, she starts to fade and doesn't seem to know what to do with herself. Eventually she disappears off to play in the hall with her dolls, and I can hear her talking to them as she moves them around the black and white squares.

I concentrate on my first mission from the company: assessing the state of the house and writing a report for them on the condition and what I think is a priority to repair. It isn't easy, not knowing what they intend to do with the place. If they want to convert it into flats or a family home, it would be as well to strip it back and start again, as far as rules and conservation regulations would allow. I walk about, taking photographs of damage and decay on my phone, then I wonder how I'm going to send it all off to them. I still haven't yet dared to turn on the internet capacity on my phone.

But if I don't, I won't know if they've contacted me. The phone is the only way they can reach me.

Standing in the bay-windowed room that looks over the drive, I stare down at the phone in my hand. It's so small and harmless-looking, but it could undo everything I've achieved if I'm not careful.

I'm sure that they can't trace me via a pay-as-you-go that they don't know I have. And if I use my fake email account, they can't possibly know it's me.

Heather's voice floats through the doorway from the hall as I take a deep breath and go to the settings. I've had all mobile data and all wi-fi connections switched off. My finger trembles slightly as it hovers over the on button, then I swipe and it's done. The phone begins to look for any networks in the area and I watch for the little symbol at the top that will indicate what strength of signal it's found. I'm expecting something very weak as the phone signal in the house is patchy, coming and going all the time – at least, down here on the ground floor. Then, to my surprise, a box flicks up on the screen. There's a wi-fi network available if I want to join it. It's a secure connection called PARADISE 1. I stare at it, baffled. A wi-fi network here? I had no idea.

Why didn't the company tell me?

I press on the network to join it but I'm immediately asked for a password.

I haven't got a clue . . . I'll try the obvious.

I type PARADISE into the box, but that doesn't work. I try it with some letters substituted for numbers: P4RAD1SE. That doesn't work either.

God only knows how many million combinations there might be. The chances of stumbling on the password are ridiculously low. But if I could find the router, the password might be there.

I set about looking for the router in the main rooms, but there's nothing obvious. I put on my raincoat in the hall. Heather watches me with solemn, questioning eyes and says nervously, 'Where are you going, Mummy?'

'Just out to see if I can spot the phone lines. Do you want to come?'

She nods, scrambles up and slips on her boots and coat, leaving her dolls on the floor.

'Come on then.' I take her hand and we go out of the huge

65

front door together, leaving it open behind us. I pull her hood over her fair hair as we step out into the pouring rain. She doesn't seem to mind it at all, turning her little face up to let the drops fall on it, sticking out her tongue to catch them. I smile, thinking that, really, I ought to keep her inside with that batty old lady wandering around, but we can't stay in the house forever. We have to be able to breathe.

We stamp about through the puddles, down the driveway to the old telegraph pole by the wall, where the phone lines swoop out over the shrubbery and encircle the house, coming in at the top left-hand side. We play about in the rain for a while, and then go back inside to dry out. When Heather is turbaned up with a towel to dry off her soaking hair, I leave her playing and start looking for the ingress of the wires in the west side of the house. I soon see it: an unobtrusive thin casing painted the same colour as the plaster, descending down through the ceiling and following the curve of cornices or creeping down the sides of doors and along the rim of skirting boards, sometimes ending in a telephone point, some- times flowing on, out of a room and along the hallway. I follow the trail back into the hall where the wires are pinned back under the plaster cornice, almost invisible. Near the kitchen, there's a small plastic junction box and a new wire splits off from the main thread. I follow this and it leads to the back stairs that descend to the basement. I go down the steps, my eyes fixed on the new wire. It runs along the ceiling, straight over to the steel door, and the wire disappears above the frame that surrounds it.

That's where the router has to be. Behind the door.

I go and stand outside it, staring at its dully reflective surface, listening hard. Then I think I hear a click and a whirr. A muffled chirrup. I'm sure I see the rapid flash of white light under the door.

My heart starts to thump hard. 'Is anyone in there?' I call loudly. 'Come out!'

There's no reply. Just a quietness that I'm sure contains small noises – tiny clicks and shifts. What if there is someone in there, behind the door, sitting still and waiting for me to leave?

'I know you're in there! Come out, show yourself!' My voice is breathless, a touch shaky.

Oh God, you're being stupid. There's no one here.

But there's all this food . . . I hurry to the freezer and open it. Is there stuff missing? I can't be sure. It certainly seems emptier but I've taken food out. Has anyone else?

Is someone here, using the wireless router? What the hell is this door?

In a rush of panic, I run back to the door and hammer on it. 'I know you're in there! Come the hell out right now, you're frightening me!'

I'm panting. There's absolute silence behind the door. Whoever is in there, I've made them shut up. *But there's no one there.* I have to believe it.

I turn on my heel and run back up the stairs as fast as I can.

Upstairs, the daylight and familiar surroundings are instantly reassuring. Heather is singing to herself on the hall floor, still playing although the game looks like a different one now. My phone has latched on to a signal and is busy downloading. I open my inbox to see what's arrived. There are two emails from Alison at ARK, and one from Caz that only arrived this morning. I open Alison's first one, sent the day after my arrival.

Hello Rachel,

I hope you had no problems moving in and are feeling settled in Paradise House. Please get in touch any time to let me know how you're getting on or if you've got any queries at all. I'd be grateful if you can let me know that you're there and all is well.

Kind regards,

Alison

It's much what I expected, so I open her second which arrived yesterday.

Hi Rachel,

I haven't heard from you, and it's just occurred to me that you haven't been given the information about the wireless network we had installed. You may be waiting until you go into town before you access email. If so, this is just to let you know that the information, including the password, is attached. I assume you won't get my messages until you've had a chance to access the internet, so do let me know as soon as you're connected.

Thanks so much.

Kind regards,

Alison

I read it over twice. It sounds normal enough, but I can't help feeling she's hiding something. I open the attachment, which takes ages with the weak signal my phone is working on, and find the password. As soon as I've tapped it into my network settings, the signal pops into full life, so I send Alison a quick reply.

I'm fine, thanks, Alison, and everything is okay here. But can you explain why there's a locked door in the basement? I found it when looking for the router, and can't open it. The router is obviously in there so it would help to be able to go in. Otherwise all is well.
  Thanks so much.
  Rachel

I feel better when I've sent it. She'll put my mind at rest, I'm sure. Then I open Caz's email, which is titled 'Are you there???'

Kate, I've been trying to reach you! I've been sending the texts to let you know I need to call you but you've not replied. Are you getting them? I tried to phone in the end, but I can't reach you that way either. Have you turned your phone off? I need to talk to you about Rory. He's definitely realised that something's wrong. Call me if you can. Hope you're okay. I'm so worried. I just don't know what to do if you don't reply. Caz x

A flicker of panic goes through me. Caz is the loose cannon in this whole thing. She used to be so reliable, so on my side

– or at least, that's what I thought. But ever since I made her into my accomplice, she seems to be crumbling under the strain. The last thing I want her to do is crack and tell Rory everything she knows.

I take a deep breath. So. It's about to begin. Well, I always knew it would. We would only get so far, and then the craziness would start. I text Caz:

Phone signal here very patchy. I'm calling you in five minutes. Go somewhere quiet.

I look over at Heather. 'Are you all right, sweetie? Would you like a biscuit?'

She stops playing and looks over her shoulder at me, her towelling turban falling a little loosely now. 'No, thank you, Mummy.'

'Really?' I smile at her. 'I've got your favourite. Chocolate creams.'

She blinks back at me and says, 'I'm not hungry.'

'Okay,' I say jokily. 'I guess I'll have to eat them all myself!'

She laughs and says, 'Don't be greedy, Mummy!'

'All right, as long as you share them with me. Listen, I have to make a call. I'll be right back when I'm done, and we'll have some biscuits together, okay?'

'Okay,' she says with a tiny shrug before turning back to her game.

I head off outside where the phone signal is better, well out of her earshot.

*

70

'Kate?'

Caz's voice comes breathless down the line.

'Yes. I'm up and running. I've got a wireless connection and I think it's safe.'

'Oh, that's good.'

'Did you email me from your home computer?'

'No. I did what you said. I waited until I was at work.'

'I said only do that if you had to. The library or an internet cafe is best.'

'I didn't have time, Kate,' she says sorrowfully.

'All right,' I say briskly. I don't want to hear more. Somewhere out there, life is going on as normal. Caz is doing the modern woman's shuttle between her workplace and home, racing about keeping everyone in clean socks and hot meals at the same time as managing a department. She doesn't even have Phil to help anymore. It used to be my shuttle too, springing from bed in the morning to make breakfasts, pack bags, empty and repack the dishwasher, then get myself ready while reminding everyone what their day held. Off I went, from home to school to railway station and the thirty-minute journey into the city. The end of the day took me in the opposite direction, this time to the minder's house to collect the children and then home, sometimes via the supermarket, to get dinner and chivvy the children through the bath and into bed. Then Rory and I would collapse in front of whatever was on at nine o'clock, watch the news at ten, and turn in.

God, it was exhausting. Mundane. I thought my life was slipping away from me in an endless round of domestic labour and work stress.

And yet . . . if I could have it all back tomorrow, I would. In a heartbeat.

'Kate? Are you there?'

'Yes . . . yes, I'm here. Did you want to talk to me about Rory?'

'Yes. He rang me last night. He's suspicious, Kate. He says he booked you a counselling session but you didn't turn up. So he went round to the house last night and there was no one in. He rang me right afterwards. He thinks you might have done a runner.'

'What did you tell him?'

'Nothing! I said I hadn't heard from you.' Caz sounds indignant, more like her old self. Then her voice drops. 'But I don't know how I'll be able to lie to him if he gets upset. He deserves to know you're all right. It's wrong to let him worry.'

'You can't tell him, Caz,' I say, my voice full of authority. 'I mean it. I don't want him to find me. I just need some time. Just let me have that.'

'But he could know you're okay. He doesn't have to know where you are. Then you'll still get the time you need.'

'Caz,' I say, my voice rising, 'it's important you do what I want. Do you understand? I don't want him to know anything at all!' I can't explain why this matters so much to me, but it does. I try to sound calmer. 'I promise I'll come home when the time is right.'

'Okay,' she replies weakly. I know she's going to be torn. Perhaps I should have got someone else to help me. I relied on her loyalty to me, but I didn't factor in that Rory would be able to tug at her heart strings and perhaps turn her to his side. If there's the faintest suggestion that she's going to give me away, I'll have to be on the move.

But then again, what can she tell him? She doesn't know where I am.

Nor does she know my alias, but she has an email and a phone number for me. Would that be enough to lead them to me?

'Swear you won't ever tell my email or number, Caz,' I say urgently. 'Swear it.'

'I . . . I swear. I won't tell.' She sounds shaky, though.

'Listen, I'm going to be fine. It's going to be all right. It'll be rough for Rory but only for a little while. Then we can all begin again. When I've got my head together. I promise, Caz. I won't make you keep this secret forever.'

'All right, I said I swear, didn't I?' But she sounds happier. I've reassured her.

'Just keep me informed of what he's going to do.'

'I think he's going to start looking for you. And I think he'll report you missing.'

'Did he say that?'

'He said he was afraid you'd done something stupid. I'm sure he'll report it if you don't get in touch.'

'Okay,' I say briefly. 'I thought he probably would.'

'You can't let them start looking for you, Kate, not when you're safe. Can't you at least tell him that? So he doesn't worry too much?'

'No, I've already told you!' I say fiercely, then add in a

gentler tone, 'Not yet, at least. Maybe. Let me think about it. All right?'

'All right.'

'Thanks, Caz. I owe you. Really. And you're saving my life. Don't forget that.'

That evening, the storm steps up a level. The wind roars around the house, whipping it hard and smacking it with rain. I have to empty the bucket in the front room and worry about leaving it all night, but there's not much else I can do. The light in our sitting room feels paltry against the great fierce darkness outside, and there are no curtains, so we can't shut out the howling blackness. We cuddle up together on the sofa, and I put some cheerful programme on the tablet to take our minds off the storm battering at the windows. Heather is transfixed, laughing at the jokes and watching the japes of the characters open-mouthed. When it's over, I say, 'Right, miss. It's time for bed. I think we'll both turn in.'

Mostly I stay up after Heather's asleep. I let myself have a glass of wine, maybe two, and then I take my pills. After that I'm too woozy to do anything but stumble along the corridor and find my way to bed. Tonight, though, I think Heather needs the reassurance of my presence. There's no denying that this old place is spookier when there's a raging tempest outside.

I take her by the hand and we go down the corridor to our sleeping quarters. Together we brush our teeth and I remind her to use the lavatory, and then we have a race to get into our pyjamas. I pretend not to be able to get my socks off, and

Heather wins, giggling. After that, we snuggle down under the duvet and listen to the storm outside.

'Isn't that weather making a silly fuss?' I whisper, holding her close. The honey scent of her hair is like a tranquilliser for me, filling me with calm and serenity. I can feel the gentle rise and fall of her breathing as she twists one fair lock around her fingers. I'm acutely aware of her presence; I can feel it healing me. It's the only thing that can. 'Lucky that we're safe and warm in here.'

'It can't get us,' she whispers back. She's clutching Sparkle-knee under one arm. The black button eyes stare at me, the woollen smile curving upwards.

'Yes. We're okay here. We're fine. Just us. You and me.'

Now is the time. She's going to ask about Rory. My stomach turns over in nervous anticipation. This is surely the moment.

There's a pause filled with the crack and thwack of rain against the window and the long whistle of wind in the chimney. Then she says, 'We're not here alone. There's Madam too.'

My stomach twists again, this time with something unpleasant. 'Madam?'

Heather had an imaginary friend in our old house. But Madam hasn't been heard of since we left and I just assumed that the disappearance was part of the trauma of the move.

Heather nods. 'Yes. Madam's here.'

'In this house? Now?' I don't know why this should fill me with such dread, but it does. I don't want Madam here. It has to be just us two.

Heather nods again and smiles a smile so sweet it makes me collapse inside at her beauty and innocence. 'Oh yes. I thought Madam was gone, but it's all right.' Then she snuggles into me and says contentedly, 'Madam's alive.'

Chapter Seven

The next day, the storm hasn't blown itself out as I expected. I look on weather sites and see that we're due more ceaseless rain.

'Another day inside, I'm afraid, sweetie,' I say to Heather as I pour cereal into a bowl for her. She eyes it suspiciously. She's getting to be pickier than ever. I add some milk, recently defrosted from the store in the basement freezer. 'Come on, we'll make it as fun as we can. Maybe we'll go upstairs and take a look around.'

She looks bored and sighs. 'Can I watch the tablet?'

'Not all day! You'll get square eyes.'

'Just for a while?'

I gaze at her as she looks up at me with a winsome expression. She would watch that thing all day long if I let her. 'How about an hour this morning and an hour this afternoon . . . You can choose when.'

'Yay. Now!'

I laugh. 'Haven't you ever heard of delayed gratification? Eat your cereal all up and you can watch it right away.'

She picks up her spoon eagerly as I put the cereal in front of her. A lash of rain against the windows makes me turn suddenly and look out towards the garden. It's properly wet out there, the water lying on the surface of the ground in big puddles, unable to soak away into already sodden earth. The trees and bushes look drenched, wet to the core. I wonder how the birds and animals are coping in the deluge. Then I blink and look again. I can't be sure but from what I can make out through the foliage, it looks as though water is actually rising up in the distance, grey and murky but still somehow shimmering as if reflecting what little light is able to penetrate the clouds. I go to the French doors and stare harder.

'I think there's water in the garden,' I say, my tone surprised.

Heather doesn't reply. She turns over a spoonful of cereal, watching it fall gently back into the milk.

'Yes. I'm sure of it.' A knob of worry tightens in my stomach and unspools out into my limbs so that my palms and fingers prickle. 'We must be near a lake or something.'

I hope that my anxiety doesn't sound in my voice but it suddenly occurs to me that the house might flood. *But how could it? We're on highish ground, aren't we?* There's still a distance for the water to cover before it's anywhere near us. It might be an isolated patch, a temporary pond caused by a soaked-out dip in the ground. No need to panic. *But I'll keep my eye on it.*

When I turn back, Heather has left the table, her cereal abandoned. She's out in the hall with the tablet. She's made herself a cosy snug out of coats she's hung off my umbrella and a broom I took out of the understairs cupboard, and I can hear the cartoons blaring out from inside it. I can't be angry. It's dull enough for her here at the moment with the weather like this. Let her watch the tablet. What harm can it really do?

I tidy up our breakfast things, then check my email. There's a reply from Alison and I click on it.

Rachel,

I'm sorry, I haven't been entirely clear. The basement is actually a private space and we'd prefer you not to go there. Obviously, you'll need to get bins, etc. (see my previous attachments for refuse information) and probably use the washing machine. Nothing else is to be touched. Do not attempt to open locked doors. Inform us of any problems with the wi-fi network and we will deal with them.

I'm looking forward to your report on the current condition of the upstairs.

Yours,

Alison

As I read it, my stomach tightens with an unpleasant feeling. So I'm not supposed to go down there. I shouldn't have touched that food. There's a secret behind that door I'm not allowed to know about it.

Instantly I wonder if my instinct is right. *Is there someone in there? Is that why it's forbidden?*

Then I shake my head. Why on earth would there be some-one down there? Why would ARK hire me if there were?

But then, why do they need me at all, when there's an internet connection and a freezer that's been recently stocked? Surely they could have assessed the place then. How much can have changed?

My rational mind tells me firmly that I'm here to deter squatters and look after the place. It's ridiculous to imagine someone hiding in the basement. Nevertheless, I can't help the shiver of fear that ripples over my skin. I look up for Heather. I always need her most when I'm afraid.

Just as my gaze lands on her makeshift tent, there's a loud banging at the front door. I gasp and freeze, and it comes again: a heavy thud on the door.

I jump up and stride out into the hallway, right up to the door. 'Who's there?' I call, hoping I sound braver than I feel.

'It's Matty!' comes a loud, cracked-sounding voice.

'Oh . . . right.' I let out a long breath. I'm relieved, even if a little irritated. Didn't I tell her to leave us alone? 'Okay, hold on. I need to find the key.'

I hurry over to Heather's little tent and peer inside. 'Sorry, darling, you have to go to the bedroom, okay? You can watch the tablet there. It won't be for long, I promise. If you're good, we'll have gummy sweets later.'

Heather looks unnerved by the banging on the door and the strange voice, and she doesn't question this, but nods and slips out, taking the tablet with her. She trots off across the hall and down the corridor towards the bedroom, and a moment later I hear the door close. She's safely hidden. I push

Heather's coat, the dolls and soft toys into the snug where they can't be seen, then go to the door, pull at the big bolts on the back of it, and turn the key. Tugging it open, I see Matty on the doorstep, looking just as she did the other day in her big brown overcoat, except that now she's wearing a black waterproof hat, like a fisherman's, and her boots are protected by galoshes. She's holding a rolled umbrella in her hand and has been using the handle to batter on the door. She's not alone, though, and my gaze slides to the woman standing just behind her on the step.

'This is my sister, Sissy,' she says, noticing. Sissy is almost exactly like Matty, but shorter and even rounder. The same grey hair escapes from beneath her hood, and she has the same dark eyes, except that her pupils have almost entirely engulfed the iris, so that they appear completely black.

'Hello, Sissy,' I say helplessly. I don't quite see how I can order away these two old ladies, wet and probably cold too. 'How can I help you?'

'You've got water climbing up your garden. The lake's flooded,' Matty says bluntly.

'The lake?'

'Down the bottom of the garden. But the overflow's blocked and it's climbing up. Nowhere else to go.' Matty stands there, staring at me.

I stare back, feeling at a loss. Are we going to keep being put in harm's way? 'I didn't know there was a lake in the garden.'

'It's a big garden,' Matty replies. 'You can't see the water from the house.'

'So do you think it will reach us?'

'It'd have to rain for a good while. I don't think so. It never has before.'

'Well, that's good then.' I'm relieved, although anxious about the idea of Heather playing out near a flooded lake. I'll have to keep an eye on her if we go out. I smile at them, hoping this will be their cue to go, but neither moves and I'm uncomfortable under the stare of their dark eyes. 'And what about you? Are you all right?'

'The electricity's stopped working,' Matty says laconically. 'And the wood's wet. We can't boil the kettle for a hot drink.'

'Oh.' My heart sinks. 'I see. Well . . . you'd better come in.' I stand back so that they can enter. Matty comes in first, holding her sister's hand, and Sissy follows just behind. Matty looks about as she enters, but Sissy only stares at her sister's back. 'Would you like some tea or coffee then? I'm afraid it's very rough here. There's not much in the way of furniture. I was supposed to bring my own but it's in storage at the moment and I haven't had the chance to arrange delivery.' It's a little lie but it explains my slightly odd circumstances. 'Here, take your wet things off and let's go to the kitchen.'

After divesting overcoats and galoshes, they are ready to follow me. I lead them down the corridor towards the westerly part of the house, where the kitchen is. Once they are in there, I say, 'Will you just excuse me for a moment? I'll be right back.' I dash to the sitting room, quickly gather up Heather's things, stash them behind the sofa, and return to the kitchen. The women haven't moved, they're standing there waiting for me. Now the coats are off I can see that they are dressed in similar rough wool skirts and jumpers.

'That's bad luck about the electricity,' I say as I come in. 'Luckily I've still got a supply. Shall I make some tea?'

'That'd be nice,' Matty says.'

I fill the kettle at the tap. 'How about you, Sissy? Tea or coffee?'

'Oh, tea, please,' says Sissy, not meeting my eye. She's still holding her sister's hand, I notice. Sissy's voice is softer than Matty's, but with the same odd accent that is not quite one thing or the other. I feel suddenly sorry for them, this pair of elderly sisters living in an isolated cottage with only each other.

'Well, do stay for tea and get warm.' I hope that they understand the implied *and then go home*. I'm worried about Heather on her own in the bedroom. I can't leave her for long.

'How are you settling in?' Matty asks, looking about with interest. Sissy keeps her gaze downwards as though paralysed with shyness.

'Very well, thank you. I mean . . . it's a big place to be in on my own but I'm getting used to it. I only use a few of the rooms. I haven't even been upstairs.' The kettle, back on the heat, is warming up quickly.

'You're the caretaker,' Matty states.

'Well, guardian is what they call it,' I say lightly. I don't know why I should mind being called a caretaker but I do a little.

'Same thing.'

She's right, of course, so I say, 'Yes. True,' and busy myself with putting teabags in mugs, while asking if they take milk and sugar. When there are three mugs of tea, two with sugar, I put them on a tray and lead the old ladies to the sitting room. 'Please, make yourself at home,' I say, handing them the mugs.

I wonder how Heather is. I hate leaving her, but there's no other option at the moment. Perhaps it wouldn't have mattered if I'd told the women straight off that I've got my daughter here. They don't look the sort to take much interest in the outside world. But I've said I'm alone now, and anyway, it would go too much against the grain to let anyone else see Heather. I sit down, feeling shaky and nervous. I can't help casting quick glances at the door. I want this to be over quickly.

'You're very distracted,' observes Matty, her dark bird-like eyes peering at me over the rim of her cup as she lifts it to her lips. 'What's wrong?'

'Well . . . I . . .'

'Leave her alone, Matty,' says her sister. 'None of our business.'

Grateful to Sissy, I change the subject. 'How is the tea?'

'Very nice,' says Sissy quickly, but still not meeting my eyes. She's looking down into her cup.

'Any word from the owner?' Matty asks.

'No . . . not so far. I'm here for the time being. I can't tell you any more than that, I'm afraid.'

'Why go to all the trouble of buying it, and not live in it?' Matty mutters, as though personally offended by the situation. 'Most people would give their eye teeth to live in a place like this.'

'It is beautiful,' I agree, looking around at the sitting room. Every day, I admire the elaborate plasterwork – the cornicing in egg-and-dart patterns and the ceiling rose of white plaster acanthus leaves curling outwards. 'If it were mine, I'd be here like a shot, restoring every part of this wonderful old place. It has real potential, if someone could spend a bit of money on it. I suppose you knew it when there were people living here – properly, I mean. Not a guardian, like me.'

Matty nods slowly and says, 'That's true. We knew it in the old days.'

'Have you lived in the cottage long?'

Matty hesitates. 'Well now. In the cottage . . . Let me see. It's been two years we've been there now.'

'Oh.' I'm surprised. I thought they would say they'd been there longer. They look as though life hasn't changed for them in decades. 'Where did you move from?'

Sissy shifts a little on the sofa, and takes another quick sip of her tea.

Matty darts a glance towards her sister. 'We didn't exactly move . . . That's to say that we moved . . . from here.'

'Here?' I blink at her, surprised. 'This house?'

Matty nods. 'Yes. This house. We were both born here, weren't we, Sissy?'

'That's right,' Sissy agrees in her gentle voice. 'Born here. Lived here all our lives.'

'Oh.' I take this in, aware of the dynamic changing. A moment ago, they were interlopers. Now I feel as though I am. 'So, this was your house?'

'Yes,' Matty says slowly. 'You might say that. As good as.'

I'm embarrassed suddenly, remembering how I've just talked about the house's potential, and how I practically ordered them off what was their own property. 'So you sold it?'

'It was too big. Once the last of the old ones went. We had to keep it on until then, even though every year we wondered how we'd manage . . . didn't we, Sissy?'

Sissy nods.

'But we were under all sorts of obligations. Things held in trusts. Stipulations and covenants. It was no easy matter to sell. It took a long time to unravel it all.'

'So you sold it to the company? To ARK?' I suggest.

'That was the name, I think. We don't know much about them. They came to us as a matter of fact. Most particular that they wanted this place, even though they've got other properties – or that's what they said.' Matty takes a long drink from her mug. When she's finished, she says, 'Anyway, it's not ours anymore, is it, Sissy?'

'Not ours anymore,' echoes Sissy. She sits hunched, tucked in beside her sister as if keeping out of sight. I like her soft gentleness, or perhaps she just seems like that in comparison with Matty's spikiness.

I wonder how much they got for the house. They could have afforded something more than an old cottage, surely . . .
'It must be strange coming back here then,' I say politely. 'You must remember how it was before.'

'It's different now,' Matty agrees. 'We took what we wanted and they told us to leave the rest. Some men came one day and stripped out the carpets and so on, took away some things and brought in others. They made a racket while they were at it. It looked like they were going to start doing it up and making it fancy. But we've hardly seen anyone since then. We wondered if it was all a ruse, a tax dodge or whatever they call it, and the place would be left to rot. Then you came.' She slides a glance across at me. 'It's a mystery, isn't it?'

I wonder if the men are the ones who put in the internet connection and stuffed the freezer. Perhaps one of them is downstairs right now, under my feet as we speak . . .

Matty looks around at the sitting room, with its delicate chinoiserie wallpaper. 'I'm glad they left the paper in here. This was a sewing room once. So pretty. On a sunny day, we often had the doors to the garden open, do you remember, Sissy?'

'Yes,' Sissy says happily. 'And there was the gold chandelier with the crystal drops. I thought it was so lovely. It was my favourite room.'

It's hard to imagine Matty and Sissy sitting in here, young women sewing, the room full of fine antique furniture, pictures on the walls. But the house is so far from what they remember that they can hardly resent me for being here. Their vision of it disappeared long ago.

'It must be strange being here when it was your home for so long,' I say.

'It's different from how it was,' says Sissy, turning her face towards the garden. 'It was so full of sound, you see. There were so many of us! But as we grew up, the older ones died off. Others left. Eventually, it was only us.'

'You must have had a very large family.'

'We did – one big, happy family in the faith.' Sissy sighs.

'In the faith?' I'm puzzled.

Sissy smiles and closes her eyes.

Matty puts her mug down abruptly. 'That's enough gossip. We've had our tea. We'll be on our way.'

'Oh.' I'm vaguely startled that the visit is over already. 'Won't you be cold in the cottage?'

'We'd be just as cold here. Come on, Sissy.'

I put my mug on the table, relieved that I'll be able to let Heather out of the bedroom. It's occurred to me that if Matty and Sissy suspect there's a child here, they might feel they should inform the owners. All the more reason to make sure she isn't spotted. I stand up. 'As long as you're sure . . .'

'Yes, I said, didn't I?' Matty looks tetchy.

'Okay.'

In a moment we're out in the hall where the raincoats and galoshes are still shiny with rain. Matty puts on her own and then helps her sister.

'I hope you weren't too upset by the way the house has changed,' I say to Sissy. 'It must be disturbing when you remember the place in its heyday.'

'Doesn't make a difference to Sissy what it looks like,' Matty says, a little breathless as she pulls the overcoat on over Sissy's thick jumper. 'She's blind.'

At the same moment, Sissy turns her gaze towards me and I'm struck by the intensity of her dark, almost entirely black eyes.

'Oh,' I say awkwardly. 'I'm sorry.'

'I've not always been blind,' Sissy says in her gentle voice.

'Only since last year,' Matty puts in. 'Not too long after we left the house.'

'That must be very hard to come to terms with,' I say, at a loss. I can't think why I haven't realised that the old woman is blind when it seems obvious now.

'No. I don't seem to mind it as much as you'd think,' Sissy says with a little smile.

'Come on, old girl,' Matty says. 'We've got to get going. It's going to be dark before we know it, with all these rain clouds. And while you won't notice it, I will if I'm to get us both through the wet.'

'Will you be all right?' I ask. I want them to leave but now I'm anxious about them. 'Do you need some fuel? You said your wood is wet.'

'Have you got some?' Matty asks, shepherding Sissy towards the door.

'I . . . don't think so . . .' I wonder if there's any wood in the basement.

'Then why'd you offer?' But she doesn't say it nastily. 'We'll be all right. I'm sure we'll find something to get the range going with.' Matty is opening the front door. The rain has stopped but the lowering clouds don't look as if they are finished yet. 'Thank you for the tea.'

'Thank you,' echoes Sissy. Then she looks straight at me and smiles. 'You've been very kind. You should come and see us. If you ever feel you need to.'

'Thank you.' I can't help thinking that Sissy knows more about me than I realise. *But how could she?*

I watch them go, the older sister leading the younger by the hand into the murky afternoon.

I can't understand why I didn't know she was blind.

Heather seems perfectly happy in the bedroom, still glued to the tablet. I hug her guiltily, climbing onto the bed beside her. She hasn't done anything today but watch that thing. But outside, the rain is still tumbling down. The water in the garden doesn't look any closer, though.

'Come on,' I say. 'Turn the cartoons off now.'

'Five more minutes?' she wheedles.

I relent just a little. 'Only while I make some sandwiches for lunch. Then off for the rest of the day.'

Heather doesn't complain, which makes me think she has secretly had enough. I leave her to it and go to the kitchen to make our lunch. I'm thinking about Alison's email and the way it forbids me to investigate the basement as I switch on the radio to catch the lunchtime news, half listening to the headlines. It's the very last item that makes me freeze, the buttery knife held in mid-air.

'. . . are seeking Kate Overman, thirty-eight, who was last seen almost a week ago at her home in . . .'

I reach out and switch it off as fast as I can. *Oh my God!* What if Heather hears it? What if Matty and Sissy are listening to it as well, and begin to wonder if there is some connection between the missing woman and my arrival?

I'm panting, my fingers shaking. *It's all out there.*

I go back over everything I've done to keep myself hidden and I can't see any way that I can be found. I'm certain no one else has seen Heather. The only chink in my armour is Caz. I have to trust that she'll stay strong.

I lean against the worktop, trembling. So it's happened. I knew it would, but the fact is terrifying. *They're looking for me. They're on my trail.*

Chapter Eight

That night I wake with a start, gasping as I jerk into consciousness. I'm certain I heard something, but the room is silent, apart from my rapid breathing. Outside there is a full moon and a clear sky, and pallid light streams in through the thin curtains. I turn automatically to make sure Heather is with me, and for a moment, I don't see her. Panic burns through me.

Where is she? Where's she gone?

But then, blinking, I realise she's there, fast asleep, her skin marble-white in the moonlight, lids closed, Sparkleknee tucked under her arm. I take control of my breathing, blowing out a soft exhalation through pursed lips, trying to calm my pounding heart. Then I smell it, just a faint trace in the air but still that unmistakable, acrid tang.

Smoke.

I don't give myself time to be frightened. I am out of the bed in an instant, on the scent, running out of the bedroom and into the corridor beyond. Around me the house is vast, soaked in darkness, and not as silent as it is in the day: there are creaks and snaps and little clicks. *What are those noises?* I lift my face and sniff. There it is again, I'm certain of it. Now I'm afraid, with a rapid, jittering terror.

It's smoke. The house is on fire.

But where is it? It can't be close; the scent is too remote, too elusive for it to be nearby. I run down the corridor, flicking switches as I go so that lightbulbs begin to glow, faint and fuzzy but enough for me to see my way. In the cold, empty hall, the marble floor is icy under my bare feet. I sniff again like a hunting dog, my nostrils flaring as I search for the smell of smoke.

Nothing. I run up the stairs to the upper landing. Nothing here, no sound, the air dull and empty. I race down the stairs again and across the hall, out into the east wing.

There it is! Did I leave something on in the kitchen?

A moment later, I'm panting in the kitchen doorway as the lights flicker into life, but there's no sign of anything amiss. The air holds only the remnants of the cooking smells from earlier: oil, onion, tomato.

I turn, with a cold sense of dread, towards the back stairs that lead down to the basement. Slowly I walk towards the rectangle of blackness that disappears into the depths of the house. As I approach it, I catch again the bitter scent of smoke, and terror washes through me, making me dizzy, but I have to go forward. I have to know. I tell myself that Heather is safe on the other side of the house, there is time to find whatever is burning and douse it. Perhaps a fuse has sparked and set something alight, or the washing machine is faulty and has burst into flames, or . . .

Did I do it? Did I leave something on?

I rush forward, down the stairs, scrabbling for the light switch as I go, certain that the smell is stronger now. The fluorescent strip flashes into life and I see that everything is quiet. Nothing is alight. The fuse board is the same as ever, the washing machine sits blameless nearby. I sniff hard, and turn to look at the steel door. Then I hear it.

Something behind it moves.

Oh my God . . . I knew it! I knew it!

I'm suddenly so furious, it dampens my terror, and I run over to the door and pound on it hard. 'Come out! Come the hell out, if you're in there!'

There's nothing. Silence. I strain to listen and think I hear a click or a snap. But there's no smell of smoke now, nothing but the musty, dampish aroma of the basement. I'm shivering, I realise. It's freezing down here, and I'm in pyjamas and bare feet. But I can't leave, not till I'm sure there's no fire down here, and no one hiding behind that door.

You must have imagined it, says a voice in my head. *Maybe it was a dream.*

Perhaps I've just woken up after sleepwalking here. I moan out loud. *What am I going to do, if I can't be sure if I'm dreaming or awake?* It was so real, the smell of smoke, the sound of something behind the door. But now, there's nothing at all.

I wait for as long as I can, until I can stand the cold and the misery no longer, and slowly I leave the basement and go back to bed, turning out the lights behind me.

*

The next morning, I try to forget the night terror that possessed me. It would be easy to wallow if it weren't for Heather, who wakes in a jolly mood, full of energy and ebullience. She eats a good breakfast – I don't have to throw away any cereal or milk – while I can only drink coffee and pick at cornflakes, ignoring the radio in the corner, which I daren't turn on. Afterwards she wants to play.

'Let's go outside, Mummy, it's not raining!' she calls, pulling on her boots.

'All right. But I think it will rain again soon,' I say. 'The clouds are still a horrible colour.' We go out together, and I find the fresh, damp air invigorating. It makes my night fears recede until I hardly remember them. But as we stomp around the house, looking for good puddles to splash in, I realise we are on the side where the room in the basement must be. I remember that the basement on this side has windows just above ground level, and start to inspect them as we pass, trying to work out if any of them might belong to the room behind the steel door.

'Go round to your den, Heather, I'll be there in a minute,' I say. 'And don't go near the end of the garden where the water is, will you?'

'Okay.' She trots off happily, keen to see how muddy her play space has become.

I get down on my knees and look through the slender window lights nearest to me. It's hard because of the darkness beyond and the veil of dirt and cobwebs on the glass but I think I can make out the edge of the washing machine. That means . . . I shift along to my left . . . Now, if I squint, I can make out the shadowy form of the stairs. I move along further, to the next small row of windows, just a thin border of glass above ground level.

Surely this is it. The room. It can't be anywhere else.

I lean forward, looking as hard as I can through the dirty glass into the murkiness beyond. I'm almost lying prone on the ground as I try to see inside. Then, suddenly, there's a flicker of light. Red. Yes – a flash. I saw it. I'm sure of it. Then . . . a green flash.

But is there anyone there?

I can't see anything else. Just more pulses of light. First red . . . then green again . . .

'Mummy!' It's Heather, coming back round. 'Where are you? You said you'd come!' She stares at me. 'What are you looking at?'

'Nothing, darling. Really. I'm coming now.' I get up, brush wet grass and mud from my coat, and follow her back to her bay tree den.

That afternoon, I go upstairs for the first time, with a sheet of paper for notes and my phone to take photographs with. Heather comes with me, clutching my hand and holding Sparkleknee under her other arm. She's muted and apprehensive, so I say in a jolly voice, 'Isn't this fun, sweetie? Our own adventure!' She doesn't look convinced, and holds my hand tighter than ever.

At the top of the stairs, on the upper landing, is a thick door of old dark wood, ornately carved and with tarnished brass furniture: a ring handle, an escutcheon and a smudged fingerplate. It takes a real effort to push it open and I know it's the sort that will swing closed behind us, shutting out any noise from below. In the corridor ahead is darkness, the kind created by shuttered windows and closed doors: shadowy, twilightish with patches of deep blackness. I'm glad Heather is with me, her hand warm in mine, her presence forcing me to show a jolly confidence I don't entirely feel.

'Shall we get some light in here?' I say, and she nods. I feel for a switch and find one. Somewhere far down the passage, a bulb begins to glow orange. Now I can see that the carpets are gone and there are only bare floorboards, a patchwork of dark original boards and light pine replacements where rotten ones have been removed. The woodwork is thick with yellowish gloss paint, chipped in places, revealing the many layers beneath. Even so, the beautiful mouldings and the fine proportions of the space cannot be disguised. It's shabby, dirty and untouched, but that can't hide the innate grace and beauty of the house.

'What a place, Heather! Look at all these rooms. I wonder who used to live here?'

Heather seems happier now the light is on; she lets go of my hand and runs her fingertips along the wall. 'There must have been lots of people,' she says. 'Lots and lots!'

'I don't think so, not recently. Just those two old ladies. I bet they ended up living downstairs, like we do, and just shut up this floor. That's why it's so much worse than downstairs.'

I start to walk around, opening doors. Behind them the rooms are all the same: bare boards, walls in a poor condition with blown and missing plaster, blocked-up fireplaces and draughty, dirty windows thick with cobwebs. I shiver in the chill air. There are bathrooms, dank and filthy with ancient fittings that look like they've not seen water for many years. The lavatories are in separate rooms, long and thin with ice-cold tiles and cisterns mounted high on the walls.

No wonder this place fell into disrepair with just the sisters to look after it all alone.

But what were they doing here? What did it use to be? With so many bedrooms, it has the feel of an institution, but it's not set out like a school and there are no traces of classrooms or dormitories.

'Look in this room, Mummy!' Heather has opened a door and stands in the light that comes from within. It's evidently a main bedroom, with a grand view from its bay window giving out over the tops of the rhododendron bushes, and, unlike the rest, some furniture remains. There's an old four-poster bed, its mattress gone but some dusty blue silk hangings swagged down from the top. An antique desk or dressing table, with an old china-backed hairbrush, its bristles holding skeins of dust, sits between two elegant windows with stone balconies beyond. On the walls are the grey outlines where pictures once hung. Heather goes over and sits at the dressing table, picking up the hairbrush.

'This can be my room!' she says happily and goes to brush her hair.

'Not that,' I say, darting over and grabbing it. 'It's filthy! Horrible.' I take another look around. 'I think it's nicer downstairs. Come on, let's finish up here and go back.'

There is not much more to see. I find another staircase,

leading up again, surely into the attics. I have no desire to go up there.

This place is sound. It's just not very comfortable.

'I'm going to take some pictures. It won't take long.'

'Okay,' Heather says. She seems more interested than frightened and wanders back towards the room with the blue silk bed.

I snap photographs of the worst decay, and of the general condition. They're the best my phone can manage. After twenty minutes, I've had enough. My skin prickles with something I can only think of as a bad vibe. I don't like the atmosphere here at all. There's a powerful sense of absence that chills me, as though all these empty rooms carry memories of the people who used to sleep in them. But I can't make out if the memories are happy or sad. I'll be glad to get back through the heavy oak door and leave the upstairs to itself.

I head back towards the main bedroom, and as I get closer I can hear Heather chatting away to herself. *Playing at being Rapunzel or something, I should think.*

It's only when I get closer that I hear her say, 'But why is Mummy doing that?'

There's a silence and then she says, 'That's not very good. I don't like that.'

I come quickly into the bedroom to see her sitting cross-legged on the floor, Sparkleknee propped up beside her.

'Who are you talking to?' I ask lightly. 'What's Sparkleknee saying now?'

Heather looks up at me from where she's sitting. 'It's not Sparkleknee. It's Madam, of course.'

Instantly I'm filled with the same nameless dread I felt last time she mentioned her invisible friend. I say breathlessly, 'I don't want you talking to Madam, Heather!'

'Why not? Madam's my friend. Anyway, it's rude not to answer,' she points out. 'You always say I have to speak when I'm spoken to.'

'No. Not this time. You have to obey me, Heather, do you understand? I'm serious. Madam might say bad things. Wrong things! Send Madam away!'

'What if I can't?' Heather asks, her eyes wide. 'What if Madam won't go?'

I gaze back at her, speechless, unable to tell if the prospect frightens her or not. I don't have the answers for her. I have no idea how to banish an imaginary presence.

Then she shrugs and says, 'It's okay, we're on our own now. Madam said there's no point in staying if you're angry, and went away.'

And she turns back to Sparkleknee, humming softly to herself as though there's been nothing at all to disconcert her.

Downstairs, I feel as though calm is restored. Heather and I are in the sitting room together; I'm doing a puzzle in an old book of crosswords while a mug of coffee cools on the table beside me, and Heather is colouring in while an audiobook plays on the tablet. I'm half picking up the adventures of a pair of twins by the seaside while I ponder my clues. Then my phone pings with a text. It's Caz. She wants to call. I text back to tell her to ring me in two minutes, and go outside so Heather can't hear the conversation.

'How are you, Kate?' Caz sounds anxious and miserable.

'I'm fine,' I say cheerfully. 'Never better.'

'Oh Kate. How can you say that?' Her voice is trembly.

'Relax. I don't mean it.'

'It's awful here,' she goes on. 'Rory is round all the time. He seems sure that I know something about where you are.'

I can see a watery sun setting over the drenched garden. The air is cool with the approaching night. 'What have you said?'

'Nothing!'

'And what's he said?'

'He's worried sick, Kate.'

'He's reported me missing – I heard it on the radio. No doubt he's got the police involved.'

'He wants you to come back. You know why.'

'For God's sake!' I hiss into the phone, full of sudden fury. 'I just want some time to myself. Is that so much to ask?'

'But why not tell him, if that's all it is—'

'You know why! You know what he did! To me! To our family! To everything I care about . . . For Christ's sake, Caz, you know . . .'

'But . . .' She gulps over the word. 'Ady,' she says in a choked voice. 'What about Ady?'

I click the call off instantly. I don't want to hear it. I refuse to hear it.

I've made a mistake. I won't talk to Caz anymore. She doesn't know where I am. She doesn't know my alias. I'll be fine without her.

My hands are shaking. I have a wild desire to go and get

my pills and wash two down with a gulp of the ice-cold white wine that's in the fridge. The phone rings again almost at once, and I put it to my ear and snap, 'Forget it, Caz, I'm not listening to that shit.'

'Rachel?' says a puzzled voice at the other end.

'What?'

'Isn't that Rachel?'

I know the voice but I'm confused. Then I remember and force myself back to normality. 'Oh, yes, sorry, Alison. I thought you were someone else.'

'Obviously,' she says drily. 'It sounds like you're not too happy with Caz, whoever she is.'

I laugh awkwardly. 'Yes. Sorry. How can I help you?'

'I was just wondering if you've got the report ready yet.'

'Yes . . . almost. I've done the survey. I'll write it up for you first thing. Is it urgent?'

'Well, I'd particularly like to know about the condition of the upstairs of the house. It wasn't much used by the previous owners, not recently anyway. It would be good to have a sense of how habitable it is.'

'All right. But I'm quite happy living in the downstairs. There's no need for it to be habitable on my account.'

'That's good but it's more for the others that I'm interested.'

'Others?' I clutch the phone a little harder and my insides clench. 'What others?'

'In case we appoint more guardians. You can't really look after that enormous place all on your own, can you?'

'Yes, yes, I'm fine—'

She goes on smoothly, 'And it gives you no flexibility in terms of leaving. What if you want a holiday? If more people do arrive, we can take steps to ensure privacy is maintained, don't worry about that.'

I say nothing, my mind whirling over the possibility of more people here and what that would mean for me.

There's a slight cool in Alison's voice when she speaks again. 'I think that if you check your contract, Rachel, you'll see that you've agreed we can bring other people in at any time.'

I wrack my brains but I can't remember seeing such a clause. 'Okay . . .'

'You're free to give notice if you want.'

'Oh no, that's fine,' I say quickly. 'But will you give me advance warning of anyone arriving?'

'We'll certainly try.' Alison sounds a little friendlier now. 'But if you can get me that report, I'd be most grateful.'

'Of course.'

'One more thing – did you get my message about the basement? There are private areas on the property, Rachel. You need to understand that.'

'Yes.' For a moment, I want to demand an explanation for the steel door, the flashes of light, the noises, the freezer. But I daren't. I need this place. 'I understand.'

'Good. I'll be in touch.'

When the call is over, I go to the bathroom and look at myself in the mirror fixed to the wall. My face, ignored and un-made-up, looks almost like a stranger's and I'm still disconcerted by the white hair, now looking dry and crackly with a faint black line emerging at the roots. Do I look like the pictures of Kate Overman that are probably this moment on the internet, on the television bulletins and maybe in the papers? I haven't had my photo taken in a while, and when I did, I had shining brown hair in blow-dried waves, well-cared-for skin, and subtle make-up. I smiled easily and had bright, untroubled eyes. Maybe they're using my work picture, a flattering portrait that had my wrinkles washed out. Or a family snap of me and Heather, maybe the one of us on the beach at Broadstairs last summer, when we're sharing a paper cone of hot, salty chips and the wind is blowing our hair out in fuzzy tentacles.

No one would connect that woman with the one I'm looking at: her skin greyish in comparison with the white hair, the eyes dull and tired, a general dryness everywhere.

I'm Rachel Capshaw. I'm an artist. I'm living here in this place on my own.

They would never see Heather, changed not one jot from that photograph. I would make sure of it. But how easy would that be?

I don't know if I'm up to the challenge.

It would change everything. I would have to leave as soon as possible. The whole point of this escape is for Heather and me to be alone and undisturbed, and for us to have the time together that other people want to stop. If others arrived, that would no longer be the case.

I'd run again. Somewhere. Anywhere.

*

That night, when Heather is asleep, I take a glass of wine into the sitting room and connect the tablet to the router, and suddenly I have access to the internet. It feels like a guilty pleasure, something forbidden, but I remind myself that there is no way this IP address could be under surveillance. There are no new emails in my Rachel Capshaw account. A search on my name brings up dozens of articles, lots in our local papers. There are pictures, of all of us. And there is our old house too. That's no surprise. These were all in print before I left. But now I can see that I'm in the national press too. My name is highlighted over and over until I can hear it chanted in my head:

Kate Overman. Kate Overman. Kate Overman.

The details are all the same. Rory is looking for me. I'm on the run. People are concerned. The police are interested in my whereabouts. There is a picture of Heather, too. The soft wavy blonde hair, the big blue eyes, the heartbreaking smile.

Kate Overman. Kate Overman. Kate Overman.

There I am. Normal, happy, smiling. Brown hair, lipstick, cashmere jumper, jeans and expensive boots. A privileged mummy in her happy life.

God, I can't stand it!

I turn off the tablet and drink my wine with a shaking hand.

I'm not Kate Overman anymore. I don't think I ever will be again.

*

The next morning, Heather comes to me, pale-faced, wan. She looks weak. I can't seem to make her eat very much and I'm worried that she's not well.

'I've got nothing to play with, Mummy,' she says, leaning against me. 'I'm bored.'

'You've got lots of toys and books,' I say, stroking her hair. She pulls lightly away so that I can't. 'Do you want to watch the tablet?'

She shakes her head and sighs. 'No.'

'What about Sparkleknee? Do you want to play with her? You like that. In the hall, on the squares.'

She looks at me, puzzled. 'Sparkleknee isn't here.'

'Yes, she is.' I smile at her. 'You brought her here, don't you remember? You've been playing with her and taking her to bed.'

Heather looks at me sadly and shakes her head again, slow and sure. 'Oh no, Mummy,' she says. 'Sparkleknee isn't here. She's gone. With all the rest.'

I stare at her, a sense of cold dread mounting in my chest. 'That's not right, darling.'

'It is, Mummy. She's not here. She was never here.' And she wanders away to find something to do.

Chapter Nine

I've been searching and searching for Sparkleknee. It's another of Heather's games, I'm sure, to pretend that she's not here. But she must be. I saw her myself. I know she was here. But I can't find her. Instead I turn up Teddington, a battered old bear that I don't remember bringing either. As soon as I show Teddington to Heather, she is delighted and tucks him under her arm. Now he is with her at night, not Sparkleknee. She doesn't mention Madam again, either, which is a relief.

While I'm searching for the doll, I'm surprised to see a white envelope lying on the hall floor beneath the letterbox opening. There has been no post here at all since I arrived. I've assumed that there is a general redirection order in place, to send all the post to ARK. I go over and pick it up. There is no name on the front. I turn it over a few times and then open it. Inside is a postcard, a very old view of a church with the words 'St James the Saviour' printed across the top. I turn it over and there is a neatly written message in an old-fashioned hand.

Thank you for letting us shelter with you and for the tea.
You were very kind. Please come and see us if you ever
need to. You can telephone us on the number below.
  Matty and Sissy

I'm comforted. I didn't expect it. I don't think I'll need their hospitality, but it's nice of them all the same. I put it back into the envelope and forget about it.

The weather starts to improve and the sunshine makes everything feel better and brighter. I send my report to Alison, but hear nothing back, so I relax and try to enjoy myself. It's easier now we can go outside for walks. We have cleaning and tidying in the morning, then a lesson with some of the reading and maths books I've brought with us, then a walk. In the afternoon, another lesson, then playing, and later, a cartoon while I read, ignoring the temptation to look myself up on the internet. I don't want to know what's going on, I'd rather not think about it. In the same way, I shut the thoughts of that mysterious downstairs room out of my mind, although I often lie awake at night, listening for noises, thinking of the flickering lights inside it. On one of those sleepless nights, towards the end of our first week at the house, something hits me.

The router, I tell myself suddenly. *That's what it is.* The thought releases me from some of my anxiety.

The next day, on impulse, while Heather is watching something, I get the easel and art box out of the car and set it up in the empty room at the front, still with its bucket under the hole in the ceiling of the bay. The light is cool but bright, and

I start painting anything that flows from my brush. In fact, my consciousness seems barely engaged in what I'm doing – it roams freely as I work automatically, smearing colours about on the paper and creating an abstract painting. It doesn't mean anything. It just is. After an hour or so, I leave the painting feeling refreshed and relaxed, as though for a short while I've been set free from everything that oppresses me. I can forget the chasers out there looking for me; Rory, and his implacable need to find me and change everything; the memories with their arsenal of pain. It all goes away and lets me be. I begin to sense very faintly that something better may lie ahead in the future, if I'm just given the time I need to get there.

But even as I begin to feel better, I am afraid that Heather is getting sicker. It's nothing I can put my finger on. She has no temperature and no particular symptoms. She seems quite happy in herself. It's just that she is getting ever so slightly weaker. She disappears for long periods of time and I find her curled up asleep on the bed in our room or hiding in the little snug she's made. Then suddenly, she'll be fine. She'll come to life and be as animated and joyful as ever, bringing me such intense happiness. Then, inexorably, the fade will come and she'll lose her high spirits.

I try not to think about it. It makes me too afraid to think about what will happen if she becomes truly sick. We're happy here. To go anywhere else would threaten all of that. I cannot face the prospect of losing her.

We have been in the house for almost two weeks. I'm painting in the bay-windowed room, Heather lolling around colouring in, when a van roars up the drive, spurting gravel out from under its tyres. I run to the window, rubbing the paint off my hands on the old apron I'm using as an artist's smock. The van is one of those cute, vintagey ones in baby blue with daisies painted on the sides. In the front are two figures, and as I watch anxiously, they climb out of the van, one from each door, and jump down onto the gravel. It's two women, young, both in jeans. One wears an expensive-looking shaggy sheepskin gilet and a beanie hat with a fur pompom, blonde hair spilling over her shoulders. The other has on a black leather bomber jacket, the kind with extra zips. She has short fair hair cut close to her scalp and wears a pair of aviator sunglasses and high-heeled boots. I have no idea what girls like these would want at a place like this.

There's a strong knocking on the front door.

'Who's that?' Heather asks, sitting up straight and looking out through the window.

'Get down!' I hiss. 'Down, Heather!'

She obediently lies flat as I retreat from sight into the shadows at the rear of the room, then scuttles over to join me, clutching at my leg.

There's another firm rapping on the door. Shivers of fear race over my back. I sense danger from these two. They don't look like they're here by accident. They don't have the benign bumbliness of Matty and Sissy. They look like they're on a mission.

'Wait in here, sweetie,' I say quietly, then slip out of the room and into the hall, shutting the door behind me.

'Hello?' The voice comes from behind the front door, followed by another sharp rapping. 'Anyone there?'

I tiptoe towards the door. I can hear them talking now.

'Shall we wait? Or go around the back, see if she's outside?' The voice is deepish, mellow, with the plummy vowels of private school and pony club.

'I say just use the key.' The answering voice is accented – it sounds Australian to me. Maybe South African. It's higher, more brusque. 'She might be out and we're wasting our time anyway.'

'Knock again. Give her a moment more. It's a big place.'

There's another strong rapping on the door and the Australian voice: 'Hello? Anyone at home?' Then, 'Get the key, Soph. She's not coming.'

I'm trembling with fright. These two are coming in whether I like it or not. How on earth have they got a key? Are they officials of some kind? I decide it's better to take the decisive course and shout, 'Hello, I'm coming! Just a second, I'll get the bolt off the door.'

The rusty old bolt isn't shut but I make a show of moving it so that it clanks and scrapes convincingly. Then, taking a deep breath and struggling to tame my beating heart, I slowly undo the latch and pull the door open. There they are, taller and slimmer now that they are right in front of me. Their youthful glamour is intimidating, both with smooth, tanned complexions and regular features. They wear it lightly, not knowing how fleeting all that easy beauty is. They probably think they'll always look like this. Beside them, I feel shrunken and wizened, my white hair drier than ever, my skin untended.

The old clothes I'm wearing, my trainers, and the paint-stained smock, make me feel dowdy and plain. But I need to appear confident, so I give them a big smile.

'Hello, ladies. How can I help you?'

'Are you Rachel Capshaw?' asks the Australian. She is the one with the short blonde hair cut close to her scalp so that it shows off sharp cheekbones and a perfectly formed skull.

'Yes. Who are you?'

'I'm Agnes. This is Sophia.'

Sophia blinks big, slanted green eyes at me and says in her drawling way, 'So lovely to meet you. Alison says you're an artist' – she looks pointedly at my smock – 'and I can see she's right. So fascinating!'

My insides seem to plummet downwards with fear. Alison has sent them. Are they here to check up on me?

'You know Alison?' I say, still smiling, my voice sounding less choked than I feel. I wonder if Heather is listening from behind the door. I hope she doesn't decide to come out, but surely she knows by now that I don't want anyone to see her.

'Yep.' Agnes slides her sunglasses down her nose, revealing china-blue eyes with heavy kohl outlines. She gazes over my shoulder into the dimness of the hall. 'Can we come in?'

'Are you here because of my report?' I say quickly, still blocking the way. 'I can do it again if Alison's not happy. I can easily take some more pictures. There's really no need for an inspection.'

Agnes laughs and says crisply, 'It's not an inspection. Didn't Alison tell you to expect us?'

I shake my head. But then, I remember, I haven't checked my email since yesterday.

Sophia says a little more sympathetically, 'Maybe she forgot. She said she was going to let you know. The plans have been brought forward. We're here to get the place ready.'

'Really?' Dread is flowing up through my body and flooding my brain. The feeling is almost overwhelming. I have an urge to fall to the floor and scream, but I fight it. 'Ready for what?'

Agnes smiles. I have the distinct feeling that she is enjoying this. 'Ready for us, of course.'

There's nothing I can do. I have to let them in. As they stride through the hall in their clacking boots, I remember with relief that I tidied Heather's scattered toys into a box this morning, so there's nothing lying about. But there will be things in the sitting room: the colouring book and pens, for a start.

And she's in the bay-windowed room. All alone. Wondering what's happening.

The women head for the stairs. They seem to know exactly where to go.

'Are you going up there?' I ask.

'Er . . . yeah,' Agnes says, her tone bored, as though I'm stating the utter obvious.

'Why?'

'To scope it.' They're on the stairs now, hardly bothering to pay me attention. I need some answers, so I follow them onto the staircase. Agnes casts a look down the banister at me. 'No need to come with us. We won't be long.'

'I'm dying for a coffee,' Sophia says with a smile, 'after that journey. If you wouldn't mind . . .'

I stop on the stairs, torn by my desire to stick with them and by my need to reassure Heather. 'Okay,' I reply reluctantly. 'I'll put some on.'

They go quickly up the stairs and disappear through the door at the top.

I put my head in my hands, my shoulders slumping with defeat. *What the hell is going on? What am I going to do?*

I'm confident they won't recognise me, but one glimpse of Heather and they'll know. If they've seen any of the pictures on the news, they'll know her in a heartbeat. And anyway, children are not part of the package here. They're not allowed. Insurance, Alison said when she mentioned it. I said it didn't matter as I wasn't bringing any children. She'd sounded pleased.

What does it matter if they chuck me out now? I can't stay. I'll have to leave. But where can I go?

I hurry back to the bay-windowed room and open the door. 'Heather?'

There's no one in there. I stare about frantically. *She was here. I left her here. Where is she? There's nowhere to hide in here . . .* 'Heather, where are you?'

I go back into the hall, looking for her. She's not there, not in the tent she made with the coats. She must have slipped out of the room while I was on the stairs with the visitors. I run down the hall into the west wing and our bedroom. It's empty but Teddington is lying on the floor and the window is open.

I hurry over and look out, just in time to see a flash of blonde hair disappearing under the bay tree.

Oh God. Poor kid. I'm making her as paranoid and fearful as I am. She'll probably stay in her den until I come to tell her the coast is clear.

I feel guilty as I go to the kitchen and fill the kettle on autopilot. What must Heather be thinking and feeling? And what will we do if these women actually move in? My options are limited. I can't take Heather on the run with nowhere to go. She's only a child, she can't live in a car. With our pictures in the press, we'd be recognised at once. The first service station we stopped at would be full of witnesses to our escape. We'd be picked up immediately. We can't go home. We can't go anywhere.

My thoughts are on an anxious loop as I finish making the coffee. I take a tray back to the hall, and hear the heavy swing of the upstairs door and voices. It's Agnes I hear first, her tone more strident.

'. . . fucking tip!' she says. 'Much worse than the photos. Those toilets are disgusting. If he thinks I'm cleaning them, he's fucking nuts. This is definitely the worst so far.'

Sophia says soothingly, 'Hey, it's okay. It's only a bit of dirt. We'll manage it. Besides, we can get help if we need it.'

'I've got your coffee,' I say, holding up the tray with its three mugs and milk jug. 'Do you take sugar?'

They both shake their heads, staring down at me as though they'd forgotten my existence.

Then Sophia says, 'Thanks, Rachel. We'll come down.'

As they descend the stairs, I nod towards the eastern side

of the house. 'Let's go in here.' I lead them into the old dining room with its table and chairs. A moment later, we're sitting down at the near end, holding our mugs of coffee. I've had time to think, and I feel more alert and more able to take the initiative.

'Why are you looking at the upstairs?' I ask lightly. 'Is it going to be renovated? I've wondered what plans the company has for the house. It's such an amazing old place.'

I mean it. This last fortnight in the house has been long enough for me to start to love it. Even though we inhabit a tiny part, I've begun to appreciate the beauty and character that lies below the dilapidation. It has a sort of sadness about it that I can't identify, but that sits well with me right now. The house and I feel a kind of sympathy for one another, with all our losses and disintegration. We both feel like once glorious structures that have faded and been abandoned, now living with ghosts and memories.

'Not exactly renovated,' Sophia says. She seems to be the more emollient of the two. Perhaps she's worried about appearing rude. That whole private school charm thing. 'But prepared.' She sends a small smile towards Agnes. 'You know how it's best to be prepared.'

'Absolutely,' I say. 'But prepared for what?'

'For events,' Agnes says in a slightly snappy way. 'And in your case that means being prepared for us.'

I frown at her, uncomprehending. 'What do you mean?'

'We'll be moving in.'

'When?'

'Soon. Tomorrow. Early.'

116

I gasp at the immediacy. 'But Alison said she'd give me notice of anyone else arriving!' I'm horrified. This is too soon. 'I don't understand why it's necessary.'

Agnes gives me a sharp look. 'There's no need for you to understand. This house belongs to the company. It has the right to put anyone in here at any time. If you don't like it, you can leave.'

Sophia shoots her a worried look and then says soothingly to me, 'But there's no need to do that. We're not here to push you out. We won't interfere with you, honestly. You'll hardly know we're here most of the time. We've got plenty to keep us busy.'

I appreciate her attempts to keep relations easy between us. 'Okay. But what will you be doing? This place is a huge amount of work if you're planning to restore it. I don't know where you'd start.'

'Don't worry about that,' Sophia says. Agnes seems a little twitchy but she keeps quiet. 'You'll know more if you decide to stay here long term. But there's no need to hurry off at once. Keep painting and we'll be quiet as mice. You never know . . .' She smiles at me. She's taken off her beanie hat and now tosses her long, caramel-blonde locks back over her shoulder. 'You might end up liking us.'

I say nothing and sip my coffee. *Tomorrow. What am I going to do?*

When they've gone, I race upstairs to see if they've left any sign to explain why they're here but there's nothing, just a few doors left open where they've been inspecting the place.

As I come downstairs, I suddenly see Heather standing in the middle of the hall, carefully placed in the exact central square. She's clutching Teddington and staring up at me, as pale as ever.

'Darling, there you are!' I rush over to her, gathering her up in my arms. 'I've missed you! I'm sorry if you were frightened. But you did the right thing going away while the ladies were here. Did you go to the den?'

'Yes,' she says, her soft voice not more than a whisper. 'And I went to the old cottage.'

I pull in a horrified breath. 'What? To Matty and Sissy? Did you see them?'

She nods.

I start shaking. 'Oh my goodness . . . Oh darling, did they see you? Talk to you? Ask questions?'

She shakes her head. 'I don't think so. I didn't let them see me. I know you don't want me to. That's why I have to hide when people come, isn't it?'

I hug her tight. 'Darling, it's only so people don't try to separate us, that's all. You want us to be together, don't you?'

She nods slowly, her eyes huge.

'Come on, you're freezing! You've been outside for ages. Let's get you warm.'

I make her supper and manage to get her to eat some of it, though I have to coax her by feeding myself alternate mouthfuls of the macaroni cheese. Then I give her a hot bath, trying to warm up her chilly limbs. She seems happy enough, just a little distant. When she's finally in bed, asleep with her teddy in her arms, I can give in to the panic that's been building inside me. I go to the kitchen and open the half-full screw-cap bottle of white wine that's in the fridge. Generally, I'm careful. I limit myself to two glasses of wine a night. Tonight, I throw caution to the wind and neck the first glass with hardly a pause, then pour another, putting another bottle in the fridge to chill in case it's needed.

I can't believe that from tomorrow my sanctuary will be invaded. My fears about someone in the room downstairs suddenly seem foolish. Of course there's no one there. The paranoia looks stupid in the face of actual, real people coming to the house. *We're happy here. It's so fucking unfair. Why do they have to come and spoil it?* They're going to ruin everything, all my careful plans. But the worst thing is that I can't see any way out. I can't think of anywhere else we can go without being seen. Everything I put in place was to bring us here. The idea that the company might recruit other guardians never crossed my mind. Even when Alison mentioned it as a possibility, I didn't really believe her.

I take stock of my situation. Heather is all right, her sickness coming and going but not seeming to get much worse. The house is liveable. We're in a calm place. Things are getting better. Until today, I would have said that I'm getting stronger, that the peace and isolation is doing its good work, giving me the space I craved.

The second glass of wine disappears only marginally slower than the first. I undo the second bottle, still warm, and pour another. I get out a sheet of paper to start drawing up my options, but I can't seem to make any sense when I write. The paper is covered in scrawls but they are haphazard, incoherent. Why can't I make a bloody plan to get us out of this mess?

I imagine police cars roaring up the drive to accost me. They'll take Heather away from me. They'll lock me up. I start to cry. I know I must be drunk when I see my third glass is empty but I pour another anyway. Soon, I'm weeping huge, choking sobs, my face running wet with tears and mucus. *I'm not allowed to escape. They won't let me escape. All I want is to get away from the hell. That's all.*

'Mummy.'

The voice is like an angel's whisper, coming from all around me. I look up. There she is in the doorway, unutterably sweet.

'Mummy.'

'Darling . . .' I stumble up but she's beside me in a moment, taking my hand, gazing up at me with those big blue eyes.

'Madam says don't cry,' Heather says. 'Everything is going to be all right. You don't need to cry. Madam says so. Don't cry.'

Chapter Ten

They said they would be back early, but everyone's definition of early is different, I suppose. I'm ready and on edge by six thirty, with the sky turning silver and my mouth dry and eyes bleary from the wine I drank last night, but the vintage camper van doesn't roar up to the front door until after midday. By then, though, I've decided on a short-term strategy. It isn't particularly clever but it's all I can think of. I will hide Heather until I can find a new place to live.

I spent the morning scoping out the ground floor and all its possibilities. There were plenty of rooms but there was no guarantee that the women wouldn't come in at any time. I went down to the cellar, but baulked at the idea of putting Heather down there. It would be too much like a prison, or a grim horror story. A child in a basement is close to cruelty. Besides, the company seems to regard it as their space. It seemed that the only realistic option was to keep her in our room. It is large with plenty of space for playing in, and there are windows overlooking the garden, with only a short drop to the outside flower bed. Heather managed it easily yesterday but I could put a box there and make it even easier for her to get out.

I improvised a step with an old packing case, then sat her down to explain.

'Sweetie, those ladies who were here yesterday are coming back and they're going to stay a while. They don't want to hurt us, but I don't want them to see you because I didn't say that you and I were going to be living here together. So I'm going to find us a new place to go. In a few days we'll have somewhere lovely to live, just you and me. But until then, I need you to stay in here, and in the den. Okay?'

I thought she would ask me more questions, but she accepted everything without demur.

'I won't come out, Mummy,' she said.

I showed her how she could get to the garden. 'You can get to your bay tree if you hide behind the hedge and go along there.'

She looked out and nodded. She seemed pleased enough.

'I'm so sorry, sweetie. It won't be for long. Maybe the ladies will leave and we can get back to normal.'

This, I realise, is my real assumption. I'm sure that one or two days in the house will be enough for those polished, glossy Amazons. What can amuse them here? How will they fill their time? I can't imagine that they will stay. Just in case, I've sent Alison an email asking how long they will be here. She hasn't answered yet.

'It's okay, Mummy,' Heather says, smiling. 'Madam will keep me company.'

I remember the previous evening, and the words of comfort

that Heather offered me from Madam, that everything would be all right. The name of the strange presence still fills me with that horrible feeling of dread but its reassurance has taken hold in my brain and given me strength. It's ridiculous. Madam isn't real. There can be no way that a figment of a six-year-old's imagination can know the future. And yet . . . I am comforted.

'Okay,' I say, holding her hand. 'You play with Madam. That's fine. And remember, I love you.'

The two women climb out of the van, looking much as they did yesterday but now carrying a large holdall each, and I can see that the van is jam-packed with stuff.

'Hello,' I call, standing out on the front steps, my hands shielding my eyes from the bright sunshine. Today is much warmer and brighter, and the air smells as though life is returning.

Agnes mutters a hello but seems intent on getting started.

'Hi there,' Sophia calls. Her long hair is pulled back into a more businesslike pony tail and she looks ready for work in jeans and a baggy sweatshirt. Agnes is already at the back of the van, opening the doors.

'Do you need a hand?' I ask casually, curious about what they've got in the van.

Sophia smiles as though she's about to accept gratefully but Agnes says quickly, 'No thanks. We're fine. We wouldn't say no to coffee, though.'

'Okay.' I go back into the house to make it. I intend to watch hard and learn as much as possible about what they are doing here. They go upstairs and prop the door open, return a few minutes later dressed in white boiler suits, then go back and forth from the van with armfuls of stuff. I give them the coffee and go into the bay-fronted room to paint, while I watch what's going on. They take out boxes, buckets and cleaning equipment, an industrial hoover, suitcases and bags. They take upstairs a mattress that looks kingsize. I wonder how they've managed to fit so much into their van; it must be a miracle of space management. Emptying it takes at least a couple of hours.

I paint without thinking while they make their interminable trips to and fro. A picture begins to emerge from under my brush but I don't even notice what it is, I'm concentrating so hard on the girls. When the van is empty, they vanish for a while, and I hear nothing from behind the closed door. I'm about to make myself a cup of tea and think about getting Heather's supper when they emerge, come downstairs without the boiler suits on, get into the van and drive away without a word of explanation. The minute they are gone, I run to the stairs and head to the second storey, my stomach fluttering with nerves. In the main corridor just behind the door there's stuff piled up neatly, but not as much as they've brought in. Going swiftly but lightly, as though they might still hear me, I open a few random doors. Most are untouched, but one large room holds all the cleaning equipment and they've already made a start on that one. Then I open another to a room with more luggage carefully piled up. But in the gracious bedroom with the four-poster bed, I find what I'm looking for. It has been cleaned thoroughly and the mattress has been put in the bed frame. It's been made up with a billowing white-covered duvet and a mound of inviting-looking snowy pillows. I feel an urge to lose myself on the feathered comfort of the bed, close my eyes and sleep. Instead, I take in the rest of the room – the suitcases against the wall – and then head out, closing the door behind me.

Are they a couple?

It hadn't crossed my mind that they might be, but there's no reason why not. And there is only one bed.

The idea humanises them a little. Until now, I've seen them as Alison's agents, spies sent to watch me. But if they're a couple, then perhaps it's not all about me after all. Maybe they're on some kind of adventure together, and Agnes is snappy because she and Sophia had a row last night, and Sophia is trying to smooth it over, and . . .

I feel a bit happier. But I still don't want to be caught snooping. I hurry back downstairs to Heather, to tell her that she can come out for a while if she wants to.

The women don't return until much later, when Heather is in bed and I'm reading in the sitting room. I come out to say hello, but they don't linger, heading up the stairs and wishing me goodnight. As I go back to the sitting room, I imagine them up there, getting undressed and climbing into that big bed together. For a moment I feel comforted. I'm not alone anymore in this vast place. Then the comfort turns into a chill of fear:

I'm not alone anymore.

*

125

Later I lie awake, staring into the blackness, Heather breathing softly beside me as she slumbers. Where can I go and what can I do? I'm terrified at the idea of leaving the house. I feel as though I belong here now. I realise that I have not yet left this place since we arrived. I've been using the frozen food from the basement.

Do Agnes and Sophia know about the food? Maybe they're expecting to use it. I'll have to replace it.

The thought is awful. Up until now I've convinced myself that at any time I can go out to the local town, to the shops, and do whatever needs doing. Now, as I lie awake with my heart thudding hard in my chest, I know that I'm afraid of going anywhere but here. My world has shrunk to this house. I haven't checked my emails. I haven't been in touch with Caz. I haven't listened to news bulletins or scanned the internet for information about the hunt that is pursuing me. I do not want to know. I want to shut myself up here for as long as I can, until they pull me kicking and screaming out of the house. That's the only way I can imagine going.

Suddenly a great wash of calm floods over me. *Maybe I've been looking at all this in the wrong way. Maybe the girls coming here is a gift to me. They have no interest in some woman on the run. They barely notice me. Perhaps they can help me . . . After all, they can come and go as they please. They don't have to worry about being spotted. They must have gone out for dinner tonight.* I imagine them sitting together in a restaurant, heedless of the looks they would attract, two good-looking women like them. They wouldn't

have bothered about what people around them were thinking.

*If we have to stay here a bit longer, at least it means I don't
have to go out.*

Soothed by this thought, I fall asleep.

The next day, I hear nothing from upstairs. I wonder what
they're doing and if they will come down at all. During the
morning, Heather plays in the sitting room, and I let her go
out into the garden, knowing she's protected from view by the
overgrown shrubs and bushes. 'It's a game,' I tell her. 'You can
go outside as long as you stay out of sight. Okay? The ladies
upstairs mustn't see you.'

'Don't worry, Mummy, they won't see me.'

'Good girl.'

I'm preparing our lunch – a defrosted chicken from the
basement freezer – when I hear footsteps coming down
the stairs. I go out, wiping my hands on a towel, and see the
two women descending the staircase. I'm taken aback by the
sight: they are both wearing long white dresses buttoned up
at the front from hem to low neckline. The sleeves are long
and bell-shaped. Sophia's hair is long and flowing and she
looks as though she has just stepped out of a Pre-Raphaelite
painting. Agnes, with her cropped hair, looks more modern,
but the effect is startling. I wonder if they're wearing their
nightdresses but the dresses are too formal for that.

They nod at me as I stand there, watching, my mouth open,
and head straight for the front door.

I find my voice before they go out. 'Where are you going?'

Agnes turns to me, one hand on the door latch. 'To church. It's Sunday.'

'Is it?' Then I laugh nervously. 'I've . . . I've forgotten the days. To church? What church?' I haven't heard any bells.

'The church here. In the grounds.' She turns back, impatient to be on her way.

'We won't be long,' Sophia says with a smile.

Then they're gone, leaving without coats. I go to the door and watch them as they head off in the direction of Matty and Sissy's cottage, through the rhododendron bushes. They seem to know exactly where they are going. But a church? In the grounds of the house? Wouldn't I have seen other people coming and going for services if that were the case? I don't understand it.

I'm sure that they are not anywhere near the back garden and Heather's den. I'm not going to follow them. Instead I go to my tablet and connect to the internet. I put in a search: 'Church at Paradise House'. But the combination of 'Church' and 'Paradise' turns up so many thousands of results, I would never have time to sift through to find what might be relevant, though I spend a while scanning them. Then, on impulse, I go to the company website and click on the details for the house, the ones I first read when I applied. There's a tab for the history of the place and I open it up to read it again.

Paradise House is a magnificent old building that was built in the 1860s by Thomas McTavish, a pupil of William Butterfield, whose neo-Gothic influence can be seen in the elaborately patterned brickwork, the chimney design and in the use of trefoil in the upper windows. It was built for the wealthy Evans family, who made their money in woollen cloth manufacture, and continued to be owned by the family into the twenty-first century. The house has had a colourful and vibrant history. It was acquired by ARK as part of its ongoing project of property development.

There is nothing more about the house's past, and certainly no mention made of a church. I wonder what the colourful history can be and why the company website did not go into any detail.

I search again for Paradise House, but nothing that comes up seems to be of interest. I can't even find it on the heritage sites that record listed buildings, which seems odd given that it appears to have some architectural significance.

But maybe I don't need the internet. After all, Matty and Sissy live right next door and they must know all about it. They said they used to live here, that their family used to live here. They must be part of the Evans family.

I call to mind the elderly sisters. They don't look like heiresses to a wool fortune. But that is probably long gone now. On the other hand, if they sold this place, they must have a bit of cash to get by on. Good for them.

I'm vaguely tickled by the idea that the internet has failed me in my quest for information but that the old girls next door might be the answer. There's something comforting in the fallibility of technology, as though we're not quite ready for human hearts and minds to be made redundant.

I'll go over there and ask them about the church.

It is more than two hours before Agnes and Sophia come back. I'm clearing up from lunch when I hear the front door slam. I want to go and ask them what they've been up to and where this church is, but it's a bit much like being a nosy neighbour to pop up every time they walk by. I still can't imagine them staying here long. I have the strongest sense that they will be leaving tomorrow, at least temporarily.

But I can't stop myself drifting quietly out into the corridor to listen as they go across the hall to the staircase and ascend. They're walking slowly, as though tired out. There is the creak of hinges as they open the door. Then I hear Sophia speak in her deep voice, its upper-class tone so clear and carrying:

'It will be all right when the Beloved gets here.'

Then the two of them disappear behind the door, which shuts out all noise so effectively it's as though a radio has been switched off.

PART TWO

Chapter Eleven

1926

Meet me at Paddington, 2.30, ticket office. Bring my green
coat. Arabella

Lettice is there on time, just as Arabella orders. Everyone does
what Arabella wants. Or at least, they did until recently. She
is clutching the coat too – bottle green with a fox-fur collar,
soft and warm. While she waits, she pushes her cheeks into
the comfort of the fur and watches the people bustling about.
A station is full of so much to observe, she thinks. The great
black trains sit docile in their platform niches, occasionally
blowing out clouds of grey and white smoke like horses puffing and eager to be off. At the end of the platforms, through
the great iron arch, is the white light of beyond, where the
rails disappear towards the places the trains will fly to as soon
as they are untethered and released. Porters push trolleys of
luggage, elderly ladies in Edwardian coats, gloves and broad
hats sail majestically to their first-class carriages, children in
their best clothes skip as they hold their anxious mothers'
hands, and men are everywhere – suits, greatcoats, hats,

cigarettes, pasty-faced, guiding their wives, reading papers, dashing by. Newspaper boys hold up the morning edition; the afternoon one has not yet arrived. A few pathetic war veterans, with bandaged or missing limbs, beg by the station doors. Filthy, ragged children cadge farthings or offer to carry bags. A vagrant wanders about in a crusted coat, with a long beard and a battered face, his feet bound with rancid cloths, carrying a dirty bundle, oblivious of the station official trying to herd him out and back to the streets.

The world is here, thinks Lettice, amazed. She rarely comes to London and this is almost overwhelming. Among the crowd she sees faces she thinks she recognises, and then realises they belong to people like the ones she knows at home: well dressed, healthy and handsome – at least compared to some of the sorry specimens she can see here. The lower classes of the city are ugly, she realises; grey- or sallow-faced, dirty-haired, missing teeth, either miserable or fierce or blank around the eyes. *But it can't be their fault. Poor things. They should come and live in the country. Oh, where is Arabella?*

As she thinks this, she's aware of a flurry nearby and the next moment, she sees Arabella approaching through the swarm of people that seems to part as she nears and then close again behind her, like a fogbank. She looks hectic, her hat pushed back on her head, her black hair uncoiffed and blowing free. She is wearing a plain tweed coat. Her cheeks have round spots of pink and her eyes glitter.

'Letty! Letty,' she squeals as she sees her sister. 'Oh, thank God you're here. Quick, quick, give me the coat!'

Letty holds out the coat dumbly. Arabella slips off the tweed coat and pulls on the bottle-green one. She bundles up the tweed and hands it to Letty. 'Here. Carry it for now. They won't be looking for you.'

She hurries into the ticket office and up to the nearest booth, Letty following. 'Two singles to Goreham, please. First class.'

'Goreham?' Lettice says. She doesn't know what she was expecting but this is still a surprise. 'Are we going home?'

'Of course. What did you think? That I'd let that scoundrel win? Hardly.' Arabella looks outraged. 'If he thinks I'll go down without a fight, he's quite wrong. Now come along. The train goes in ten minutes. Platform six.' She reaches up and presses her hat forward so that it sits better, and tucks up her loose hair, stuffing it up under the hat. 'Let's go, Letty, we mustn't miss it.'

Letty follows her, feeling helpless in the face of Arabella's determination. But then, if it's not Arabella's, it's Cecily's. She doesn't know which side she is on, each is so powerful and so convincing. *I must be very weak*, she tells herself. *Or else they are very strong*.

It's a mystery she must get to the bottom of one day, but it doesn't look as though it will be today. She follows obediently in Arabella's wake as she marches out into the station where grey light filters down through the curved glass roof strutted with iron.

They hurry through the crowd, Arabella tip-tapping ahead, pulling the fox fur close around her neck, and they are almost at platform six when Letty hears it: the slap of leather shoes on the concourse, the shouts, the murmur of surprise among the crowd.

'Hi! You there! Stop!'

Heads turn, eyes wide, mouths open, as three men, two in gabardines, one in a wool coat, all with dark hats and moustaches, come running up. They are in a wild rush but once they reach Letty and Arabella, they stop, wary and uncertain of what to do. They don't want to grab the women in public. Instead, they stand in Arabella's way, blocking the entrance to platform six, panting.

'Get out of my way,' Arabella says in a voice of ice. 'This instant.'

'You're to return with us, miss. You know you're not permitted to travel. We know Mrs Porter let you out.' One of the men, a fellow in green gabardine, is speaking. He has a ratty look, Letty thinks. His eyes are close together and rimmed in red.

'You have no jurisdiction over me,' Arabella says majestically. 'Let me pass.'

'Now, come along, Arabella, don't be so silly.' It's the man in the wool coat. He's got a persuasive, deep voice, and a well-spoken accent. 'You know this is a foolish escapade. Come back and we can talk about it.'

'There is nothing to talk about, Mr Barrett,' she says. 'You are an agent of evil, as you well know. I do not answer to you. You have no power over me.' Arabella takes a step forward. The men close ranks, blocking the way to the platform. As if in protest, the train puffs a cloud of smoke and chunters out a huge mechanical sigh.

Mr Barrett, his moustache rather thin but very black, smiles, one corner of his mouth sloping upwards. 'An agent of evil, am I? I think that rather proves my point. Now, let's be a good girl—'

'A good girl?' Scorn drips through Arabella's voice. 'Who do you think you are, Mr Barrett? You're nothing. No one. You have no right to speak to me, let alone stand in my way.'

'I act on behalf of Mr Ford, as you are aware.' The smile looks less convincing now, Letty thinks.

'Mr Ford has no right to prevent me doing anything,' spits Arabella. Her cheeks are even more hectic and her eyes sparkle with fury.

Edward? thinks Lettice. *This is all Edward's doing?* She is mortified by the scene they are making. All around, people are turning to stare and murmur. A small circle of observers is forming. The men look like police in plain clothes, and she can feel the shame of guilt even though she's innocent. *What do they think I've done?* It looks so bad; everyone must assume they've stolen something, or worse, though she can't imagine what that might be.

'Get out of my way!' orders Arabella, drawing herself up tall, every inch of her resplendent with dignity. 'Do you not understand? You have no power over me. If you attempt to prevent me catching the train, I will sue you! I will sue for abduction, for false imprisonment! You know what you're doing is illegal, and I know very well what my rights are. You may no longer prevent me from following the dictates of my own mind. I will appeal to the Commissioners for Lunacy!'

There is a pause as the men absorb this. Lettice sees that

they are shaken and that Arabella senses this. She says imperiously, 'Let me pass!'

The hands of the clock that hangs huge above the platforms move a jot further on. There is one minute before the train leaves. They must hurry or miss it.

Barrett steps back to let them pass. 'Very well,' he says reluctantly. 'We must pursue this matter at a later date.'

'Consider yourself lucky you have not been arrested!' Arabella strides past him. 'Come, Letty!'

The train is being held for them, realises Lettice, trotting in her sister's wake, still carrying the tweed bundle. The station official is holding up his flag, his whistle in his mouth, waiting for them to reach their first-class carriage. A porter dashes forward to open the door and then they are in, settling into facing seats, with only one elderly lady to share the carriage with them. The whistle blows, the slow turn of the wheels begins, the windows are veiled with steam, and they jerk forward.

'There,' says Arabella with satisfaction. 'That showed them!'

Arabella explains what has happened as the train makes it way west, out of London and away. 'Didn't you wonder where I was?' she asks, disbelieving.

'They said you were taking a cure,' Lettice says, aware now how flimsy it sounds. 'I knew you'd had the influenza at Christmas. I thought you were recovering somewhere nice.'

'Nice? Hardly!' Arabella snorts. 'No, my dear. They shut me up.'

'What?'

'Yes. Under the Mental Deficiency Act. My darling sister and her caring husband, wanting only what's best for me, naturally! Nothing to do with my twenty thousand a year, and my ownership of Hanthorpe.' She frowns and narrows her eyes at Letty. 'Did you really not know?'

'No!' Lettice gasps. She is truly shocked, but she is well aware of her sister's tendency to indulge in high drama and flights of fancy. The scene at the station is meat and drink to Arabella. She has to be careful believing everything her sister says. It has led her into trouble in the past.

'I've been in Moorcroft Asylum at Hillingdon. A lovely place, I must declare,' she says, sarcasm dripping from her voice. 'I was taken against my will, bundled off the moment I came out of church. Thanks to Cecily and Edward, my capacities were considered too weak for the everyday world and I was shut away with the real lunatics and deficients!' Her eyes fill with angry tears. 'I could have spent my life there with no one the wiser. But of course, the Beloved would never permit it. He sent the Reverend Ashley as my rescuer.'

'Reverend Ashley?' Lettice says faintly. Another stranger. Another influence. She knew that Cecily and Edward were concerned about Arabella. How could she not? She was not witness to the interview that must have convinced them to have Arabella committed but she knew only too well what precipitated it. Arabella, frank and honest to the point of endangering herself, would have had no idea that she was playing into their hands.

'That's right. A good man, a man of faith! A recent convert

to our cause. He knows the Beloved, he understands. He intends to join us in good time. Until then, he is able to work undetected to protect those of us that need it. He ensured that I was moved out of the asylum to the home of Mrs Porter in Peckham. She is a kindly lady, a widow who takes in patients not suited to the asylum but who are not permitted to live alone. She supervises them. Well, it took five minutes for her to know that I wasn't in the least bit mad. She had a poor unfortunate with her – gentle but raving, compulsively washing every two minutes, unable to speak, crooning away to herself. The contrast could hardly be greater, and Reverend Ashley soon persuaded her to release me. So I telegraphed to you to meet me.' Arabella's face twists into an ugly scowl. 'But the wretched Hannah – her daughter – I'm quite sure is in the pay of the authorities. She must have alerted them to my plans. I never trusted her! I explained to Mrs Porter that it is illegal to detain me, when I'm in my right mind. I'm neither a harm to myself, nor to others. It doesn't matter if others don't agree with my beliefs. That means I should be at liberty, Letty. The courts have said so, there is a precedent! And Reverend Ashley knows it; he's the one who told me that I'm free to leave if I wish. And now . . .' Arabella draws herself up again, inspired by her own noble speech. 'I am going home to take back what is mine.'

Oh dear, Lettice thinks. *This means trouble.* She is not sure which side she should be on – neither is particularly appealing. She knows that Cecily and Edward's outward respectability masks their desire to take control of the family fortune for their own benefit, but the fact that they have gone to these lengths frightens her. If they're prepared to lock Arabella away, might they do the same to her? After all, Arabella has taken her to one of the church meetings . . .

Admittedly, she has nothing like Arabella's inheritance. Ten thousand a year is a good sum, but nowhere near her sister's riches, which include ownership of the house. Still, she knows Edward would have it all, if he could, the house as well.

The house most of all.

She knows her brother-in-law wants it, considers it rightfully his, as he is head of the family with Papa gone and the other sisters unmarried.

Arabella is lost in happy fantasies of the battle ahead, oblivious to the shocked expression on the face of the elderly lady opposite, who has grasped that she is travelling in the same carriage as a lunatic. Lettice smiles consolingly at her and tries to convey in her eyes that Arabella is not dangerous.

At least, not to others, she thinks mournfully. *What she is doing to herself is another matter.*

Her oldest sister was always eccentric and prone to fancy. From communing with fairies in the sand dunes on their seaside holidays to consulting mediums in order to talk to the spirit world and, more particularly, their mother, Arabella has been seeking something all her life. And now she has found it. A fervent, unshakeable belief in the man who now guides her in every part of her life, to whom she was willing to devote herself without question, the one she calls the Beloved.

I never wanted to be at everyone's mercy, Lettice thinks. Outside, the fields fly past, edged by the distant inky green forests.

Arabella has fallen asleep, one cheek buried in emerald fur, her hat askew. *But somehow that is how it's ended up.*

Perhaps it began in her earliest life, with the nurse who pulled her hair viciously and slapped her if she did anything but sit quietly and do as she was told without demur. The one after that was no better, but she was slovenly and lazy, and forgot to feed the children at times. If they complained, they were smacked with the hairbrush and sent to bed. Lettice felt that she and her sisters existed in a strange kingdom far from their parents, where all the rules were reversed. Downstairs, the family was in charge, the servants bustling to fulfil their orders, keep the house clean, ease the life of their masters. But upstairs, behind the nursery door, the children were at the mercy of the servants and whatever they wished. Letty cowered and hid when the footman came up to lounge in the nursery armchair, his feet on the fender, sometimes pulling Nurse onto his knee, wrapping his hand around her waist and kissing her. Once Letty peeped through the crack in the door and saw him pushing his tongue into Nurse's mouth, and his hand up under her skirts. She'd been so shocked, she'd dropped the tin toy she was holding and it clattered on the bare floor. The couple had jerked apart, pulling their clothes straight, Nurse smoothing her hair before hurrying into the passage. When she saw Letty, she screamed at her that she was wicked, dragging her by the arm into the bedroom and beating her hard until Letty was sobbing and cowering, trying to dodge the blows.

'You see what happens when you don't do what you're told?' cried Nurse, her face flushed with anger and excitement. 'Now lie here till I get you, and don't you breathe a word or I swear I'll flay you.'

Letty, shaking with pain and fear, lay as still as she could and said nothing for hours, until, when she was freezing cold and bursting with her need for the lavatory, Nurse had finally come back to release her. There was no sign of the footman when she returned to the nursery.

That Nurse disappeared one day as well. They often did. People who'd been part of their lives forever were gone one morning and never seen again, a stranger taking the empty place without explanation. Sometimes Letty wondered if such a thing could happen to her, or Arabella or Cecily. They might wake up and discover that one had been replaced with a more pleasing model, less likely to cause disruption. More obedient.

But if that were to happen to any of them, surely it would be Arabella. She could tell that the servants disliked Arabella most of all; she wasn't pretty like Cecily, with her dark untameable hair that frizzed out in all directions, her sharp brown eyes and her pointed chin. She was dreamy and yet dramatic, a thudding, unmissable presence with a loud voice and a fearless way of retorting at anyone who upbraided her. The nurses were careful in their punishments with Arabella, but Letty could see them reining themselves in, as though she was the one they most wanted to lash. Letty suspected it was Arabella who had told the grown-ups about the crimes of the worst nurses, and it was a relief when at last they ended up with Nanny Hughes, slow and ponderous but loving in her own way. At least there were no more slaps and there was always dinner.

'You wouldn't say boo to a goose,' she'd say to Letty. 'What a little mousey you are.'

But to Arabella she said, 'No one will want such a galumphing hoyden, miss! Mind yourself and your manners, if you please.'

Arabella paid no attention at all.

Cecily was the darling, as she was to their parents. Cecily's brown hair didn't stick out in all directions but emerged from the rags and pins in shining ringlets that Letty, with her kinks and flattened bits, envied. Cecily's brown eyes sparkled hazel in the light and she danced very well. Her tendency to tell lies was never remarked upon, in a house full of people living in dream worlds. Besides, no one was really sure what was true and what wasn't, with so many versions of events floating around. Nanny said one thing, the girls three different things. The housemaid saw something they'd none of them witnessed, and the parlour maid had seen nothing at all, but could make a good guess. Mama knew nothing of the nursery and believed whatever had been said to her last. And Papa laughed it all away and told them they were ninnies and would they please all be quiet?

It was Cecily's most bitter moment when the house had been left entirely to Arabella, and ten thousand to Lettice. Cecily received eight thousand because, Letty suspected, she had a husband whereas she and Arabella had not. Until then, Cecily had enjoyed the charmed existence of being pretty – in comparison to the others, at least – and engaged at eighteen to the younger son of a prosperous farmer whose only mistake had been to father seven boys, of whom Edward was the youngest, and eight girls. It had made sense, with Mama dead and Papa ailing, for the young couple to live in the large house, now without such a phalanx of servants as there used to be. Papa got rid of the butler and most of the footmen to avoid the manservant tax, and kept the gardeners, grooms and the driver, who didn't count as taxable. Cecily seemed to have got used to her position in charge of Hanthorpe, chivvying Papa from armchair to bedroom and then, Arabella said, to death. The terms of his will came as a shock to Cecily. She'd assumed that she was evidently fitted to running the house and was preparing to fill it with children, and was loudly outraged that it had been left to Arabella, though what she had expected, Lettice didn't know. The house could hardly be divided into three. Even though Arabella was its mistress, they all continued to live in it together, in a scratchy, rough kind of way, getting along but without much joy. Cecily and Edward must have always suspected that if Arabella married, they would have to leave, but perhaps they counted on her remaining a spinster. Marriageable men were at a premium these days. Edward had lost four brothers in the war, and three of his sisters had resigned themselves to their single fate and taken holy orders. Cecily would have been delighted if Arabella had done something so convenient and docile. But no. Arabella would never submit in that way. Whatever path she took would be full of adventure of some kind.

And she has not disappointed.

For one day, Arabella walked into a chapel in Farmouth

and stumbled upon her revelation. She fell at once into utter and absolute devotion to the Beloved and his cause. She intended to be his most faithful disciple.

The train rocked as it hurtled along the rails, chugging and snapping as it went. Letty was weary from her recent travel. She'd already spent three hours on the train this morning, and now another three in the afternoon.

I don't think Cecily and Edward would accept the Beloved. Even if the Beloved wanted them.

The Beloved was a white-haired man who seemed ordinary enough until he turned those eyes to you. Like shafts of bright sunlight, their gaze seemed to flare out and pierce all they touched, as though he could see to the heart of everything. The Beloved had something magic about him, an undeniable charisma. Lettice had seen him only once, when Arabella had persuaded her to make the trip down to Farmouth to the chapel. 'You must come,' she urged. 'I don't know how long he'll be allowed to preach there. The bishop is already talking of defrocking him.'

'Why?' Lettice asked, surprised.

'Because he's a fool, like all the rest,' Arabella said impatiently. 'They can't see the truth. They're blinded by evil, naturally. But you'll understand when you listen to him.'

The chapel was in a back street, some way out of the main part of town and far from the seafront where families were walking and taking the air. They went into its single storey, though it had a balcony level running around the three walls and facing the altar. The Beloved conducted the service, which began familiarly enough: a welcome, prayers, a collect and a shriving. Then a hymn was sung, and a reading given from the Bible, along with a psalm and a New Testament passage. A hymn and then the Gospel. After that, the Beloved – *I mean, the Reverend Phillips, of course, I must stop calling him the Beloved* – climbed into the pulpit and began to speak. He was ordinary enough to look at, except for his snow-white hair, unusual for a man in his forties, which surprisingly gave him an air of youthfulness, helped by his slightly tanned complexion. He wore the sober black clothes of a minister and seemed no different to any other man of God – but when he began to speak and his eyes to flash and his arms to lift to heaven, he was spellbinding. Afterwards, Letty never could remember what had been said in any detail, only what it had felt like to listen. He had started quietly enough, in a tone of hushed reverence, as he began to describe the Gospel story they had heard that day, and to make the link to the Old Testament reading, which had been the story of the near-sacrifice of Isaac. What was it in the way he told it, Letty wondered afterwards, that made it so thrillingly exciting? By the time he described Abraham freeing the beast in the thicket and sacrificing it in his son's stead, the whole place was aquiver, a kind of shifting and breathing testifying to the pent-up emotion inside them all. When Letty looked about, she noticed that there seemed to be more women than men in the congregation, respectable widows who'd lost husbands in the war, and women who would have wed if there'd only been the men to marry when they were at their ripest. They all sat together in the pews, cheeks flushed under their best hats. Then, when Letty could practically feel the thrill that moved through them

147

all, the anticipation of release, it began. In the pulpit, the Beloved started to groan and moan, and then to move. His shoulders jerked as if he were being shaken by an unknown force. His head flew from side to side as though an unseen hand were slapping each cheek in turn. The congregation was still, transfixed as he began to shudder and moan, then to shout. His hands clasped the pulpit as if to stop himself being thrown right out of it, and he cried out, his eyes squeezed tight shut as if better to commune with whatever was inside him.

Arabella seized Letty's hand and squeezed it hard, her chest rising quickly, her eyes ablaze as she stared at the Beloved, murmuring, 'Yes! Amen!' with increasing fervour, and the other women around them did the same, panting and trembling and crying out. Letty found herself stirred up by all the excitement and passion, clutching the pew in front as the Beloved shook and shouted and raised his face to heaven.

The Beloved's words, the exact words, she forgot almost at once, but he spoke powerfully of the Lamb, about the blood, and the nearness of judgement and salvation. She knew he had denounced sin, the way they all lived, and declared that he saw visions as clear as day, the vision of what the Lamb wanted, and what the Lamb wanted was—

'Letty?'

Arabella's voice breaks into her thoughts, springing her out of them. She is flustered, as though she's been caught in some lurid private fantasy of her own, something rather vulgar that ought not to happen in public. 'Yes?'

Arabella blinks sleepily. 'What time is it? Aren't we there yet?'

'We will be soon,' Letty answers, looking at her watch. 'We're nearly there.'

The scene at home is not what Lettice expected, nor, by the looks of it, what Arabella expected either. The motor was, naturally, not at the station to meet them, and the one taxi was absent. By chance they found Billy Miller, the boy from Ashtree Farm, returning from collecting parcels for his mistress, and he said he could easily take them back on his cart. They didn't talk of private matters while sitting up on the seat with Billy, and the pony went at a slow pace, which took some of the wind out of Arabella's sails. Nonetheless, when they arrive at the house, she manages to fire herself up again, jump down without Billy's help, and rap on the front door with satisfied force.

'Let me in at once!' she demands, as though they've barricaded the front door against her. It is opened a moment later by a timid-looking maid, who gasps to see the familiar face of Arabella, and Lettice wide-eyed and apprehensive behind her.

'Enid,' says Arabella, her nose high in the air. 'Where are my sister and brother-in-law?'

'Mr and Mrs Ford are in the drawing room,' stammers Enid, unable to prevent herself bobbing to Arabella as though she is a returning queen.

'Thank you, Enid,' says Letty, unable to keep the note of

apology out of her voice as Arabella marches past, saying, 'I shall surprise them there!'

'Will you want tea, miss?' whispers Enid.

'No, thank you,' Letty says, fearing broken china and hot spills in the fray that will follow, and hurries after Arabella as she reaches the drawing room door and flings it open.

The afternoon light coming in through the large bay window, filtered through the dark green leaves of the rhododendron bushes outside, is pale grey and anaemic. Cecily sits on the sofa sewing her embroidery, while Edward stands by the fire, leaning on the marble mantleshelf, one hand thrust into the pockets of his tweed trousers, a country gentleman at home. Cecily lifts her head and Edward turns as Arabella pushes the door open and strikes an attitude in the doorway.

'Ha!' she cries. 'You didn't expect this, did you? Your plan has failed. I am home.'

'So I see,' Cecily says, putting down her embroidery. She has a studiedly dignified air. 'Welcome back, Arabella. We're very glad you're well again. And as for it being a surprise, I'm afraid we've been expecting you. Mr Barrett telephoned a few hours ago to let us know you were coming home.'

'And, naturally, we are delighted,' Edward adds in a grave tone.

Arabella blinks at them. Then she frowns. 'What do you have to say for yourselves? You have behaved outrageously – criminally! I am within my rights to sue you, as well you know.' She advances into the room, her chin still held high. 'Perhaps I shall.'

'I don't think there's any need for that,' Edward says in a

placatory way. He gestures at an armchair. 'Sit down. We can talk about this amicably, can't we? After all, we're family, aren't we?'

'Family?' Arabella looks scornfully at the armchair. 'No true family would do what you have done.'

'Please, Arabella,' Cecily says with a sweet smile, 'you know we only acted in your best interests, for your own good. We did what we thought was right, and if it was mistaken, then I'm sure we both heartily apologise. We are delighted that you are well and home.'

Arabella looks at them suspiciously, and then casts a quick glance to Letty, who has followed her sister in, as if to see what she makes of this. 'You two only act in your own interests,' she says, 'so forgive me if I don't fall weeping into your arms. I know very well what's going on, and I won't stand for it. I'm as sane as you are, probably more, and I am the mistress of this house.' She draws herself up again so that she stands very straight. 'I think the time has come for you to leave and form your own household elsewhere. After what has happened, I do not believe that we can live harmoniously together.'

There is a long silence. Letty looks from Cecily to Edward, trying to read the expressions on their faces. After all, this was what they'd been trying to avoid all along, and now Arabella has made her decision – unmaking her mind has always been next to impossible.

Edward spreads his hands wide and smiles. 'Arabella, I believe you're right. The cause of this trouble has been an over-proximity between us. It's not always easy to rub along, and religion, like politics, can divide the fondest families. The time has come for us to go. We shall start to look for another house immediately. Won't we, my love?' He appeals to Cecily with raised eyebrows.

'Yes, Edward,' Cecily answers meekly.

Arabella stares, surprised at the way things are turning out, taken aback that her desire for a confrontation is to be thwarted after all. 'Very well,' she says at last. 'Good.'

Letty wonders where this leaves her. Will she stay here with Arabella, the two of them alone in this huge place, a pair of spinsters, one of whom is obsessed with the Beloved and the Day of Judgement? Or will she go with Cecily and Edward, no doubt to end up running their household, governing their children, her days disappearing in myriad tasks, requests and instructions? Is it better to be anchored in this life, or the next?

But I wonder what Edward has in mind. It's not like him to be docile, or to give up easily.

She must not be unfair to them, though. They may have decided that the better course was to accept that the house belonged to Arabella, and to relinquish it to her.

Cecily stands up. 'Shall I ring for tea? You must be thirsty after your journey. Sit down, Arabella, you too, Letty, and we'll have tea together.'

Considering that two of the party have attempted to have another committed to a lunatic asylum, tea is very civilised. Arabella is unable to resist talking of her adventures, telling the story of her spell in the Moorcroft, her removal to Peckham and her escape, as though it was all a lark in which her cleverness triumphed. Cecily and Edward listen, rapt, as they absorb it all, almost applauding when Arabella reaches the part about her victory over Barrett and his men, as though Barrett were not their own agent.

There is something very strange about all this, Letty thinks, watching them over the rim of her teacup. *The game is not yet finished. Edward and Cecily have another plan.* Her gaze slides to her older sister, animated and vibrant, full of talk, unaware that she's been speaking for a full thirty minutes without a pause and is still going, words falling from her like water from a tap. Arabella is no fool and yet she can be so blind. Will they manage to persuade her of their good intentions? But she is determined that they should go. They will have to work hard to change her mind on that front.

Nevertheless, by the end of the day, it seems that good relations have been restored and the unpleasantness is put behind them. Arabella even kisses her sister goodnight before returning to her bedroom, tired out from her long and exciting day.

Letty goes to her room, also exhausted. She is certain that Cecily will punish her for her part in Arabella's return. But how, she is not sure.

Chapter Twelve

Hello Rachel,

You'll know by now that two other guardians have arrived. Sophia and Agnes are terrific people – I'm sure you'll enjoy having them around. Thanks for your report. It was invaluable in preparing for their arrival. I trust you've been able to maintain your privacy. Please do tell me if there are any issues at all but I have every confidence that the arrangement will work. Sophia tells me you're painting in the front room! That's great to hear. I'd love to see your artwork one day. Meanwhile, please ask if you've got any questions.

All best wishes,

Alison

Yes. I have a question. Who or what is the Beloved, and when might it be arriving?

I close Alison's email, deciding not to reply. I'm beginning to realise that communicating with Alison is a one-way affair. My worries and queries bounce off her and she pursues her own course whatever. I might as well not bother fretting over who might arrive at the house or when. It will happen when it happens.

I laugh drily to myself when I imagine Alison arriving and inspecting my art. The paper is covered in great splodges and splotches of paint, mostly black and yellow as though I'm a bee fanatic, applied in fierce whirls and abstract slashes. It means nothing. It's an almighty mess. But no doubt she'd consider it thoughtfully, compliment my talent and lie herself blue in the face about how good it is, while privately thinking I'm a total fraud.

It's a bright morning, the sky clear and cerulean except for wisps of cloud that look like they've escaped from a bigger bank somewhere and have floated off to find new horizons. The bite in the air has softened, and I've spotted some yellow trumpets of daffodils in the garden. I sent Heather out to play this morning, well wrapped up in jumpers, a coat and a hat. I worry about her fragile health, but I also know that fresh air is good for youngsters, so I think on balance it's better for her to go out. Anyway, she'll go stir-crazy if she's kept in. I'm sure that she won't be spotted by the women upstairs; I suspect Agnes and Sophia sleep late, in the way of people without children. Years of rising between five and seven o'clock in the morning to tend to babies has irreversibly altered my body clock and now I think of eight o'clock as a lie-in. I envy their ability to sleep on through the morning, and I'm glad it gives me a window of freedom.

I feel the urge to be out there myself, breathing in the spring air, smelling the scents of the garden. I jump up, fetch my coat and let myself out of the French windows into the morass of overgrown shrubbery, making my way to Heather's little den under the bay tree.

'Heather?' I stoop down to look into the hollow underneath. 'Sweetie?'

There's no reply and no sign of her. A pile of old withered leaves that were once her plates and cups sits abandoned near small heaps of damp earth. There are scuff marks in the ground, but she isn't here.

'Heather?' I don't want to raise my voice too much in case the women upstairs hear me and look out. 'Where are you?'

I listen hard for her. Amidst the sound of the spring birdsong, I think I can hear a faint answering call. 'Mummy!' Her voice, soft as a breeze, carrying over to me.

'Heather, are you okay?'

I hear the reply: 'Yes!'

'I'm going over to the cottage next door, sweetie. I'll be half an hour. Go back inside if you get cold. You can watch the tablet if you like. All right?'

There it is again. '*Yeeesss!*'

Where is she? The wind must be carrying her voice in a strange way. I am not worried about her, though. I'm sure she's safe enough here in the garden, and she's spent too long hiding away in the bedroom in case the women come downstairs and see her.

'Okay, darling. See you later.' I straighten up and wonder how I'm going to find Matty's cottage. I only have the vaguest idea of which direction it's in. But they told me it was easy enough to find. I set off towards where I think the boundary of the garden must be. The tangle of bare branches and over-grown bushes is sometimes too much to overcome and I have to make my way around it, where the route is easier. I've soon lost my sense of direction and just keep moving forward, clearing the way ahead by stamping down brambles and foli-age, feeling like an explorer advancing through the virgin jungle with a machete in hand.

Soon I come to a long, thick hedge, too regular to be an overgrown shrub. It seems to form a border, and I guess that beyond this must lie another property, surely that of Matty and Sissy. I walk along the hedge, trampling down long, damp grasses as I go, looking for a thin patch where I might be able to wriggle through. No doubt the sisters know a civilised way around much nearer to the house, which is now completely obscured. I spot what looks like a hole in the hedge, and head towards it only to see, to my surprise, a rotten gate on a pair of rusted hinges, locked with a bolt that looks as though it has not been opened for a very long time. It is tightly shut and all my efforts cannot open it, the cold, rust-pocked metal hurting my hands until I wrap them in my scarf. After that, with a great heave, I'm able to edge the bolt bit by bit out of its home until I can tug the gate open wide enough to sidle through. I'm out of our garden and into a kind of meadow, the grass much shorter, speckled with wild flowers and heather. The ground feels waterlogged underfoot, and I guess I'm near the lake. I look over to my right and see a small cot-tage up the slight rise, its roof thatched, smoke rising from the chimney.

'Bingo,' I say, pleased with myself. 'That must be it.'

I head off towards it, the going easier now that I'm out of the overgrowth. There is a satisfying squelchy noise as I stride up the hill, enjoying the sensation of the walk. It's so long since I've been out. Even before we got here, I stayed inside for months. I've been closeted away for so long and I feel now the mood-lifting magic of exercise. I consider walking on and on, away from the cottage, the house and everything, just walking on forever. But I know I can't. I'm needed. I have to go back.

When I finally reach the cottage, it loses a little of the charm it had from a distance. It's dilapidated and seems to be gently and slowly falling down. A few skinny chickens peck about in the area in front of it – not quite a garden and not quite a yard. But there are also well-tended flower beds and I can see, through a gate, a range of raised beds with the dark green and purple splodges of winter greens, and others that will no doubt be full of produce later in the year. Empty fruit frames dwarf the pruned-back canes. By the door that sits under a porch so wonky it could be from a fairy tale is a herb bed with a huge rosemary bush. I pick a stem of grey-green spikes, crush them absentmindedly and inhale the earthy scent that brings back vague memories of Sunday roasts and Easter lunches. I throw it quickly away and go to the door. An old iron ring serves as a knocker and I bang it hard.

'Hello? Anyone home?'

A voice sounds faintly inside. Then footsteps, and I hear it more clearly. 'All right, I'm coming. Hold on.'

A moment later, the old door opens slowly and reveals Matty standing there, wearing a cherry-red jumper with a huge droopy rollneck, and a tartan kilt. She wears thick stockings and a pair of woolly slippers. Her grey and white streaked hair falls freely over her shoulders. Her dark eyes fix me with their inscrutable blackness at the core. 'Oh,' she says flatly. 'It's you. You'd better come in.'

I follow her in as she heads back into the cottage's interior. The floor is worn grey slabs, the ceiling low and fretted, like the walls, with dark wooden beams. There is stuff everywhere: huge pieces of furniture clearly not suited for the small dimensions of the cottage, loaded with ornaments and bric-a-brac, and half-open drawers spilling their contents. Baskets against the wall are stuffed with tottering piles of newspapers and magazines, or folds of fabric, or assorted junk. Every bit of plaster has a picture hanging from it – all sorts, from large, grand gilt-framed oil portraits and landscapes to amateur-looking watercolours, along with prints, engravings, woodcuts, framed pages from books, and photographs of stiff-looking Victorians and Edwardians in their best clothes: leg-of-mutton sleeves, wasp waists, straw boaters and unsmiling expressions.

Are they hoarders?

I recall stories of people unable to jettison anything, who end up crawling through tunnels of rubbish, slotting themselves into tiny gaps between it and the ceiling, until one day they are struck by a tumbling avalanche of detritus that buries them alive. I look around. It's bad, but not that bad. They could just do with a bit of decluttering.

No wonder their belongings don't fit in here if they came from the big house. But there's so much tat. They could lose most of it without even noticing. Then you might be able to see the nice stuff.

We emerge into a kitchen, where I'm enveloped by a cloud of warmth made fuggy by the washing that hangs on a rack above the range. What draws my eye at once is a sideboard on which sits a bonsai tree, absolutely adorable in its minia-ture perfection, the tiny gnarled trunk and outstretched branches in perfect proportion. There are leaves of dark glossy green unfurling next to little green buds, the tips show-ing the white of the petals within.

Next to the range, in a wooden rocking chair, sits Sissy, knitting. She looks up as I come in and smiles as though she can see me.

'Hello,' she says cheerily.

'It's the caretaker from the house, Sissy,' explains Matty. I wonder if she is teasing me.

'Hello,' I say. 'I hope you don't mind me dropping in.'

Sissy still seems to be staring straight at me. 'I knew you'd come,' she says almost confidingly, her needles clacking on, her fingers twisting the dark wool with fast, deft movements.

I look back at the bonsai tree. 'That's very pretty. What a lovely tree. It's so tiny but so perfect.'

Sissy says, 'Oh, our little snow rose. She's a fussy one, that one. The others live in the sitting room but not the snow rose. She likes it here. She likes the warmth of the range and the way the sink and the washing keep the air moist. She hates to dry out! But worse is being too damp. She knows exactly how she likes things, and she likes it here. My theory is that she is a sociable little thing and enjoys hearing our chatter. She's modest but when she decides to open herself out, she's the most beautiful of all.'

I smile. 'You're obviously very fond of it. I'd love to see it flower.'

'You might,' Sissy says. 'You might. All it does is flower. It will never grow any bigger. It will always stay this way: small and sweet.'

Matty says, 'Tea?'

'Thank you.'

She fills a huge bell-shaped kettle from a tap at the sink, takes it to the range, lifts a lid and places the kettle on the hotplate beneath. She nods towards the small square scrubbed table in the middle of the room, which I take to mean I should sit down, so I pull out one of the chairs and sink onto it, glad to rest after my walk.

'What brings you here?' Matty asks, leaning back against the range while she waits for the kettle. 'Everything all right at the house?'

'Yes, fine. The house is just the same. But . . . I've got some visitors.'

The knitting needles stop clacking and there is a sudden silence. Then they resume and Matty says stiffly, 'Visitors?'

'More guardians. Sent from the company. Two girls. Well, women. Two women.'

Matty glances over at her sister, who inclines her head towards her as if they are swapping looks, even though that's impossible. 'Oh,' she says.

'They're called Sophia and Agnes.'

'Oh,' Matty says, frowning. 'Greek. As usual. That's a bad sign.'

'Is it? Why?' I ask.

'Don't worry about that,' says Sissy in her gentle voice. 'It doesn't mean a thing.' But her needles have slowed, her fingers curling the wool around them less rapidly. She's staring at the length of knitted wool as if counting rows. She must be lost in her own thoughts.

I continue, 'Well, they're here, and there might be others coming. I had to take stock of the condition of the house, and it made me think a bit more about what it used to be like. In the past. When you lived there.'

After a pause, Matty says, 'That was a long time ago.'

'So . . . I'd be interested if you could tell me a little about it. About its history. There's nothing I could find on the internet about Paradise House, just a bit about the architect.'

'Paradise House, is it?' Matty shakes her head. 'Well, well.'

'Didn't you call it that?'

'*We* did. But that wasn't its official name, not on the deeds. They're calling it Paradise, are they?'

'Yes, I don't know any other name for it. Well, that explains why I couldn't find out anything about it! And the women told me there's a church in the grounds. Do you know about that?'

Now the silence that greets my words is deep and unmistakably loaded.

'We know about the church,' says Matty at last.

'Oh yes, we know about the church,' echoes Sissy in her soft way.

'Where is it?' I ask, curious. 'I haven't heard any bells.'

'No, you won't hear bells. Or see people going to it. It's not used anymore.'

'But the women told me they were going to a service there.'

The atmosphere grows suddenly tense and I sense an anxiety that hasn't been present until now. Matty starts to move, turning to the kettle, lifting it and putting it back. Sissy drops her knitting to her side and begins to rock in her chair, her brow puckering into a scowl.

'Is something wrong?' I ask.

Matty replaces the kettle, tapping her nails for a moment on its metal side, before turning back to me. She stares at me with those almost rimless eyes. 'So,' she says. 'It's what we thought. It's all starting again.'

'What is starting again?'

Sissy says quietly, 'History. History is starting all over again.'

They are careful about what they say in answer to my questions. I soon realise that in fact I am the one answering questions. They want to know how I heard of the place, on what terms I was engaged to come here and who it is that engaged me. I try to stick with the version of events that ties in with what I told Alison, just in case the stories are compared at some point in the future.

'I'm an artist,' I tell them.

'Are you?' Sissy says it quickly, directly. 'Really?'

I hesitate. 'Yes.'

'You exhibit? Sell work?' She seems suspicious.

163

'Well . . . no. Not yet.'

This seems to reassure her, though I can't think why. 'And you've come here to paint?'

'Yes. In peace and quiet.'

'All on your own,' says Matty.

'That's right.'

'Don't you have a husband? A family?'

'My husband and I are separated,' I reply stiffly.

They absorb this silently. They don't ask about children after that. They want to know more about Sophia and Agnes. I can only assume it's because they feel so protective of their old home that they want to understand what's going on there now. After all, they came to scrutinise me not long after I arrived. Now I'm doing that for them with the newcomers.

'And they went to the church,' Matty says.

'That's right,' I say. 'Wearing very pretty white dresses.'

Matty nods, looking not at all surprised, and says, 'Well, they would.' She has made the tea, lifting the kettle off the plate just before it begins to whistle, and pouring the water into a bright yellow china teapot. After a moment, she tips the pot over the waiting cups, and then adds milk to the tea. She pushes one in my direction. 'There.' Then she walks over to Sissy, lifts her hand and folds her sister's fingers around the handle of the cup. 'That's for you, old girl.'

'Thank you,' Sissy says.

I thank Matty and sip the tea. It's unexpectedly delicious, exactly what I wanted after my walk. *Perhaps it's the fresh air, after so long inside.*

'You still haven't told me about your time in the house,' I

say, smiling. All this talk about the newcomers has formed a bond between us – at least, that's what I hope. Now we're united against the strangers. Aren't we?

Matty sighs while Sissy sips her tea. She sits down slowly in the chair opposite me. She stares at me for a moment, and says, 'I don't think you're a religious person, are you?'

I blink at her, uncertain what to say. I want to keep our bond alive, so I'll say whatever will make her happy. But I'm not sure what that would be. Then I think: *am I? Am I religious?*

It's not something I've thought about for years. I went to a convent school, taught by nuns and spinsters, and our entire school lives revolved around the Church calendar and the school chapel. We had lots of lessons on religion – 'divinity' it was called, as though teaching us to be angels – but of the utterly unquestioning kind.

Sister Martha would make us recite the Magnificat or the Nunc Dimittis. Or The Beatitudes. *Blessed are the poor in heart . . . Blessed are the meek . . . Blessed are those who mourn . . .*

And we were in that chapel twice a day, for morning service and in the evening for compline. I dreamed through the morning service, but the evening one I liked: the dimness of the chapel, the orange-gold candlelight flickering on the walls, turning them salmon pink; the calmness of the short service and its plea for safety. *Defend us from all the perils and dangers of this night.* Like an invocation, a spell, a magic charm.

I never really questioned religion. I simply accepted it. Why, after all, would we go to all this bother if there were nothing at all to it? Why would it be so integral to official, grown-up life if it were all just a fairy story? Everyone whom I was supposed to respect and obey believed it. And I liked hymns, and Easter and Christmas, Lent and Harvest Festival, the rolling round of the liturgical year. I liked the stories of saints and the Bible tales. And who could disagree that we should love our neighbour and try very hard to be good?

But after I left school, I drifted away. With no one to make me, I never went to church, except the occasional midnight mass, half drunk on Christmas Eve, to bellow out the old favourites, doing the descant on 'O Come, All Ye Faithful'. The old rituals faded and were forgotten. It was all a story told long ago that I used to know well, but not anymore.

I'm struck by a sudden horrible thought. Perhaps if I had continued going – begging for forgiveness, trying to be good – things might have been different.

Defend us from all the perils and dangers of this night.

Oh no.

It's like an arrow piercing me. Where I went wrong. I never asked for protection. I never said the spell. I forgot that I needed to be safe from the dangers of the night. That we all did.

I forgot to protect us all. Is that what went wrong? Is that why I'm still going wrong?

I feel faint, a horrible wooziness in my head, threatening to drag me down into the dark. Into the perils and dangers.

'Are you all right?' Matty is leaning forward, frowning as she stares at me. 'Do you feel ill?'

My eyes flutter closed as I gasp for breath, and I reach forward to clutch the table. There's a kind of howling in my mind, a sort of shriek that's so high I can hear it as a vile, mosquito wail that makes my skin prickle and my mouth taste bitter. I can't speak; I try to breathe, as though that's the only thing that can restore me.

'Help her, Matty.' It's Sissy's soft voice, now urgent. 'Help her.'

I feel strong hands clasp me under my arms and pull me upwards so that I'm straight in my chair. My head lolls back. *Breathe, breathe*, I command myself.

'Come on, now,' Matty says firmly. I feel a light slap on my cheek and then on the other. 'It's close to hysteria, that's what it is. Listen to her!'

I'm gasping for air, each inhalation accompanied by a strange high sound that comes from the depths of my throat. The knowledge of what I've failed to do seems to be strangling me. My neck is blocked with something solid and impassable.

'Don't hurt her,' cries Sissy.

'I'm not. It won't hurt her. But she needs to snap out of it now.'

Then I feel it – a hot, broad sting on my face as Matty slaps me hard. It shocks me but the pain cuts through the block-age in my throat and opens my lungs to the sweet air beyond it.

'There,' Matty says, releasing me. My shoulders slump as I pull in long, deep breaths. 'That's done it.'

When I raise my eyes to them, I'm embarrassed at what just happened but they don't seem in the least disconcerted by it. There's no sense that my near-faint was in any way unusual.

'There's something there, Matty,' whispers Sissy. She's picked up her knitting and is stroking it with one hand while the black eyes seem to stare right through the wool. 'Don't you think?'

Matty nods, her gaze fixed on me. 'Oh yes,' she agrees. 'There's something there. Something there right enough.'

Chapter Thirteen

As soon as I've recovered myself, I tell the sisters I have to be going. I'm still mortified at almost passing out at their kitchen table. All they did was ask if I was religious, and I almost had a fit. They must think I'm a nutter.

I'm frustrated too. I still don't have any idea what their connection with the house is, or why there is a church in the garden somewhere. All I know is that, according to them, history is repeating itself. But I don't know what that history is, or whether it's a good or bad thing that it is happening again. If it is.

Back at the house, the upstairs windows are all wide open. They must be airing the whole place. I can see movements from time to time – the flit of a shadow as someone passes in front of a window. What can they be doing up there? Cleaning, I suppose. There's not much else to do.

I'm in the kitchen making lunch for Heather and me when I'm startled by the rapid approach of footsteps. I just have time to stash Heather's sandwich in the cupboard when

Agnes puts her head around the kitchen door, her eyes blazing.

'Have you been helping yourself to the stores downstairs?'

I feel my face flame red.

'Well?' Her voice is harsh and fierce.

'I . . .' My eyes drop. I can't meet her gaze.

'Don't try and lie. It's obvious it's you. There's no one bloody else here, is there?'

'I'll replace it all,' I say, wishing I'd got round to doing that before now. I feel like a naughty child being upbraided. 'There was no one else here to use it. I thought it wouldn't matter. I've kept a note of everything I've used—'

'That's not the point!' shouts Agnes. Her cheeks are pink with anger. 'We could need that stuff at any time. At any time! What do you think it's here for?'

'Well, I've got no idea. Why would anyone stuff a freezer in an empty house? And . . .' My own voice starts to rise. My guilty embarrassment is turning into annoyance. 'Haven't you ever heard of a supermarket? You can actually go out and buy anything you need! You don't have to stockpile a load of food. I mean, it's not exactly the back of beyond here. There's a supermarket just a few miles away. What does it matter, if I replace it?'

'It's not yours to touch!' yells Agnes. 'We could need it at any point, don't you realise? It's precious! Precious resources we could rely on at a moment's notice.'

I start to quail under her blazing anger. I'm as sensitive as a child, with paper-thin resistance to rage and blame. 'I'm sorry,' I say, my voice choked. Tears erupt from my eyes, pouring hot down my face.

'Why don't you just go away, Rachel? No one wants you here! The others are coming, you're not needed!' Agnes takes another step towards me, almost relishing her fury with me, her excuse to let rip, and enjoying the sight of my tears.

'You don't understand,' I say, but the words are thick with weeping. I want to stop but I can't, it's pouring out of me. 'Please don't shout at me.'

Agnes's eyes harden. 'Why don't you go to the shops yourself?' she asks in an ominously quiet voice. 'I mean, I don't think you've been out for ages. Your car hasn't been moved. It's bone dry underneath it. There are no tyre marks on the gravel that weren't made by our van. What's the problem, Rachel? Huh?'

She's standing very close to me. I can see the soft hairs on her cheeks, the thick coats of black mascara on her lashes, and the oily pink slick of gloss on her lips. I smell the citrus tang of the scent she's wearing. Her presence is hyper real and threatening. I'm terrified of her.

'Please,' I say, trying desperately to stop crying.

'I've seen you outside, peering about, creeping under bushes. I've heard you when you think we're not there, talking away. Who are you talking to, huh? You're hiding something, Rachel, and I'm going to make it my business to find out what it is, do you understand?' hisses Agnes. 'I'm not going to take my eyes off you. I'm going to find out about you, because I think you're here to cause trouble—'

'Ag, what the hell is going on?' It's Sophia, standing in the doorway, her expression appalled. 'Rachel, why are you crying?'

She strides over and puts her arm around me, reaching at the same time for a small pack of tissues in her pocket. As she offers me one, Agnes turns to her, her Australian accent strong in her indignation. 'She's taken loads of stuff from the freezer. The stores are severely depleted. There's less than half of it left. I always thought it was a terrible idea to put a stranger in here.'

'Shut up, Ag.' Sophia looks at me, her expression more disappointed than accusing. 'Is this true? Did you?'

'I . . . Yes. I'll replace it of course.'

Sophia turns back to Agnes. 'And the . . .' She drops her voice, pulls the other woman close and murmurs in her ear so that I can't hear.

Agnes listens and shakes her head. 'No.'

'Okay then.' She smiles at me. 'So no harm is done. But, Rachel, I'm afraid you won't be able to help yourself to the stores in future. They're there for a reason. You mustn't touch them. Okay?'

'Okay.' I'm indisputably in the wrong, but I want to ask why. Why do they need a freezer full of food that mustn't be used? What exactly is going on here?

Sophia looks at me carefully, her head tipped to one side. 'Are you okay with that? Can you restock the freezer for us?'

'Of course. I kept a note of everything I took.'

Agnes seems calmer. She shoots me a look. 'When did you last go out, huh?'

'I haven't needed to go out,' I reply, sniffing. My crying has stopped. Sophia's presence has soothed the whole situation. 'I've been settling in, painting, doing my report. When I found the stores downstairs while I was using the washing machine, I realised that I could put off the boredom of shopping for a while. That's all. I'll go out and get whatever you need.'

'Today?' Agnes's eyes seem to glitter as she asks.

I shrug. 'Yes. Today. If you want.'

'There's no need to be hasty,' Sophia says, in her placatory way.

'Really?' Agnes turns on her. 'No one knows the hour. No one.'

'The Beloved will know,' Sophia says simply. 'Nothing will happen before he gets here.'

'I think we need him here *now*.'

'He'll come when the time is right. All will be well.'

Agnes is silent as she takes this in. 'Okay,' she says at last. 'Okay.' Then she looks back at me. 'Just make sure you do it soon. And don't forget. I'm watching you.'

I'm shaking as I sit down on the bed and put Heather's sandwich in front of her. She's sitting against the pillow, a book open on the duvet. She reaches out and absentmindedly picks up the sandwich, and I watch as she holds it, still reading. She's so pale, almost as white as the pillowcase. I reach out and stroke her hair. It's cool but soft under my touch.

'What are we going to do, darling?' I ask in a half-whisper. 'Everything is changing. I don't know how long we can stay here with them. But where can we go? Where will we be safe?'

Heather doesn't seem to hear me, she's lost in her book.

I start to hear words echoing in my mind. 'Defend us from all the perils and dangers of this night.' They sound again, louder this time. Then again. I realise I'm saying them myself. 'Defend us . . . defend us . . .' Am I praying?

Heather looks up at me, curious. She listens as I say the words faster and faster until they are rattling out of my mouth. 'Defend us, defend us, from all the perils and dangers, the perils and dangers, the dangers, the dangers . . .'

I can feel that blot of panic building in my throat again. I'm afraid that I will start to scream, or begin to fight for breath, or that I will faint. Then Heather reaches out, smiling, and puts her hand on mine.

She says gently, 'Madam says don't be afraid. You're going to be all right. Madam says help is coming.'

'Oh darling.' I smile at her, but my eyes are filling with tears. 'I wish that were true.'

'It is true,' she says simply.

I stroke her cheek. 'I only want what's best for you. Do you know that?'

'Yes, Mummy.' She gazes up at me.

'I love you so much,' I say softly.

She smiles. 'I love you more.'

I hug her close and kiss her cool cheek. 'I love you most.'

In the afternoon Sophia and Agnes come back downstairs and head out to their van. A moment later, its engine roars into life and the gravel crunches as they drive away. I wonder if they've gone to replenish the stocks of food and when they'll be back. But I sigh with relief as soon as the sound of the van fades away. I'm alone again.

I put on a coat and my boots and head out through the rhododendron bushes in the direction I saw the women head on Sunday. It's still damp between the dense trees, the sun unable to penetrate through the thick glossy green leaves. I shiver a little as I make my way onwards, through the mud and mess of fallen leaves and rotting sludge. It occurs to me to wonder how big this garden is, exactly. I get the strange feeling that I could walk all day and still, somehow, be in it.

This isn't a garden. It's an estate.

Then, ahead, I see a pointed slate roof, and rising from it a small steeple topped with a cross. So there it is. The church.

I emerge out of the thicket and see the whole thing before me. It's a simple building, like a child's drawing in its neat straight lines and rectangular shape. What makes it a church is the huge arched door beneath a large, extravagant glass window, alive with a rainbow of jewel tones and detailed pictures: I spot doves, lambs, an ark, trumpets and angels, rays of heavenly light, a triumphant messiah in a white robe descending to the upturned faces of the faithful.

It's a church all right.

I go forward, curious, and reach the front door. The church is more impressive up close than at first sight. The door is thick oak, bound with black iron hinges and with handles of ornate iron rings. I lift one and it moves easily under my hand. The door swings open.

It's light inside. Around the top of the building are round trefoil portholes with clear glass. At the far end above the altar is another vast stained-glass window, casting rosy light down upon the wooden table beneath. The table, which must be the altar, is on a raised dais, and below that are a few rows of wooden chairs, the kind with slots for hymn and prayer books on the back. But there are no more than twenty or thirty. The rest of the space, from just inside the door to near the back row of chairs, is more like a sitting room, or even a games room. Around the edges are dusty red velvet sofas and button-backed chairs on neat turned legs. There are bookshelves, a piano, a harpsichord, and, to my surprise, a glass cabinet containing a collection of small crystal sherry glasses.

I laugh out loud.

'What's so funny?'

I jump violently and spin round. There, in the doorway, is Sissy, her hair all around her face, one hand holding on to the iron ring on the door.

'Oh, Sissy! You frightened me. Nothing . . . nothing's funny.' I walk towards her. 'It's me, by the way. Rachel.'

'I know,' she says simply. Her dark eyes stare past me, towards the rays of softly coloured light falling on the altar. 'I knew you'd come here. I've been waiting.'

I laugh again, awkward this time. 'I suppose you guessed my curiosity would get the better of me.' I look back around at the dusty old church. It's hard to imagine what on earth Sophia and Agnes got up to in here on their own on Sunday. 'Did you use to come here when you were a girl?' I ask, turning back to Sissy.

She smiles. 'Oh yes. All the time. But it was getting emptier even then. As the ladies passed over. It was only ladies by then.'

'What denomination is it?' I point to the sherry glasses. 'Not Methodist!'

'No. Not that.' She smiles gently, not glancing in the direction I'm pointing. *Of course, she wouldn't. She's blind.*

'Not Church of England?'

'No, not that either.'

'So, what then?'

'Not one particular thing.' Sissy's voice is dreamy suddenly. 'And yet, many things.' She lets go of the handle and takes a few steps into the old place, as though she knows it well enough not to have to see it. 'This is where we children came, after the others were inside. We came in together in our white robes, two by two. Matty and I came last, as we were part of the holy family, descendants of the Beloved. They looked at us in awe. They looked at our brother in awe. They believed that we would never die.' She laughs, a strange sound with a harsh edge to it. 'Well, Matty and I are still here. The only ones who are. But David is dead. I'm afraid even the faith could not keep him going. But by then they knew that. Once the Beloved himself was gone, they knew.'

I listen, trying to make sense of what she's telling me.

'The faith was shaken by death. It was not supposed to happen, not to us. We were the wheat. The chaff would be destroyed, thrown on the fire, but we would ripen and live until the harvest came. The harvest of souls. But it never happened.' She sighs heavily. 'Some promises were kept, I suppose. The promise of respite from the world, the happiness of

177

living here, untouched by the disappointments of life outside. But I think gradually we realised that the greatest promise of all was no more than a dream. Death came for us, like it comes for everyone.'

She shuffles further forward into the room, feeling her way past the glass cabinet. I wonder if she is going to go all the way up to the altar but when she reaches the last row of chairs, she grips the back of one and turns to face me. She stares right at me with those big black sightless eyes.

'Now,' she says, and smiles. 'Why don't you tell me about your little girl? How is she?'

Chapter Fourteen

Letty watches as the Reverend Phillips walks around the house – at least, the ground floor of it – seeming very pleased. Satisfied, Letty thinks. Arabella follows him wherever he goes, so close as to seem almost stuck to him. She's breathless and excited. Letty follows with the reverend's wife, Sarah, a much older lady with a kindly face and a low, comforting voice.

'What a lovely home you have,' she says to Letty as they walk behind the others.

'Thank you.'

'Your sister is the kindest woman in the world.'

Letty says, 'She can be very generous, Mrs Phillips.'

'Please, call me Sarah. After all, we're going to be family.' The older woman smiles. She doesn't seem to mind over-excited Arabella pressing close to her husband.

'I suppose we are,' Letty says faintly.

'This is fine,' Reverend Phillips is saying. 'It is magnificent, Miss Evans.'

They stop to look into the library, and the reverend gazes about at rows of leather-bound books, expensive furniture, the brass and leather club fender around the fireplace. He evidently sees much to please him, and he already has a proprietorial air, as though he can envisage himself in this room, behind the great walnut desk with its inlaid red leather top.

'A splendid room,' he says in his deep voice. Letty cannot help herself responding to it, with its mellow tone and the timbre that seems to touch something in her bones. She doesn't know why this should be. The Reverend Phillips is not a particularly handsome man, or a young one, though he is younger than his wife, but he has an undefinable glamour. Perhaps it is his white hair, which makes his skin appear youthful in contrast, despite the deep lines that run from the side of his nose past his mouth, and the great notch between his eyebrows. Lettice thinks he might be forty-five, perhaps a little more, but his wife, with her serenity reflected in the neatness of her dress and the smoothness of her grey hair in its tidy bun, must surely be at least fifty.

And yet, there is no mistaking his magnetism. It comes partly from the voice, partly from those eyes of the most piercing blue surmounted by black brows, and partly from his presence. He carries himself with an unusual dignity and confidence. He has an aura of wisdom and . . . and . . . *grace* is the word supplied by Letty's mind. Grace is a curious word to apply to a man in a thick black overcoat, carrying an ivory-topped walking stick which seems more for effect than any practical use. And yet it is what he has. The air around him seems to buzz with energy and what Letty can only think of as similar to the charisma of a great actor.

She can understand why Arabella is as enchanted as she appears. And now she is fluttering about him, showing him the house with a puppyish eagerness, as though she longs to be patted on the head and told she is good. More than that, she has the air of true reverence. Worship, even.

They continue the inspection of the house, even visiting the scullery and laundry, while Arabella explains that there are more cottages on the estate and boasts excitedly of the extent of the grounds. The reverend listens with an air of pleased complacency. When at last they return to the drawing room, where Enid has laid out tea, the reverend clasps Arabella's hands in his and stares into her face. Sarah sits serenely on the sofa sipping her tea, observing calmly as her husband works his magic on Arabella. Lettice watches as her sister twitches with excitement, her cheeks flushing dark pink and her mouth falling open.

'The Lamb is with you, Miss Evans,' says the reverend in his rich, rolling voice. 'He has inspired you and called you to his holy work. You are a part of his plan, a vital part, in calling the elect to salvation! And here, in this marvellous place, the chosen will begin to realise his mission of grace. You are truly blessed, Miss Evans. I see the marvels of the spirit working in you and through you!'

Arabella is trembling, her eyes shining. 'Yes, Beloved. Yes. I feel it . . . oh, I feel it.'

'Then let us pray.' Still clutching Arabella's hands, he bows his head, and the other women follow suit: Sarah shuts her eyes and presses her palms together as the reverend begins to address the Almighty, and Lettice peeks out from under her lids, watching as Arabella is lost in the ecstasy of prayer.

'You cannot do this, Arabella, I won't allow it!' Cecily is pacing the drawing room, her expression taut with fury and fear.

'I don't believe you can stop me,' returns Arabella coolly. She has an impregnable air and they can all sense it.

'Letty, are you part of this nonsense?' demands Cecily, turning her burning gaze on her.

Lettice opens her mouth to speak but as she does, Arabella says, 'Of course she is. And it's not nonsense. It's deadly serious.'

'I can't believe it!' Cecily puts her hands to her face and shakes her head. 'This is madness, sheer madness.'

'The Beloved says you are an unbeliever, Cecily. You and Edward. You're both destined for the fires of hell, even your children when they come,' Arabella says as calmly as if she's telling Cecily that the weather is inclement for the time of year. 'But you still have a chance to join the elect. If only you'd see the truth. Listen to the Beloved and understand.'

Cecily suddenly looks utterly bewildered. 'But Arabella, you're going to give him this house! All of it – lock, stock and barrel. What am I supposed to make of it? You must realise that it's a ridiculous thing to do.'

'On the contrary, it's a very sensible thing to do,' Arabella returns. 'The Day of Judgement is close at hand. The Beloved has made it all very plain to us. The signs are clear that the end of time is nigh.'

'What signs?' Cecily demands, her voice angry again. 'Don't tell me of war and plague and all the rest of it. They are as eternal as the moon! What do they signify?'

Letty goes to the window, standing in the curve of the bay and gazing out at the drive and the garden. She knows there is no point in arguing with Arabella. Cecily has not seen the Beloved, she does not know anything of the power he exerts and of the way that Arabella responds to him; she is bewitched by him, utterly in his power. And Letty can feel the power creeping into her as well. It's something to do with the thrill in the belly his voice engenders, along with the feeling of absolute safety that comes from his certainty of their imperviousness to death and destruction. She doesn't want it to be so, but the force of his gaze on her makes her skin prickle and the tips of her fingers shake, just as she sees Arabella tremble when she's near him. She hasn't been able to stop herself imagining the reverend embracing his wife, taking her into his arms and pressing his mouth on hers. What must that be like? To be one with the Beloved?

'The greatest sign of all is the Beloved himself,' replies Arabella, her voice serene. 'He is the fifth incarnation.'

'The what?' asks Cecily.

Letty turns a little, concentrating hard on her sister's words.

'The fifth what?' demands Cecily again.

'First there was Adam. Then Noah. Then Abraham. Then Christ. And now—'

Cecily gasps and says in a horrified voice, 'No, Arabella! Don't dare say it! He can't claim such a thing! He daren't!'

What about Moses? thinks Letty. *Why has he been missed out?*

'The Beloved is the next incarnation,' Arabella says proudly.

Cecily leaps to her feet. 'It's blasphemy, Arabella! Wicked blasphemy! Does the bishop know?'

'The time is not yet right for the world to know. Only we his followers have had the precious knowledge vouchsafed to us.' Arabella leans forward to her sister, the excitement possessing her again. 'Can't you see the honour, the glory of it? The incarnation, here in this house! Where we will await the Coming, where we will be immune to death! Oh Cecily, that we've been chosen! Can't you see it?' She stands up and opens her arms wide, a beatific look on her face. 'Believe, Cecily! Believe and be saved! Join us!'

As Cecily stares in horrified outrage, Letty feels a thrill down her back as she responds to her sister's words. *Yes,* she thinks, without even meaning to. She has no desire now to go and live with Cecily and Edward as their unpaid companion. She wants to remain here, in the house she loves, with Arabella. *And the Beloved.* The thought makes her feel light-headed and she closes her eyes. *What's happening to me?*

'This is madness, Arabella!' Cecily is saying loudly. 'You can't get away with it.'

'I can and I will.' Arabella smiles and raises her eyes to heaven, moving her lips in prayer.

Words float into Letty's mind. *For I am my Beloved's. And he is mine.*

*

Letty has her ear pressed against the door of the library. Cecily and Edward are in there with the lawyer while Arabella is away for the day, attending to tasks the Beloved has given her. Mr Simpson's voice is easy to hear, though she cannot make out her sister's questions. The answers are enough, though.

'I'm afraid that religious mania is not sufficient to prove insanity. It's perfectly possible to be sane and yet believe in the most arrant nonsense. Throughout human history people have been convinced that they are living in the end of days. Strong personalities exploit the credulous. This knave is no different to many who've gone before him.'

'But' – it's Edward's voice, aggrieved – 'he claims to be some kind of divine manifestation! It's blasphemy. I've written to the bishop. He cannot continue to allow this man to make these claims and remain in the Church. It's sheer wickedness.'

'That may be so. It's the bishop's decision. But whatever he rules, it makes no difference to your sister's power to make over all her property to the Reverend Phillips if she so chooses.'

Letty hears Cecily say something and the reply from Mr Simpson.

'Then I'm afraid you have no choice but to leave.'

'But it's my home too!' The shout from Cecily penetrates the oak door of the library with its anguish.

'I'm afraid not. Perhaps morally. But not legally. If she wishes you to leave, you must go.'

Letty hears quick footsteps and stands back just in time to be out of the way when Cecily flings open the door and runs across the black and white chequerboard floor of the hallway, sobbing violently, and heads upstairs.

The lawyer says, 'All I can suggest, Mr Ford, is that perhaps you ought to do as Arabella suggests and become followers yourselves. Then you could stay.'

'That's not funny, Simpson,' Edward replies. 'This is a tragedy for us all.'

'Of course it is. Forgive me.'

Letty walks slowly across the hall. *I'll go upstairs and find Cecily*, she thinks. *I must comfort her.* But she's already beginning to imagine a life here without her sister and brother-in-law. She's starting to think of them as lost to the cause. *Blind. Wilfully blind. Condemned.*

But she and Arabella will be saved.

'The flock gathers!' cries the Beloved. He stands on the bottom step of the staircase, his arms flung wide as they come: from the outposts of the Beloved's journey through ministry. Wherever he has been, he has gathered followers, from country parishes to city churches, from the Isle of Wight, where his words brought a dying man back to life, to the Army of the Redeemed, a small London sect that swiftly became part of the Beloved's own army.

Where will they all sleep? wonders Letty. The rooms that belonged to her parents are now those of the Beloved and Sarah, his wife. But Arabella has it all in hand. Enid is watching, horrified, from behind the green baize door. The cook has already given notice.

'You are the elect!' calls the Beloved. His expression is joyful, his eyes bright with blue rapture. He wears a white shirt open at the neck, and a black waistcoat and black trousers that show off his fine, strong limbs. There is something about the majesty of his white hair and his physical strength that makes him appear ineffably wise and full of youthful vigour at the same time. It is a potent mix. Letty feels that strange rush of excitement that she can't suppress when she sees him. He will be living here. They all will. A bright new future is beginning, and at its end the joyous Day of Judgement when all will be taken up to the house of the Almighty to live in bliss for eternity. Until then, they will exist in the peace and fellowship outlined by the Beloved, and worship in the church that Arabella is already having built in the grounds. And when the church is finished, the name of the house will be changed from Hanthorpe to Paradise House.

The gardeners carry in boxes and trunks belonging to the new arrivals. The ladies come, long skirts rustling – for the Beloved has decreed that women will wear long white skirts and white blouses buttoned to the neck. And it is nearly all ladies, none younger than thirty by the looks of it, most a good deal older. Certainly they are much older than Arabella, who is only twenty-five, and Letty, who is twenty-one on her next birthday. Some are not yet in their designated clothes, but have arrived in dark dresses, coats and hats. Some have shabby coats and worn hats, and the tired expressions that speak of a life of physical labour. It is evident that the Beloved exerts his power over all the classes of society, loving all his followers with equal fervour.

'These are glory days, my children,' the Beloved says. 'Glory days. Hallelujah.'

'Hallelujah!' chorus the ladies nearest to him.

'Praise be,' the Beloved murmurs. 'The time is at hand. I am almost ready to be revealed to my people.'

'Praise be,' call the ladies.

'Praise be,' Letty says obediently.

Chapter Fifteen

'You're not blind!' I shout at Sissy, my voice ringing with accusation. Panic is gushing up inside me. *How does she know about Heather? Did Heather get seen at the cottage after all? But . . . it's not possible, it's not!*

Sissy and I stand in the church, staring at each other. Except that she shouldn't be able to see me. And she can. I know it.

'Yes, I am, dear. I can't see a thing.'

'You're lying!' I shout. 'I know you are. How did you get here on your own if you can't see? How do you know when I'm with you and I haven't spoken? You sent that card, didn't you? You wrote it. How could you do that, if you can't see?'

'I can still remember how to write,' she says reasonably.

'A blind person wouldn't write in perfect neat lines like that, with no mistakes! You can see. Why don't you just admit it? It's obvious!' I'm shaking, but whether with fear or anger, I don't know. I've always noticed the way Sissy's eyes follow movement. Now I know why. She isn't blind. Maybe she thinks she is – but she isn't. But I'm not going to admit any-thing.

'My child,' she says, coming towards me, holding out her arms. Her eyes are black. I can't tell if they're empty or not. She could be staring at me, or looking straight through me into infinity. 'My poor child. I understand. I can sense your pain. You can talk to me about it.'

'Shut up!' I cry. I haven't run this far and worked this hard to give it all up to this strange woman. I'm afraid of her – all that compassion, the open arms, the kindly warmth. I'm afraid of what she might make me see. I realise that she could be the one who opens the door I've been leaning so hard against, trying with all my might to keep it closed. I hold up my hands. 'Stay away from me!'

Sissy is still moving towards me, her black eyes full of sympathy, shimmering with wetness. 'You poor girl. I can help you—'

'No!' This can't happen. I won't permit it. I've done every-thing I can to stop it. But already I can sense that it may be too late. 'Leave me alone! You don't know anything about it!' I turn and run, my feet loud on the bare wooden floor, then wrench open the door and bolt through it, straight into the person on the other side. I scream as I cannon into them, and a pair of strong hands grabs my upper arms and holds me steady.

'Hey! Are you okay?'

I pull back and I'm staring up into ice-blue eyes rimmed with dark lashes. They are in a man's face, with a mass of thick brown hair falling around his ears and a beard and moustache obscuring half his face. He's wearing a black T-shirt and jeans, and he's well built, broad-chested with muscled, tanned arms. I'm shaking like a leaf and my teeth are chattering. He looks concerned and says again, 'Are you okay?'

I nod, aware his hands are still firm on my upper arms.

'You must be Rachel,' he says, smiling. His teeth are perfectly straight and white, gleaming with magazine perfection. He lets go of my arms. 'I wondered when we'd meet.'

'Wh-who are you?' I ask. Then I glance over my shoulder to the church behind me. I don't want to see Sissy and I'm afraid that she's shuffling towards me, feeling her way along the room as though she can't see perfectly well. 'I want to get away from here.'

'Of course. I'll take you back to the house. You look a bit shaken.' He seems concerned for me, taking my arm and linking it through his as he turns to accompany me. 'What happened in there?'

'Nothing, nothing.' We start walking in the direction of the house, the man steering me onto a path I don't know which looks as though it will efficiently edge the thicket I fought my way through earlier. 'Sorry . . . who are you?'

'My name is Archer.' He smiles again. The blue eyes light up with friendliness; he beams with affection, even though I'm a stranger to him. The face behind the beard is olive-skinned, and the nose and mouth have a kind of Grecian perfection to them. 'The girls told me about you.'

'Sophia and Agnes?'

'That's right. I've just arrived. I've brought some friends with me. Dora and Daphne.'

More! I can't cope with it . . . 'How many of you are there now?'

'Oh. Just me and the girls. So five of us altogether.' He smiles at me. 'I got a message from Agnes. She said it was time to get here. And you know what? I was already on my way.'

We're approaching the house now. I can hardly hear him, or understand what he's saying to me. I'm numb with the shock of what Sissy said to me. Her words are thudding against my mind, pounding at me. They're like battering rams, hitting at the walls I've erected in my head. The walls are weakening. Soon they'll break and all the things I've carefully shut behind them will come flooding out.

It will kill me! I can't, I can't.

I need to decide what to do now but even as I scrabble for strength, for all the resources I've called on up until now, I feel as though, finally, I'm at a loss. I don't know what to do. The danger is both within me and without. There are more people in the house. How can I carry on there? How can it be what I wanted and needed so badly? I thought I'd found a place where Heather and I could be alone. But it doesn't seem possible. It can't happen. There's nowhere to go. I've reached my limit.

I'm suddenly icy cold. I feel as though my breathing might stop altogether. I stand still.

Am I at the end? Is this it?

Archer takes a few steps forward and realises I'm not

moving so he turns back to me. 'Hey, Rachel, are you all right?'

I'm staring at the ground, my head full of a hissing white noise, feeling as though my heart is going to explode inside me. The world is in a conspiracy to take Heather away from me. All my plans, everything I've done, all the work I've put into finding a place where we can be together undisturbed – it's all wasted. It's over. It can never work.

I realise that I've known it's over for a while.

'Heather,' I say miserably. 'I'm so sorry, darling. I tried so hard. I'm so sorry. I've failed you again.'

'Who's Heather?' Archer says, looking around as if to see someone emerging from the thicket.

A terrible sadness sweeps over me. 'My daughter.'

He looks surprised. 'I didn't know you had a daughter. Is she here?'

I reach out with everything inside me to feel Heather's presence. Lately, she's been fading from me. Harder and harder to find her. There's no trace of her around me now. I can't even hear that gentle whisper, the soft sound of her calling 'Mummy' to me.

'No,' I say slowly.

'Is she at home? With her dad?'

'No.' I can see her now as I last saw her. In her bed, hugging me. Smiling. *I love you more.*

I love you most.

I close my eyes. Inside me a silent scream is building. I manage to speak. 'She's nowhere.' My mouth is dry. I've not said it. I've not thought it. I've not admitted it to myself. I've not permitted myself to make it real. But now, at last, I have no choice. I have to say it. My world will stop. 'She's gone. She's dead.'

I don't know what happens after that. Blackness, enveloping and forgiving, takes me away from the pain. I've not let myself feel it. It's been a massive act of will, to stop the terror of it touching me. I can't do it anymore but I have a small respite left. Unconsciousness. And I'm grateful when it claims me.

Much later, without wanting to, I rise up through the darkness like a swimmer ascending through layers of water to the surface. I'm lying on the bed in our room and as I open my eyes, I see the small pile of Heather's things next to me: the books, her pyjamas, the stuffed puffin on the top.

Black despair settles on me and, without meaning to, I groan. There's a stirring in the room and I realise that I'm not alone.

'Heather?' I say, hoping against hope that somehow I've managed to summon her back, that the spell I worked so hard to magic is still working. My hunger for her is almost unendurable.

'No,' says a soft voice, not one I recognise. 'Not Heather.'

Sharp pain stabs at me in my core. My eyes close, wetness dripping down my face from under my lids, and I sink back into the pillows. I'm freezing cold, right to my centre, as though everything in me is dying. I don't care now. I don't care about anything. I don't want it, I don't want this world. I can't bear the pain. I shouldn't have to suffer it.

Women are talking together somewhere nearby, their voices low, no more than a buzz of sound without words. There's a tap at the door and someone goes over to it and opens it. I hear a man's voice.

'How is she?'

'She's coming round a bit now. But she's really ill. She's in terrible shock. I don't think she wants to live.'

The man says, 'Rachel needs healing.'

'She does indeed.'

'That's why she's been brought to us. That's what we can give her.'

I close my mind to all of them and sink away. I hope I won't wake up because I don't want to know this agony anymore.

But I wake again later, when it's dark. Someone is beside me and a warm hand is on my shoulder. I can hear a voice, low, rich and mellifluous.

'I bless this servant, Rachel. I reach out to her in her time of grief and heal her wounded soul. I give her the sure and certain knowledge of the salvation to come and the hope that all will be made well, and all souls shall be reunited in love. I show her the path. I will take her with us on the journey to glory.'

The hand seems to be channelling warmth. It feels like a golden light that contains radiance and heat, passing from that hand into me. It cannot penetrate my frozen core but the warmth forms a layer all over me, with an invisible vibration. I'm comforted, just a little. The voice goes on. It's that man,

Archer. He continues murmuring his incantation, and I think about healing and about souls meeting again, and just for a second the hideous sadness is leavened with a moment of hope.

I sigh deeply.

'We're here for you, Rachel. You're all right. You're with us now. You're one of us.'

For a brief moment I feel safe again. I wonder if this will make the pain go away, and free me from the knowledge of what I've lost, and how I lost it and . . . and the other awful thing.

But I mustn't think about that.

My mind is still obedient in some ways. It cannot protect me from losing Heather anymore, but it can hold back the last, darkest things. At least, I hope it can.

They bring me meals in my room, bowls of soup mostly, and take turns in feeding me. Sometimes it's Sophia or Agnes. Once I wake to find a strange woman with me; she's examining me, feeling my forehead and pressing a stethoscope to my chest where my top has been pushed down.

'Who are you?' I ask, breathless with surprise and shock.

'I'm Dora. Don't worry, please. I'm a doctor. Well . . . a medical student.' She smiles at me. I can hardly make out her features in the murk of the darkened room, but I can see brown eyes behind a pair of rimless glasses, and brown hair pulled back. 'The good news is you seem physically okay. But you've had a shock, haven't you? Do you want to talk about it?'

I shake my head. I wouldn't know where to start.

'Do you have any family or friends? Is anyone worried about you?'

'No.' My lips are dry and the word comes out as a whisper. 'No one.'

'Okay. Good.' Dora smiles. 'That always makes it easier. Now, you need to rest.'

The man, Archer, never tends to me as the women do. They are the ones who feed me, take me carefully to the bathroom, hold me up while the bedding is changed and the bed remade. They bring me tea and water, check my temperature and open the windows to air the room. But Archer comes in the afternoon and I begin to particularly look forward to his visits. He holds his hands over me, and every time I feel that nourishing warmth penetrate my skin and soak through to my bones. He murmurs prayers, calling on a greater power to heal my grief, and offers me the promise I long to hear: that I will see Heather again.

'You can be with us now, Rachel,' he says with a smile. 'You've been brought to the right place. It's the will of the Lamb that you should be protected at the end of days. It's not long now. Bliss is at hand.'

What is bliss? Perhaps it's death, and being with Heather. A longing for this bliss fills me up. It is the only thing that can defeat the sadness that holds me in its painful grip whenever I'm alone. I turn to him. 'Do you promise?'

'Oh yes,' Archer says. He smiles. 'You're safe here. I promise.'

Chapter Sixteen

Once the great influx is complete, there are thirty followers living in the house. To Letty's surprise, this number soon seems quite normal, and the house appears to absorb them easily.

'Of course it does,' Arabella says happily. 'The Beloved would not suggest anything that isn't possible. He *makes* it possible.'

'Yes,' Letty answers. It is true enough, but the success of the whole thing has really depended on the willingness of the followers to do as they are told and to accept that within the house is a mirroring of the hierarchies that govern them in the outside world. The poorer women, with their shapeless coats and battered suitcases, have brought nothing to the communal pot except their labour, so they are housed in the attics, in the old servants' rooms, plentiful from the days when there were lots of staff, and they fulfil that role now, each given duties to ensure the smooth running of the house. They clean, wash, cook and tend to the gentlefolk so that they and, of course, most particularly the Beloved, live in comfort. Although it is clear to all that they are unpaid servants, they are not called by such a term. Instead they are called the Angels, which Letty finds rather funny considering that most of them are over forty and with the rough hands of working women. *Perhaps it makes it easier, if you're called such a pretty name.* The bedrooms on the upper floors are distributed depending on what level of donation has been made to the community. Arabella, of course, is in a position of magnificence, and retains her well-appointed room overlooking the front drive. Letty has kept her, smaller, bedroom and tiny dressing room. Other ladies, who've signed over their incomes from stocks and shares or trusts, occupy the nicer rooms, but the grandest suite is saved for the Beloved and Sarah, where they are able to retire to relative privacy if they desire. But for the most part, life is lived communally.

'Letty, come with me, I must talk to you.' Arabella beckons Letty from the drawing room, where she is sewing while listening to Maud Digby playing the piano. It's Chopin, and the music is wonderfully relaxing. *One of the things I'm enjoying about the new arrangements*, she reflects. In fact, the house seems to have come to life with its many occupants. She looks up at the sound of her sister's voice.

'Hurry up, Letty!' Arabella says.

'What is it?' Letty follows her out. 'Is there trouble?' She wonders if it is anything to do with Cecily and Edward, who have taken their expulsion from the house with great bitterness. Their initial acceptance, it has turned out, was a bluff, a way to gain time to see what they could do to stop Arabella's schemes. Angry letters have been exchanged. Cecily cut Arabella dead when they passed in the street and could hardly bring herself to nod to Letty. And from the looks that the villagers are giving anyone from the big house, the rumours must be in overdrive. Letty fears that evil gossip is being spread and suspects her sister is behind it.

Arabella says, 'No, no, no trouble. But I must talk to you. Come on, the library's empty.' She pulls open the door and leads Letty inside. The light from the garden is obscured by the heavy red velvet curtains and as a result the library is swathed in gloom. Arabella goes and sits on the desk, swinging her legs underneath it like a schoolgirl. This is where the Beloved sits to do his correspondence and read great tomes of biblical study. Arabella is showing her power. Despite having given the house to the community, she considers it her fiefdom still. She is wearing the white dress stipulated by the reverend, but hers is not the long skirt and buttoned-up blouse that the older ladies wear. She has a white silk dress with a drop waist and a neckline that shows a small but noticeable expanse of smooth pale skin. A long pearl necklace is twisted several times around her neck. In a community of unadorned ladies, Arabella's appearance makes quite an impact.

'So?' asks Letty. 'What is it?'

'I'm afraid you're going to have to give up your rooms.'

'What?' She suddenly sees herself banished up to the servants' quarters in the attic, given chores, turned into an Angel rather than a lady. 'But why?'

'They're needed. Not for long. The Beloved is expecting some special guests who intend to join us. A family. Mr and Mrs Kendall and their son. We must have your room because it has a dressing room, where the son can sleep. It's only until one of the cottages has been made suitable for them.'

'The Beloved doesn't want them to live in the house?'

'Oh no. That would be quite unsuitable, considering they are a married couple and they have an unmarried son. They'll move out when the cottage is ready. Mr Kendall is a most distinguished lawyer. His joining us has been incredibly important for the Beloved's mission.'

'And where will I sleep?'

'You can move into my dressing room. I'll ask one of the Angels to set up a bed for you. I'm sure you can make this one small sacrifice, when you think of what others have given up to be here.'

'Of course.' But Arabella barely waits to hear the reply. She knows Letty will be malleable. When has Letty ever said no to anything? She has accepted all the many changes that life has brought. *Well, Arabella has brought, really.*

Arabella goes on. 'Anyway, you ought to think about the fact that you haven't made your income over to the Beloved yet. It has been noticed. You ought to get around to it soon. Will you think about it?'

'Of course.' Letty knows it's a condition of staying here. They've all done it, and she must too.

Arabella gets down from the desk and straightens her white dress. 'Now, I must go to the Beloved. He needs me.'

Letty has noticed that the Beloved leans on Arabella more than any other woman here. He asks for her to be with him when he prays, because her spiritual gifts allow him greater access to the Divine. Letty wonders what Sarah makes of that, and whether he used to be content just with her spiritual gifts, before Arabella appeared on the scene. Sarah is never ruffled, though. She radiates a kind of goodness and serenity that draws people to her. She seems to float above them all on a cloud of holiness and the Angels adore her and minister to her whenever they can, as though by being close to her, some of her qualities might rub off on them. Letty can't help thinking, in her heart, that it's hard to understand how Arabella is considered of a greater spiritual merit than Sarah. But the Beloved must know what he's doing.

As Arabella makes for the door, Letty says absently, 'It will be strange to have men around the place, won't it?' Apart from the gardener, the odd-job boy and the groom, there are two aged priests, the Reverend Silas and the Reverend Gilbert, who have taken up residence in the lodge by the eastern gates, and a few doddery old fellows from the Army of the Redeemed, who are living in the lodgings over the garages and who like playing their brass instruments and marching around the grounds. Everyone else is a woman. Letty laughs. 'So many females. It's rather like a harem here!'

Arabella stops and turns back, her face flushing violently. 'How dare you say that, Letty! How dare you! The Beloved is above – way, way above – such thoughts, such things! He has fewer male followers because not many of those brutes can accept the strictures of our life.'

'Strictures?' Letty thinks of the almost pleasant idleness in which the days are passed. She thinks of the piano tinkling music, the Angels labouring away to keep the house comfortable, the tea served every day at four in the drawing room, and the plentiful meals. Arabella has shown her plans for new electricity, heating and water systems so that the house can be made yet more luxurious. 'What strictures?'

Arabella opens her mouth and closes it again. 'I can't say. But it will all become clear. The Beloved is about to reveal everything.'

The change in sleeping arrangements is made within a few days. Arabella's dressing room is rearranged and a small bed put up by the door. Once inside, Letty can only leave by going through Arabella's bedroom, which isn't too much of a problem but it is unlike her previous independence. She has nowhere she particularly wants to go, but knowing she cannot come and go without being seen is strangely confining.

Letty clears her drawers, puts some things into boxes to be stored and others into piles for one of the Angels to move. In the event, it is Kitty who comes. Letty likes Kitty; she is thirty-four but looks younger with a round face and a button nose, and cheerful eyes.

'Thank you, Kitty,' Lettice says, when the other woman loads up a basket of clothing to take to Arabella's.

'It's no bother to me,' Kitty announces. 'Everything here is part of the plan.' She grins. 'I've never been so cheerful to do work before in my whole life. In fact, I like it. As long as the Beloved wants it done, I know it's the Divine Will, and that makes it a pleasure.'

'Yes, Kitty,' Lettice says warmly. 'You've got it exactly right. The Beloved can't do wrong.'

She believes that more and more. It is hard not to, when she spends her days among others who believe it so fervently. Surrounded by the utterly convinced, she too is convinced. The Beloved is wise. He is an incarnation. To think that she should be so lucky as to be able to spend her life close to a man like that.

When she leaves her room, Kitty is setting up the bed in the dressing room for the Kendalls' son – a canvas strip with metal legs laboriously threaded through the sides. Letty wonders about the person who will be sleeping there, and what he will make of the small room with its walnut burr wardrobe, dressing table and mirror.

In the other dressing room, her own canvas bed awaits. Kitty has done her best to make it comfortable, with large cushions as a mattress and the best bedlinen.

Really, I don't suffer, Letty tells herself. *Imagine what the Angels are putting up with, two or three to a room in the attic.*

Arabella is in the bedroom when Letty emerges from the dressing room, looking at herself in the mirror on her dressing table. She has wrapped a white silk shawl around her shoulders, with long, soft tassels falling over her arms. She turns as Letty comes in. Behind her in the mirror is the reflection of Arabella's four-poster bed, hung with blue silk and trimmed in gold braid.

'There you are,' she says. 'Is everything ready for the Kendalls?'

'Yes, Kitty has seen to it.'

'Good.' Arabella goes back to examining her reflection. Her dark looks aren't beautiful but they are dramatic, and she doesn't need any enhancements to give her face character. Her lips are naturally red, her dark eyelashes give her eyes a strong frame. 'They must be well looked after.'

'Why are they so important?' asks Letty.

'They're important to the plan, that's all. You'll understand in time.' Arabella can't conceal her pride at knowing the Beloved's secrets.

'When do they arrive?'

'On Friday. Just at the time the church will be opened to us all for the first time.' Arabella smiles happily. 'It's almost ready.'

Letty, like everyone else but the Beloved and Arabella, has not been allowed to see the progress on the church. She knows that windows were commissioned at great expense and have been installed over the last fortnight. The interior remains mysterious but she is excited to see what the final result is, and to hear what the Beloved says when he addresses them all for the first time as the leader of their flock. There is an atmosphere of anticipation and barely repressed excitement; all of them know that they are the chosen ones, with the good fortune to be allowed to exist alongside a great and holy man.

'Many are called,' the ladies murmur to each other, and reply, 'But few are chosen.'

We are the chosen ones, Letty thinks now. The thought brings great comfort.

As the end of the week approaches, there is a festival air in the house. The church is almost ready and preparations are being made for its opening, and the feast that will follow it. But Tuesday brings a letter for the Beloved, the envelope bearing the address of the Bishop's Palace and an engraved mitre on the front. It is brought to the Beloved at breakfast, where the Angels lay out bacon, eggs, mushrooms, kippers and porridge, and hot coffee in a silver urn. He picks it up and laughs as he notices the symbol. All eyes are on him as he opens it and reads the letter inside. The Beloved stares at the letter for some time, reading it over several times, and then throws back his head to laugh again, even more heartily.

'As I thought,' he says when his laughter has subsided. 'The fools don't realise how much they play the Devil's game. They do his work for him! Isn't it as I said, Sarah?'

'Yes, my love,' his wife returns from her end of the table. She is, as usual, utterly calm and unflappable.

'Well, if he wants to see me, I shall certainly go. But we can be sure that whatever is said will make no difference to the plan.'

'You're going to see the bishop?' Arabella asks. She always sits next to the Beloved, and she cranes to see what is written on the letter, but the Beloved smooths it away from her sight.

'It is as I prophesied,' the Beloved says to her, with a smile. 'It is as I have foreseen.'

Other ladies around the table murmur, 'Amen.'

'When do you go?' Arabella asks, buttering a slice of toast.

'We shall leave tomorrow and return on Friday.'

'Friday?' Arabella looks dismayed. 'But the service! The church!'

'I shall be back in time. Everything will go ahead as planned.'

*

The following day, the Beloved and Sarah leave, collected in the motor and driven to the station. Sarah wears a fur-trimmed coat and black felt hat with a diamond brooch pinned at the front. The Beloved looks magnificent as usual in a black great-coat, gloves and a top hat. He carries his cane with the ivory head. As soon as they are gone with their luggage, the house feels desolate. The mood sinks and the ladies wander about all day with miserable expressions. Even the Angels seem to flag in their work and afternoon tea is served late. It's as though the heart of the community, the source of its energy and pur-pose, has gone.

Letty is astounded by how low she is. She had not realised how vital the Beloved has become to her. She's sometimes wondered what it would be like if Arabella decided to change her mind about the house, and everything went back to the way it was. Now she knows. It would be horrible. The Beloved brings with him so much of value, but most of all he brings his precious self.

The hunger for the Beloved's presence grows as the time of his return draws closer. There was excitement before, but now the celebration of his return adds a new thrilling flavour to the preparations. The Angels start to plan the feast that will be served, reinvigorated with the task ahead. The tea arrives in the drawing room on time. The kitchen fills with food and the reception rooms are vigorously cleaned. Arabella wanders about, giving orders and going to the church to ensure that all is well. The organ, ordered from a famous company in Som-erset, is having its final checks ready for its inauguration. Maud Digby teaches the ladies the new hymns she has written for the community's songbook, and they spend hours trilling them out until they are as familiar as the old ones.

> *The Beloved brings joy and gladness to all*
> *We heed his voice, we heed his call*
> *For his is the word the Almighty doth speak*
> *He uses his arm to strengthen the weak . . .*

It is almost as though the Almighty is speaking the Beloved's words rather than the other way around, Letty thinks as she sings. But Maud has done her best, and the hymns are pleasing enough.

On Friday morning, all hands are on deck and even the ladies are working, dusting the best furniture or arranging flowers, to make sure that all is ready. A telegram arrives from the Beloved to say that he and Sarah will be with them later that day, and Letty is filled with excitement at the thought of his return. When the doorbell rings that afternoon, she's in the hall dusting the gilt-framed mirror and, thinking it could be the Beloved, she rushes to open it before any of the Angels can arrive. But standing on the doorstep is a quite different man: rather plump and red-faced, his coat buttons straining over his stomach, and wearing a trilby hat. Next to him is a small fair lady with anxious eyes, holding a valise. Behind them both lurks a figure in a dark coat, a hat pulled low over his face, hands stuffed deep into his pockets.

'You must be the Kendalls!' cries Letty. She had forgotten all about them in the Beloved's absence but now she recalls in a rush.

'Yes.' The man smiles, his plump cheeks rising up like little red cushions. 'I'm Mr Kendall. This is my wife. And this is my son, Arthur.' He nods to the figure skulking on the steps behind him.

'Please come in!' Letty stands back, beaming, to let them into the hall. 'Where is your luggage?'

'It's being brought later from the station.'

The trio enter the hall, blinking in the bright light after the gloom of the descending evening outside. Mr Kendall looks about. 'Is the Reverend Phillips here?'

Letty doesn't understand for a moment, and then says, 'Oh, you mean the Beloved! I'm afraid he was called away. But he'll be back any moment. Please come and I'll show you to your room.'

'This is quite a house,' remarks Mrs Kendall, taking off her shawl. She seems impressed by the chequerboard floor and the vast mirrors, the marble busts standing on the torchières either side of the drawing room door. On the round mahogany table in the centre, hothouse flowers spill over a huge pink and gold porcelain vase.

'I hope you'll be comfortable here,' Letty says politely. Both Mr and Mrs Kendall are dressed well, in expensive clothes, and she suspects their standards are high. The house, gleaming in anticipation of the evening's celebrations, is looking its very best.

She leads them upstairs and shows them to what used to be her room; it already feels as though it is not her own, even though it looks the same: decorated in pale blue with silk hangings around the bed, and heavy damask curtains.

'Very pretty,' says Mrs Kendall, happier than ever as she notes the well-made French furniture and the gilt lamps with pleated shades.

'The dressing room is made up for you, Arthur,' Letty says, looking at the boy. He's not really a boy, she notices, too tall for that, but it's hard to see much of him. He flicks a gaze at her from under the low brim of his hat and grunts.

Mrs Kendall says, 'I'm sure he'll be most comfortable, Miss . . . ?'

'Oh, I'm sorry, I should have said. I'm Miss Evans. Lettice Evans.'

Mrs Kendall raises her eyebrows and Mr Kendall says, 'Then this was your house?'

'No . . . well, I've always lived here. But it belonged to my sister, Arabella. You will meet her very soon.' Letty thinks that Arabella is probably taking a long, scented bath in order to be ready for the Beloved's return. 'I'll leave you to settle in. Please come down when you're ready and there will be some tea for you. Our inaugural service is due to begin at eight o'clock.'

'And the reverend will be back?' Mr Kendall casts a glance at his watch.

'Oh yes. He promised.'

The hours move on and the Beloved does not return. As eight o'clock nears, the community begins to gather in the hall, murmuring and nervous.

'Have faith!' declares Arabella. 'He will be here.' She is in a white gown, with a high neck and long, tight sleeves. The full-ish skirt ends at the calf, the hem fringed in white feathers. It's not like anything Letty's seen before. The other ladies are in the prescribed uniform of white blouses and long skirts, some very plain and others adorned with lace and jewellery.

'What if he's been prevented from returning?' asks Ethel Channing-Davies, who is a fretful sort. 'He was seeing the bishop, wasn't he?'

Everybody knows that the bishop is at loggerheads with the Beloved. There has been talk of defrocking. Could it be any worse than that? A nervous flutter goes through the assembled women. The idea of the community without its beating heart is unsupportable.

The ancient Reverend Silas lifts a trembling finger. 'I can take the service if, for any reason, our leader is unable to be with us.'

'That's ridiculous,' declares Arabella, shooting him a furious look, 'and utterly unnecessary. He will be here.' With her chin high in the air, she stalks out in a flounce of shaking feathers.

The Kendall family have come downstairs, dressed according to the Beloved's instructions: the men in plain black trousers and a double-breasted waistcoat over a white shirt. Mr Kendall wears a bow tie with his, but his son Arthur has a sombre necktie in black satin. Mrs Kendall's sober white dress is belted at the middle but her large bust and bottom give her the appearance of an Edwardian matron. All three stand together watching proceedings with a grave wariness. Arabella has hardly noticed them, she is so preoccupied with the evening ahead and the whereabouts of the Beloved.

The Angels move among them all, handing out glasses of

barley water and plain biscuits, to help sustain the congregation until the feast. Letty watches the son Arthur take a biscuit with an expression of scorn on his face. He is taller than both of his parents and their soft, plump features have taken an unexpectedly craggy turn in his face; or perhaps, she thinks, it is just his youth that gives him hollows in each cheek and a hungry look. He must be around twenty, she thinks. His hair is long at the top and combed back, some kind of oil giving it a burnished appearance, but it looks as though it is dark blonde in its natural state. His slate-grey eyes wander over the crowd of middle-aged women and ancient men without interest, then they land on Letty and for a moment they stare at each other. Despite their ignorance of one another, they acknowledge their common bond of youth. But in Arthur's eyes is a resentment that she guesses is his lack of desire to be here. He shifts his gaze away carelessly.

Letty looks at the grandfather clock. It shows almost a quarter to eight. *What are we to do? Is the Beloved not coming then?* She can hardly bear to think it, not because of the fact that he will not be able to lead their service, but because he promised. Surely, surely, he is not capable of breaking a promise.

'Listen to me!' Arabella stands at the top of the stairs, looking out over them all. 'Everyone! Please listen. We will go now to the church. We will prepare for him. For he will surely come. We must have faith.'

Her strident, confident voice calms and restores them all. Arabella descends the stairs with majestic poise, and the crowd in the hall parts to let her through, then forms behind her into a procession. Kitty rushes forward to open the door and Arabella marches through, the band of followers behind her. One of the Army of the Redeemed, a Mr Wilson, has brought his trumpet and he starts to toot away while a few of the ladies clap along, and soon they are all processing jauntily along, clapping.

Letty joins in, her spirits rising. She checked her reflection before she came downstairs, and was content with it. Her dark brown hair, thick and hard to tame, has not been bobbed, much as she would like it, and she has to be content with tucking it back hard and crimping the front to imitate the fashionable hairstyles. It is probably vanity, but she can't help wanting to make the most of herself. Her looks are somewhere between Arabella's sharp, dark drama and Cecily's softer prettiness. She has a pert chin and upturned nose that she wishes were straight, but her complexion is good and she's glad that her black lashes give boldness to her slightly too pale and rather slanting, catlike green eyes. Perhaps it is living among so many older ladies, but today she feels young and fresh and bright. She is wearing a white woollen skirt and a soft white jersey silk top, the prettiest and most festive things she has in the right colour. No one has stopped for a coat but the evening air is balmy enough. It is May and the day has been a warm one. Arabella leads on and they follow, heading along the newly made path around the rhododendron thicket towards the church.

'Come, come,' calls Arabella, her tone excited and happy. 'See the holy place ahead!'

They all gasp as they come around the side of the thicket to see the new church, with its lights blazing from within, the great stained-glass window glowing like a jewel. By some unseen cue, the organ within strikes up and a riotous peal of music flows out into the night. The trumpet stops, and the clapping, as they listen to the wonderful noise.

But where is he? Where can he be? Letty is aware that this holiday mood, infectious though it is, will come crashing down if Arabella's promise is not fulfilled.

Arabella doesn't stop on the threshold, but continues on into the bright new interior, every chair polished, the red velvet-pile carpet pristine, the brass chandeliers glimmering. Up at the organ sits Maud, pounding away on the keys, her feet dancing across the pedals as she peers over the top of her glasses to read her music. When they reach the front of the church, the followers begin to take their places in the chairs. Letty sidles into a seat, and sees the Kendall family on the opposite side, the parents with their faces aglow, Arthur's expression still stony but with a hint of interest at what will happen next.

Arabella stands before the altar, her back to everyone and her head bowed, the hem of feathers swinging about her calves, her pearls glimmering. Then the moment comes: the organ finishes with a flourish and the notes fade away. There is silence, heavy with expectation. Slowly Arabella raises her head, turning her face to the great window over the altar. She lifts her arms high, spreading out her palms to the image of the lamb in the centre of the window, the lamb with the flag carried in its mouth and the sword beneath its feet.

'Oh Beloved!' she cries, her voice loud and piercing. 'Oh

Beloved, come to us! Do not leave your children hungering for your presence! Thirsting for your presence!' She takes a deep breath and begins to recite:

'By night on my bed I sought him whom my soul loveth:
I sought him, but I found him not.
I will rise now, and go about the city in the streets,
and in the broad ways I will seek him whom my soul loveth:
I sought him but I found him not.'

There is a kind of sigh from the listening congregation, a wispy sound of longing.

Letty thinks, *It's the 'Song of Solomon'. Spoken like an invocation.*

Arabella turns to them all, her arms still aloft. She stares down the aisle of the church between the rows of people. Then a radiant smile bursts over her face and a great voice bellows from the doors.

'I am here. I am come!'

They turn as one and there in the doorway stands the Beloved, his arms also held high.

Arabella cries ecstatically, 'The voice of my Beloved! Behold, he cometh leaping on the mountains and skipping on the hills!'

For a moment, Letty has a vision of the Beloved skipping up a hill in his black suit and is seized by an impulse to laugh, but it is replaced by an overwhelming sense of relief and joy. The Beloved is home, as he promised. All is well. Around her, the followers sigh and moan with happiness and fulfilment.

Maud squints at her music and starts up with the hymn they have all been practising in order to welcome him home, and everybody begins to sing. The Beloved walks slowly up the aisle, blessing those he passes, touching their outstretched hands, nodding and smiling, listening to the hymn in his praise. Behind him walks his wife, Sarah, her face tired and drawn but her eyes as serene as ever.

When the hymn is over, the Beloved has reached the altar, and he turns to them and motions for them all to sit. Letty sinks down, unable to take her eyes off him. They have missed him more than she ever thought possible in such a short time. She hopes that he will never go again.

We cannot survive without him. She knows it's true. Then her soul is filled with joy, because she knows that the Beloved's promise is that death is conquered. They shall never, any of them, be separated from him.

The Beloved is speaking, his magnificent voice filling the room. 'Today, I did battle with dark forces. With evil forces! Today I have finally cut my binds to the old ways. I am free. And so, my brothers and sisters, are you. We are free to live as the truth demands! It was no longer possible for me to conceal myself from you all. Some of you already know, you have had the knowledge vouchsafed to you, most from divine visions.' He pauses, then says loudly, 'Today I cease to be the Reverend Phillips. I gave the bishop back the symbols of my allegiance to his way. I go now on a greater path. A holy path. The path to salvation! And you are my chosen to accompany me on this road.'

A tremor of excitement passes over the congregation.

'This path will not be easy. There will be trials. There will be sacrifices. The day is at hand, and much is asked of the elect. It is required that we re-enact the mystical union of the Lamb and his people. I myself am married, as you know, to Sarah. Our union is the holiest of holy. It is a spiritual union only, like that of the Lamb with his Church.' The Beloved's eyes flash and he points at his wife, now sitting in the front row. 'That woman and I refrain from physical intimacy! We reject it!'

There is a muffled gasp among his listeners.

'Yes.' He begins to walk back and forth in front of the altar. 'That's right. We have renounced the flesh, and so must you all. The kingdom is at hand. The Devil is putting up his strongest fight in his frenzy to hold this world in his grasp. Do you think he wants to give up this prize, this sordid den of iniquity in which every vice brings him pleasure? Of course not. We must fight him at every turn. We have no need to bring children into this world, not when the day is near, the day when we will all be judged. We must concentrate our efforts on battling the Devil, and on saving the souls that exist today. Now! Here!' The Beloved slams his hand down on a hymn book. Letty jumps at the sound.

There is a breathless silence as the Beloved stalks back and forth, staring at them all with blazing eyes.

'We will begin our fight with spiritual marriages that will bring our brothers and sisters together and yet deny the Devil his pleasure in carnality. I announce here that our first couple to be united will be Reverend Silas and Albertina Johnson.'

Letty gasps, as everyone else does, and no one can help turning to look at the astonished couple in their different pews. The Reverend Silas, aged and bent and held up by his walking stick, almost bald with just a fringe of white hair around his ears, appears quite bewildered, while his betrothed, a sedate lady in her mid-forties with grey hair and fat, soft hands, looks fearful. But the jubilation of the people around them, and the immediate congratulations, seem to buoy them up and soon they are smiling and happy, nodding and waving to each other from their places.

The Beloved quietens them down with a gesture. 'There will be more unions, brothers and sisters.'

Letty can't help darting a glance around the church. There are many more women than men. One of the men is Reverend Gilbert, almost as aged as Reverend Silas. There are old boys from the Army of the Redeemed, but one of those is already married. Apart from that, there are the gardeners, a groom, a handyman and the boy who does the errands.

Surely he can't mean us to marry them? Letty thinks, puzzled. Then her gaze falls on Arthur Kendall. He is staring directly back at her. At once, she flushes bright red and she looks away.

By the altar, Arabella is watching the Beloved with shining eyes.

PART THREE

Chapter Seventeen

'Hi, Caz,' Rory says, standing in the doorway. He's trying to smile, but his expression is tortured. 'Can I come in? I've got some news.'

Caz stares at him. *Has he found out where Kate is?* She can't help hoping he has. Then she won't feel so torn anymore between her promise to Kate, and Rory's pain. She knows deep down she's ready to break. She's so worried about Kate and the fact that there's been no word, no communication. The phone is off. The emails are unanswered. 'Of course. Come in,' she says.

In the kitchen, Rory slumps down onto one of the chairs.

'Two weeks she's been gone,' he says. 'More than two weeks. They can't find a trace of her. Where the hell can she be?'

Caz stares at him. *I have to stay loyal. I promised.* She takes a deep breath. 'I don't know.' It's true. She doesn't know. But what she does know is tearing her up inside. 'What's the news?'

'It's Ady. He's woken up.' Rory's mouth tightens and she

221

can see he's still fighting the emotions that threaten to tumble out.

Caz gasps and breaks into a smile. 'But that's brilliant! He's awake! Oh Rory, I'm so happy for you, and for him. How is he? What do they say about his progress?'

'It happened yesterday. They told me to expect it when they started to reduce the drugs keeping him under. It was an amazing moment, Caz, to see his eyes open after all this time.' Rory manages to smile at the memory. 'He's fuzzy. He's not fully aware yet. But they think he's going to be all right.' Then his expression contorts and his voice trembles. 'He wants his mother, though. He's asking for her. He needs her. And . . . I don't know where she is. I can't get her for him. Do you know how that feels? Why should he have to lose his mother as well?'

'Oh God . . .' Caz goes round the table to him, putting her arms around him. 'Oh Rory. It's too terrible. I'm so sorry.'

As long as Ady was in his comatose state, Kate's absence made no difference to him. But now . . . This makes it all different. *But I swore. I swore I wouldn't tell.*

Another voice in her head says, *But she doesn't know about Ady.*

Does she want to know? She wouldn't talk about him. She wouldn't mention him. She wouldn't mention Heather either. Both of them were off limits, as though the only way she could cope was to erase them from her mind. Except, Caz remembers . . . one time on the phone, Kate said to her, 'They want to take Heather away from me.' And she thought, how can they do that when she's already been taken away?

She pulls away from Rory and sits down next to him.

'I don't know what to feel,' he says huskily. 'I haven't told him about Heather yet. I can't. I've just said that Mum and Heather can't be with us right now. I'm happy I have him, that he's going to be all right. But, Caz . . . when I think about what I've lost.'

She hushes him gently, putting a comforting hand on his. She looks into his eyes and they are full of tears. 'Oh Rory,' she says, her heart aching for him. 'You've been through so much. I'm sorry it's still so terrible. But Ady is back with us. That's wonderful.'

'It's not complete without Kate.' He looks up at her, agonised. 'Caz, I've always been your friend, haven't I?'

She nods. It's true. When Philip left, Rory was there for her. He came round whenever she needed him, mending the boiler or putting up shelves, just helping out. He didn't ask about Philip, just said, 'Are you all right?', accepted the coffee or beer she offered him, and got on with sorting out her problems. The practical ones, at least.

But Kate is my best friend. She has been right from the start, when I was pregnant with Leia and Kate had Ady on the way.

They met at their antenatal group. About the same age, with similar backgrounds, both working in those hectic office environments where the to-do list is never quite ticked off and the desk never completely clear, they hit it off at once and became firm friends. Two years later, they had their second children just a few months apart. Caz had Mika before Kate had Heather, and Kate helped out, taking Leia when Caz desperately needed to focus on the baby. Later, when Heather came, Caz did the same for her. As things returned to an even keel, they used the same nurseries and minders so that they could share runs. Their children were in the same class at school, and they passed each other tissues at nativity plays and assemblies. They discussed kitchen blinds, the merits of almond milk, causes of eczema and how to get rid of nits – they always had to delouse at the same time, with spending so much time together. They jogged in the park when they were feeling energised, and sat about watching reality TV with wine and snacks when they weren't. They invented the rolling babysit: one couple took the other's children from Friday night until Saturday afternoon, when the other couple took delivery of all four until Sunday afternoon. They took turns for the plum prize of Saturday night and Sunday morning; the first shift was easier knowing the pleasure that lay ahead: a Saturday night out and a lazy Sunday morning with the papers and breakfast, made all the sweeter by the knowledge that in the other house, there were screaming demands for pancakes and cushion fights in front of a Pixar movie.

Caz and Kate seemed to feel the same things as if by instinct. They moaned and laughed together, but never argued, except over reality show contestants. If they were irritated with each other, they took it home, offloaded on their husbands and let it go. They showed apology by suggesting a night out at their favourite bar, eating pickled anchovies and drinking Prosecco, giggling and gossiping until the cause of the discord was forgotten.

It was a happy time. We were so close, Caz thinks wistfully.

Those carefree times ended when Phil left. It was different when they were no longer two couples. Now Caz needed Kate more than the other way around, and she rose to it. The two of them spent hours talking about Philip and the woman he'd gone off with.

'Fucking internet fucking dating!' Caz would say with feeling, pouring out another glass of wine.

'Amen!' said Kate, raising her glass.

'I can't believe someone was so stupid as to take him on.'

'I expect they'll be miserable,' Kate consoled her. 'Or happy in the way that idiots can be when they pair up.'

'Yeah.' She gulped her wine down.

'He'll regret it,' declared Kate. 'It's obviously a midlife crisis. We should have seen it coming when he took up cycling and Lycra-wearing.'

'He probably wanted me to find those messages to the floozy. I bet he left the phone at home on purpose. And then ringing me and asking me to look for it! He might as well have just taken out an advert in *The Times*: "I am having an affair and intend to leave my wife immediately."' Caz laughed bitterly. When she'd discovered the affair, she'd called Kate in tears. Kate had come straight round with emergency wine and tissues. Don't do anything rash, she counselled. Wait and see what happens. You might be able to get through this.

Phil came home that night and he guessed at once that she knew, and she sensed he was glad it was all out in the open. He was gone within the week. Caz begged him to stay, desperate to keep the family together. She even invited him round, cooked him supper, opened some champagne, and tried to seduce him. He turned her down. It was the most humiliating experience of her life. But she knew then it was truly over.

Kate was there for the hours and hours Caz needed to talk it through and start coming to terms with what had happened, and to help her bear the awful act of handing over the girls to Phil every other weekend. She listened to the same stories over and over, analysed Phil's behaviour, and hugged her when she cried, while gently pushing Caz towards letting go of the whole horrible mess. The comfort, the talking, the bolstering – Kate did it all.

When Kate moaned about Rory, as she did sometimes, Caz couldn't understand it. Ever since she'd known them both, she'd been envious of what they had. It was true that Rory wasn't exactly dynamic. He was one of those men who are content with their lot: he loved their beautiful house, their children and, obviously, Kate. He didn't want more than he had. He told Caz once that he'd have been content to stay in the tiny flat they started out in. Kate had got them where they were: she earned more than he did and was always the one pushing for the bigger car, the nicer house, the things to go inside it. She wanted life just so, and she loved decorating their home, making it exactly right. She had strong ideas, vivid pictures in her head of how life should be lived, and Rory was happy to go along with it. Kate could be firm, there was no doubt about that. And Rory was the opposite – malleable and adaptable, eager to keep the peace. At first that seemed to work well but it was also, Caz supposed, how they'd got into trouble. He didn't want to rock the boat. He didn't want to tell her that everything she'd worked so hard for was at risk.

But sometimes in the course of those long nights, over the open bottle, when they'd talked about Phil for hours on end, it was Kate's turn.

'The problem with Rory . . .' she would say, and she'd be off. It was his silence that drove her mad, his introverted ways, his preference for communicating through hints and inference rather than straightforward dialogue. The way he kept his opinions to himself and let hers just wash over him, agreeing to everything for the sake of an easy life.

'But didn't you realise what he was like when you married him?' Caz asked, in half-disbelief.

'No. Honestly, I didn't. I think maybe I was talking for the first decade,' Kate said wryly, 'and I didn't notice when he didn't say much in return.'

Now that she had noticed, she couldn't unnotice it. Their relationship, like most, had started with mutual enchantment and the certainty that life together would be full of lazy, sexy, laughter-filled afternoons, and then moved to the realisation that the other person, married with such conviction, was pretty much a stranger.

'I never knew Phil!' Caz exclaimed. 'Not a bit. He was a complete mystery to me, the whole bloody time. That's obvious now.'

'But maybe you knew Phil at a certain point in his life. And he isn't that person anymore.'

'Maybe. Or maybe marriage is just a complete illusion. An

attempt to pretend we're not totally alone in the world with only a pretend togetherness to comfort us.'

'That's a downbeat assessment, isn't it?' Kate thought for a moment and said, 'So marriage might be a duff. But what about children? That's more than pretend togetherness, isn't it?'

Caz nodded slowly. 'Yes, maybe it is. That's the only love you can rely on lasting. You always love your children – at least, I can't imagine not loving Leia and Mika.' She laughed wryly. 'Okay, maybe if they were really ghastly serial killers, it would be tricky.'

'But it's bittersweet,' Kate remarked, 'because they're always going away from you. From the minute they're born, they are growing up and away. All you can do is treasure every moment with them while you're the centre of their worlds.'

'True.'

They were both quiet, considering their own children. Caz said, 'I'm still at the lioness stage – you know, I would savage anyone who hurt them. I suppose as they grow up, that feeling must subside.'

Kate nodded. 'It has to. I can't imagine my mother savaging anyone who hurt me these days.' They both laughed, because Kate's mother was notoriously lazy and found it hard to get off the sofa unless it was to refresh her gin and tonic. 'She prefers to savage me instead,' Kate added and they laughed some more, because Kate's mother had started sending emails late at night when she was, presumably, drunk and wanted to share some home truths about why Kate had turned out so disappointing.

Even though Caz understood some of Kate's frustrations with Rory, she couldn't help thinking that he seemed a perfectly lovely husband. Rory was completely uxorious. He never went to the pub, barely drank, never leered or flirted or patted nearby behinds. He liked being at home with the family, cooking meals for them all, pottering about, helping Kate in her latest desire to paint this room or rearrange that one. Kate had begun to take it all for granted. Caz's guess was that Rory's gentleness and tick-tock predictability had lulled Kate into a false sense of security. She had grown to think that her husband had no other life than what she saw, no secrets at all.

Now, when Caz thinks of how they were, she's crushed by pain for them. No matter how much Kate moaned about Rory and thought that somehow he could be better, or do better by her, she's sure Kate would go back to that old life in a second. Now she must know how happy she was.

'Caz?'

It's Rory, sitting across the kitchen table from her.

'Yes?' she says, snapping back to him.

'Do you know anything you're not telling me?'

She can't meet his eye. She wants to look at him, into his slightly downturned eyes that make her think of a friendly dog. He's got brown eyes with darker speckles in them.

'Can we go through it all again?' he asks, slowly now. 'Just to be sure?'

'Of course.' She goes to the fridge, gets a bottle of Gavi that's chilling there, and collects two glasses from the cupboard. As she pours out some wine, Rory says, 'I'm driving.'

'Just one then,' Caz says. 'Keep me company.'

'All right.' He lets her push one of the glasses over to him, but doesn't drink anything, just watches as the glass mists with the chill from the wine. 'So, let's get this straight. You spoke to her three weeks ago. On a Monday. Right?'

Caz takes a big gulp of mineral-crisp liquid, then says, 'Yes, that's right.'

He pulls a piece of paper out of his pocket and picks up a stray pen so that he can start scribbling. 'According to the neighbours, they saw her that day. But on the Tuesday, the car was gone and the curtains closed, and she hasn't been seen since. So she left sometime between when you spoke to her, and Tuesday morning.'

'Yes, she must have.' She wishes he would pick up the glass and have a drink.

'What was her mood like? What did she say?'

Caz thinks back to the last conversation with Kate before she put her plan into action. She could say, 'Well, Rory, she was a bit like a general about to embark on a campaign, issuing orders and fixing her last-minute hitches. She gave me my instructions about how I was to contact her and left.' She doesn't say that. She feels helpless, unable to tell the truth and not wanting to lie.

'Caz!' Rory puts his hand out and covers hers. She jumps slightly, surprised by its soft, smooth warmth and the way it feels so human. 'I've been round here several times, asking you the same things over and over. You say you don't know anything but I don't believe you. I think you're hiding something. You and Kate are best friends, you tell each other everything. I just can't believe you have no idea what's happened to her.'

She drags her gaze up to meet his. His brown eyes, usually so soft and almost pleading, are burning and bright. 'This is serious,' he says. 'Ady needs her. The police are looking for her. I'm concerned about her. You know what her mental state was like. Aren't you worried about her?'

Caz takes another drink. 'Yes, of course. I'm desperately worried.'

'We both know she was in a bad way when she left. All the pills she was on.' Rory's eyes are expressive, although he doesn't say out loud what he must be thinking: that Kate was intending to kill herself when she disappeared.

Caz feels wretched. She wants to tell him everything – that as far as she knows, Kate's alive and there's a chance she might come back. The silence from Kate is beginning to worry her deeply and she yearns to share the anxiety with someone who cares as much as she does. And surely now that Ady is awake and asking for Kate, that means she, Caz, has a whole new and different obligation to a boy who needs his mother . . .

But I promised Kate. I need to think about it. I need to be sure before I betray her.

Rory stands up, his wine glass untouched. 'If anything happens, if she gets in touch, you call me at any time. Day or night. Okay?'

Caz nods, not trusting herself to speak.

'If I don't answer, I'm probably in the hospital with Ady. So text me and I'll pick it up as soon as.'

'Okay,' she manages to whisper. 'I will.'

'Thanks, Caz.' He looks at her, those brown eyes more intense than she's ever seen them before. In fact, she's never known Rory be so insistent and forceful before now. 'Take care. I'll be in touch.'

She watches him go and then pours another glass of wine with a trembling hand.

Oh Kate. Please, please, please get in touch. I don't know how much longer I can keep your secret.

Chapter Eighteen

Letty is going down the high street on her way to the hardware shop when she sees Cecily, walking towards her with a friend. They are bound to pass.

'Cecily!' she calls and waves.

Her sister doesn't appear to hear or see her, but carries on talking to her friend and walking sedately on.

'Cecily! It's me, over here!'

Cecily looks up now, her expression stony, and without a smile or any acknowledgement, she crosses the road with her friend and they pass by on the other side, not once turning to Letty.

Letty watches her go open-mouthed. So it is not only Arabella who is now considered beyond the pale. She too is to be shunned. When she goes into the hardware shop, Mr Baker, who has known her since she was a girl, is polite but cool and unsmiling too. After she's bought her bits and pieces she leaves, and gets only a nod and a murmur in response to her cheery farewell. It is no different in the bakery, where she stops to buy a couple of rock cakes from the plate in the

233

window, except that the reception is even chillier. Mrs Higgins flushes brick red as Letty comes in and can't look her in the eye. She puts the rock cakes into a bag while straining to avoid any contact with her.

'Mrs Higgins,' she says loudly, 'is something wrong?'

'No, miss. Here are your cakes, miss.' Mrs Higgins takes the money Letty holds out and is evidently deeply relieved when she takes the bag and goes.

After that, she notices all the villagers are giving her the same treatment. *What can the problem be?* she wonders. She cannot help feeling hurt at this unexpected shunning. She has always been a popular figure in the village, greeted by the tradespeople and the gentry alike. It's very unpleasant to think that, for some reason, she is now persona non grata.

The next day, unable to stop thinking about what is happening in the village, she goes out again, bicycling the two miles, and, although she fears she may be a little oversensitive, she is sure that the situation is even worse than the day before. Doors slam at her approach and the road is crossed abruptly. She is certain that unseen eyes are following her progress and that she is being whispered about as she goes by shop windows. She walks on, indignant at this treatment and more than a little wounded. At last, she reaches the church, props her bicycle against the wall and goes through the lych-gate and into its cool interior. It is, she realises, a long while since she's been here. She used to come every Sunday, and sit in the family pew, but since the Beloved's arrival, it's been prayer meetings in the drawing room, services in the hall, and now in the new church.

Perhaps I'll never come back here, she thinks, looking about at the marble monuments, the pulpit, the altar in its red and gold covering, the brass eagle lectern. All so familiar and, once, so awe-inspiring. But now it has lost its magic. It is like being in a theatre after a marvellous play, and going back-stage to see the props are cheap and fake, and the costumes dirty and torn close up. She can't believe she was ever taken in by all this. But now the Beloved has shown her the truth, she feels nothing in this place is real.

I must go home.

As she comes out of the door, something whizzes past her ear and smashes into the stone archway. She gasps and jumps, and turns to see a clod of earth has exploded against the church wall. Another lands beside it with a thud, making her duck with fright.

'Yah, yah, heathen!' comes a jeering call and she looks over to see a group of dirty-kneed boys in the churchyard, grinning at her, their hands full of earth.

'Stop it, you horrible boys!' she shouts, trying to sound braver than she feels. 'You nasty little wretches. Go home at once, or I'll tell your mothers.'

'My mother won't talk to the likes of you,' retorts one. 'She says you're all Devil worshippers up there, should be burnt at the stake.'

Letty gasps, horrified to hear such things in the mouth of a child. 'What awful nonsense, she shouldn't say such a thing! It's wicked and wrong.'

'Yah!' shouts another, and, determined not to miss out,

hurls his fistful of mud at her. It lands some way in front of her. He is a bad shot.

'Stop it,' cries Letty again. 'How dare you?'

'Our dad says you ought to be whipped,' jeers another. 'Shall we whip her, boys?'

For a moment, Letty feels frightened. There are about eight of them, strong young things, and they seem to think they have some kind of permission from their elders to torment her. What if they take it in their heads to hurt her for real? *I mustn't let them see I'm afraid.* As she gathers herself to sound authoritative, she hears another voice.

'Go home at once, young Stanley. Go home right now, do you hear?' Coming through the lychgate is a familiar figure, waving her arms at the children. 'All of you, clear off! Troublemakers!'

The boys grumble but drop their dirt and wander away to whatever adventures they interrupted to enjoy a bit of sport with her.

'Oh Enid,' Letty says with relief, smiling at the former housemaid. 'Thank you, thank you so much.'

Enid's gaze meets hers for a moment and then slides away. 'You're all right, miss. I couldn't help hearing them. They shouldn't talk to you like that, no matter what.'

'How are you, Enid? Have you found another place since you left us?'

'Yes, miss. I've a place up at the hall in Wilmington. It's my day off and I'm visiting my mother.'

'That's good. Do you like it there?'

Enid opens her mouth to answer and then closes it. A

moment later, she says, 'I'm sorry, miss, I'm not allowed to talk to you.'

Letty goes towards her slowly as if afraid of scaring her off. 'Enid, do you know why all this is happening? No one in the village will speak to me. They're all cutting me dead. What's wrong with everyone?'

Enid looks a little exasperated. 'You can't pretend you don't know, miss! I'm fond of you, I always have been. You've always been good to me. But what's going on up at your house . . .'

'What do you mean?' Letty is genuinely surprised. 'It's a good and holy life we're living at the house.'

Enid laughs. 'Holy? That's not what we've been hearing.'

'What have you heard?' Letty asks, a trifle coldly.

'That you're all getting married to each other, for one. They say it's a free-for-all.'

'What?' Letty is horrified.

Enid nods. 'We've heard it. That you're being exhorted to do unmentionable things up there. And' – she flushes pink – 'that reverend, the one the bishop has sent back in disgrace, he's making claims that are very wicked. He wants to be Jesus. That's what we've heard.'

'Oh. And who have you heard it from?' Letty feels a little faint. 'No, don't worry. I can guess.'

It must be Cecily and Edward, fanning the flames of gossip and misunderstanding. They want the community to fail. They care only for the family's wealth, not for the good of their immortal souls.

'Listen, Enid,' she says urgently, 'you must tell people they are quite mistaken. First, there have been two marriages, it is true. The Reverend Silas married Albertina and the Reverend Gilbert married Nancy Nuttall. But they are *spiritual* unions only. Believe me, there is no immorality at the house. The Beloved would not allow it. He believes that all fleshly temptations are the work of the Devil. And' – she laughs to show the ludicrousness of the suggestion – 'we don't worship the Devil! We follow the Lamb like everyone else.'

Enid looks suspicious. 'Really, miss?'

'Of course.' Letty laughs again. 'Do you think I look like a Devil worshipper?'

'Why d'you go to your own church then? Why not our church? Isn't it good enough for you?'

'Of course it is. But, Enid, the Beloved knows some truths that others don't or won't believe. That's why we have to be separate.' She puts her hand out and touches Enid's sleeve. 'You should come and join us. Be saved. We are happy and you can be too.'

Enid shakes her head. 'No. No. I couldn't.' She stares at Letty for a moment and says, 'I'm glad you're all right. I've been worried about you. I didn't like to think of you dancing about naked in that church, or doing unmentionables on the altar while begging to be Satan's bride.'

Letty gasps and then laughs in horror. 'Oh Enid, you couldn't think that?'

Enid flushes. 'Well. It's what they're saying. And worse. But I can't repeat it so don't ask me to.' She looks about quickly and guiltily. 'I have to go now. But, miss, you ought to know that they're turning ugly against you all. There's mutterings

238

that your place ought to be burnt down, and everyone in it. You should get out while you can.'

'That's ridiculous. No one would do anything so wicked!'

Enid shakes her head, her eyes fearful. 'Don't you believe it, miss. They think you're worshipping Beelzebub up there and that burning's too good for you.'

'Tell people they're wrong!' cries Letty. 'You mustn't let them believe such awful lies.'

'I'll try,' Enid throws over her shoulder. 'But I don't think it will do no good.'

Back at the house, Letty feels almost as though she has a dirty secret. As she crosses the hall, glimpsing several ladies reading sedately in the drawing room, she feels suddenly angry that such awful things should be whispered about them all.

'Nasty, horrible gossip!' she says to herself crossly as she goes up the stairs. 'They should all mind their own business. Besides, anyone can come here at any time and see for themselves.' She has a sudden mental image of herself as Enid described: writhing on the altar, begging to be the bride of Satan, and she is sickened. 'How can people say such vile things?'

'Letty! Letty.' Kitty is coming up the stairs behind her, pounding and breathless. 'You're wanted in the library.'

A rush of pleasure warms her stomach, along with apprehension. 'Me? The Beloved wants to see me? Are you sure?'

'Of course I am. He's asked for you particularly.'

'Then I'll go at once.' She hands Kitty her packages. 'Could you take these to my room, please, Kitty?' She straightens her skirt – brown tweed as she has just been out – smooths down her unruly hair as best she can, and runs lightly down the stairs to the library door, where she knocks.

'Come in,' booms the Beloved's voice, and she opens the door and goes in.

It is gloomy as ever in the library, and the Beloved is at his desk, which is scattered with papers and great leather-bound books.

'Ah, Letty,' says the Beloved. 'Thank you for coming to see me.'

Letty is almost overcome with the honour of an interview all on her own. She has never, she realises, been alone with the Beloved before. The magnetism of his presence focused entirely on her is almost too much to bear.

'Come here.' He gestures to the red leather chair in front of his desk. 'Sit down.'

Letty obeys, and makes herself as comfortable as she can while feeling so awkward.

'How are you, my child?'

'Very well, thank you, Beloved.'

'I'm glad to hear it. I've been watching your progress here. You are doing so very well, so very well.'

Letty flushes with pleasure. 'Thank you.'

'Your quiet good sense, your dutiful obedience, the way you open your spirit to my words. I have seen it all.'

She feels a swell of pleasure within. She knows that the Beloved sees all.

'Thank you,' she says humbly. 'I have taken my first steps along the path.'

'Of course, of course. But never forget, you are of the elect. You are guaranteed to stay with me for the glorious transition from this life to the next.'

'Yes, yes,' she whispers, thrilled at the thought.

'Here we wait, in the sure and certain hope of eternal life,' the Beloved says, smiling. Then he leans towards Letty, stretching one long arm over the leather desktop. 'But there is something I would like you to do for me, Letty. Will you help me in my mission?'

'Of course,' she says at once. 'Anything, Beloved.'

'Very well. I have been receiving messages from the Lamb – in fact, we are in constant contact. I'm speaking to him now, this very second. Do you know how that is possible?'

Letty shakes her head.

'It is because the Lamb and I are one,' he says softly. His white hair and side whiskers seem to glow in the murky light and his blue eyes glint. 'You know this. Soon all shall know. Because of this, our wills are as one. And the Lamb has made it plain to me that I must augment my spiritual gifts.'

'Really?' Letty asks, wondering how the Beloved could possibly be more gifted than he is already.

He nods. 'Yes. I must have a helpmeet.'

'Oh. But . . . your wife . . . Sarah . . .' ventures Letty.

'Yes, of course. Sarah is a great help, but there are limitations on what she is able to do for me. I must have further assistance. And the Lamb has deemed that your sister, Arabella, is to be that person.'

Letty is confused. 'I don't understand. She already helps

241

you, doesn't she?' They are all used to Arabella and the Beloved being constantly together.

'That's quite right, but, my dear child, there must be a stronger union between us. Do you understand? It is necessary for my great mission. Is it for us to question the will of the Lamb?'

'No,' Letty says sincerely. 'Of course not.'

'Then you will understand. But not all have your great sagacity and perception. Not all have your pure faith. And that is why the Lamb and I need your help. It must never be said that I wish this for myself. It must be clear that it is divinely ordained.'

'I'm sorry, Beloved, I'm being very stupid. I still don't understand . . .'

The Beloved smiles. 'You will, my dear. I will explain exactly what needs to be done.'

That evening, during the Friday night service, Letty is in the front row, next to Arabella, waiting for her cue. They sing one of Maud's more rousing hymns, with a bouncy military jauntiness that gets them all bobbing. When it is over, the Beloved begins to speak. This is what they all enjoy the most: the way he takes them with him on a journey towards absolute conviction mixed with a shaky excitement that leaves them flushed and breathless. The future he paints for them is so wonderful, so glorious, so brilliant that they can hardly wait to get there. But life until then is so marvellous too; the sense of happiness wells up and fills them all with the desire to praise and sing.

Letty watches the Beloved, waiting till he begins to crescendo. He takes off his black jacket – a signal that things are heating up – and stalks about, his white shirtsleeves billowing as he waves his arms and declaims, showing his fine figure as he marches here and there. When he cries out, 'They shall hear me on the mountains! They shall hear me in the valleys!' Letty jumps to her feet and shouts, 'I have seen a vision! I have seen a holy vision!'

There are gasps and all eyes are on her, as the Beloved stops, and turns to face her, his eyes blazing.

'What have you seen, sister?' he demands.

'A holy vision, a sacred union, a spiritual marriage!' she cries.

'Amen!' shouts the Beloved. 'This is what is ordained. We are enriched by our spiritual unions. Who do you see, sister?'

Letty turns and sweeps her gaze over the congregation, aflutter now with the anticipation of who shall be next to be married. There is apprehension too. The ladies have spoken among themselves of their anxiety at the possibility of being spiritually joined to one of the labourers and how difficult it would be to fulfil the Divine Will in that event. 'I see as clear as day,' she calls. 'The Lamb has shown me what must be done. The bridegroom is . . .' She swings back to face him. 'It is you, Beloved!'

A shocked inhalation and a murmur of surprise. Eyes turn at once to Sarah, who goes very still but her expression does not change. The Beloved quietens the muttering with a gesture.

'How can this be, sister, when I'm already married?' he asks.

'I cannot say, I can only tell you the will of the Lamb. He has shown me that you should be joined in the spirit to . . .' – Letty points at Arabella beside her – 'to my sister, Arabella! So that your gifts may be united to the great glory of us all.'

Arabella looks as though she might faint, her expression utterly bewildered. She turns to look at Sarah in the row across the aisle but the Beloved's wife stares straight ahead, her face as white as marble. 'I . . . I . . . don't understand,' says Arabella, stunned. She looks afraid, as though a pet tiger she has been taming has suddenly turned on her with a snarl and a desire to eat her.

'We must listen to the will of the Lamb,' the Beloved declares. 'But I am not yet sure that this is meant. Let us all pray for guidance on this most vital, most extraordinary of matters. What we can know is that the Lamb asks not for fleshly union, but only spiritual. Amen. Amen.'

They murmur obediently in answer, and the service continues.

'Did you really have that vision?' demands Arabella, when they are alone in her bedroom. She has grabbed Letty's arm, holding it with a fierce grip. 'Did you really see those things?'

'Yes. Of course,' Letty says. What else can she say? She will not betray the Beloved, not even to Arabella.

'I'm to marry him?' Arabella asks wonderingly. 'But Sarah . . .'

They look at each other, both unable to understand how it could be.

'I suppose it doesn't matter if it's spiritual,' Letty says slowly. 'You're lucky, Arabella, to be considered his helpmeet.'

'Yes . . . yes, I suppose I am.'

On the Sunday, Letty stands up and cries out her vision again. She has seen a sacred wedding in the lily fields of heaven, where the souls of the Beloved and her sister were joined eternally and formed a gateway for the believers to enter. The Beloved seems more convinced but insists further prayers must be offered. In the next week, three other ladies stand up to report their visions of the Beloved wed to Arabella. On the Friday night, Sarah herself stands up and says:

'My brothers and sisters, it is clear to me that it is the Divine Will that this should happen. Let it not be said that I would stand in the way of this. Husband, I demand you take this woman as your spiritual wife. I relinquish my hold over you and offer you to her, that she may accompany you on the next stage of this great journey.'

The Beloved bows his head and accepts the inevitable. He must put aside his old wife and take on the new. It is ordained and it must be.

Letty hears voices from the library as she passes, and realises that one of them is Mr Kendall and his voice is raised. She doesn't mean to stop and listen, but she does.

'. . . sir, that is why we are most concerned, most concerned.'

'You've heard, as we all have, that this is not my will, but that of the Lamb,' the Beloved replies smoothly. 'You do understand that, don't you?'

'But sir, can this be anything other than bigamy?'

'It's a *spiritual* union, Kendall. Not a union of law or of flesh, but of pure, godly spirit. I can assure you of that. It is a holy marriage only. No laws will be broken, no bigamy committed, no corporeal . . . connection.'

When Kendall speaks again, he is quieter. 'Very well. You reassure me. I see your point exactly. Precisely. And in truth, I support it wholeheartedly. But my wife is . . . she is nervous, sir. She thinks it's possible that the Lamb may ordain a spiritual marriage for me, or for her, and she is unhappy at the thought.'

'Of course. I understand. I will assure her that I see no such likelihood in any vision vouchsafed to me. Your gifts and hers are perfectly matched. There is no need for further union.'

'She will be glad to hear that, sir.'

'And I will ensure that the cottage is ready for your habitation directly. I believe that your spiritual needs require it. And it's been too long for your boy to camp out in a female dressing room.'

'Yes . . .' Mr Kendall gives an anxious cough. 'Sir, my son is not yet a committed member of our group. He is closing his heart to your words. We are afraid for him.'

'I've sensed it. I've prayed for him, Kendall. I believe the Lamb has his scheme almost ready to reveal.'

'Thank you. Thank you, sir. We don't want to lose him—'

'Letty?' It's Arabella, walking swiftly across the hall towards her. 'Are you all right? What are you doing?'

Letty jumps, and moves away from the library door, hoping she doesn't look guilty. Eavesdropping is a nasty habit. 'Nothing, nothing.' She shakes her head. 'I'm going upstairs. Shall we go together?'

'Yes. I want to talk to you about what I'm going to wear on Sunday.' Arabella has accepted her path to the Beloved's side. She has a new air of holiness, like a nun on the verge of taking her vows. Letty thinks she is happy. Certainly, she seems it.

The wedding takes place with a great air of festivity and joyous celebration. The church is decked out in large arrangements of white flowers. The day is bright and sunny, and Arabella makes a beautiful bride, in a long white silk gown, a veil and a wreath of orange blossom. She wears white satin shoes and carries white roses. The Beloved is majestic in a white suit. It is Sarah who joins their hands together, reads the vows and hears the responses, and blesses the rings. It is she who marries them. Her face shines with joy as she presents the couple to the congregation, and announces that the Lamb's will has been done.

The Beloved cries, 'But the Lamb's will is not yet fulfilled! There is more! Last night, I saw a mighty vision. A vision of delight where a holy soul brought a wavering one to the fold, the great and happy fold.'

The atmosphere instantly becomes electric with anticipation.

What is this? What is about to happen? The congregation holds its breath.

The Beloved leaves his new bride and walks down the aisle. As he goes, he puts out a hand to Letty, and she automatically takes it. He leads her out from her row and into the aisle, then reaches out to . . . for an awful second she thinks it is Mr Kendall, and she remembers the Beloved's promise to him and his wife. And then she sees that it is not Mr Kendall, but Arthur who is being grasped and led out into the aisle as well. Now they are both being taken back to the top of the church, to stand before the altar.

'Here they are,' calls the Beloved. 'The Lamb desires their union and so it shall be, right here, right now. Let us make this a doubly joyous day. Stand and face each other and take your hands.'

Letty can hardly believe what is happening. She is standing before them all, her hand held by Arthur Kendall. The Beloved has produced two rings from his pocket, and the ceremony is beginning. The Beloved is marrying her to the sulky boy, who has moped and sloped about the place for weeks, not speaking, not joining in, resisting it all.

It will be my job to save his soul, she thinks numbly, and realises as she looks into his grey eyes that he is staring back at her in fury and disgust. But he does as she does, and obeys.

Chapter Nineteen

I am in a very dark place, and because they have taken away my wine and my pills – the things that used to help keep the worst of it at bay – there is nothing to numb the pain. I lie on the bed for hours, hugging Heather's stuffed puffin close, burying my nose in it in case I can get some trace of her scent. Tears come and go, ambushing me in gusts and floods. It's almost easier when they're carrying the grief out of me than when I'm dry-eyed. When I cry and howl, I feel bigger than the grief. When I lie silent, it grows – huge, vile and black. It becomes bigger than I am and encloses me like a terrible prison cell. In those moments, I only want to die. The loss of Heather is too much. Too dreadful. I can't bear it, and no one should expect me to.

How did I get here? How did this happen to me?

It started before that awful night, of course. The roots of every huge event are buried far below it, deep in the earth. Did ours begin to grow in the months before, or the years before, or should I go back to the day Rory asked me to marry him? Was that really when we were set inexorably on the path to our tragedy?

I remember telling Caz all the things about Rory that drove me mad, but of course I didn't see them at first. We were so happy in those early years, feeling as though we'd won some kind of amazing lottery, finding each other and falling in love, then having our gorgeous children. We were both full of wonder at our good fortune, and completely accepting of it. Of course our lives were going to be happy. We were the lucky ones. I had a good job with prospects, and brought home more money than Rory did in his job as a finance director of a small charity. That was fine. I didn't resent it. I knew he loved his work and I was glad that I earned enough to make sure we could have the things that were important to me: a pretty house in a pleasant area that I could decorate as I liked, decent holidays, things for the children, from bicycles to tennis lessons. I was perfectly okay with it all.

But then . . .

I'd thought we were as close as any married couple could be. I trusted him completely, partly because I knew he could never do anything as low, stupid and predictable as Phil had. I was certain that Rory would never have an affair, or even look at another woman. He was a kind, loving husband, a wonderful father, a dependable friend.

But I didn't see that he was also deceitful. He hid things. His tendency to silence should have told me to be wary of what he concealed. I never saw it coming.

One day, when I was gathering up abandoned bits of paper on the sideboard to chuck in the recycling, I found the draft of a letter, typed up and printed out. I picked it up and read it, as I would anything in the house because there were no secrets here. It was Rory's response to his bosses' decision to make him redundant.

I frowned as I read, trying to take it in. Rory finished his letter by saying, *I have a family – a wife and two young children. This sector is losing jobs and there's no guarantee I can get another. Please, I beg you, don't do this. Please let me keep my job and I will work twice as hard as ever, I guarantee it.*

But had he sent it? Had they made him redundant?

I was shaky and frightened as I dialled his office number. I never used it. Rory had suggested ages ago that we communicate only via our home email addresses or an online app, so that we could never be accused of using our work inboxes for personal issues.

The voice on the other end sang out the charity's name and then: 'Can I help you?'

'Can I speak to Rory Overman please?'

'Oh . . . I don't think . . . Let me just check for you.' There was a long pause. 'Sorry, I'm afraid no one of that name works here.'

My stomach plummeted with a sickening swoop. 'But he did, didn't he? Until . . . ?'

'Yes, until . . . er . . . March, according to the list. But he's no longer here.'

March! Six months ago! 'Do you know where he works now?'

'I'm afraid not. Is there someone else that can help you?'

'No. Thank you. Goodbye.' My hand shook as I put the

251

phone down. I looked around the empty house. I was supposed to be working from home, and I had been until I started clearing up while the kettle was boiling for coffee. The children were at school. I had no idea, I realised with a start, where Rory was. He wasn't where I thought he'd be. *Where is he? What's he doing?*

I had no clue of his whereabouts when five minutes ago I'd been certain. The shock of realising that he'd been deceiving me so thoroughly made my world rock on its axis, and I was dazed, uncomprehending.

But I'm here on my own.

I went to the study, where all our papers and bank statements and household files were kept, and started to go through everything on the desk, letter by letter.

I was determined to find out what the hell was going on.

That evening, when Rory came in, wearing his suit and carrying a briefcase as usual, I smiled and pretended to know nothing. I'd already found out that there was more to this than a job loss, and I wanted to be sure of myself before I confronted him, in case he tried to spin more lies. I asked some casual questions about his day and he responded with answers that once would have washed lightly over me, only half registered, but that now burnt into my mind. They were lies, all of them: the throwaway remarks about his lunch hour, and the rubbish baked potato he ate in the canteen, the flight delays for So-and-So who's just back from holiday, the conference call with the Scottish branch. All made up. Fantasy.

I don't know how I stayed calm and let him do it. Perhaps it was unfair and I shouldn't have. But I did and he went on, digging a deeper and deeper hole that would be, eventually, impossible to get out of.

Of course, now it all seems so stupid. There I was, making dinner, all of us safe and alive, in our beautiful home. It was all still okay. But I didn't see it like that: I was frightened. I thought we were going to lose everything, and it would all be Rory's fault. Worse than that, I thought my marriage was over. How could he lie to me about something like that, so huge, so momentous? We had been so happy once, but it must have turned sour somewhere when I wasn't looking. It was the abruptness of the reversal that was so shocking. Was I such an awful wife, such a terrible person, that he couldn't tell me that things had gone wrong for him?

Now that I understand what loss really is, all of it seems so trivial. What is a house? Nothing that can't be rebuilt. Even a lost marriage can be replaced. But a child . . .

I sigh in the darkness, alone in the prison cell of grief. Now Heather has gone, irrevocably and forever. My mind won't make her live anymore, and I wish I could go out like a candle and know nothing more.

I want it to stop. Forever.

Chapter Twenty

The phone rings, startling Caz out of sleep, and she's grabbing for it instantly before she's even awake. Her first thought, her fear, is that something is wrong with the girls and Phil is calling to say there's been an accident. Ever since the fire, she's been afraid. Bad things do happen after all.

'Yes, yes? Who is it?'

'It's me, it's Kate!'

'Kate?' She sits up, blinking in the darkness. 'I'm so glad you called! Are you okay? What's wrong?'

'Oh Caz.' Kate starts to wail. 'It's Heather!'

'I know, darling. I know, sweetheart. It's terrible. So terrible.' Caz's heart aches for her, for what she must be suffering.

She doesn't seem to hear her. 'Caz, it's Heather. I can't find her! I've lost her.' She starts to sob. 'They wanted to take her away from me and now they have. You have to look for her, Caz. Tell her I'm sorry. Tell her I want to be with her but they won't let me.'

'But, Kate . . .' She's helpless. 'I don't know where she is either. Because she isn't anywhere anymore, you know that.'

'She might be at the house, Caz. Go to the house.'

'But the house is gone. It's burnt. It's all gone. Remember?'

'No,' Kate insists. 'It's not gone. You're there now. Find Heather, will you?'

The phone goes dead and Caz looks around. She's not in her room at all, but in Kate and Rory's bedroom in their old house. She always liked it, with its pale green walls, the old-fashioned brass bedstead, and the thick cream curtains. She thought it had burnt away to a shell, but here she is. And in the bed, Rory is sleeping beside her, his dark head turned away from her on the pillow.

This isn't real. I'm dreaming.

She gets out of bed. The wooden floorboards are smooth and solid under her feet as she goes slowly across the room to the door. Outside the corridor is just as she remembers, and there are the two doors. One goes to Ady's room, and one into Heather's room. She turns the handle of Heather's bedroom. At first it won't move, then she hears a soft, sweet voice singing inside and is filled with delight. It's Heather, she knows it. She fumbles at the handle and it moves suddenly, the door swinging open. The room inside is not like the rest of the house. It's what remained after the fire: dripping, blackened, open to the sky and reeking of smoke, burnt fabric and charred wood. But there she is, standing with her back to Caz looking out over the garden below, her fair hair glowing in the moonlight.

'Heather, baby!' Caz rushes to her and kneels down in the ashy, soggy mess to embrace her. She can feel Heather under her hands: she's soft and warm and so incredibly real. Caz starts to cry with joy at seeing her again. She's grieved for her too, the little girl she knew from a baby, her goddaughter. Even if this isn't real, she wants it to be, so, so much, just for now.

Heather turns round and puts her arms around Caz's neck. 'Godma Caz,' she says, pressing a cheek against hers.

'Heather, we love you. We miss you so much. Your mummy and daddy miss you.'

'I miss you too.'

'Can't you come back to us? Can't you?'

She doesn't say anything but hums lightly into Caz's ear. Then she says softly, 'Mummy needs your help. You have to help her.'

'I want to, but I don't know what to do. What shall I do?'

'You have to help her,' says Heather again.

'Yes . . . Tell me what to do, sweetheart, please . . .' Then suddenly, in the other room, Caz's phone starts ringing again, blaring out into the night. She gets to her feet, thinking of Rory asleep there. She doesn't want to wake him. He mustn't be disturbed. 'Wait here,' she says to Heather. 'I'll only be a second.' She runs out of the burnt-out room and back towards the main bedroom. There is her phone on the bedside table, the display lit up, and the ringtone cutting through the air. Rory stirs. He mustn't be woken. She reaches for the phone, grabs for it but she can't get hold of it—

Then she wakes, rushing up to the surface of reality, knowing she's left Heather behind in her dreams. She's instantly frustrated. *We weren't finished. I'm still in the dark. There was something I didn't manage to do but I can't remember what it is.*

She's dazed, still almost able to feel Heather under her hands, and smell the sweet scent of her hair. Caz is breathless from the force of her dream and its sudden end. Then she's filled with the deepest misery she's ever known, and starts to weep.

She can't sleep after that, so she goes downstairs to the kitchen, making tea as if sleepwalking. The vivid dream has brought it all back to her: the intensity of the grief and loss they all felt on that awful night, that terrible night.

Caz got a call from Rory at four o'clock in the morning to say that they needed her. There had been a fire at the house. He sounded shaky.

'Oh God, Rory, that's awful. Are you all okay? Has much been lost?' For some reason, she imagined something small and contained: the utility room burnt out, or the new kitchen charred to a crisp and the ceiling smeared with sooty stains, firemen rushing past while the family stood shivering on the front lawn in their night things.

But he began to wail, a sound that made her skin creep and her joints go weak. 'It's all gone, Caz! The house . . . everything . . . You've got to come to us. We've lost her, we've lost her.'

'Kate? You've lost Kate?'

'No . . . no . . . Heather. It's Heather.' Then he couldn't speak anymore.

Caz got to the hospital twenty minutes later, speeding through the empty streets and not caring if she got stopped because she wouldn't stop, she'd do anything to get to them. Kate was there, blank-eyed, her face and hands blackened where she'd fought to get to the children. Ady had woken up and, tall and strong for nine years old, had managed to get his window open and jumped out. He was alive but in an induced coma while they assessed the state of his injuries. He had a broken leg, a fractured wrist and a punctured spleen at the very least, but they were concentrating on his head and neck where they feared there was trauma.

A policewoman, quiet, sympathetic, sat with them, observing, occasionally talking into the radio on her shoulder.

Rory was weeping uncontrollably. Caz hugged him and stroked his hair, then went to Kate and took her hand. She turned to look at her with those dead eyes. The house was now taped off while the fire service and police forensics began their investigation.

'I'm so sorry,' Caz whispered. It seemed hardly enough, and yet it was all there was to say.

'I went to get her out,' Kate said clearly. 'I tried to get to her room.'

'Oh Kate. I'm . . . so sorry.' Hot acid tears burnt Caz's eyes. She couldn't bring herself to picture Heather in her bedroom, or think of her at all in case she dissolved and couldn't be strong for Kate and Rory. 'Sweetheart, I can't imagine what you're going through.'

'They had to stop her running back in,' Rory said through his tears. 'She tried, but even though she wanted to, she couldn't have. It was physically impossible to get back up the stairs.'

'Are you injured, Kate?' Caz asked, wondering if she too jumped from the upper floor. 'Have you seen a doctor?'

She looked impatient. 'Yes, yes. I'm fine.'

Rory said, 'She's okay. We don't know yet where she was when it started, but it was the back that went up. Where the kids were. Oh Christ.' He knuckles his eyes. 'I can't believe it. I can't believe we'll never see her again.'

Kate got up and paced about, muttering something to herself. Caz watched her anxiously, feeling helpless, not knowing where to begin. What do you say to someone when something like this happens? All she could think of was practicalities: how to get them hot drinks and food; where they would sleep and what they would wear; how to arrange visits to Ady in hospital. And there would be the funeral to sort out. Presumably an inquest. She wasn't sure how it all worked. More than anything she wanted to gather Leia and Mika into her arms and hold them tight and never let them go.

Caz thinks it began that very night, though, even before she reached the hospital. Kate's uncoupling from everyone else. She seemed to enter into her own world, a place where there was no Ady at all. The old Kate disappeared. Of course she would change. Caz expected shock, grief and trauma, and perhaps a long road to the acceptance of what had happened. But Kate was not only utterly changed, she seemed completely removed from what was taking place around her.

From the start, Kate went through what had to be done not like someone in shock but like someone simply unaware of what was going on. When Caz tried to talk to her about Ady and persuade her to go to the hospital and see him, Kate seemed not to have any idea of who or what she was referring to, and soon began to forbid all mention of him. His name sent her into a kind of hysteria and they soon learned not to say it in front of her.

'It's grief,' her friends told each other. 'Soon she'll come out of it and want to see him.'

But there was no sign of that.

The coroner adjourned the inquest and released the body. At Heather's funeral, Kate did not so much seem zombified with grief or the tranquillisers she was on, as uncomprehending of why she was there. Rory, in utter white-faced agony, held it together as best he could as people hugged him, offered condolences for the unbearable, but Kate stood apart, as though she'd been invited to the funeral of a stranger. She showed no emotion at any point. Caz even saw her glance at her watch as if hoping the whole thing would be over quickly.

She felt so sorry for her friend, and so desperate to do whatever she could, yet there didn't seem to be any way to help. She tried to be practical, finding a place for Kate to live – a tiny modern house on the estate just outside the town – and helping to get her settled. She offered to go to the old house and see what was left to salvage and Kate blinked at her as though she didn't know what Caz was talking about. The police investigation was completed when they were satisfied there had been no crime. After the insurance people had done their assessment, Rory and Caz collected up the remnants and Caz brought around boxes of what had been saved from the house.

'Oh, thank you,' Kate said, her eyes lighting on a box that held what had been taken from the playroom: some books and toys that had survived the deluge of water from the fire hoses. 'I'm going to need those.'

Caz looked about the room and thought then that if she hadn't known Heather was dead, she would have imagined the little girl was still here. A small blue coat covered in white stars hung on the peg in the hall, with a pair of boots underneath it. On the table was a plastic plate with a ham sandwich on it, and a peeled satsuma in a bowl next to it.

'Are you sure you're all right?' she asked Kate.

'Yes. I'm fine.' She seemed remarkably okay in many ways. If one didn't think too much about her refusal to see Ady. 'But Rory came round again last night.' Her eyes filled with coldness. 'I wish he'd just leave me alone. He must know it's all over. He's on and on at me to see a counsellor. That's what he calls it, but I think he means a psychotherapist. I don't see the point. I'd be fine, if I were left alone to get on with things in my own way. I just need some time. Some space. Maybe some time away.'

'Really?' Caz ventured. She could see a row of pill bottles on the windowsill in the kitchen. 'Would that help?'

For a moment, she looked like the old Kate again: the vivacious, pretty, energetic woman Caz loved, before the horror drained her of everything and left the dead-eyed automaton in her place. 'I think it would,' she said. 'I really think it would.'

'How long would you need?'

She shrugged. 'A couple of months.' Then she leaned towards her, her eyes intense, with more emotion in her than Caz had seen for a long time. 'Caz, I know I can do it. I can get away. But Rory doesn't want me to – and he's got all of them on side. The doctors. My mother, my sister. They want to keep tabs on me, maybe even get me on a ward or in a secure unit. I can't cope with that, Caz. I absolutely can't. I don't know what I'd do if that happened. I've got a plan but I'll need some help with it. I need someone I can trust. Will you help me?'

She must have known Caz would. She was desperate to help. She understood that Kate's agony was only just beginning, and that she needed to get through this strange, disconnected stage so that she could begin to accept what had happened and come to terms with it. She had to do it before they brought Ady round. He would need her when she came back.

'Of course I will.'

And that was when she committed herself to Kate's escape. But now everything has changed.

Chapter Twenty-One

Letty cannot quite believe she is celebrating her own wedding when the community makes its way back to the house for the feast in honour of the Beloved's union. The Angels have been busy and have conjured up a magnificent banquet, set out on a huge trestle table in the hall, where everybody sits, the happy couples in the position of honour.

It is strange to see Arabella at the Beloved's side, Sarah now moved a few places away. The Beloved himself looks invigorated by his marriage ceremony, and often glances at his new bride, who appears flushed and happy, almost at ease in her place as consort. Of course, in many ways, she has held the position already. As owner of the house and the Beloved's favourite, she has always been accorded a high status. Now, though, she has no challenge to her role as the most important woman in the community. There is a deference from everyone that wasn't there before. And Sarah, while still treated with every courtesy, has the unmistakable air of the dowager about her.

Letty sits beside her new husband, and next to him are the

Kendalls, happy in a bewildered way at the turn events have taken. Their son is now the spiritual brother-in-law of the Beloved, and surely this will bring him truly into the fold. Letty can see it in their eyes: the desire that this honour will help soften Arthur towards the Beloved, and give him a status in the community that makes it more appealing to him. She can guess that they yearn for his soul to be saved along with theirs.

Arthur, though, doesn't appear to be softening very much at all. His demeanour is no different to what it has been over the weeks since his arrival: reserved and taciturn, with a touch of sulkiness about his mouth and the air of someone wishing he were somewhere else.

Letty wonders how many marriages begin in absolute silence, with the groom unwilling to look at his bride.

'May I pass you something?' she asks in as friendly a way as she can. 'The pressed tongue is excellent. You should try it.'

He grunts and takes the plate she offers, forks some tongue onto his plate and passes it on to his mother on his other side.

She leans towards him and says in a low voice, 'I had no idea that this was the will of the Lamb. I'm as surprised as you are. But it cannot have been ordained without purpose. I'm sure that if we pray and persevere, we shall begin to understand the plan.'

He turns his cool grey gaze upon her and says, 'You can't honestly believe that we're married. The little farce we've all just been through doesn't mean a thing. I might as well have married the table.'

She gasps and pulls back, reddening. Then she remembers herself. Her role is to bring this lost soul to the fold. He is going to resist, that's obvious. She must learn not to take what he says personally, and to forgive him if he is brusque or insulting.

'The union is a spiritual one,' she reminds him. 'So you're right in a way. I hope you might, in time, come to understand, though, that it is more precious because of it.'

He looks at her with something like pity. 'You are happy to be given away without being consulted or offering your consent?'

'It's the will of the Lamb,' she says. Surely he can understand that her consent or consultation is nothing compared to that. The will must be accepted, embraced. It is an honour to be chosen for holy work.

Arthur shrugs. 'Believe it if you want to, it makes no difference to me.'

The Beloved gets to his feet and calls for quiet, then begins his bridegroom's speech, a rousing oration on the nature of a spiritual union. He reminds them that their purpose no longer includes the need to procreate, when the Day of Judgement is so close at hand. He quotes from the Bible: 'For, behold, the days are coming, in which they shall say, blessed are the barren, and the wombs that never bore, and the paps which never gave suck.' He tells them that this holy community, chosen for endless life, shall not know death and therefore does not need to know birth either. He praises them for their acceptance. 'You are blessed. For I am among you! I am working out my plan. The day is coming soon when I shall be known and accepted in truth, and the world will marvel.'

An expectant silence falls. There is the sense that the Beloved is about to say something that will change everything for them, make it all fall into place. But he does not. He leads them in a group prayer and declares that the party must go on. The evening ends with a singsong around the piano of the community's favourite hymns. Then, at last, it is time to retire. Letty bids goodnight to her husband, and makes her way to the little dressing room where she is still sleeping on the camp bed. Arabella comes in while she is undressing.

'Congratulations!' She hugs Letty hard and stands back, beaming. 'Who would have thought we'd be married on the same day, at the same hour!'

'Yes. I had no idea!' Letty smiles back. It seems a little strange to be married when nothing has changed. Here they both are, getting ready for bed as usual.

'I'm sorry Arthur cannot join you tonight,' Arabella says lightly, unpinning the veil from her head.

Letty looks up at her, surprised. 'What do you mean?' Arthur has gone up with his parents, as he has every night. She expected no different now.

'The Beloved says that when the cottage is ready in a couple of days, the Kendalls will move there, and you can return to your own room. Arthur can join you then.'

Letty gapes at her, and says, 'But I don't understand. Why would he join me? The marriages are spiritual ones. The Beloved has said from the start that there is no union, no physical union. So we don't need to share a room. Why would we?'

'Sometimes you're very dense, Letty,' Arabella says, looking exasperated. 'Here, help me unbutton my dress, won't you? I can't reach. What's the point of renouncing the flesh if you are not tempted? Where is the triumph over the Devil in that? The Beloved has explained it all to me. We're only doing truly holy work if we allow temptation near us and resist it. It's obvious when you think about it.'

Letty stands very still, but her face flushes bright red. 'You mean . . . you will share a bed with the Beloved?'

'Yes,' Arabella says airily, and Letty cannot tell whether she is as insouciant as she pretends or not. 'That's right. And you'll share with Arthur. In time.'

Letty cannot speak as she unbuttons Arabella's dress, and watches as she wanders out to the bedroom, but as soon as she is gone, Letty shuts the door and leans against it. She breathes fast, feeling a little ill. She had no idea she would be expected to share such intimacy with that young man. He is a stranger to her, and he has no affection for her at all. For a moment, she feels a flash of indignation, and she thinks of Arthur asking if she is happy to be given away like this. A surge of rebellious anger goes through her. Then she exerts her will, pushing it down and saying to herself, *It's only because I don't understand the plan properly. If I obey, it will be made clear. The Beloved cannot do wrong. Whatever he decides must be right.*

*

That night, she lies on her camp bed and wills herself to go to sleep, but she cannot. Despite the heavy door between the dressing room and the bedroom, she can hear sounds from Arabella's room. At first, it is Arabella padding about, and then a long stretch of quiet when she must have climbed into her four-poster bed. Letty squeezes her eyes shut in the darkness and tries to summon sleep, but it will not come.

After about twenty minutes, she hears a door open and close, and footsteps across the floor. She hears the low murmur of the Beloved's voice and knows he is there, with her sister, in her bedroom. She tries not to picture Arabella in her nightdress tucked under the sheets and the Beloved in his nightshirt, climbing in beside her. She waits for the noise next door to stop as they go to sleep, but it does not subside for some long time. There is the squeak of a spring and the creak of wood, murmured voices, and a cry that is quickly stifled. Letty pushes her fingers into her ears and listens to the loud rush of her own breathing and the thud of her own heartbeat. When at last she pulls them out, all is quiet.

It is three more nights before Mr and Mrs Kendall move out of Letty's room and go to the cottage that has been made ready for them. It is a signal mark of favour that they have been accorded their own place to live, and Arabella remarks idly that it is because Mr Kendall has made a huge donation to the cause, and has promised more.

Letty scans her sister's face for signs of any change since her marriage to the Beloved, but there is nothing obvious. She seems much the same as ever, healthy and serene. But each night is the same: the creaks and groans that come from Arabella's bedroom, lasting around ten minutes at most, that Letty can only suspect are sounds of married love. This she can scarcely believe. It is against all that the Beloved has proclaimed about spiritual unions. It makes no sense at all.

Perhaps then, she reasons, it is not what she thinks, but something else. Perhaps it is in fact the Beloved and Arabella resisting temptation – praying together, embracing as they fight the urges placed in them by the Devil. That's what it must be, she tells herself. And it is a stain on her that she might even think otherwise.

She and her new husband have little to do with one another. She makes a point of greeting him politely but he only grunts a response, although once or twice, she thinks she sees a look of something like pity in his eyes. When she suggests they pray together, he is resistant and refuses to join her. Letty is embarrassed that the other community members, watching with interest, see her rebuffed but she comforts herself with the reassurance that in time she will prevail with him. Sometimes, when she looks for Arthur, he is nowhere to be found, and then she sees him coming in through the front door in his coat and boots.

'Just out for a walk,' he says when she asks him where he has been. 'Getting the air.'

It's not surprising a young man needs exercise. She understands. When she offers to join him for a walk around the grounds, he refuses, and hurries away to his room.

My room, she thinks. *At least, it was and it will be again soon.*

Mr and Mrs Kendall are almost overly polite to her, eager to be friendly and to make excuses for their son's recalcitrance.

'You will be the making of him, Miss Evans,' says his mother, grasping her hand when they meet over tea in the drawing room.

'Please, call me Letty.'

'We know you've been chosen to save his soul,' says his father. 'You have our eternal gratitude.'

'I will do my best,' Letty says. 'I can do no more.'

She expects Arthur to resist when it is explained to him that he will be expected to share the blue bedroom with her, now that his parents are moving out of it. She imagines he will be furious and demand to be given his independence. He will want to go to the cottage, where there is a bedroom he could have as his own. But, on the contrary, he is docile and seems happy to go along with it.

At this, Letty feels her first flicker of hope. He has given her an opportunity to make friends with him, and surely from that will come the path to salvation. After all, can they share something so intimate as a bed without growing close to one another? Surely not.

The night she is to return to her room, she gathers up her things to take back there. Kitty comes in to help her.

'Are you all right?' she asks, seeing Letty's white face.

'Oh yes.' She smiles bravely. 'Yes, I am.'

'Nervous, are you?' Kitty looks sympathetic as she loads cushions into her arms from the camp bed. 'I'm not surprised. You don't even know him, do you?'

'Yes. It will be a challenge.' Letty hopes she sounds more courageous than she feels. 'I know it won't be easy. But this is the first step on the way.'

'All right,' Kitty says laconically. 'Just you make sure he understands the terms. The Beloved was clear. This is a marriage of spirits. If he tries it on with you, you let me know, that's all.'

Letty blushes. She can't help thinking of the sounds that come from Arabella's room at night. 'We will resist all temptation,' she says quickly. 'We will pray together that we escape the torments of the flesh.'

Kitty gives her a sideways look. 'Yes. You do that. But if you find he wants to do more than pray, don't be afraid of shouting out and letting us all know. He's not a true believer, that one. We've all noticed it. We don't know why the Beloved puts up with him. Talk about the viper in the bosom.'

'The Beloved wants to save his soul,' Letty reminds her.

'Or for you to.' Kitty sniffs. 'It's not for me to question the will, but I'm still puzzled, that's all. I can't help it, I'll be quite honest about it.'

'You must try, Kitty,' Letty says gently. 'Try and accept. As I have.'

'You're too good,' Kitty replies, shaking her head. 'A pattern to us all.' She turns to take her pile of cushions away. 'Just look out for yourself, though. Don't let yourself get taken advantage of.'

'I won't,' Letty promises, but she feels more afraid than before. Why would the Beloved put her in the position of making herself vulnerable to a man who doesn't love her?

I must not question. He knows all. He would never put me in danger. I am under his protection.

The hands on the clock take flight, and spin outrageously fast. Before she feels in the least ready, the bell is ringing for dinner and they are all in the big dining room, the Angels serving up the plentiful and wholesome food: roasted chicken, three types of potato, garden vegetables and thick, aromatic gravy. Letty can barely swallow a mouthful. She is only aware of Arthur at her side, as he always is now. He seems larger than ever, a great broad shape that dwarfs her own – *what can it be like to take up so much room in the world?* – and large, long-fingered hands. As he cuts up his food, she can't help watching them and wondering what they would feel like on her body. She banishes the thought at once.

You see how quickly the Devil works! I have no desire for him at all and already my thoughts are polluted!

She darts her gaze around, hoping that no one has seen her look at Arthur's hands, as if fearful that they can read her mind.

Does she have no desire for him? She has given no thought to it, aware only that life here in the house means shunning the flesh. She is ready for a different kind of bliss – if married relations are bliss. Cecily once said, in a moment of candour, that it was something to be endured – not pleasant and not dignified but necessary for a man – and so she has felt that she must be lucky to be spared it at the same time as guaranteed a place in paradise in the near future. Now she is forced to think about it, and she is confused. And scared.

When the meal is over, she goes upstairs quickly but not so

quickly that it seems she is eager to get to her marriage chamber. Once in her room, she races about, preparing for bed, and within five minutes is buttoned into her long nightdress and under the covers of the bed, her heart beating fast and her eyes screwed tight. She wants to appear asleep. It's the only way she can think of to avoid the embarrassment they will surely both feel.

Arthur spoils her plan by knocking on the door and waiting for her to answer it. She can't go on pretending to sleep when he knocks more loudly, but gets out, dashes to the door, opens it and dashes back. He comes in slowly, watching as she flurries about in the sheets, trying to cover herself up. He goes wordlessly to the suitcase on the stand in the corner, removes some things from it and shuts himself in the dressing room. She hears water in the sink, and movements, and then the door opens again and he comes out.

She slams her eyes shut, her pulse racing again, clutching at the sheets and pulling them up under her chin. She can sense him standing in the middle of the room, observing her. She can hardly bear it; then at last he speaks.

'I can sleep on the chaise longue if you like. Or on the floor in the dressing room if that would make you feel better.'

She opens her eyes and turns her head to look at him, blinking in the lamplight. 'But,' she says feebly, 'won't you be cold? There isn't any other bedding.'

'I can fetch some,' he says. 'Or take the blanket from you, and leave you the coverlet. It's not cold tonight.'

'Whatever you wish,' she says faintly.

Arthur takes a step towards the bed and she can't prevent

273

herself starting and making a nervous squeak. He stops and regards her again.

'You needn't worry. I don't intend to touch you. As far as I'm concerned, we're not married and I wouldn't dream of engaging in marital relations with you, even if you didn't believe that all these marriages are purely *spiritual*.' He says it with an unconcealed sneer in his voice.

'Then what are you doing here? Why are you in my room at all?' Her voice comes out a little quavery but she is glad she sounds stronger than she feels. He stands there, thinking, and she looks at him, in his flannel striped pyjamas, his face still damp from his wash. He looks so boyish, with his dark fringe flopping forward, his skin fresh and clear of any whiskers. The grey eyes are sober and candid and he is less sulky than he appears when they are all downstairs together.

'It's a good question,' he says. 'Well, here's the thing. I need to keep my parents happy. And for some strange reason, this seems to make them happy. They weren't pleased at all when I had a girlfriend before, and she was a perfectly decent sort, even if she was a dancer. But now that I'm married to a complete stranger by a religious maniac, all is well with the world. Crazy, isn't it?' He reveals an unexpectedly beautiful smile that makes his eyes crinkle at the corners and shows his even teeth. She'd never noticed them before. He is not such a boy, suddenly, but a hybrid creature on his way out of youth and into the first real flourish of manhood.

'You had a girlfriend?' she asks, curious.

'Oh yes. I've had a few, actually. But they only knew about that one. Dear Susan. A lovely girl and not her fault that she happened to have a stevedore for a dad and a seamstress for a mother.'

'How did they find out about her?'

Arthur shrugs. 'I got myself into a bit of trouble at the university. Quite a lot came out then – about how I was having fun and who with. I've been rusticated.'

'Rusti . . . ?'

'Sent down for a year. My father will only let me go back on condition that I stay with him and my mother for the entire time. And that meant coming to this place.' Arthur rolls his eyes. 'And they think *I've* been mixing with a bad crowd.'

'What do you mean?' Letty demands, sitting up, the sheet still held tightly under her chin.

He laughs. 'Look at you. All fired up with the desire to protect that charlatan.'

'He's not a charlatan!' she says hotly.

'Of course he is. Clever and convincing, but an utter fraud. I can't help admiring what he's done, though, the way he's built all of this, got you all absolutely gulled by it. And now he's managed to swap that old wife of his for a younger, sweeter one as well. All in the name of spiritual marriages!' Arthur guffaws and shakes his head. 'Like I said, very clever.'

'How dare you speak like that?' If Arthur's words bring on the tiniest moment of doubt about the Beloved, all she has to do is imagine his face, the fire in his eyes when he preaches, the utter conviction he possesses and passes on to them all. She knows without doubt that he is genuine. 'He wants to save your soul!' she declares.

'He wants to save something,' Arthur remarks, 'but I don't

think it's my soul. Now, let me take that blanket and I'll curl up here. I'll be perfectly comfortable.' He comes up and takes the blanket, sweeping it off the bed like a magician removing a tablecloth, and goes to the chaise longue. A moment later, with the cushion plumped up for his head, he breathes out loudly and seems to fall directly asleep.

Letty reaches out to turn off the lamp, seething. She cannot sleep now because of the anger racing through her. *Charlatan! How dare he? He knows nothing about the Beloved. He's just some jumped-up boy who thinks he's sophisticated because he's done a term at Oxford or Cambridge or wherever.* Then she tries to calm herself. *I'm being tested. He's not going to make this easy for me, that much is obvious. But I will save his soul. I can see now that it is my mission.*

Chapter Twenty-Two

My life unspools in front of my closed lids, as though my brain refuses to accept the decision I've made: to sink into oblivion. For more than a day I've not opened my eyes, whether I'm lying in bed, being supported to the bathroom or having hot broth pressed between my lips on the edge of a spoon. I don't want to eat. I don't want to function. I just want to cease. But my mind won't have it. It keeps delivering crystal-clear replays of episodes in my life as though they're all stored on discs, playable as easily as a favourite sitcom.

I can see myself as I was. I'm in my post-work clothes – jeans and a sloppy shirt, my hair pulled back in a ponytail, standing in our kitchen, stirring something – risotto? – at our baby-blue range cooker. My face is drawn and I'm tight-lipped, waiting for Rory to come home from wherever he's been. Heather and . . . the other one . . . the one I can't picture . . . are at Caz's. Caz knows something huge has happened but I can't bring myself to tell her yet. It's the first thing I haven't confided in her since we became friends.

The front door slams, and my stomach turns over with

nervous anticipation. I've tried to plan this, but it's been impossible. Every turn of the conversation, every phrase, will depend on Rory and how he reacts.

'Hi!' he calls from the hall. I hear his keys clink down on the sideboard. 'I'm home!'

'I'm in the kitchen,' I say, unnecessarily. It's where I always am when he comes home, with the others around me. Heather is often watching the television while she plays and someone else is usually sitting at the kitchen table doing homework.

Who is that other person? It's someone I know well . . . but . . . they won't come into the frame.

Rory is striding into the kitchen, loosening his tie. 'Where are the kids?' he asks, looking about.

'At Caz's.'

'Oh.' He looks surprised. Heading to the cupboard to get a glass for a drink of water, he says, 'I didn't know they were going to be out this evening.'

'I arranged it. I think we need to have a talk.'

He seems blithe, unconcerned. 'Oh. Okay. Anything in particular?' He runs the tap into his glass and goes to sit down at the kitchen table, looking up at me, the picture of innocence. If I didn't know better, I would suspect nothing at all.

I move the risotto off the heat, put the spoon down very carefully, then go and sit opposite him. 'How was work today?'

He shrugs lightly. 'You know. Same old.'

'Was Andy there?'

'Er . . . yeah. As usual.'

'Uh huh.' I nod. 'How was Sally?'

'She was fine.'

'And Stuart? Was he there?'

'Yes. Of course.'

'Okay.' I stare at him, hoping that my questioning will alert him to the fact that maybe something is wrong. 'What if I tell you that Stuart wasn't at work today? Gill called me and told me he was home ill.'

'Really?' Rory looks surprised, then nervous, but he quickly recovers himself. 'Maybe he was. I can't say I always know when Stu's in the office.'

He holds my gaze. Those gentle brown eyes, just a bit downturned at the edges. He's a good man in so many ways. Does he even know he's lying to me? Has he somehow managed to convince himself that he's telling the truth? I will him to break, and to say, 'You know what, Kate? I've made a huge almighty fuck-up and I'm so sorry. I really need to tell you about it.' I feel as though I could forgive everything if he just said that. Every moment that goes by when he doesn't is depressing me further.

'What if I told you that Andy wasn't in the office either?'

He doesn't say, 'How would you know that?' He stares down at the table instead, frowning. 'Well . . . I don't know.' He's paling just a little. He senses that something is about to happen, some seismic shift that will change everything.

And the stupid thing is that by pretending none of this is happening, he's made it a thousand times worse than it needed to be.

I can't help giving him another chance. 'Is there anything you want to tell me? Anything at all?'

He looks me straight in the eye. 'No,' he says firmly.

'Oh Rory.' Huge sadness fills my heart. He must, surely, know that he's delivering slow, certain deathblows to our marriage. 'Are you sure? Nothing you think I should know?'

'Nope.' He looks over at the stove, striving for normality. 'Is that risotto? I'm starving.'

'I have to tell you something.' I'm calm. I hope that by being calm he'll realise that this isn't a silly row, a bit of shouting that blows over and is soon forgotten, but something too serious to get hysterical about. 'I know.'

'Know what?' He gets up. 'Shall I get the dishes? I can finish the cooking if you like.'

'Sit down. I know that you haven't been at work today.'

He looks paler suddenly and sinks down into his seat. He clasps his hands and stares at them.

'I know you haven't been at work since March. You were made redundant then, weren't you?'

He goes as still as a stone and doesn't lift his eyes, and there's a defeated air about him.

'Six months ago, Rory. What have you been doing all day?'

He shrugs.

'Why didn't you tell me?'

There's a long pause and then he says in a low voice, 'I don't know.'

'You don't know?' I'm disbelieving. 'Didn't it ever occur to you that you should have told me?'

'Yes.'

'So . . . why didn't you?' I know, from our arguments in the past, that Rory will resist my efforts to get him to explain himself. Monosyllabic answers will follow one after the other, or else it will be the usual 'I don't know', turning what should be a dialogue into an inquisition with him as the hapless victim of me, the inquisitor. But surely this is too big for that kind of stonewalling? Surely he owes it to me to tell me what's been going on in his head? At least to try?

He flicks a gaze up at me. Then he says, 'I don't know.'

'No. Wait.' The anger begins to build. 'You can't fob me off with that. I won't have it, not this time. You must know! Every day when you walked out the house in your suit and carrying your briefcase, you must have made a conscious decision to hide this thing from me.' I can't stop hurt and fury entering my voice. 'When you signed the papers for the loan for the kitchen, even though you didn't have an income, you must have known what you were doing. Well? Didn't you?'

His shoulders hunch. I can sense him turning inward, into himself. He won't engage with me, or look at me, and every fibre of his being is telling me to go away and leave him alone. It's more than I can stand. All the frustration of the last few years, all the worry, anxiety and despair of the last week as I've realised the extent of what's been going on behind my back . . . it bubbles up inside me. All I want is for him to talk to me. Just tell me. *Just say sorry.*

He's not even going to do that. His gaze is fixed on the table, he's stony still. Someone has to speak, has to tell the story, and it's going to be me.

'So you pretended to go to the office every day, hiding all

this from me, using the redundancy money to act as your salary? Were you hoping you'd get another job before I found out?'

Silence. No reply. No look, no glance.

'Were you?' I leap to my feet. 'Please, Rory, talk to me. Talk to me!'

'I suppose so,' he says with a dull lack of conviction.

I want to weep. Here, at this awful time, he can't muster the strength to look inside himself and tell me what's going on there. It's as though he expects me, even wants me, to be angry, and he'll do all he can to make that happen. Is it perhaps because there he feels safe? He's not the sinner or the adult who's failed to take responsibility for himself, but the helpless child, the victim of the grown-up's fury.

'I can't take this, Rory. I can't take the lies and the deception. Even now you won't explain it, or apologise or try to make me understand. Don't you realise what you've done to us, what you're doing right now? You won't even explain or ask for my sympathy. Can't you see how much it hurts that you couldn't share your troubles with me?' I gaze at him, but he won't lift his eyes from the table. I feel utterly hopeless. He's a good man, a good friend. But is that enough? What kind of marriage is based on a lie like this? I say quietly, 'What would you do if I asked you to go?'

He's still, then shrugs like a man who can no longer fight his battles. 'I would go, I suppose.'

'That's it? You wouldn't try to stay? To convince me I'm wrong? To win back my trust?'

'What's the point, when you want me to go?'

We're both defeated, I see that now. I've gone wrong some-where but I don't know where. Somewhere along the way, when I thought I was doing the best for us both, I was dam-aging us. And so was he. We both were. I don't know how we can go on.

I can hear voices. There are people in my room, the ones who come every now and then. Perhaps the man is here, the one who holds his hands over me and tries to warm my frozen core. The episode is still playing even while I become aware of people with me. I can see the woman stand up. She talks passionately, gesticulating, expressive, while the man listens, his expression growing ever sadder. Now he stands up. I know what's happening. She's told him to go, to leave her and the children while they all come to terms with what has happened and decide if it can be mended. He's agreed to go. He'll stay with a friend. He goes upstairs to pack.

From behind my closed lids and dry lips, I want to shout, *Don't go! Don't leave them alone! You don't know what happens next. Don't leave them.*

But I'm powerless to change it now.

Chapter Twenty-Three

The day after her powerful dream of Heather, Caz sends a message to Rory.

> **When you're out of the hospital, come and see me. I need to talk to you.**

She's nervous about seeing him. Rory, once so easy-going and placid, has found a new intensity, as though everything he has been through has broken down the walls between him and the world – or between him and himself. She has seen Rory annoyed and seen him retreat into himself, but she's never seen him angry.

But I have to be brave. I can't back out of this.

He texts not long after:

> **Sure. I'll be there around seven.**

When he arrives, she's ready. The girls are at their father's house. She's put out some food and a couple of chilled bottles of beer, even though Rory rarely drinks. When he comes in, though, he opens one at once and sits down at the kitchen table, looking tired.

Caz sits down opposite with a glass of wine. 'How's Ady?'

Rory gulps some cold beer before he answers. 'He's fine. Doing well. They think he'll be out before too long. Another fortnight or so to be sure. He's in good spirits.'

'I'll go and see him,' Caz says.

'He'd like that.' Rory's gaze slides over to her, hopeful. 'So . . . have you heard from Kate?'

'No,' she says honestly. 'I haven't.'

He looks defeated. 'This is so bloody terrible. She's in a bad way, Caz. I'm worried sick.'

'Me too.'

'If only we knew more about her state of mind.' He takes another gulp of beer, then says, 'Did she confide much in you before she left?'

'Well . . . a bit. But she wasn't making all that much sense. She wouldn't talk about Ady.'

Rory shakes his head. 'That's what I can't understand,' he says, almost wonderingly. 'She wouldn't go to the hospital. She wouldn't talk about him. It was as though he didn't exist.'

'She's still in shock. She's been driven crazy with grief. Maybe it's the only way she can cope.'

Caz can't understand it herself. How do you just erase a child like that? In her heart, it's the most worrying thing about all of this. Grief over Heather is explicable. Taking flight when Ady needs her, refusing to talk about him . . . that's the mystery.

Rory says, 'I try to understand it, even though it makes no sense. I have to realise that it's not the real Kate right now. She refused any counselling, brushed aside any idea that she might need professional help. Her mother and I both felt she needed medical care but she refused, and she was still so articulate, so functioning, that they couldn't force her. She'd only agree to the antidepressants.' He frowns. 'Do you think she's had some kind of reaction to them?'

Caz hesitates before she speaks. 'But she's not been herself for a long time. Even before that night, I mean.'

'I know.' Rory bites his lip. 'After she found out about . . . my situation.'

'Yes. That's when she started to change.'

Caz remembers when Kate came round to the house, icy calm, and told her everything: the hidden redundancy, the credit card bill run up to keep up appearances, the talk at home and Rory going.

'Oh Kate.' Caz had shaken her head, stunned. 'I can't believe it. Rory doesn't seem the type! I would never think it of him.' Caz knew it was awful, but she couldn't help feeling sorry for Rory. Kate had such high standards. Fine when everything was going okay, but not so good when it wasn't. Rory hated confrontation. He must have dreaded telling her. He must have somehow decided not to. That habit of silence of his. 'You must feel terrible.'

'Why did he lie to me?' Kate asked, pale, her eyes questioning. She seemed outraged and floored by it at the same time. 'Am I so awful? Why couldn't he tell me he was in trouble?'

'He should have told you,' Caz said adamantly. Of course he should have. But she had a sudden vision of Rory leaving home every day, pretending to go to work, maybe going back after Kate and the children had left, or else spending the hours in the library or in a cafe, and felt a rush of sympathy for him. 'Maybe he didn't want to disappoint you.'

Kate looked up at Caz, uncomprehending, hurt, torn between fury and despair. 'How could he not tell me? I don't understand. It changes everything between us! I feel like I don't know him anymore.'

Now Caz says, 'Why didn't you tell her?'

Rory sighs. 'I was a coward, I suppose. I just wanted everything to be all right. I couldn't bear to spoil it for her when everything was going so well. I thought I could make it all right without her ever knowing. The irony was that when she found out, I'd just applied for a new job and I got an interview the week after. So I thought I could see the way out. If I got the job, I'd be earning again, and able to sort it all without worrying her. I did get it but it was too late.'

'You'd still have been lying to her. You know you should have told her. She was devastated by the secrecy. She said it was like your whole marriage had been a sham, because you weren't able to confide in her, or tell her when things went wrong. She thought she must be an awful wife, if you were so scared of telling her you'd lost your job. She didn't understand why you couldn't turn to her for help.'

There's a pause before Rory says, 'I never thought of it that way. I was trying to protect her.'

'And . . . yourself?'

He thinks for a moment. 'Yes. I suppose that's true. I hardly even admitted to myself what was happening. I wouldn't let myself think about what I was doing. It was easier to maintain the facade, act like I really did have a job and a salary and all the stuff I needed to keep it going. It was like being in a dream, and I just didn't want to wake up.'

'I know Kate isn't always easy. She's headstrong and seems absolutely sure of herself. But she's as needy as anyone else. Perhaps you didn't realise, but what you did shook her to the core because she began to think that nothing was safe, and that her happy life was just an illusion. And then—'

Rory looks agonised. 'I've wished a million times that I'd told her. Because if I had, maybe it would never have happened. Maybe Heather would still be here.'

'That was an accident,' Caz says firmly. 'It had nothing to do with what happened with your job. You mustn't blame yourself for it.'

'But Kate thinks it. She blames me because I wasn't there that night. If I had been, maybe I could have saved Heather.' He covers his face with his hands. 'I have to live with that.'

The dream flashes into Caz's mind again – the gorgeous sweetness of Heather's presence, her whispered command: *Mummy needs you. You have to help Mummy.*

The emotions of the dream ripple through her: the shock, the confusion, the strangeness of being somewhere so familiar that has gone. But they pass over her in an instant and vanish. Caz says slowly, 'I only wanted to do what was best for Kate.'

'Of course.' Rory rubs his face and looks over at her wearily. 'You've always been there for her.'

'I thought she was out of it – disconnected – because of the pills. She just wasn't with us, was she? Not at the funeral, or the inquest. It was like she was focused somewhere else, on something we didn't know about or couldn't see. In another place.'

'Yes,' Rory says thoughtfully. 'She seemed to be afraid of being . . . persecuted. I don't know if that's the right word. She seemed to think we were all out to get her.'

'Paranoid?'

'Yes. But not like someone with schizophrenia or anything. She was too businesslike for that. It was honestly as though she was exasperated that people expected her to be anything other than normal, after what happened. She just seemed untouched by it, but afraid that our assumptions that she must be suffering were going to force her into something she didn't want.' Rory shakes his head. 'I don't know. It was like a cold disconnection.'

'So determined,' Caz says.

Rory smiles sadly. 'So like Kate. She always knew exactly what she wanted, and she made things happen. It's how she copes with things.'

'I thought I *was* helping her. But . . . maybe I wasn't.' Caz stares at the table. 'When she went away.'

He looks over at her, frowning. 'What do you mean?' Then he goes very still. 'What do you mean, Caz? Is there something you want to tell me?'

She looks up. 'She was so commanding. I didn't know how to say no to anything – not considering what she had been through. She promised me that this was her way to get better.

289

It wouldn't be for long. All she needed was a little time. So . . . so I said I would help her.'

'Okay . . . When? When was this?'

'I suppose it started about a month before she left. She had to make arrangements, you see, because she was determined that she wouldn't be found. So she had to plan it.' She starts fiddling with her fingers, nervous and guilty. She feels simultaneously disloyal to both of them – to Rory for not speaking earlier, and to Kate, for telling him when she swore she wouldn't.

He stares at Caz, astonished. 'You've known all this time? You haven't told me?'

'I promised I wouldn't.'

He slams his palm down on the table and she jumps violently. 'For God's sake, Caz! You must have known she wasn't in her right mind, that she wasn't capable of making a rational decision! She was using you, manipulating you to do what she wanted. Christ knows what she was thinking.' Then his expression changes from furious to pleading. 'How could you see me suffering like this and not help?'

'I was just trying to do the right thing, for both of you,' she whispers. 'But Kate was so . . . so implacable. She would have done it whether I helped her or not.'

'What did she get you to do?'

'She wanted to use my address as hers, in order to get a credit card that wasn't connected with her.'

'So . . .' He frowns. 'In a fake name?'

Caz nods.

'What's the name?'

'She didn't say.'

'And she didn't tell you where she was going?'

Caz shakes her head. 'No. She was very careful about that. She mentioned a company. That was the only thing. She said "The company's expecting me . . ." or something like that. But she was very careful with what she said.'

Rory stares at the table, tapping the top with his fingertips. 'Do you think she was planning to go abroad?'

'I have no idea. But I don't think so. Because . . .' Something floats into her mind, a throwaway remark which she can't quite recall. 'I got the impression that she was driving somewhere. And the ringtone isn't foreign either.'

She's spoken without thinking, and it's only when Rory's face changes that she realises what she's said. His look of concentration is replaced by one of astonishment and then of hard anger.

'What? The ringtone? The fucking ringtone, Caz?' His voice is climbing the register, as what she's said sinks in. 'You mean you've spoken to her?'

Caz is mortified. Of course she planned to tell him everything, she just hadn't got there quite yet. She stammers out, 'W-well, I . . . I . . .'

He gets to his feet. 'How the hell could you? How could you do this behind my back, knowing what I've been going through?' He stops and looks at her with a terrible disappointment. 'I had no idea you could do something like this.'

'Please, Rory.' She gets up as well, her hands out to placate him. 'I'm telling you now! Don't you understand? Kate made me promise. She swore she was all right, that she was doing the right thing. I believed her.'

'You wanted to believe her. We both know she's far from all right! I've been in her house, I've looked on her computer and in her email. There's a load of stuff quite obviously designed to be blind alleys. She booked tickets to Spain and to France and never showed up for any of them. But there's nothing else to tell me what she might actually have planned.' He stops, puts his palms on the table and leans forward to stare hard at her. The look in his eyes makes her want to back away. 'So, what do you know?'

She starts to talk, faltering at first, and then it comes pouring out. That Kate has an email account – not one with a name like jane doe at hotmail, but just a few numbers and letters – and that Caz can contact her through that. She tells him that she has a mobile number, and that she's spoken to Kate three times on it since she left.

'Oh my God,' Rory says, running his hands through his hair again. 'You've got a number for her.' He shakes his head. 'You better hope the police don't find out what you've been withholding from them. They've been putting out enquiries all over the country. They could have just phoned her up!'

'It's not that simple,' Caz protests. 'And I told her . . . I told her she was doing the wrong thing, that it wasn't right to let the police look for her, or to let you worry. She wouldn't listen! You can't blame me for this, Rory. I can't change it, I've tried! And when I mentioned Ady, she just hung up on me! I haven't heard from her since.'

'Have you tried to reach her?' he asks, in a low, intense

voice. Caz is sure he knows in his heart that she's right and that there was nothing she could have done to change Kate's mind, but he needs a focus for his frustration and anger. And she has lied to him.

Or is it in the same way he lied to Kate? Not so much outright deception as by omission. I haven't told untruths, but I've also volunteered nothing. Rory, of all people, ought to know how easy it is to do that.

Caz says, 'Yes. I've tried to reach her. But it all went quiet over a week ago.' She leans back in her seat, exhausted from it all. She's been worrying about it so much, and she's tired of it.

Rory sighs, and looks as defeated as Caz feels. 'Then we're back where we started,' he says. 'She could have dumped that phone and that email account.' He shakes his head. 'Why were there no records on her computer?'

'She was very careful,' Caz says quietly. 'She used internet cafes and libraries, so she couldn't be traced.'

Rory slumps in his chair. 'What's the point? She doesn't want to be found. Look at how hard she's tried to get away. Maybe we should just let her go.'

Caz leans towards him, suddenly intense. 'We can't give up,' she says firmly. She's not about to tell Rory of her dream. It would be a cruelty to bring his dead daughter into all of this. But she can use what it gave her to sort out this horrible mess. 'We're going to find her. Let's start right away.' She pulls her mobile phone towards her. 'I'll text her first. We'll keep going until she replies. She'll have to, in the end.'

Rory looks at her miserably. 'What if we're too late? What if she's already dead? That's probably what she was planning.'

'I'm not sure about that. She didn't sound suicidal. Until we have evidence, we assume she's alive and that we can find her. Someone has to have seen her. Someone knows where she is. Come on. We can do this. For you and her, and Ady.'

'Okay.' Rory musters a smile, trying to look confident. 'What have we got to lose?'

Chapter Twenty-Four

Arthur barely speaks to Letty during the day, and maintains his exterior of a bored and sulky young man, the Arthur she knew before their marriage. He slopes about, occasionally disappearing for one of his walks, or reading wherever he can find somewhere private without too many women flocking about. He is treated with a kind of remote respect by the ladies, but the Angels do not like him at all. They evidently suspect his motives.

'He's walking about the village,' Kitty tells Letty when she is overseeing the organisation of the linen cupboard. Sometimes, Letty feels like she's running a good-sized hotel, with the amount of household work that needs doing: fifteen bedrooms to be changed and cleaned; the endless replenishment of the generous larder, and the planning and ordering of meals; the maintenance of the house and grounds. Arabella is content to leave it to Letty to manage. She is more queenly than ever, growing into her place at the Beloved's side. And Sarah, that calm and serene presence, has been moved further away: two more places down at the table, the row behind in the church. Arabella seems to wish the distance to be widened, as though eventually everyone might forget that Sarah was ever anything other than one of many middle-aged ladies devoted to the welfare of the Beloved and keen to hang on his every word. Sarah appears to be suffering, though no one knows if it is a result of her treatment. She is increasingly unwell, grey-faced, tired and in pain. She is spending many hours alone in her small bedroom, tended by the Angels.

'Arthur walks about the village?' Letty asks carelessly. She points at the upper shelf. 'Single sheets only on there, Kitty, please. I suppose he's entitled. After all, no one is forbidden from leaving. It is a matter of choice to be here.'

'But once you're in, you're in,' Kitty replies, pressing a mound of fresh white sheets onto the upper shelf. 'I don't think he is in. And you know what's going on in the village.'

Letty remembers Enid and her outlandish accusations. *She said they're all saying it.* 'You mean the gossip about us?'

Kitty nods. 'It's not healthy. I don't go there myself at all anymore. The other girls say it's not pleasant doing the shopping down there right now.'

'Well,' says Letty crisply, 'if they don't want our custom, I'm perfectly content to use other tradesmen, and take deliveries from further afield. We put a lot of business their way, don't we? I don't see what life here has to do with them.'

'You know what people are like,' Kitty answers, patting down a pile of pillowcases. 'They like to be shocked. They'd be disappointed if they could see us as we really are.' She grins and leans over to Letty and murmurs, 'I expect they think we do the housework in the altogether.'

Letty gasps and then laughs. 'Kitty . . . stop it. Well, if Arthur is going down to the village, perhaps he can help counter the rumours. They might listen to him.'

'Have you had any luck with him?' Kitty enquires. 'Is he hearing the word?'

Letty sighs. 'I don't think so, not yet. But at least we're a little more friendly than we were. He wants to leave by the end of the summer, so if he goes then, I'll have failed.'

Kitty shakes her head. 'He is a mighty challenge. You'll have to fight the Devil hard for that one, his grip is so firm on his heart.'

Letty knows it's true, and yet she has found herself looking forward more and more to the evenings, when she retires to the blue bedroom and Arthur joins her there. He always gives her time to go up alone, use the dressing room and change so that she is safely in bed when he comes in. He seems to understand that this gives her the security she needs. He preserves his own modesty, always changing in the dressing room and insisting on sleeping on the chaise longue at the end of the bed. But from their separate posts, they have long conversations, and sometimes, in order to hear him better, she turns around and wiggles down to the end of the bed. There she makes him out dimly in the darkness – the shadow of his profile, the glimmer of his eyes – and hears him speak in a low voice, punctuated by throaty laughs when he says something that amuses him. The darkness seems to liberate them in a way that is not possible in the daytime. Sometimes, when they are downstairs in the dining room and she glances at him, stiff and silent beside her, she finds it hard to believe that their nocturnal conversations actually happen. But then, darkness comes and he is back, and their whispered confidences begin again.

He tells her about his life: a boyhood in Buckinghamshire and then a move to London with his father's work. As the family prosperity increased, so did the expectations of his achievement. He is the only child, the sole focus of all ambitions. He was sent to Harrow and from there to Oxford – 'where I had the best fun in the world. Only I suppose it had to come to an end, it was all going so fast. It couldn't be maintained.' He thinks for a moment. 'I've got through all this by pretending I'm on a curious kind of rest cure. Like being sent into a sanatorium for a seaside convalescence.'

Letty listens to his tales of Oxford with fascination. She's never heard of such a wicked, dissolute life. It makes her feel so very provincial and innocent when she hears of gambling clubs and dancing, and girls and motorcars and huge amounts of food and drink and money.

'The old man wanted it that way,' Arthur says carelessly into the darkness. 'He gave me a decent allowance so that I could keep up with the smart set. He wanted more than anything for me to have position in society, perhaps marry an earl's daughter or something. Money can get you that, sometimes, if you're clever and not too pushy. But when it came down to it, he didn't like it. I told him what they all got up to, all the nobs he was so desperate for me to make friends with, and he couldn't believe it. Dissolute, he thought. Immoral. He doesn't understand high jinks, or the fact that it's a rite of passage. We'll all be respectable when we settle down and get married. What he couldn't stomach was the idea that half the boys were sissies and the other half were sleeping with other men's wives or actresses.'

Letty is shocked but says nothing, just stays still in the darkness.

'It didn't help that he fell into religion. Not the good old C of E, that's harmless enough. All this fire and brimstone stuff. Doom. End of the world is nigh. All of that.'

'You mean, the Beloved's teaching,' Letty says softly. There's a pause and then she says with a tone of gentle accusation, 'You don't believe it.'

'Not a word. Not a bloody word.' Arthur laughs. 'There's always been someone who says the Day of Judgement is due tomorrow at twelve, let's all get our sackcloth and ashes out as they'll be needed directly. Christ's disciples thought they were living in the final days, almost two thousand years ago. And here we are still, and no sign yet of anything ever happening. Why? Because it's not going to.'

Letty trembles in the presence of such blasphemy. She reminds herself that she is being tested. She has to stay firm in the face of Arthur's heresy, because that is the way the Devil is trying to find her weakness. It would be easier if he weren't so confident and so sure of himself. She can't think how she is going to begin to break down the walls of his unbelief so that the Beloved's truth and goodness can pour in.

'But my father and mother have fallen for it, hook, line and sinker.' Arthur whistles out through his teeth. 'Just my luck they should find a rascal like Phillips, ready to fleece them of my inheritance.'

Letty frowns. She can't stand to hear the Beloved talked of in this way. It causes almost physical pain. But she has to listen if she's to understand the way that Arthur thinks. 'Is that so? Would they disinherit you?'

'The slightest hint that I'm not playing ball and my father is perfectly capable of cutting me out and signing the lot over to this place. In fact, he probably can't wait to. Thinks it might buy him a cushy berth in heaven, I expect. Even cushier than here.' He pauses. 'I imagine your family were none too pleased when your sister decided to make the house over to him, were they?'

'Well . . . our parents are dead. We don't have much in the way of family. But my sister, Cecily, was the most upset at what Arabella did. She hasn't been able to forgive it. This was her home until then, you see.'

'Yes. That must have been trying,' Arthur says slowly. 'And you? What did you make of it?'

'Me?' Letty is surprised. No one has ever asked her opinion about it. 'Well, it made no difference what I thought.'

'That may be true, but you could still have a view on it, couldn't you? What did you think about your sister giving this house and the estate and everything to a strange man? Spending her money on building churches and putting up a gaggle of old men and women like this?'

Letty says, 'It's not like that. It sounds so simple and stupid, the way you describe things. But they aren't simple at all, they're very complicated, and what sounds stupid is not. The

Beloved is inspired by the Divine – but that doesn't make his message easy to hear.'

'I don't know how you put up with it,' Arthur mutters. 'I'd have lost patience with it at once. And as for this marriage he made us go through . . . you've never once said it was an outrage to have it sprung on you, or an insult to your dignity. Which it is.'

'Because it was the will,' Letty says gently. 'It is part of the plan. I must obey and accept.'

He says nothing for a moment, and she knows he's lying still, staring into the darkness, but she senses that pity again, the same that she's seen in his eyes once or twice before.

'Tell me,' he says suddenly, turning towards her in the gloom. 'That vision you claimed to have – about your sister marrying Phillips. Did you really have it? Lily fields of heaven and all the rest of it?'

'Oh,' she says. A repulsive feeling curls in her stomach. It's the shame of her complicity in the Beloved's lie. 'Oh . . . that.'

'Yes. That. You were very convincing. I liked watching you, standing up there, your cheeks all flushed, declaiming what you'd seen. But I didn't entirely believe you . . . and I didn't entirely believe that *he* had nothing to do it. Phillips. It was all too convenient for him. The rascal.'

'Don't call him that. He's the Beloved.'

'I'd rather rip my own tongue out than call him that,' declares Arthur. 'The man should be ashamed of himself, dubbing himself that way. It's not manly.'

Letty thinks of the Beloved, striding about, tall and masculine, showing his fine figure to them all, while Arthur is hardly more than a boy. *Of course the Beloved is manly. He's the ideal of manliness. He's what everyone aspires to.*

It occurs to her that she doesn't know many men. It floats across her mind that, compared to the gardener, groom, odd-job boy, the relics from the Army of the Redeemed and the ancient reverends, the Beloved could hardly look anything other than impressive. She subdues the thought at once.

'So,' he persists, 'you did have those visions?'

Letty is silent. Lying is anathema to her. But she's tried so hard to do what the Beloved wanted that she's come to believe that she did see something. 'In a way,' she says at last. 'I came to see what the will wanted.'

'You poor scrap,' he says suddenly, his voice sad. 'You're a good girl, aren't you? You didn't ask for any of this. And now you're as deep in as any of them.' He sighs into the darkness. 'I thought it was going to be hard enough getting myself out of all this. Now I can see it's going to be even trickier than I thought.'

Letty is aware that she has begun to think of Arthur all day long. Where once he was a shadowy presence around the place, one that she barely registered, now any room that does not contain him seems empty and lacking in life. When she sees him, he seems brighter and more alive than anything else in the house, and the sight of him fills her with bubbles of pleasure, lifting her mood and making her walk more lightly. Her tasks seem more manageable and life has been given a kind of sparkle she hasn't known before. At the same time, she has begun to feel strangely awkward around him. When she sits next to him at mealtimes, she can barely lift her eyes to him, and her fingers tremble when she inadvertently touches him.

When he says solemnly, 'Can you please pass me the salt, wife?' she knows, as she would never have known before, that he is teasing her, but the words send tiny jolts of excitement over her skin.

Occasionally she feels the eyes of the Beloved on her at these times, and more than once she has looked up to see him watching her appraisingly, and she senses that he is observing Arthur as well.

What does he want? What is the will?

Each night, Arthur tells her a little more of himself and he asks about her as well. He asks to know about her childhood here at the house and what she wants for herself.

'Don't you hope to see more of the world than this place?' he asks.

'I suppose I did. I had plans to study once. I thought of nursing, or teaching. But that's all changed since the Beloved came here.'

'Why should it change?' Arthur asks impatiently. 'You're not his vassal!'

'Because the world is here now,' she says simply. 'And what is the point of studying or work if the Day of Judgement is at hand? That's why we're here. We'll be ready when the day comes. It is imminent. The Beloved says so.'

Arthur is silent.

'I wish you would believe,' she says softly. 'I would like you to be saved.'

'I would like you to be saved too. I suppose we have different ideas about what that means.'

She is touched by his words, her heart swelling with pleasure at the thought that he wishes her well. But how they are ever to reconcile what they believe, she does not know.

At least he is here now, she thinks. *He's safe with me. He must not leave.*

Arabella does not come down for breakfast and stays in her room all day. She says she is perfectly all right but that she has a headache. The next day, she is absent again and Letty goes up to see her, concerned for her health. When she lets herself into the bedroom, quietly so as not to disturb her sister, the bed is empty, its sheets rumpled and the counterpane thrown aside. From the dressing room comes the sound of retching. Letty hurries over and sees Arabella bent over the sink, being violently sick.

'Arabella!' She rushes over to pull back her sister's hair and put a comforting arm around her shoulders. 'You're ill. I must call a doctor.'

'No. No.' Arabella spits into the basin and straightens up wearily. 'Don't. There's no point.'

'What do you mean? You're obviously unwell. How long have you been like this?'

'I've been nauseous for a couple of weeks but since yesterday, I've felt truly ill for most of the day.'

'Most of the day?' Letty is wide-eyed with concern. 'Come on, let's get you back to bed. What on earth can it be? You've barely eaten for the last two days, you can't be poisoned by anything, can you?'

Arabella says nothing but lets Letty help her back into bed and tuck her up.

'Please allow me to call the doctor,' Letty begs, when Arabella seems to be comfortable again.

'No! No! Not yet. I don't want anyone knowing yet,' she says.

'Knowing what? That you're ill?'

Arabella shoots her a look that is simultaneously scornful and defiant. 'No, you goose. Can't you see what's in front of you? I'm ill because I'm going to have a child. It's the sickness that comes in early pregnancy. It will go after a time. I hope.'

Letty stares as she absorbs this. 'A . . . a child? Are you sure?'

'I think I know the signs. And I have them all.'

'But how can you be expecting?'

'Don't be so stupid. How do you think? I have a husband, don't I?'

Letty doesn't know what to say. She can see the fear in Arabella's eyes, behind the snappish irritation. Letty is thinking what they will all think: how can this be, after everything the Beloved has said? He has been adamant that the community's marriages are untainted by the flesh. Children are a sin. But all that must be . . . has to be . . . can it be . . . *a lie*?

Arabella blanches and groans. She jumps out of bed to run for the dressing room again. When she has finished heaving up bile, Letty holding her hair clear, she sighs and says, 'The

Devil can win sometimes, Letty. The fight is a violent one –
and sometimes he wins.'

Letty doesn't tell Arthur what she has discovered, and he
doesn't seem to notice that she's quieter than before when
they are together at night. Instead, he talks of his friends at
Oxford and their adventures, something he likes to dwell on,
partly because he enjoys her shocked reaction, she thinks. But
also he seems to be reminding himself of that other life, the
one that still awaits him if only he can break free of this place.
She is so quiet that he thinks she has gone to sleep and soon
he is also quiet and she hears the regular sounds of his breathing.

She lies awake, thinking of what this might mean, and how
the community will receive the news when it becomes obvious
that Arabella is expecting. It can hardly be hidden from them.

She feels a tremor of something unpleasant and utterly
undesired. It is, she realises, doubt – nasty, creeping, sickening
doubt. With it would come the destruction of all the safety
and certainty that underpins their world. She does her best to
suppress it.

It is a Friday evening service, the most exciting of the week.
While Sundays are solemn, Fridays have a more festive air,
filled with a sense of joy and something like hedonism. Arabella manages to get there; she tells Letty that the sickness
goes away towards the evening, but the experience of the day
is so horribly draining, she is still good for very little. But
Sarah does not attend. Kitty says that she is sicker than ever,

confined to her room with a painful complaint, something to do with her kidneys.

Letty sits with Arthur during services now. His parents are usually just behind them, watching anxiously to see if Arthur is yet exhibiting any signs of faith. Arthur seems unusually docile during the services. He sings the hymns in his tuneful voice and listens to the sermon. While he doesn't say 'Amen!' or 'Praise be!' with the others, he doesn't dissent either. There are no grunts of scorn or whispered comments. Letty is glad of it. She is still shaken inside, and the sight of Arabella, so obviously pregnant now that Letty knows and yet no more than off colour to everyone else, reminds her of the creeping serpent of doubt that is writhing inside her.

I want to believe so badly, she thinks, fervent. *I have to.*

Everything is built on the Beloved's words and on the belief he has engendered in them. There would be no one here, no church at all, if it weren't for that. As it is, there are new members of the congregation now. There are more men and women, called to hear the word, desperate to be saved, attracted by life in the community where there is comfort and plenty and a promise of safety until the end of the world and beyond. Tonight the church is packed.

The Beloved is in fine fettle. Since his marriage to Arabella, he has been filled with a new strength. The ladies talk with awe of his spiritual gifts and the awakening of a new depth of passion and conviction within him. He certainly seems more magnificently physical than ever, clearly glorying in the charisma of his own presence.

Tonight, he lets rip upon the congregation, declaiming

loudly about the wickedness in the world and the divine inspiration vouchsafed to him that means he can see clearly who is wheat and who is chaff. 'We await the great moment of retribution!' he thunders. 'I can see into your hearts! I can see who will be saved and who will not. I can see those who burn in torment for eternity! To be saved you must *believe. Believe!'*

The congregation is full of sighs and tremors as the Beloved begins to walk among them, fixing them in turn with his burning blue gaze and pressing his hand to their chests as if to feel the heart beating within. Sometimes he shouts, 'You, sister, are saved!' or 'Brother, you shall see salvation!' and sometimes he says nothing and then hisses, 'Believe!'

Even Arthur is unable to take his eyes off the spectacle as the Beloved, in billowing shirtsleeves and black trousers, marches around, causing women to scream as he pronounces them saved, or howl if he does not. Then he puts his hand to the heaving chest of Emily Payne, a humble girl, one of the younger Angels, come to join her older sister in the community. She is not more than seventeen, with big blue eyes and a sweet face, with large buck teeth that mar her prettiness. The Beloved stares furiously into her face. 'Believe!' he roars. 'Sister Emily, believe!'

'I do believe!' she yells, and to everybody's amazement, she falls to the floor and begins rolling wildly about, frothing at the mouth and crying, 'I believe, I'm saved!'

Moments later, several others are doing the same. The atmosphere is intense, dramatic, and wild. Letty is carried away by it all, sure that she is witnessing divine transports.

Arthur grabs her by the arm, his expression half amused, half appalled.

'By God,' he whispers through the racket, 'it's like something you'd see at the asylum.'

'Believe, Arthur!' cries Letty ecstatically.

'They believe,' he says, looking around at the writhing women and dumbstruck men. 'They believe only too well.'

Letty ignores him. She has forgotten all her doubts. *I believe.*

The next morning, when Letty comes in for breakfast, the atmosphere is sombre but no one will say why. Arabella is absent again. Arthur frowns as he cuts his bread, but he doesn't seem to know any more than Letty does. The Beloved is not there either, and Letty hears a whisper that there have been official visitors to the house.

'What is it, Kitty?' Letty asks, as she passes her in the corridor. 'What's going on?'

Kitty is grim-faced. 'It's Emily Payne. It seems she left the service last night, and drowned herself in the lake.'

Letty gasps. 'What? How awful! Why would she do such a thing?' She recalls Emily's ecstasy of the night before, her sure and certain belief that she was saved.

'Perhaps she couldn't wait for paradise,' Kitty says soberly. 'The policeman is here. The coroner's been sent for. Poor Emily.'

'Amen. Rest her soul,' whispers Letty.

Then she goes upstairs to her room and sits down on the bed. To her astonishment, the door bursts open and Arthur comes in, red-faced. *He never comes here in the daytime!* But he marches over and takes her hands.

'Letty,' he says urgently. 'I've just heard the news. Enough is enough. This has to stop. It was amusing enough to start with, but real people will be hurt. They have been hurt! That poor girl has drowned herself because of that man.'

'What?' She only half hears him, she is so astounded by the fact of her hands in his and the way that touch is making her feel.

'Don't you see it, Letty? He's so busy preaching hellfire and damnation, he's sending them mad. She killed herself, the deluded fool! He has to be stopped. I can't stand by any longer, and nor should you.'

'But . . .' She looks up at him helplessly. 'She must have been possessed to do such a thing. The Beloved never wished it for her!'

'Of course not. He needs them alive, not dead.'

'She must have been a sinner,' Letty says, sounding firmer. That was surely the only explanation. The Beloved has banished death. If death came, it must be as a punishment.

Arthur sits beside her on the bed, still holding her hands. His nearness is confusing her, making her feel odd. 'Letty,' he says gently, 'I shouldn't care what happens to you. You're so completely enmeshed in all this. But I do. I want to free you.'

'I am free,' she says fiercely. 'Freer than you, with your gambling and girlfriends! I want to free *you*!'

They stare at one another angrily, then he bursts out laughing.

'I never in my life thought something so ridiculous could

happen.' Then he is grave again. 'But that poor woman's death is not ridiculous, and if he goes on like this, it will happen to others. Something must be done.'

She feels that gnawing sense of doubt deep inside her again. She knows that Emily should not be dead, Arthur is right about that. Perhaps . . . perhaps the Beloved is not as in control as he promised. And if he is not, then what can be relied upon? 'What can we do?' she asks.

Arthur tightens his hold around her hand, his grey eyes grave.

How did I ever think he was a boy? Everything in her responds to him.

'I don't know,' he says at last. 'But I have an idea. All I want you to do is to be ready.'

The Beloved summons them all to the church, where Maud plays sombre tunes. He speaks to them for long hours, so long that it is hard to remember exactly what he has said. All that Letty knows is that the Devil claimed Emily Payne as his own, and that the rest of them must be firmer and stronger as a result. The Beloved will soon reveal the truth to them all. The other thing she knows is that Arthur is not there, but she has no idea where he might have gone. She misses him far more than she'd ever imagined she could.

PART FOUR

Chapter Twenty-Five

One day I wake and some of the darkness has lifted. I am not better, whatever that means, but I don't seem to be in the depths that have contained me for . . . I'm not sure how long. Some days, at least. Perhaps weeks. But I don't feel like my old self either. I'm someone else.

In the bedroom, I see that Heather's things have been taken off my bed. They are propped on a chair nearby. There is no Sparkleknee, or Teddington. Those two beloved toys were burnt. There is only the stuffed puffin I found in the box Caz brought over. Heather's little suitcase is closed. Grief thuds through me. It is like a steamroller, and there is no hope that it will ever leave me. But perhaps I might learn to exist with it.

That is the thing that I never thought I could do. It was unendurable. Unsupportable. I couldn't bear it. I decided that I wouldn't bear it. The one thing I hoped – that I could have been in that bedroom with Heather when it was finally engulfed, instead of fighting the wall of furnace-hot smoke outside – was not possible. So I created another reality and I stepped inside that one instead. It was easier to live there.

I sigh heavily. The pulling away of my created reality has left me raw and exposed to the truth about my life. I'm not strong enough to deal with it yet. Words are whispering through my mind – *Home . . . you have to go home . . . remember? . . .* But I can't listen. Not yet. Maybe one day. Maybe soon.

There is a knock on the door and a woman comes in. She is young, maybe early twenties, with brown hair pulled back and brown eyes behind a pair of glasses. 'Oh, hi, you're awake,' she says, smiling. 'I'm on breakfast duty today. Hungry?' She lifts up the tray she's carrying and shows it to me.

'Not really.' I sit up, shifting myself up against the pillows.

'I suppose that's not surprising. You've not eaten much lately. Your stomach has probably shrunk. Have some coffee at least.' She places the tray on my knees and sits down herself on the bedside. 'If you can, you could try and eat some toast. It's got marmalade on it. Yum yum.'

I smile back at her, though not through amusement. I'm touched by her solicitude, and I get the feeling she knows me better than I know her. She looks at me with interest as I sip the coffee.

'You seem different,' she remarks. 'Something's changed.'

'Yes.' I nod. 'I guess I'm a bit more like my old self. I'm sorry. I can't remember your name.'

'Dora.' She pats her own chest, smiling again. 'It means "gift". Archer's funny. I always said he thought he was God's gift, so he called me Dora. Theadora, actually. It's shortened to Dora. Of course, it turns out he is actually God's gift, so the joke's on me.'

I smile at her in bewilderment. I have no idea what she's talking about. 'How long have I been ill?'

'It's been just over a week. You've been in a bad place. I don't know what's happened to you but the Beloved says it's not good.'

'The Beloved?' I ask, remembering I've heard that before somewhere.

'Yeah, sorry, I mean Archer. We also call him the Beloved. I know it sounds weird, but it all makes sense really. You'll understand if you stay here. He's been healing you, hasn't he?'

I suddenly remember the channelling of a bright warmth from the hands of a man, how it entered my skin and soaked downwards into my core. 'Yes . . . I suppose so. He must have.'

Dora nods. 'He's amazing at that. It still gets me every time. I am just in so much awe.' She reaches out and puts a hand on my leg, smiling broadly. 'We're lucky, aren't we, Rachel? To be born at a time like this?'

Rachel? My name is . . . it's . . . Kate. That's right.

Fragments of recollection are falling into my mind. *Wait . . . I've been Rachel Capshaw for the last month or so. I left Kate behind.*

For a moment I'm filled with pleasure at the idea of escaping the pain of my previous life. And then I remember, with a dull sensation of fatalism, that it isn't possible.

I tried. I tried my best. I did everything I could. I failed.

317

'Drink up, Rachel, and I'll take the tray away. But you have to promise me you'll have some soup at lunchtime. You've lost so much weight. You need to start rebuilding your strength.' Dora smiles at me. 'Do you have any diagnosis for your recent ill health?'

I shake my head. 'No. Nothing. Just depression, I suppose.'

'Yeah. I saw your pills in the bathroom. Heavy-duty. You've been suffering.' She looks sympathetic. 'Archer told me you lost your daughter. I'm so sorry.'

'Thanks. ' I don't want to talk about it with her. 'Where are the pills now?'

'Archer took them and flushed them away. He doesn't believe in that shit. He knew he could heal you without them.'

'Oh. I see.'

'You're in the best place now, Rachel. Honestly. You'll be your old self, and more. You've been brought here for a reason.' She smiles again and gets up to go, taking the tray and its cold toast with her, leaving me the cup of coffee. As she goes out, I hear the whisper of a powerful voice in my mind: *You can be with us now, Rachel. You've been brought to the right place. It's the will of the Lamb that you should be protected at the end of days. It's not long now. I promise you that bliss is at hand.*

I feel a rush of that golden warmth in my stomach, and an echo of some lovely feeling I once knew, before everything beautiful in the world died. And for a second, I get the sensation of something like hope.

*

During the morning, I practise getting out of bed and walking around the room. I feel weak and shaky at first, and climb gratefully back into bed. I sleep again, and wake to find Sophia at my bedside, with a bowl of steaming soup on a tray.

'Hi,' she says in her well-educated drawl. 'So lovely to see you awake again. You had us all quite worried for a bit there. I've got some munchies for you, and you're under strict instructions to have it *all*. No arguments.'

I don't want to argue with her. I can hardly take my eyes off her, she's so beautiful. Her long gold hair spills over her shoulders and she has perfectly smooth tanned skin like something from a make-up advert. I knew she was good-looking before, but now she seems almost supernaturally lovely. I must have been shut in a darkened room for far too long.

Sophia leaves me the soup and I manage to eat it, nearly all of it. With it comes a new burst of energy and I get out of bed and walk around the room, now with more strength. Emboldened, I head out of the bedroom for the bathroom next door, glad that I won't have to rely on helpers to get me there anymore. I have shadowy recollections of being brought here with someone supporting me under each arm, lowering me gently down onto the lavatory and taking me off again.

How humiliating. At the very least I've got to be able to take care of that again on my own.

It all goes well until I'm out in the corridor once more on my way back to my room, when the energy that's sustained me there vanishes, and I'm left leaning against the wall, breathing hard and trying to fight the dizziness that threatens to overwhelm me.

'Hey, hey!' It's Agnes, hurrying down the corridor towards me. 'Are you okay?' The next moment her arms are around me and she's lifting me up. She's surprisingly strong and as she helps me stagger towards my bedroom, she talks to me, her Australian accent sounding friendly for the first time since I met her. 'You don't want to push yourself. Archer says you're just recovering, you're still really weak. I'm going to tell him he needs to do another session with you.'

'What does he do?' I ask, still breathless, as she guides me to the bed and sits me down. 'What's it called?'

'I don't know if it has a name. I guess it's a combination of disciplines. There's some reiki in there. Here, down we go . . . now, is that better? It's something Archer's created on his own. He's like that. He does everything in his own way. He's a leader, not a follower. A pioneer. That's kind of how he describes himself to us – a captain of a ship going out into the unknown. Except that he seems to know quite a lot.' She grins at me. I've never seen Agnes looking so cheerful. 'Now, how are you?'

'Better, thanks.'

'That's good. Those old sisters have been round wanting to see you. Archer said no. He doesn't like outsiders coming in. Especially not now we're filling up.'

'Filling up?'

Agnes nods. 'Yeah. We've been busy while you've been recovering from . . . getting better.' She flushes lightly and rushes on. 'People have been coming from our other houses to start preparing this one. I think Archer wants it to be his headquarters. There are a lot more faces here now, so don't be surprised if you hear a bit of a racket from time to time. There's work going on all over the place.'

'Really? Are you all guardians?' I ask, surprised.

'Kind of.' Agnes smiles.

'And the company doesn't mind if you do work to the house?'

'Not a bit.' She laughs now, quite merrily. Her mood has vastly improved since I first saw her. 'They approve. Guaranteed. Now, shall I take that soup bowl away?'

In the afternoon, I sleep again. I don't know why I'm so tired but I feel as if I've been hit by a truck. Or as though I've been running some kind of enormous marathon, pushing myself on and on to finish until, suddenly, I've collapsed, with no more energy in me, no reserves to draw on.

The dull thumping of grief still marches in time with my heartbeat. I feel a terrible sense of guilt, that I've let Heather down twice. First, by not being able to reach her that night. And then by bringing her here and losing her again.

It was so real. She was so real. She was alive again. I know she was.

But now her presence has completely disappeared. She's gone. The things I brought with me, that I watched her play with, are just detritus of a life that's vanished.

I'm sorry, my darling. I thought I could make it work.

And yet, I feel a vague sense of triumph too. For those precious days, she was with me. She did live again. I had the chance to read to her, play with her, do all the things I loved so much. She was able to restore something in me, and give me the strength to face the truth – that she was gone.

But there's something else.

A dark knowledge throbs away in the depths of my mind. Something I don't want to see or know about. It's best if I keep looking forward, and not downwards into the abyss. I will think about Heather and saying farewell to her. I won't go to where something terrible still seethes and moves.

Healing is what I need.

Agnes is as good as her word, and as the sun is turning white-gold with the approaching evening, Archer comes to my room. He puts Heather's toys carefully on the floor and pulls the chair over so he can sit close to my bed and look me straight in the eye.

I'm surrounded by ravishing young people, I think. The girls are all gorgeous and now here is Archer, a young Adonis, as casually, ripplingly attractive as a lion. His thick brown hair falls in waves to his shoulders and the beard does nothing to distract from his well-formed mouth and those magnetic ice-blue eyes. He's wearing a sort of grey tracksuit, with white trainers. It ought to look awful but of course he looks effortlessly stylish. He's brought me a cup of steaming liquid: clear and pale green.

'So, Rachel, how are you?' He's got the same patrician tones as Sophia, and the core-deep self-confidence of someone who knows that they matter in the world.

'I'm . . . okay. I'm a bit better.'

'Great, that's good news. I've got some herbal tea for you.' He hands me the cup. It smells fragrant and grassy. 'It will soothe you. Drink it.' He watches while I take a sip. 'That's right. It'll start to work soon. You've had quite a trauma, haven't you?'

I nod. His voice is so kind and understanding, I feel a sudden rush of tears, but I gulp them back, and say thickly, 'Yes, that's right.'

'I want to help you.'

'You have helped me.'

'The healing?'

I nod again, and take another drink of the tea. He's right. It is soothing.

He smiles, his mouth curving up like a pirate's. 'Good. That's good to hear. Would you like me to heal you some more?'

'Yes. Yes please.'

'Okay.' He stands up. 'Lie back and relax. Actually this will work better if you take off your top.'

I flinch slightly.

'Do you mind about that? Sorry, I didn't think. We're very relaxed about nudity here. You'll see a lot of it about. It's our natural state, and we don't judge each other. I mean, clothes are cool too. But so is our skin. We need light just like plants do. You know that, don't you, Rachel? So if you're bothered, you could just lie on your front and I can work on your back.'

'Okay,' I say, a little muffled. I have no idea what I'll look like after a week in bed, but I know it won't be tanned and smooth and delectable like the girls upstairs. But I don't want to seem like a prude. I put down my tea, take a deep breath and pull off my T-shirt, revealing my pale chest and stomach beneath, then turn quickly over so that he can only see my back.

'Well done. That was brave. All right. Close your eyes and relax.'

He comes very close to me. I can feel the warmth of his body close to mine, and then the heat of his hands just centimetres above the bare skin of my back. He leaves them there for a long time and I can feel the heat radiating out, spreading over my skin, until it is almost as though his palms are burning me without touching my flesh.

He begins to speak, his voice low and hypnotic. 'That's so good, Rachel. You're responding beautifully. You're sucking up my healing, I can feel you drawing it out of me. My life force is entering you, going deep inside you and making you better. Can you feel that, Rachel?'

I make a sound of assent, but I can hardly speak, I'm so focused on what I can feel. The heat is spreading through me, oozing over me like honey, running down the backs of my legs and warming my heels and the soles of my feet, up and over my scalp, releasing the taut muscles around my neck and shoulders, relaxing the knots in my belly, easing everything out. It's a beautiful feeling. Now he's moving his hands, still not making contact with me, but taking that glorious warmth all over me. It's burning its way into my core and bringing my body back to life in prickling, uncomfortable and yet pleasant ways.

He starts to speak again, his tone still mellifluous. 'I'm

blessing you, Rachel. I'm filling you with the bliss of my presence and giving you the sure and certain knowledge that
you're on the path to paradise. Come with us, Rachel. Join
us. You can have our love, you can share in our love.' There's
a pause and he says softly, 'Turn over, Rachel.'

I have no sense of embarrassment now. I turn over, my eyes
still shut, exposing myself to him, not caring, just wanting
more of that healing warmth. Now his hands hover over my
belly, heating it up. I feel myself opening out like a flower
in the sunshine, turning towards the light like a sunflower
following the path of the sun with its face.

'You are coming towards us now, aren't you? You're ready
to accept us. We can offer you what you need. We can offer
you peace and contentment and healing.'

His words are like a soft, soothing balm on sunburnt skin.
I want so much to have the things he says he can give me.

'I will tell you,' he says in that murmuringly mesmeric
voice of his, 'how you can reach it.'

The next day I leave my room. Someone has been in while
I've been asleep and laid out some clothes for me: baggy
white linen trousers and a white T-shirt, and a pair of slip-on
white leather sandals. I put them on and then, because it's still
cold outside, I pull on a jumper over the top, rather spoiling
the all-white palette with its red and pink stripes. Then I head
back out into the house, feeling as though I've been away a
very long time.

Agnes is right, there is more noise. I think back to the
silence here when I first arrived. The atmosphere is completely

different. There's a buzz of energy about the place, and a kind of irrepressible good mood. I can hear music coming down the stairs, from a radio or a sound system, and every now and then a cheery voice calls and is answered by another. There are men here now – I can hear the deeper tones of male voices, even loud singing in a booming bass voice. Everywhere there seems to be activity. I catch glimpses of people busy in rooms, carrying things, fixing things, the banging of hammers and the whirr of drills. In the hall, I see a scaffold tower set up inside, against the windows. They're high and many-paned. A young man at the top of the scaffold is drilling what look like shutters into place, while another works at the bottom. They are not beautiful wooden shutters but heavy steel. They look thick.

The man at the bottom of the scaffold looks round and sees me. He grins. He's another youthfully good-looking boy with a supremely fit body, tanned and muscly, as they all seem to be. *Is it a requirement of being here?* I wonder. *All this physical beauty? And if it is, how the hell did they let me in?*

'You must be Rachel!' he calls in an American accent. 'Hi! Good to meet you.'

'That's right.' I go forward to him, smiling shyly. The man on the top level of the scaffold is still whirring away with his drill. Then it stops and he lifts up a pair of goggles and turns to look down at the sound of our voices. 'What's your name?'

'I'm Rocky.' He gestures upwards. 'Up there – that's Fisher.'

Fisher, swarthy and stubbled, looks down through the planks of the scaffold and grunts a greeting. He looks back at the shutter as if keen to return to work but he holds off as long as I am there.

'What are you doing?' I ask.

'Fixing up a bit of internal support,' Rocky says, smiling at me.

'It's rather industrial, isn't it?' I frown. 'Are you allowed to do that? I mean, I would have assumed this place is protected . . . listed . . . whatever it's called.'

Rocky shrugs. 'I dunno. I have no idea. We just do as we're told. You'd have to ask Archer about that.'

'What do you need great thick shutters like that for?' I go closer to the scaffold, curious.

'They're going on all the windows. And we've got Linus – he's a real tech expert. He's designed it so that they can be controlled from inside with the touch of a button. One sense of danger and pow, down come the shutters. The doors will be reinforced too. In about ten seconds, you have yourself a safe house.'

'Oh. Right. I see. Why do you need one of those?'

Rocky laughs as though I've just cracked a really good joke. 'Yeah, sure . . . I'd better get on now, if you'll excuse me, but very nice to make your acquaintance. See you round.'

Fisher is already pulling down his goggles, ready to drill again. A second later the whining cut of the drill fills the hall and sparks fly around the top of the window.

I go towards the small sitting room that was my refuge when I was here alone. Opening the door, I find a group of women sitting around the table, each with a computer open in front of her. Another couple sit on the sofa, which has been covered with a blue woollen blanket, and they seem to be sewing something large and intricate. All of them turn to look at me, their chatter stopping at once.

'Hi,' says one, getting up. 'You are . . . ?'

'I'm Rachel,' I say, intimidated. They all seem so confident and sure of themselves, sitting here in the room I considered my own not so long ago. 'Archer . . . knows me.'

'The sick old woman,' one whispers under her breath to her neighbour.

'Okay,' says the woman, standing. She looks Chinese but her accent is pure, well-bred English. She's wearing tight white jeans and an equally tight white T-shirt with 'Genius' written across it. 'Yeah. He did talk about you. Didn't he, girls?'

They all nod and chime in with their agreement.

'We hope you're feeling better,' says another, a friendly, round-faced girl with pink cheeks and a mass of messy fair hair gathered up in a hairband.

'Yes, thanks, I am.' I look around at them. 'What are you all doing?'

'Chores,' says one from the sofa, putting down her needle and making a face. 'My finger really hurts. I'm going to have to stop for a bit.'

'We've all got work to do,' says the Chinese girl reprovingly.

'Yeah, but you guys are on your computers. I'm fucking sewing!'

'That's enough, Kaia.'

'Sorry,' says Kaia. 'But I'd challenge anyone not to go out of their mind doing embroidery.'

'I like it,' murmurs the girl next to her, still sewing away in red silk, her tiny exquisite stitches making up the petal of a rose.

'What are you sewing?' I ask pleasantly. 'It looks very pretty.'

'An altar cloth,' replies Kaia, shaking it out so I can see the intricate pattern they are creating. In the centre is a white lamb, its front hoof raised, a blazing crown on its head. It stands in a field of beautiful flowers, and angels hover over it. There must be hours of painstaking work in it.

The Chinese girl is watching me intently as I examine it. Then she says, 'Will you excuse us? We really have to get back to work.'

'Yes, of course. I'll be on my way.' I smile at Kaia, who seems very friendly. 'When do you hope to have it finished?'

'Oh, it's nearly done. It'll be ready for the ceremony on Friday. Are you coming to that?'

'Kaia,' says the other woman, warningly.

'I don't know,' I reply. 'Maybe. We'll see what Archer says.'

'Maybe see you there. If not before.' Kaia starts threading her needle with more silk, green this time.

'See you later, Rachel,' the Chinese girl says and I can hear the note of dismissal in her voice.

'Yes. See you later.'

Chapter Twenty-Six

'Arthur! Where have you been?'

Letty sits up in bed, all worries about wrapping the sheets around her to preserve her modesty long since gone. Instead she's been driven frantic with worry about Arthur, whom she has not seen all day. He was not at lunch, or at dinner, but his empty place was not remarked upon. Everyone was still taken up with the shock and unpleasantness of Emily's death. There is a rumour that she left a note but no one has seen it. Letty went up to bed, miserable.

I shouldn't care so much. At least, not until his soul is saved.

But she can't help it. She's grown to need his presence. Without it, the house is lustreless.

Now, at last, here he is, panting and still in his outdoor things. 'I went for a walk,' he says, striding in, smiling.

'Did you? All day?'

'Yes,' he says, 'a very long walk. A horribly long one. And now I'm ravenous and dinner is over. What shall I do?'

'I suppose one of the Angels might bring something,' Letty

says doubtfully. The Angels do a wonderful job of ministering to them all, but they don't like any inference that they are no more than servants or waiting staff.

'No. Let's go down and see what we can scavenge.'

Letty cannot stay cross for long, she is so delighted to have him back. His eyes sparkle and he is full of life and vitality. She is like a vampire now, needing his youth and freshness to invigorate her. The desiccated ladies around her are drying her out. As they go downstairs, he takes her hand and they skip down together, laughing.

'Why are you in such a good mood?' she asks. 'Have you been to a party?'

At once her smile falls as she's struck by the thought that he's been off meeting some of his university friends. He's had time to take the train somewhere and then come back. Perhaps he's been drinking, dancing with beautiful girls with tight dresses and loose morals. The thought fills her with violent jealousy.

'No,' he says, not noticing her change in mood. 'Not a party, I'm afraid. It's been so long since I've been at one of those that I've forgotten what they're like. I say, why don't we go up to London one day? I'll take you to the Savoy and we'll drink cocktails and watch the world go by.'

'Yes, perhaps!' she says brightly, feeling better. Could it happen? The Beloved would not permit it, but there's no harm in pretending just for a moment. Is there? She knows that the Beloved's grip upon her is loosening as her need for Arthur grows. Does that make her a fool?

I won't think about it. I only want to be with Arthur.

She leads him to the kitchens, which are now in darkness except for the fire glowing in the range that sends a red flickering light over the slate floor. The evening work has been done and the place restored to order.

'Let's see what we can find,' Arthur says, going to the larder and switching on the light. 'Ah, a meat pie. How delicious, and just the thing. Whatever you might say about this place, the grub is first rate. And there's some bread and butter too. Why, it's a veritable feast.'

He brings out plates balanced precariously on one another, and puts them on the scrubbed pine table. He sits down and starts to eat hungrily. Letty goes to find him some wine and brings a glass for him, then sits down to join him.

'I've decided to be very positive about all of this,' Arthur says, munching on the meat pie. 'I'm going to turn it to my advantage. When it's all over – and it will be – I'm going to write a book about my experiences here. It might be a novel or it might be non-fiction, I haven't decided yet. Anyway, it will cause a sensation and make me a fortune and a celebrated author. This has cheered me up no end.'

'I can tell,' Letty says, laughing.

He looks over at her mischievously. 'You do believe me, don't you?'

'Well, yes . . . in a way.'

'In a way?'

'I believe you want to,' she says, admiring the way that the firelight is gilding his cheekbones and his hair and making his grey eyes almost honey-gold. 'I believe that if things were different, then you could.'

'If things were different?'

She can't let it all go, just like that, no matter what Arthur might want. It is still her truth. She says slowly, 'If it weren't for the fact that it won't be long before we move beyond this world, and into the next.'

His smile fades a little and he turns back to his meal for a moment. Then he takes a gulp of his wine and says heartily, 'My dear little missionary, I'm always forgetting that we are diametrically opposed to one another. It's a sad thing, but there it is. I'm amazed that you can go on with your very touching and absolute faith in someone who says one thing, and right in front of you does another.'

'What do you mean?'

'Spiritual marriages! Denying the flesh! Repudiating this, that and the other! All the while, raking in other people's riches, driving them mad with threats of hellfire, and bedding whoever he wants.'

Letty gasps in horror. 'What do you mean?'

Arthur leans forward and says in a low voice, 'Emily Payne didn't drown herself because she was possessed by the Devil. She did it because when Phillips wasn't enjoying your sister's bed, he was in hers. And she won't be the only one. I've seen his kind. He's a practised seducer, unable to resist the temptations of the pretty girls around him. He'll be worse with the servants, mark my words. There's nothing like a nubile laundress to get a man like him hot for the chase.'

Letty puts her hands over her ears. 'No! It's not true. I won't hear it.'

'You may not hear it, but you'll have to see it with your

333

own eyes soon.' Arthur takes another bite of his pie, a vicious one this time. 'Come on, we both know perfectly well you can hear me. You'll have to admit it when your sister actually gives birth to the old fraud's child.'

She is dumbfounded. How did he guess? Arabella isn't showing yet, and her sickness is subsiding. She is able to attend meals, though she still looks grey and tired.

He can read her thoughts on her face. 'So you know already? Well, you're not the only one. Rumours, my dear child. Rumours. How do you think I found out about Emily Payne? The old rogue isn't the only one who can charm laundresses. So you see, my darling wife, soon you'll have to admit to yourself that your hero isn't so pure after all.'

The jokiness between them is gone, though Arthur still seems happy enough as they go upstairs together. He takes his place on the chaise longue and is soon fast asleep, while Letty stares unhappily into the darkness. It feels as though, with Emily's death, something has shifted. She has grown to believe what the Beloved has said, week after week, in his raging sermons: that death has been banished, and that here, at the house, they will not know suffering. And yet, here is death. Here is the prospect of a child. It seems that the same mortal cycle goes on, whatever the Beloved says.

That serpent of doubt uncoils within her and begins to hiss its message in her ear.

Until now she has been able to put the picture of the Beloved in bed with Arabella out of her mind, though she knows deep down that he has been unable to resist the fleshly temptations of a carnal marriage. She closed her mind to the truth. But after what Arthur told her about Emily Payne, she cannot shift images from her brain.

These, she is sure, come from some diseased part of her: a place owned by evil. What else would conjure up the lewd pictures of the Beloved arranging meetings with the younger Angels, in quiet places where they won't be disturbed, for the saving of their souls – a process that requires the swift unbuttoning of their white blouses, the lifting of their white skirts, the Beloved's strong brown hands rifling in their drawers, a pushing back against the wall while he takes his pleasure . . .

No! Stop it! It sickens her. The hot excitement that sometimes roils through her when she thinks of it appals and disgusts her even more. One night she is tormented by a dream when, instead of an Angel, hands wet from the mangle and hair askew, it is she, Letty, that the Beloved desires. He finds her in the church, and presses her down on the altar, kissing her with hot, fierce kisses as she resists, trying to tell him to stop but muffled by the force of his lips. Then she realises that it is not the Beloved after all, but Arthur, and she is flooded with happiness, surrendering to it with pleasure . . . only to wake breathless and ashamed, with the sound of Arthur's breathing filling the dark room.

After that, she can hardly look the Beloved in the eye, and finds it easier if she avoids him. That magnetic presence and the great force of will that once drew her to him now repels her, reminding her that it brings with it other qualities: selfish desire and a need to control all around him.

Kitty finds her in the sewing room, with its pretty Chinese wallpaper and view of the garden, mending some stockings. 'The Beloved wants to see you. In the library.'

'Ouch . . . Bother, I've pricked my finger. Never mind, it's nothing.' She sucks off the blob of scarlet blood on her fingertip, then says, 'Very well. I'll go at once.'

Flutters of apprehension whirl in her stomach, but she makes an effort to suppress them and appear normal. *Well, I am normal. Nothing has changed.*

Nothing outwardly, anyway.

But the Beloved has a way of knowing. Suddenly, with certainty, she knows that this is his secret: his intuition, and ability to read the minds of those in his thrall. He can sense the slightest hint of dissent in a glance. He must have a reason to want to see her. And that must be . . .

He knows.

The Beloved sits behind his huge desk, as imposing and impressive as ever, with piles of books in front of him. 'Ah, Letty. Here you are.' He stands up, turning the full force of his smile upon her. 'Bless you, child. It's good to see you.'

'Thank you, Beloved.'

'Please sit down.' When they are facing each other over the red leather top of the desk, he says, 'It feels as though I haven't seen you for a long time, not alone at any rate. But I've perceived lately that you're troubled. I want to help you. Tell me your worries.'

'I'm not troubled,' she says, and smiles.

'Now, come, come, I can sense that you are.' He fixes her with the piercing blue gaze that makes her feel as though he can read every thought in her head. 'Is it because of . . . Emily?'

She looks down at her hands. 'Well . . . yes. Of course I'm saddened. I don't understand what happened to her, why she did it.'

'The Devil wins many battles, even here, in this holy place. I myself do constant battle and I do not always succeed in conquering. If I can fail, how much more can others fail?' He leans across the desk towards her. 'Are you failing, Letty? Is that what is making you unhappy? Is the evil one triumphing over you, despite your prayers?'

She blushes. He knows what she's been thinking, how she's been imagining him, and how she's been feeling about Arthur. She lifts her eyes to him. 'Yes,' she whispers.

'As I thought.' The Beloved sits back with a satisfied smile. 'You have been unable to resist the temptations of the flesh. Your husband has persuaded you to fulfil his desire, hasn't he? He's not one of us, not yet. And you've been unable to force him to pray the lust out, haven't you?' His eyes glitter.

'No, not at all!' Letty says indignantly. 'We are pure!'

He stares at her, eyebrows lifted in surprise. 'You are?'

'Yes, Beloved, I swear it. We have remained chaste, as you commanded.'

'Well . . . that is good, Letty. That is very good.' The Beloved stands up and paces behind his desk, thinking. Then he stops and turns to look at her suddenly. 'But pure in heart, Letty? Do your thoughts and desires remain clean?'

She opens her mouth to insist that they do, then looks away in awkward embarrassment.

'Of course they don't.' The Beloved comes around the desk and crosses to her, kneeling beside her and grasping her hands. Letty is astonished to find him in such a supplicatory position in front of her, and cannot look into his burning gaze. 'You are not alone, my child. I myself am subject to thoughts and desires and sometimes I am impure. I confess it, and I repent and I am still saved. You may do the same. If Arthur's carnal needs demand satisfaction and you must obey despite your desire to remain a spiritual bride, then you may surrender in the full and certain knowledge of forgiveness. I will forgive you, my child, and that is the same as the Lamb forgiving you, is it not? The plan is mysterious. Sometimes we must appear to do evil, if we are to do good.'

Letty is confused. 'You mean . . . I should give myself to Arthur?'

'I believe it may be a way to save his soul. To keep him among us and bind him to us. That's what you want, isn't it?'

Letty nods. Her hands are burning where the Beloved is still clutching them. 'I see.' Her heart falls within her with disappointment. No, something stronger than that. Disillusion.

The Beloved seems to sense it. He peers even more closely at her. 'Is your faith still strong, my child? Are you still of my flock?'

'Yes, of course, Beloved,' she says obediently.

He does not seem convinced. But he lets go of her hands and stands up. 'Then go on your way. I will pray for you. Come to me whenever you waver and I will give you strength.'

*

That night in the church, the Beloved does not deliver his usual fierce sermon, with its shouts and frenzy. Instead, when the time comes for him to address his congregation, he gives a signal and the lights are dimmed so that the candles on the altar provide the only illumination: tongues of flickering golden fire behind the Beloved. The atmosphere is intense and expectant. The Beloved disappears and when he returns, he is dressed entirely in white: a long robe that falls snowily to the floor. He spreads his arms and turns his face upwards. He begins to speak in a low but thrilling voice and they all listen intently.

'The time has come to reveal the next step in the plan, the manifestation of the will. We must listen and accept it. What I say to you now comes from that great power. It flows through me. Yea, it is me. I know that you are weak, that you falter on the path. That is why I tell you now the great revelation, so that you will understand what we are bound to here, why you are the elect. I am He. You know of whom I speak! I am He, come again in my own body to save. Behold! I live forever more! And I am the holy bridegroom, and the great judge, and every one of you will be judged by me. And you find me here, among you. You are truly the blessed, the new disciples. Come to me if you wish to know truth and know glory and have everlasting life!'

Letty gasps and the whole congregation quivers but no one speaks after this great declaration. The Beloved stands, his arms outspread, his head drooped on his breast, unmoving.

Then one of the ladies gets to her feet and says in a shakily joyful voice, 'It is true! I see it, the glorious day has dawned. He is here.'

Another stands. It is Mr Kendall, his face alight. 'Hail!' he shouts. 'Hail to thee!' Then he drops to his knees and begins to pray loudly.

More of them stand, declaring their belief and faith. Letty can only stare. Each one of them present has heard, and must now make a choice – to turn back or go on. She knows what she has heard, and finally, at last, she can fool herself no more. She turns to Arthur, whose eyes are shining with triumph. His hand reaches for hers.

'It's time,' he says to her, his voice more intense than she's ever heard it. 'Can you do it?'

She can't speak, only nod. The serpent of doubt has unwound and disappeared. Now she is certain.

'At last,' he says. 'We can blow this place wide open.'

Chapter Twenty-Seven

'Any luck?'

Caz shakes her head. 'No. Nothing. I've sent six texts today. I've emailed. No reply.'

Rory sits back on the sofa and sighs heavily. 'Oh God. We're wasting our time.' He looks over with blank, defeated eyes. 'I think she's dead, Caz.'

'Hey.' Caz goes over and sits on the arm of the sofa, her phone in her hand. 'Don't say that. There's absolutely no evidence that she's dead. Someone would have seen her, they'd know something. It's not that easy to kill yourself with no one knowing.' She rubs his shoulder comfortingly. 'I think we should assume she's out there somewhere. She took her pills with her. Why would someone suicidal do that? She was just adamant she needed some time. I think she's turned off her phone and her computer, and she doesn't even know I've been in touch.'

'I want to believe that,' he says. 'But even if it's true, it doesn't help. It doesn't bring us any closer to finding her.'

'I think we can find out more,' Caz says. 'We have her email address. We should hack it.'

'How are we going to do that?' Rory shrugs. 'Caz, I really think we should take all this to the police. They're the ones with the systems to sort this out. They'll help us find her.'

'We can try that,' Caz says, 'but think about how hard it was to get them interested in the first place.'

Rory has told her how reluctant the police were to start a hunt for Kate. Grown women are at liberty to go off in their cars whether their separated husbands like it or not. It was only when Rory managed to get the local press interested – 'Tragic local woman in fire death hell vanishes' – that the police issued a formal request for information on Kate's whereabouts through the media. There was a brief flurry of human interest – the pictures of Heather they put alongside Kate's were enough to touch the hardest heart – as the press speculated about whether she was suicidal but then the story faded quickly away from sight.

'But now we have this new information,' Rory says, frowning. 'Surely they'll listen to that.'

'It will only make them more likely to think that she's perfectly safe,' Caz says. She believes it but she's also aware that the police might not look kindly on her concealing what she knew when they went public with Kate's disappearance. 'Don't you see? They'll be even less interested if they think she's busy phoning and emailing. They'll never see our point of view.'

'You're probably right,' says Rory despairingly. 'There's nothing we can do.'

'Don't give up, Rory. I know someone who might be able to help.'

Lucas looks at Caz coldly. 'Just because I'm in tech does not mean I'm a hacker for hire. I'm not one of these wikileaks types. I happen to respect privacy. And the law.'

'I know that, and I wouldn't usually ask. But this is an emergency.' Lucas has always been her friend in the IT department, happy to come and fix whatever problem afflicts her work computer. She feels as though she can trust him. She outlines some of Kate's story. It would take a heart of stone not to be moved by it, and she can see that Lucas is as horrified as you'd expect. 'She's ill now, Lucas, suffering from depression and on her own. She doesn't even know that her little boy has woken up. Can you imagine that?'

He lets out a long breath. 'Jeez. That's pretty bloody awful.' His expression is grave. 'I've got a daughter. She's four. If anything happened to her . . .' He shakes his head, unable to go on. They sit in contemplative silence for a moment, offering thanks to the universe that so far they've been spared that horror.

'So what do you want me to do?' he asks.

'I've got an email address. I just want you to break into it so we can see what's there. It might give us some clue about how to find her.'

'It's not that simple, I'm afraid. I'll need more than an email address. Any ideas about a password?'

Caz shakes her head. 'If I did, I wouldn't need you.'

'Well, you might.' He sighs again. 'It would be easier if she were going on the internet and accessing the account herself.'

'I don't think she is. Unless she's purposefully ignoring my messages. I have a mobile number too; is there any chance we can find her with that?'

Lucas shakes his head. 'You'd need official clearance to get that data. Look, without being able to access her computer, or the network she's using, it's going to be pretty near impossible to hack into her email in the way you imagine. But . . . there is something we can do. It relies on her picking up her texts, and on her security settings.'

'I don't think she's doing that.'

Lucas shrugs. 'Caz, it's illegal to hack someone's email. I'm prepared to help you, though, bearing in mind what you've told me. I'll set a simple trap and you can sit back and wait. If it springs, well and good. If not, that's as far as I'm prepared to go.'

'Okay,' she says helplessly. 'Let's do it.'

Lucas opens up the email provider for Kate's account and taps in her email address. 'Right, we're pretending that we're Kate, and we've forgotten our password.' He clicks on the link for a forgotten password. It asks for verification using a mobile phone number. He types in the number Caz has written down for him and pushes send. 'There.'

'What good will that do?' she asks, confused. 'It's going to send a message to Kate's mobile, isn't it?'

'Yep. So now we send her a message as well, pretending to be her email provider. We'll say that there's been unusual activity on her account and that she needs to send her verification code to us.'

'And if she does?'

'Then we'll have access to her account. We can reset the password, then go in, change the settings to forward emails to another address, then send the reset password to Kate as a temporary password. She can change that if she likes. Unless she suspects it's not the provider or she checks her settings, you'll carry on receiving all the messages she gets and sends.'

'Clever. But how will we text her? She knows my number.'

'Okay. We'll use mine. If she texts me, I'll send it on to you immediately. I'll show you how to change settings now. After that, you're on your own. All right?'

'Thanks, Lucas. I really owe you one. And so does Kate's family.'

Rory is on compassionate leave from work, now that Ady has woken up and Kate has disappeared.

'I get a new job and spend most of the time away from it. Thank goodness they're understanding.'

'That's what charities are like, aren't they?' asks Caz. 'Understanding?'

Rory nods ruefully. 'Sometimes. When they're not making you redundant.'

She tells Rory what Lucas did for them.

'That's it?' he says, disbelieving. 'He didn't hack straight in?'

'He couldn't. And anyway, it's not fair to ask him to do something illegal. He agreed to set this trap for us and it's pretty much fraud. But it all depends on whether Kate falls for it or not.'

Rory sighs helplessly. 'Great. That might never happen. And meanwhile, I'm spending all day with Ady telling him that she's going to be back soon.' His face contorts with pain.

Caz puts her hand onto his over the kitchen table. 'Are you okay?'

'Yes . . . no. I had to tell him today. About Heather.'

'Oh God.' She squeezes his hand, gripped by sorrow for them both. 'How did he take it?'

'He just looked me in the eye and said he already knew.'

'How?'

'He guessed, I suppose.'

'Poor boy. Poor thing.'

'He seemed very calm about it. Weirdly calm. I mean . . . sad, of course. But accepting. I don't think it will sink in for a while.' Rory frowns. 'The strange thing is how confident he seemed about Kate as well. When I said she'd be back soon, he nodded and said yes, he knew that too. Then he said . . . he said, "You and Aunty Caz are going to get her, aren't you?"'

Caz stares at him. 'That's strange. Have you mentioned me to him?'

'No. Well, I said you might visit him and bring Leia and Mika when they're back from their dad's, and the hospital said it was okay. But that's all.'

She smiles. 'It's a good omen. Maybe we will bring her back.'

'Check your phone,' he says, and they bend over it together. There's nothing from Lucas.

'Give it time,' she says comfortingly. 'We'll get Kate home where she belongs. Keep the faith.'

'I'll try.'

Caz's boss looks pained. 'You know how it is, Caz. We like at least two months' notice of any holiday booked.'

'I know. And I wouldn't usually ask. But these are exceptional circumstances.' She explains, and once again Kate's history has that strange talismanic power. People are fascinated by it, attracted and repelled at the same time. They want to know and yet, it's too much to take in. They can't make themselves empathise too closely, or they'd be on the floor, sobbing, in bits. Each time she tells it, she understands Kate and what she's done just a little more. If you don't realise how vile and cruel reality can be, you can't comprehend the mechanisms our spirits can use to cope. She'd thought she was in unbearable agony when Phil left. But she can see now that it was nothing, not really. The best things in her life went on: the children, her health, her job. She lost someone who wasn't really worth keeping, that was all.

The thing that she doesn't understand is why Kate has cut Ady out of her life. Surely he was the only thing that could bring her back, bring her joy after losing Heather. Yet, she won't even hear his name.

Caz secretly believes that if Kate laid eyes on Ady, she would come back to her old self and break out of the tough armoured shell she's created for herself. She thinks Rory believes this too. But for Ady's sake, it has to happen soon. It's that urgency that has pressed Caz to ask for time off, and that gave her the strength to ring Phil up last night and ask him if he would keep the girls for longer.

'You don't want them back?' he said, disbelieving.

'Of course I want them back – but I have something I have to do. I'm helping Kate and Rory.'

'Oh. Yeah.' He sounded guilty. He should, considering they had all been friends for years, and although he had sent a card and a bunch of flowers, he didn't go to Heather's funeral. He said he wouldn't come without his girlfriend, and he didn't think it would be appropriate. Caz thinks he was right. The day was terrible enough without that. 'How are they?'

'Not so good,' she said briefly. He didn't really have the right to know more than that. He hasn't even rung Rory. 'So can you keep the girls for the next week? I'll drop their uniform off and everything they'll need for school. Leia knows when their ballet lessons are.'

There was a pause and she knew Phil was considering saying no. Maybe he had a couple of nights out planned, and the girls would get in the way. White-hot rage rose up inside her, but then, to his small credit, he agreed.

Her boss pulls open the staff holiday calendar. 'It's not easy because Steph's off already.'

'Annabel can cover. She's volunteered.'

'Well . . .' He hates breaking the rules. Give one an inch, he thinks, and they'll all expect a mile. But he knows Caz's request is as close to compassionate as you can get without actually fulfilling the criteria. 'Okay. I'll allow it this time. But don't spread it around, will you?'

'No. Of course not. Thanks.'

'I hope you find her.' He gives her an encouraging smile. 'You're a good friend, Caz.'

Caz thinks about that in the car on the way home. Is she a good friend? Really?

Outwardly, yes. But when Kate found out about Rory's hidden redundancy, Caz couldn't help seeing it from Rory's point of view. Yes, he'd omitted to tell Kate some very important things, and he was wrong in that. But it was plain that he wasn't acting out of selfishness, like Phil had. He wasn't being maliciously destructive, the way Phil must have known he was. He was, after all, being protective. He just didn't realise how much it would rock his marriage when it did all come out at last. He was wilfully blind, and stupidly naive and, yes, in the wrong. But it wasn't straightforward.

Kate wanted Caz to rip him to shreds with her.

And I couldn't. I was torn between pity for them both and envy of Kate's emotional security because, in the end, it wasn't a matter of whether or not Rory loved her. It was just how he showed it.

They both looked at it through different sides of the lens. The lie was the worst thing to Kate. To Rory, it was the shame of losing his job and the stress of finding a new one, and managing to keep afloat financially, that nearly clawed him under.

'He won't say he's sorry,' Kate said tearfully. 'Where's the remorse? I can't forgive him till he says he's sorry.'

'Perhaps he doesn't understand that,' Caz suggested. 'Maybe he's being practical. Trying to show he's sorry by solving the problem.'

'He should understand it! It should be obvious. How can I ever trust him or feel secure in our life together if he doesn't understand that?'

Caz did her best to talk the talk, but her heart was divided from Kate's for the first time. She thought Kate was lucky. She daydreamed about a life where she had a man who treasured the humdrum companionship of family life, who didn't need to look beyond it for excitement.

But now the positions are reversed, and Caz is the lucky one. She would not wish herself in Kate's position for anything.

I owe it to her to find her and bring her home to Ady. She's my friend. I don't have a choice. But before that can happen, Kate has to answer the text.

Chapter Twenty-Eight

Arthur disappears after the great church service, with everyone still stunned by the Beloved's revelation. They knew that he was part of the great dispensation to mankind, the next in line after Adam, Noah, Abraham and Christ. But to be not just the preparer of the way, but the way itself is unexpected, and overwhelming.

Life has offered all members of the community a great boon: to be born at the same time as the Beloved, and to know him. Like those Galilean fishermen of centuries ago, they are now called to bear witness, and it is the most exciting thing ever to happen.

Letty watches the jubilation, the way they all crowd around the Beloved, eager for his touch, and she feels apart from it all. Arabella, shocked but apparently happy, moves among them, accepting the congratulations with a remote air, as if it is on the news of her husband's promotion to a more senior position in his office, rather than that she is married to the Divine.

The congregation are in a buzzing state of anticipation, for

351

now it seems certain that the Day of Judgement cannot be far off. It looks as though their devotion to the Beloved and his promises is about to be repaid.

Letty leaves them and goes to the house to look for Arthur but she cannot find him anywhere. Checking the cloakroom, she finds his heavy greatcoat gone, and comes out into the hall disconsolate.

'I want him here,' she says out loud. She wants to talk to him about what he said in the church and what he meant to do. How can the place be blown wide open, and what will it mean for them all? Letty is not sure she wants that to happen, even with her faith in the Beloved melting away. But it seems she is too late and he's gone off to do whatever it is he means to do. The house is empty, with everyone still at the church, and she wanders about the hall, wondering what it will be like when they come back. Almost without thinking, she goes to the library door and opens it. This used to be her father's domain and now it is the Beloved's, his private study entered only at his invitation.

Why is it his? she thinks. *What did he do to deserve it? It's only his because Arabella gave it to him. And she only gave it to him because he worked his spell on her, like he does on all of them.*

The words that Arthur uses about him float through her mind: charlatan, fraud, rogue and rascal. She sees it suddenly as Arthur painted it for her – the way everything the Beloved wanted fell into his lap because of the way he manipulates people.

She walks over to the desk and looks at the papers on the

top. There are half-written letters, others received from lawyers and bankers to do with the running of the house and the estate. Then she sees, beneath a jade paperweight, a small scrap of paper folded up and tucked there. She lifts it out and opens it. It's written in frantic handwriting:

I know I'm too wicked to be allowed to live. He said if I believed, I'd be saved, but I can't believe. I want to, but I can't because if it is all true as he says, then why does he do such things to me, such as he says the Devil wants? He says I make him do it with my original sin and my tempting ways and because the Devil is in me. I'm sorry, I'm too wicked to live.

Letty stares and reads it again, twice, three times. *Oh Emily. I didn't want to believe it.* She feels agonised with pity for the poor girl. *Why did he torment her by telling her it was all her fault?* She recalls him beating on the girl's chest and Emily falling to the floor in a fit. *As though he was trying to cast out a demon. Poor child, she must have thought she was possessed.* A thought occurs to her. *But the Beloved has read this. He knows.* Perhaps this is why he decided that now was the time to make the greatest claim of all, to keep his flock close. To distract them from asking him awkward questions. No doubt more than one other has seen this note. Someone found it and brought it to the Beloved. No wonder he is asserting his power.

I don't believe it can go on. Surely they must see what he's really like?

But where is Arthur? What is he doing? If only he'd waited, they could have found this note together, and used it to show the Beloved for what he really is.

'Letty! What are you doing in here?'

Letty looks up swiftly to see Arabella in the doorway, watching her in horror. She says quickly, 'Arabella. We have to talk about the Beloved.'

'Should I tell him you are nosing among his private papers?' Arabella advances, her expression sternly outraged. 'What on earth can you be thinking?'

Letty holds out the scrap of paper to her sister. 'You have to see this, Arabella. It's a note from Emily Payne, explaining why she jumped into the lake. It isn't what we thought. He's fooling us all. He's not the new Moses or the next dispensation, or the . . . one we are expecting to come back.' She can't bring herself to say it. There has been too much blasphemy in this house already and she's ashamed of it. 'He's been . . . having his way with the girls here, the same as he has with you. He told me to sleep with Arthur too! Just to keep him here.'

'I expect you relished that little instruction, didn't you, dear sister?' Arabella says with spite, ignoring the other accusations. 'We've all seen the way you look at him. You're quite enraptured, aren't you? I don't expect you quibble too much with the Beloved's decision on that matter. I wouldn't be surprised if you haven't been bounding about with him since the very first night.'

'Arabella!' Letty stares at her in horror. 'How can you say such a thing?'

'It's clear that wicked young man has dripped his poison into your ear. You were supposed to save him, you fool! But no. You're too weak willed for that, aren't you? You've allowed yourself to be made an agent of darkness instead. You two are clearly in cahoots. Well, it won't last much longer. I'm going to put a stop to it.' Arabella's dark eyes flash dangerously. 'And the Beloved agrees with me. It's time Mr and Mrs Kendall know what kind of serpent they've bred. And he'll lose the inheritance he's so eager to get his hands on. They'll disown him in a second, now that the Beloved has made known the truth.'

'The truth? Do you . . . do you believe it, Arabella?' Now that the scales have fallen from her own eyes, it is hard to believe that anyone could be so wilfully blind as to find any of it credible. The Beloved has banished death? He has forbidden carnal relations? Then why is Emily dead? Why is Sarah ill upstairs? And why is there a child kindling inside Arabella?

'Of course I believe!' cries Arabella. She throws her arms wide. 'I have been chosen! I am the favoured bride. I am the womb.'

Letty's mouth drops open. She never believed Arabella insane, not when Cecily and Edward had her bundled off to the asylum and not when she came so triumphantly back. But now, staring into her sister's wild eyes, she wonders if perhaps it is the answer, the reason why Arabella fell so thoroughly into her belief in the first place. And all that the Beloved has said and done has played directly into her madness. It must make perfect sense to her; it always did. And now that the Beloved has taken the ultimate masculine role for himself, it falls to her to fulfil the ultimate female one. The queen of heaven.

'Arabella, please.' She holds out the note. 'Read this. You'll understand then, you'll see the truth.'

Arabella snatches the note and tears it into tiny pieces, throwing them up and scattering them around. 'That's what I think of your forgery. No doubt you and Arthur cooked it up between you. Though you ought to be ashamed of what you're doing to poor Emily's memory!'

Letty watches the torn paper fall with dismay. The evidence she wanted to give Arthur has gone. Now there is only her testimony. 'You know that's a lie,' she says firmly.

'It's your word against mine and against the Beloved's. And now, you little troublemaker, now that you've gone to the Devil, you shall have to be contained until we've decided what to do with you!' Arabella goes to her sister and grabs her around the arms. 'Help, someone! Help me!'

'Let me go!' shouts Letty, struggling, but Arabella is too strong to shake off, even with the residue of her tiredness. 'Let me go!'

'Help me!' yells Arabella, and in a moment, the door opens and three Angels rush in, one of them Kitty, then stop, astonished to see the sisters struggling together. 'Well, don't just stand there! I caught her spying on the Beloved. She's plotting with that Kendall boy for his downfall. Help me take her!'

The Angels hesitate only for a second, then join Arabella in restraining Letty. Kitty holds Letty's arms with sadness in her eyes.

'Now come, miss. It's for your own good. It won't be for long, just until you come to your senses.'

They bundle her up and take her upstairs to the blue bedroom, where she is dumped on the bed and locked in, the key taken away.

Letty manages to sleep during the night, in between fits of trembling outrage and fear. The speed with which the tables have been turned against her is startling. Will the Beloved allow this treatment of her? But once he is told that she took Emily Payne's note from his desk, he will no doubt concur with Arabella that she has turned against the community. What will they do with her? Will she be locked up, as Arabella once was, and the world told she has lost her reason?

At other times, she worries about Arthur and where on earth he might be. There is no doubt that he is under suspicion; Arabella confirmed that the Beloved has given up on his attempts to win him over. Arthur will be banished, that's inevitable. The rumour that they are in cahoots will no doubt spread quickly. She finds it strange that gossip about the Beloved's behaviour changes nothing, but one word from Arabella and she is accepted as a traitor.

But will Arthur be able to help me?

She doesn't see how. Their marriage has no legal standing. He has no rights over her. She sees suddenly that she is powerless, at the mercy of her sister and the Beloved, and whatever they decide to do with her.

The next day dawns bright and warm. Letty has slept in her clothes and feels uncomfortable so she washes in the dressing room, putting on a plain brown skirt, blouse and jumper and sensible laced shoes.

One of the Angels, not Kitty, brings in a tray of breakfast for her – a typically hearty meal even though she is in disgrace – and leaves her to eat it. The Angel's injured air and refusal to meet her eye reveals the extent of the feeling against Letty downstairs. She can hear frantic activity going on all around her. Carpets are beaten outside, and there is the clank of a bucket and the splash of dirty water being thrown away.

They are cleaning. Then she laughs out loud. *They are cleaning for the last days! They're expecting heavenly visitors very soon.* She has a ridiculous picture in her head of an avenging angel with a fiery sword coming in, looking about and saying, 'Oh, I do like what you've done in this room! Delightful choice of curtains.'

Poor silly fools. Poor trusting people.

It wouldn't be so bad if they weren't destined for disappointment. How long would they all wait here for the day to come? How long would they go on believing in the Beloved in the face of all the evidence to his humanity, mortality and fallibility?

She spends the day looking out of the window, reading and wondering where Arthur can possibly be.

Meals are brought at lunch time and supper time, an unfriendly Angel delivering and then coming back to collect the tray. Apart from that, she sees no one. When the supper tray is collected, she senses a change in the atmosphere. 'Paula, what's going on downstairs?' she asks.

Paula looks strained. 'I can't say.'

'Is there trouble?'

Paula hesitates, obviously wanting to tell her. 'A difficulty,' she finally says. 'But not one we can't overcome with prayer and faith.'

'What is it? I hope it's nothing serious . . .'

Paula can't resist. She leans in, checking first over her shoulder as if there might be someone listening. 'It's the village,' she mutters. 'There's going to be a big meeting round the war memorial tomorrow. Dickie's been down there and says it's tense as you like. They're being stirred up something terrible. Dickie says they shouted some awful things at him. We none of us know what they'll do.' Paula, agitated by her own careless talk, picks up the tray and hurries off, not forgetting to lock the door behind her.

Letty can only wait and wonder, though she is not afraid of the foment in the village. It's gossip and nonsense, that's all.

It is much later and she is asleep in bed when a noise disturbs her. It's coming from outside her window, not on the ground but somewhere nearer. For a moment she's frozen with fright, staring at the pillow and listening as hard as she can. Then she hears a grunt and a muttered 'Ouch!' and she leaps out of bed and hurries to the window. Pushing it open, she sticks out her head and sees a large shape stretching itself down from the roof and onto the small stone balcony outside her window while hanging on tightly to the iron downpipe.

'Arthur!' she whispers loudly, happiness filling her with delicious warmth.

'Yes!' he whispers back. 'This is all very *Romeo and Juliet*, isn't it? Is my foot near the ledge?'

'Swing a little to your left and you're there.'

A second later, he drops, breathless, into the balcony and scrambles through the window. As soon as he is in her room, he wraps her in his tight embrace, kissing her hard, then letting her go and standing back to look at her.

'You're a sight for sore eyes, Letty, sweet.'

'You came back!' she says joyfully.

'Of course I did. I climbed the fire escape ladder at the back, got up onto the roof and came round the flat part at the front. The only tricky bit was getting to your window. You didn't think I'd leave you here, did you?'

She clasps his hands tightly. 'But where have you been?'

'I've been in London, working on getting the fraud exposed. You'll see what will happen. We'll put a stop to all the nonsense here, just wait.'

'But how?'

Arthur shakes his head. 'Not yet. It's a surprise.' His gaze travels appreciatively over her nightgown. 'Looks like I woke you up.'

She flushes. 'That doesn't matter.'

His eyes become intense as he looks at her. 'I've missed you, Letty.'

'I've missed you too.'

He pulls her to him and kisses her. The sensation sets every nerve in her body tingling, and her stomach swooping with almost painful excitement. When he pulls away, breathless, she knows that he feels the same.

'Letty,' he says, his voice choked. 'Oh Letty.'

They kiss again, lingering now over the delicious sweetness. She longs to be pressed against him, but when they part at last, he steps away from her.

'You know I would never take advantage of you, Letty,' he says, his tone more serious than she has ever heard from him before.

She nods and smiles softly. 'Of course, I am your wife.'

He laughs wryly. 'That is the irony. But until the law and the Church of England say so, I'm afraid that it doesn't count. But I'm happy just to be with you while I can.'

There is a creak outside the bedroom door and they both stand statue-still, listening hard. Footsteps move slowly past in the corridor. Letty's heart is thumping and she holds her breath as the sound fades.

'We mustn't be discovered,' she whispers. 'The atmosphere here is very strange.'

'He knows he's in trouble,' Arthur whispers back. He takes Letty's hand. 'Come on. We can cosy up together. They won't hear us talk that way.'

Letty climbs into bed, covering herself up with the sheets, but Arthur, once his boots are off, stays on the outside, one arm around her. She loves being so close to him, her nose almost touching his cheek so that he can turn for small kisses between words. Letty hasn't counted exactly how many nights they've spent together in this room without ever touching, but she knows now that each one has been a terrible waste. Arthur beside her, his arms around her, his mouth close to hers, is so blissful she can't believe they have denied themselves for so long.

Arthur says, 'If my plan comes off, this bounder will be exposed for what he is.'

'What is your plan?'

He looks down at her soberly. 'I shan't say now. I'll explain later.'

She nestles into him. 'Arthur, you've always known, haven't you?'

'Of course. When my parents got involved with Phillips, I made a study of him. He's the usual sort – an inferior type of man, attracted to the theatre and stardom of his brand of evangelical religion. There are people like him all over the world. Always have been, and always will be. Some are saints, no doubt, but most are not. Not men like Phillips. They enjoy the feeling of destiny and of controlling others, and getting what they can from the whole racket. Including lots of lovely cash.'

'I can't believe he's so wicked,' Letty whispers, marvelling at the beauty of Arthur's jawline as she runs her fingertips along it.

'He may not be really wicked. Flawed, like all of us. Careless of his power over others and how it can damage them. Emily won't be the last person to hear about hellfire and brimstone and all of that, and be driven to death by it.'

'Do you think he believes it?'

'I think, like many of us, he's able to believe two things at once, even completely contradictory things. At the same time as he is convincing himself that he really does feel divine power coursing through him and that he's immune to death, he knows that his earthly appetites are worth fulfilling just in case.'

'But I can't hate him, despite everything,' Letty says, lifting her chin to kiss him again, 'because he brought me you.'

They go to sleep, wrapped in each other's arms. When Letty wakes early the next morning, the bed is empty beside her and she can hear the splashing of water in the dressing room. A few minutes later, Arthur comes out, washed and dressed.

'I have to leave now,' Arthur says gravely. 'I shouldn't have stayed so long. I daren't be discovered here. I think Phillips has a good idea of what I'm up to, and that could put you in harm's way.'

'I don't want you to leave,' she says, disappointed.

He comes over to the bed and leans down to kiss her tenderly again.

'And I don't want to leave you. I'm sorry, my sweetheart, but I must go. I haven't finished the work I have to do.' He sits down on the bed beside her. 'I had to come back to see you again and ask you if you would consider coming with me.'

'With you?' she says, almost wonderingly.

'Yes. I can't simply leave you here, knowing what I know of Phillips.'

'I suppose I'm not exactly persona grata here.' She tells him about Emily Payne's note and Arabella's response. 'They think we're in league and probably imagine that I'm just as wicked as you are. They locked me in here all day yesterday. It's almost menacing.'

Arthur frowns. 'Then what are we waiting for? You must come away with me at once. I'm not leaving you here. I'm going to try my hand at being a journalist in London. I'm afraid I'm going to need a job now that my father is bound to cut me off without a sou. I shouldn't think I'll be going back to Oxford, not without money. And after that, I've an idea that we really ought to be properly married, if you'd like it.'

'I'd love it,' she cries, hugging him.

'Excellent.' He kisses her again, with a great smacking kiss. 'Do you think you can bear to be a poor man's wife?'

'We won't be all that poor,' Letty says delightedly, 'because I've got money!'

'Have you?' He looks surprised. 'I thought it was all given to the old goat.'

'Not mine. I never signed it over. I intended to, of course. At least, I think I did. But I didn't.'

'Well, that's wonderful. Then as long as we have enough to put the odd bunch of roses on the table to cheer ourselves up, I'll be happy.'

She loves him for not asking how much it is. She savours the picture of them in a little terraced house somewhere, perhaps near the river in London, with Arthur going off to work while she keeps their home beautiful and teaches orphan children. *Or something like that.* She'll fill in the details later.

He goes on: 'So, you must get your things together. We can

be off before they all wake up. I've got a place where we can stay.'

'No, no, Arthur, I can't come with you. Not yet.'

'Why not?' He looks hurt and anxious at the same time. 'I told you, I can't leave you.'

'You must. I'll be fine. The Beloved won't hurt me, he really won't. But I have to stay close to Arabella, just for a while longer. I want to say goodbye to her, if I can. Once I leave, I will probably never return. Come back tomorrow and I'll be ready to go, I promise.'

He gazes at her for a while and then says, 'All right. I understand. But you must promise that you'll stay away from Phillips. I will be able to meet you at the gates tomorrow evening. Be there at six. I don't think anything can happen before then.' He stands up reluctantly. 'Now, I must go.'

She clings to him, suddenly afraid. 'But you'll be careful, won't you?'

'Of course. And you too. We'll be together tomorrow night. Stay in here until then.'

Letty nods, her eyes filling with tears. 'Till tomorrow,' she says, holding his hand until at last his fingertips leave hers and he gives her one last smile before heading to the window.

'Remember, six o'clock,' he says, as he opens the sash.

'I'll remember. Six o'clock.'

The only thing that can comfort her when he's gone is the memory of his beautiful kisses and the promise of their future together. It's only later that she remembers that she meant to tell him about the meeting in the village.

Oh well. It'll all be over by tomorrow.

Chapter Twenty-Nine

I feel apart from the community I now find myself in. The house seems to be packed with young people, all unfeasibly good-looking as far as I can tell, but maybe it's just the glow of their youth and the strange happiness that pervades the place. They all seem so untouched by life, while I feel as though I'm wearing a great black mark on my forehead that signifies all that's happened to me and the grief I'm carrying with me.

Although perhaps that's only because I can't see what they've suffered in their lives.

But it's overwhelming after so long by myself. I eat alone in my room, Sophia bringing me a plate of the delicious curry they're sharing in the dining room. I've never tasted anything like it; it seems to contain only vegetables and some kind of flower, but it's fresh, spicy and satisfying, served on wild rice, with a beaker of water on the side. There's also a yogurt with a passion fruit curd topping and a biscuit made of something I can't identify but that might be buckwheat, or one of those strange not-quite grains. The food feels healthy and very now.

I'm sure it contains spirulina or algae or seaweed, and strange powders and proteins to ensure optimum gut health. These young people don't get to be as bright-eyed and bushy-tailed as they are on pizza and chips and beer. There's also a cup of that soothing herbal tea, and I drink it down, enjoying the fuzzy, slightly disconnected feeling that comes with it. I used to get that from cold white wine, and I like the idea that I get the same numbing effect from a healthy drink like tea.

After I've eaten, I go and look out of the window at the garden, and see beneath it the box that I put there for Heather to escape by. I feel a pang somewhere, but not too sharp, thanks to the tea. Part of me wants to be back there, in that state when I could conjure Heather up and make her so real I could touch her and smell her. Feeding her was more difficult. I never quite managed to make her eat. But we did so much else. Under the bay tree is the little hideout we built together. I wonder now what I looked like: a grown woman scrabbling about in the dirt, talking to herself, acting as though someone was with her. Agnes saw me. She could tell something was wrong. But she couldn't guess what.

It was when people began to invade this place that I was forced to come out from my fantasy world into cold, hard reality. After that I found it harder and harder to make Heather live with me. She began to fade and vanish. And then, when Sissy shattered the illusion completely, the pain came. The guilt. Unbearable. Everything I'd been running so hard from. It threatened to destroy me.

And then . . .

Lately the suffering hasn't been so acute and tormenting,

because the mysterious Archer is able to take away the pain, with his tea and his healing. I don't understand what gift he has exactly, but it's powerful, whatever it is. And he is certainly the leader here, and whatever is happening is under his aegis. I remember hearing Sophia say something to Agnes, before all the people started arriving. Something about the Beloved. They meant Archer. And Dora called him the Beloved too.

The garden looks different, I notice. I open the window and climb out, using the box to step down onto the terrace, and wander onto the lawn. It's been changed dramatically in just a few days: the overgrowth has been cut back and trees pruned, and I can see that large beds have been cleared in preparation for the next stage. They look as though they are planned for fruit and vegetables.

It's so different that I can't even imagine Heather here. I'm glad about that. I start to walk and soon see a gateway out of the garden to a small stone path, and that leads to a cottage.

Nursery Cottage.

I almost laugh. I must have fought my way down the garden, through the gate at the bottom and back up the meadow behind in order to get to what was just outside. I went in a huge circle. I wonder what the sisters are up to, and how their little bonsai flowers are flourishing. I think about the perfection of the snow rose, with its tiny trunk and exquisite petals in the bud, and its sensitive, demanding nature.

It will never grow any bigger, Sissy said. *It will always stay this way.*

368

The thought sends a fresh bolt of grief through me. I feel so tired again, because I know I'll have to live this way every day for the rest of my life, and it would be easier in so many ways not to bother and not to go on at all.

I look down the garden towards the marshy ground of the meadow. There's a lake nearby, I know that. I wonder if I could walk down to it, and find some stones to put in my pocket, like Virginia Woolf, and just wade out, knowing that at the end of my walk I'll find a blessed relief from the suffering.

Maybe that's the thing to do.

'Rachel!'

I turn to see Archer, now in a sloppy hooded zip-up jacket, walking towards me, smiling. 'Hi.' The sight of him boosts my spirits at once. There's something so positive about him and his aura of serenity.

'How are you?'

'Fine.' I smile.

'Really?' He looks concerned and as he approaches me, he puts out his arms and envelops me in a hug. I'm surprised, but that's quickly replaced by a warm feeling of comfort and connection. 'I'm worried about you,' he murmurs in my ear.

'You don't have to be.' I push the idea of my lake walk out of my mind. 'Honestly.'

'Well, I am. I think you're here for a reason, Rachel.' He releases me, but takes my hand and says, 'Come on. Let's walk.'

We move in harmony, taking identical steps, our feet

landing at the same time, and I watch that for a while, enjoying the pattern of it.

'Are you wondering what's going on here?' he asks almost idly, sliding his strong blue gaze to me around the edge of his hood.

'Well, yes. I suppose I am. You're forming a collective of some kind. That's my guess, anyway.'

'Yes. It's a good guess. We are a community; we share the same beliefs and the same vision of the future. All of the people here are bright, recruited from the top universities, and they all bring their different talents to the table.'

'And most of them are very attractive,' I say, hoping I don't sound like a lecherous middle-aged woman.

He laughs. 'Yeah, that's no accident either. We want the children of the future to be good-looking, don't we?'

'Er . . . I suppose so.' I laugh too. 'You're not carrying out genetic engineering here, are you?'

He shrugs, still smiling. 'Not exactly. But there's no harm in making sure you've got the best possible material, is there? It's not about race or anything sinister like that. It's about health and brains, the things which ensure survival – more than that, they ensure a thriving, prosperous people. But there's something else too.' He gives me one of his sideways looks. 'They're all blessed with spiritual gifts.'

'Are they? How do you know?'

'They wouldn't be here otherwise. Everyone is here because they believe.'

'Believe in what?'

He smiles at me again and I can't help being charmed by

the row of even teeth, the beguiling curve of his lips, the dark beard. 'Believe in me, of course.'

I'm taken aback. I wasn't expecting that. I thought he was going to say that they believe in sustainable living or vegetarianism mixed with Buddhism, or the new medievalism or something. But believe in him? What is there to believe?

Archer goes on carelessly: 'It might be a bit of a shock to you, but this is my house.'

I'm surprised, frowning as I absorb what he's saying. 'Your house? So . . . you're not guardians, employed by ARK?'

'No. Actually, ARK is me. Archer Richard Kendall. Actually Lord Kendall of Broxton.' He laughs. 'Hard to believe, isn't it? But that's who I am. My grandpa, Arthur Kendall, did some notable fighting in the Second World War, and then went into the civil service where he had an excellent diplomatic career, with the result that he was given a hereditary life peerage. That went to my dad, his son, who had me very late in life with his third wife, having only had girls before that. And he died last year, making me the new Lord Kendall and happy possessor of the family cash.' He gives a self-mocking grin. 'You don't have to curtsey. It's fine.'

'That's why this is your house?' I ask, confused. I suppose all the well-bred accents make sense now. He's been recruiting from among his own.

'Yep. At least, I didn't inherit this house itself. It went years ago, thanks to my great-aunt. When I saw the chance to buy it, I jumped at it. It was obvious that it was meant to be. I even changed the name back to Paradise. All part of the plan, you see.'

371

'What's the plan?'

We've come to the end of the garden and now we turn around and look at the house from the back. I've never seen it quite as clearly as this before, the shrubbery was always too high, but now that's neatly trimmed the beauty of the place can be clearly seen. It's a gracious house, with a calm symmetry and a good line. No wonder people are drawn to it. It seems to offer boundless shelter and comfort.

'Ah,' he says. 'The plan.'

'Are you a cult?' I ask bluntly. 'Is that what I've wandered into?'

'A cult?' He laughs loudly. 'No, I'm not a cult. At least, I don't think I am. But I suppose cults never do, it's such a pejorative term. And' – he's more thoughtful now – 'I think cults have ideas that other people can't believe in. Whereas we base our beliefs on things everyone knows to be true.'

'Oh? Things like the sky being blue?' I'm being ironic but he seems to take me seriously.

'Yes . . . yes. A bit like that.' He goes over to a rackety wooden bench and sits down. I sit down beside him and he turns to face me, his expression intense. 'Rachel, what do we know for sure about the world?'

I'm thinking of an answer but he goes on without waiting for one.

'It's a consensus that we humans have managed to get ourselves into a bit of a pickle. We've mucked up our environment pretty much past the point of no return. Climate change is happening and fast. It's going to bring with it unprecedented geological change, with seas rising, ice caps melting, huge and frequent weather events and changes in temperature. We could see hurricanes and tornados as commonplace events here, where we've never known them before. We'll certainly have floods and bizarre weather patterns. We might even find the seasons reversed, with warm winters and icy summers.'

'Will we?' I've heard so much about the dangers of climate change that I've ceased listening to much of it. There's so much squabbling about what is and isn't true, and so many sensational headlines, I don't know what to think. It's the hottest year on record, or one of the coldest, or it hasn't changed a bit – depending on who you listen to. 'And there's a definite consensus on this?'

'Oh yes. Unless you're a denier. You're not a denier, are you, Rachel?' There's a tiny sinister barb in his voice despite the silkiness of his tone.

'No. No. Of course not.' Denying definitely does not sound good.

'Good. I'm glad we agree on that. It makes it a lot easier.' He gets up and starts to walk again and I walk beside him. Now we're skirting the bottom of the garden, heading in a direction I've not been in before.

'So,' I say, wanting to understand, 'we're in a time of severe man-made weather changes.'

'Yes, we are. And that's going to bring with it political change. Did you know that we've been living through what's known as the Great Peace? Ever since the Second World War ended. Yes, there have been wars but on the whole, the world has been at peace. We haven't seen a great global conflict. Well, that peace is about to end. In fact, it already has.'

'You mean . . . Syria?'

'Yes, Syria. But before that, in Darfur, we saw the same thing. A war, as the result of climate change. Drought causes famine, and famine causes radicalisation as well as movement of population, and that makes war.' He shrugs again. 'It's simple. We spend a lot of time arguing about it but when you stand back and look, it's clear as day. Scientists have already proved that the great drought of the early 2000s across what's known as the Fertile Crescent, from Russia to Saudi Arabia, was more than likely caused by man-made climate change. Now look at what we've seen in precisely that area. War.'

I blink at him. It sounds convincing. 'Yes, I can see that.'

He warms to his theme. 'The war isn't confined to the Middle East either; we can't go and visit it like war tourists. We can't go in and bomb whichever side we feel like support-ing – the ones with the oil usually – and then go home and sleep safe in our beds at night. It doesn't work like that. The war is coming to us, in the form of migrants and refugees, and in the form of radicalisation, terrorism and bombs. Look at Paris. Look at Istanbul and Ankara. Look at Brussels. It'll be London again soon. Maybe Oslo or Copenhagen. Washing-ton. Somewhere, because they can't be stopped every time. The anger of the people will grow with each outrage. After the Great Peace comes the Great Conflict, and this will be like nothing we've ever known. Political and religious war will engulf the globe and destroy trade and agriculture and our energy extraction industries. Climate change will destroy crops and bring starvation. There'll be no coffee, no bananas, no chocolate, no oranges – just for starters. As the world's resources shrink, we'll begin a life-or-death struggle for what remains. And we're about to discover that mankind's supremacy over disease is being threatened too. Antibiotics have been so abused by the human race that they're going to stop working. When that happens, disease will ravage us in a way we haven't known in well over a century. You'll cut your finger and die of sepsis because there aren't any pills to kill the infection. Death rates in childbirth will shoot back up to Victorian levels. Influenza – new strains of bird flu, swine flu and whatever – will rage across the world as it did in 1918 and kill millions. The plague will return. Huge, threatening global events are guaranteed and soon. We're going to be fighting for our lives.'

'You're not exactly cheering me up,' I joke weakly.

He turns on me, his blue eyes alight with passion. 'This is so, so serious, Rachel. Can you hear what I'm saying? We're on the brink. You must see it.'

'Yes . . . I can see it.' And I do. Everything he says makes sense. I feel afraid, even though my life counts for so little now.

Archer takes my hand again, holding it in his large, smooth palm. I like the way it transmits strength and warmth to me, making me feel less shaken by his vision of the future. 'But don't worry. I have a plan.'

'Are you going to tell me what it is?'

'Soon, Rachel. I want to see if you're going to be a permanent part of our lives first.'

I lie awake in bed that night, listening to someone playing the guitar outside. It's not exactly warm enough for outdoor parties yet, but it's not freezing either. Someone has lit a brazier in an old steel drum and several people sit outside after dinner, talking quietly and smoking. Fragrant smells creep into my room and I think that they must be smoking some kind of cannabis but I don't know enough to identify it. At some point, the music starts. It's restful and pleasant and I like lying awake and listening, wallowing in the numbness brought on by my bedtime herbal tea. The lyrics sound familiar, but I have no idea where they come from:

'Arise, my love, my fair one
And come away.
For the winter is over and the rain is passed and gone.
Flowers appear on the earth;
And the time of birds is come,
The voice of the turtledove is heard in our land . . .'

The voice is a man's, beautiful, gentle. I am sure it is Archer's voice and I close my eyes to listen better. The things he said today resonated with me. He pulled together so many disparate things in the world and gave them sense and a pattern. The vision of the world outside my own experience and my own trials has put everything I've suffered into proportion: millions of parents will lose children in the coming disasters, through sickness, hunger and war.

We ought to try and stop it. Or at least work out what to do about it.

Archer has shown me a nightmare vision and yet, he has also given me the first glimmer of hope, the first will to survive, I've felt in a long time.

I want to know what the plan is.

Chapter Thirty

The next morning the door is unlocked by a tearful Kitty, her eyes red-rimmed and her nose shiny, carrying Letty's breakfast tray with shaking hands.

'What is it? What's wrong, Kitty?'

'Oh, miss . . .' Kitty's eyes well up with fresh tears. 'It's the mistress.'

'Arabella?' Letty says, anxious at once.

'No . . . no, the old mistress. Mrs Sarah. She's . . . dead.' Kitty chokes on a sob.

Letty gasps. 'How terrible! Poor Sarah. Oh, I'm so sorry.' Tears spring to her eyes. She hasn't seen much of Sarah since the Beloved married Arabella, no one has except her faithful Angels. But it is said that Sarah refused a doctor, or any relief for her pain, but suffered slowly and without resistance. 'Do you think she willed it, Kitty?'

'She didn't fight it, poor lady,' says Kitty with a sniff.

'Poor, poor Sarah.' Letty blinks but a tear escapes and runs down her cheek. Sarah was never anything but gracious and kind, and Letty is sure the house has lost something precious. 'God rest her soul.'

She wonders if Sarah's giving up on life was caused by the Beloved's decision to marry Arabella. *Perhaps he even told her it was time for her to make way for a proper marriage, a legal marriage, to enshrine the Beloved's right to the estate in law, and the heir Arabella is carrying. After all, the Beloved can talk people into doing almost anything. Why not dying, in order to make his life easier?*

It is a horrible thought. It makes Letty more determined than ever to get away. 'Can I come out?' she asks.

Kitty shrugs. 'I have no orders. The Beloved went off early on business. Miss Arabella's still abed. Come out if you wish.'

Letty emerges to quite a different house. The mood is sombre and depressed. She goes downstairs to the dining room to find that it hasn't been set for breakfast, for the first time since the Angels began ministering to them. A pair of ladies pass her, both sobbing into lace-edged handkerchiefs.

'Maud, Thomasina, I'm sorry . . .' Letty says, wanting to offer comfort, but they don't answer her, just head towards the drawing room from where the sound of crying emerges. *I'm still in Coventry then.* Just then she spies Paula trailing along the corridor and also weeping plaintively. She hurries towards her. 'Paula, please don't cry so! You'll be ill. The mistress wouldn't have wanted that.'

Paula howls. 'Oh, our sweet lady! How we'll miss her! Oh!' She throws her apron over her head and weeps noisily.

Letty puts a hand on her arm. 'Yes, poor Sarah. Poor lady.

We must offer prayers for her. Be brave, Paula. It comes to us all.'

'But that's not so,' cries Paula, muffled under the apron. Then she pulls it off, to show tears flowing down her face. 'The Beloved said that we'd none of us die. We'd live here in bliss and harmony till the Day came. But the sweet lady – his own wife before the mistress – she's gone from us before the Day. What can it mean? She can't have been taken by the Devil, like Emily, can she?'

'I'm sure she wasn't taken by the Devil. She was a good and kind person, and never less than holy. She'll be in heaven now, I'm certain of it. The Beloved will explain everything.'

He'll have to, Letty thinks grimly, as she goes about making a breakfast for those who want it. The atmosphere is grief-stricken, but also full of shock and confusion. The usual trusting, confident happiness that the community members carry about with them is completely gone.

Letty herself does not feel it, and she wonders why. *Perhaps it's because I'm young. I never expected to die very soon anyway.* She'd always imagined the plan would be resolved within her lifetime, and certainly within that of the Beloved. But perhaps, for some of the older people, the Beloved offered a comfortable cushion against the fear of encroaching old age, illness and extinction. Sarah's death has proved that there is no bulwark against it after all.

Arabella is nowhere to be seen. No one will speak to Letty at all. It is obvious that they've been warned about her.

She is in the hall, taking down an arrangement of flowers that seem far too celebratory now that Sarah lies dead upstairs, when Mrs Kendall comes in, her eyes red and tiny from weeping. When she sees Letty, she stops still, then comes striding as purposefully as she can in her long white skirt. 'You!' she shouts, pointing at Letty. 'You were supposed to save him for us!'

'Mrs Kendall . . .' begins Letty, turning to face her, flushing. 'Arthur—'

'Is lost . . . because of you! We had such hopes. The Beloved assured us you would bring him to the fold. And yet you've failed, failed us all!'

'Please, Mrs Kendall, there was nothing I could have done. Arthur never wanted to be here, you know that. He only did it to please you.'

'Oh, I suppose you now know my son better than I do!' Mrs Kendall's eyes flash with anger. 'You will have nothing further to do with him.'

Letty stares at her and then says sweetly, 'But, dear mother-in-law, we are married.'

Mrs Kendall narrows her eyes, aware that if she disputes this, she will be going against the authority of the Beloved. 'We know you are a pernicious influence, Miss Evans. We've heard that it is probably you who is spreading vile nonsense full of sordid lies around the village! You have truly been taken by the evil one, and the Beloved will cast you out like the viper you are! Any holy union with my son will be dissolved.'

'Mrs Kendall,' Letty says slowly but firmly, 'this will not bring Arthur back. He's gone and he will not return, not to live here at least. You must respect his decision and his faith.'

Mrs Kendall turns brick-red and spits as she talks. 'He'll regret listening to your blandishments! He'll be disinherited if he does.' She comes up close to Letty. 'You were supposed to save his soul. You have done the opposite.'

'Oh no,' Letty replies with a smile. There's nothing they can do to hurt her or Arthur, she is sure of that. 'You're wrong. I haven't done anything at all. He has saved *me*.'

No one attempts to lock her back in her bedroom, she notices. With the Beloved absent, she is treated with a kind of reluctant respect, as though no one has forgotten, deep down, that this is her childhood home.

By midday, the shock and grief have worn off to the extent that the Angels are able to go about their work again, and the comforting routine of meals is re-established. Ladies huddle in corners, talking about where the Beloved has gone and what is to be done with Sarah, lying cold in her bed upstairs.

They really are lost without him. All of them relinquished control of their lives to him. Now they don't know how to take a decision.

She remembers her own sense of loss when the Beloved went away just before the opening of the church, the day the Kendalls came here. *When he was defrocked by the bishop.* So she can well understand their dependence on him. *And the power it gives him.*

Arabella remains in her room and is not to be seen, perhaps out of delicacy with Sarah's death uppermost in everyone's minds, or perhaps because she is not well.

Letty suspects that it is something to do with the pregnancy, which is becoming more visible daily, although it has not yet been publicly acknowledged. She hopes Arabella is all right. Despite everything, she still loves her sister.

I will go and see her if she doesn't come down before tea time.

Letty goes to her room and packs her soft carpet bag with everything she thinks she might need for a few days. The rest of her things she piles neatly for Kitty to pack in a trunk and send on in due course. She feels a thrill of excitement at the life that awaits her: the cottage in London, Arthur to share it with. But before that can happen, she must make sure all the business is taken care of. She sits at her desk and writes to the family lawyer, outlining everything that has happened so far, as she feels, obscurely, that it is important to be a witness to what has taken place in the house. She tries not to be emotional or judgemental, but to let the events she records speak for themselves. Anyone reading it will see the extent of the Beloved's manipulation and his breath-taking blasphemy – there is no need to say what is so obvious. This letter takes two hours to write, and when it is done, she folds it up and puts it in an envelope. She takes it downstairs to put on the tray for posting, and is surprised to see a letter there addressed to herself in Cecily's handwriting. She scoops it up and opens it, reading as she walks slowly back up the stairs to her room.

Dear Lettice,

Arthur Kendall has told us you have come to your senses at last. We are delighted to hear it, even if still

*deeply disappointed that Arabella has not yet seen the
light. He says, however, that you insist on remaining
among the gang of lunatics another day. I don't know
how you can stand another hour. Edward and I strongly
caution you to leave at once. Come to us at High Hill
Farm as soon as possible. There is the possibility of
imminent trouble and I do not want you present. Please
do as we ask and come immediately.*

    Your sister,

    Cecily

Letty stares at the letter. *Trouble? What can she mean?*
Letty remembers the meeting in the village that is happening
today. Can that be what she is referring to? It's hardly likely,
surely. But her instinct is telling her that Cecily is right. Come
what may, it's time to leave. The atmosphere here is all wrong.
Sarah lies dead in her bed. No one is speaking to Letty; even
Kitty is turning against her. But she must try, one last time, to
help Arabella see the truth.

Racing up the stairs, she passes no one and in a few minutes she is at Arabella's door. She does not knock but goes
straight in. Arabella is sitting on the stool in front of her
mirror, brushing out her dark hair and humming to herself.
She turns as Letty comes in, and Letty can see the bulge of her
belly sticking out. How far advanced is she? Five months?
Six?

'What on earth are you doing?' she says coldly to Letty.
'You're not permitted in here anymore.'

'But, Arabella, I have to speak to you. I have to try and

persuade you, perhaps for the last time, that you're mixed up in something terrible.' She goes over and kneels down at her sister's feet, clutching her hand. 'Please, please listen to me!'

Something in Letty's dramatic pose seems to appeal to Arabella. She looks down a little more kindly and says, 'I will listen to you if you like, but I warn you, it will make no difference. I already know that you speak with the Devil's tongue.'

'Don't think about that for a moment, please, just listen.'

'Very well.' Arabella seems strangely calm, so different from her excitable self during the early days of the Beloved's arrival. 'Say what you wish.'

Letty stares up at her. There was so much to say, but now she has her sister's ear, it all seems hopeless. It won't make a blind bit of difference, she can see that. 'What the Beloved says isn't always true,' she says carefully. 'He claims divinity, but really he's as mortal as the rest of us. He's no saint. He gives into temptations of all kinds. He lies. He's taken your house, your money and made you pregnant, and you're not even married.'

'Of course we're married,' Arabella says indignantly.

'Not in the eyes of the law. The child will be illegitimate.'

'It really doesn't matter, Letty.' Arabella is evidently trying to sound patient. 'All of that won't matter soon. Long before the child is grown, the Day will be at hand. Property, legitimacy, all the rest of it, won't matter a scrap.' She looks sadly at her sister. 'The Beloved is right about you, Letty. He says your heart is hardened to the truth. You've renounced the way. You cannot rid yourself of material concerns.'

'That's rich coming from him,' Letty retorts. 'He's the one making sure he marries an heiress and has a child with her. He's the one suggesting everyone hands over their money and belongings to him.'

'He is acting for the good of us all, making a place where we can wait for the final judgement.'

'That's all he's made – a comfortable bed where you can all luxuriate doing nothing, with the Angels to look after you unpaid, waiting for the day he says is nigh, but which he knows nothing of. What has he said that is true? That there will be no death? Look at Emily and Sarah. That he's renounced the flesh? Arabella, you are pregnant with his child, and Emily was his mistress too! He has even claimed he is . . .' She still cannot say it, it's too blasphemous to utter.

'He has explained it all. I understand it because of my spiritual gifts. You have not been so blessed.'

Letty gazes at her helplessly. It's quite clear that nothing will change Arabella's mind. She is deeply, utterly committed to the Beloved, and it will be impossible to convince her that he is an imposter.

Suddenly, Arabella smiles. 'Don't you understand, Letty? He makes me happy. I was so miserable before, and now, at last, I have a purpose and a meaning in my life. I have love as well. What I believe in has made my life good. Isn't that enough for you? Do I have to be right as well? All I want is to be happy.'

'But, Arabella, the belief has made *you* happy, if you say it has. But it is also powerful and destructive. It can drive others mad, drive them to their deaths. I think Sarah died of misery, knowing you were there to take her place. And look at Emily, thinking she was too wicked to live. Is your happiness worth it?'

Arabella considers for a moment, picking up her brush and drawing it through her long hair again. 'It is like wine,' she says at last. 'For some, one sip can lead the way to destruction. For others, they can drink the wine and never be mastered by it. Instead, they take what is good and make it enhance their lives. Can you blame the wine for that?'

'I see,' Letty says. 'You must stay and drink the wine and see what happens. I understand that now. I'm leaving, but I wish you every happiness.'

'And I you,' Arabella says absently.

Letty stands up and kisses her sister's cheek. 'Goodbye, Arabella.'

'Goodbye.'

Letty turns to go. She will collect her things and leave. It won't take so very long to get to High Hill Farm, even lugging her bags. But there, in the doorway of Arabella's room, is the Beloved, and his expression is full of cold fury. She gasps.

His eyes blaze with ire as he says loudly, 'You, Miss Lettice Evans, are going nowhere, until you have answered to me.'

'Let me pass,' commands Letty, hiding her fear as best she can.

He laughs. 'After all this time, do you really think I will obey you? You're a little fool, and a treacherous one too. I know your plans to destroy us, with the Kendall boy. It will not work. The evil one will never triumph over the chosen!'

'I don't know what you're talking about. I said, let me pass.'

'Oh, you shall pass. You are to face this whole community to answer for your wickedness. You've brought sin and death into this house!'

She sees suddenly how clever he is. Sarah's death will be laid at her feet, not at his. 'You can't blame me for what's happened to Sarah,' she retorts.

His eyes glitter dangerously and she knows that this is the kind of situation he most relishes. High theatre, intense drama, with himself at the heart of it, directing it like a maestro.

'You shall be taken from here and tried,' says the Beloved with a chilly smile on his lips. 'The trial will be before us all. I shall be the judge. But you will be condemned by your own mouth. And I shall glory in your subjugation.'

Chapter Thirty-One

'Do you want to see around, Rachel? You ought to, if you're going to be one of us.'

'Yes, I'd like that.' I've guessed that this is more than the glorified and slightly odd holiday home it seemed at first. Archer is the lynchpin of the place; everything revolves around him and wherever he goes he's surrounded by a kind of adoration. He reaches out to everyone he sees. I've already felt the power of his gaze on me, and the way he makes me feel like I'm the most important thing in the world to him. From the expressions on the faces of the young people around him, he does that to all of them.

'There are two parts to our life here, Rachel.' He greets everyone we pass cheerily, asking them what they're up to and how they are, and then smoothly continues. 'One part is striving to achieve the highest goal: perfect love and understanding of the Divine. The other part is preparing for what lies ahead. When the trouble comes, how do you think most of the population will cope?' He leads me out through the French windows in the sitting room into the garden. It's a bright sunny day. The season has certainly changed from when I arrived with Heather on that cold winter night. The winter has gone, and she's gone. I hear the lilting lyric from the song last night again: *The winter is over and the rain is passed and gone.* Archer is taking away the winter – at least, that's how it feels.

He is talking passionately about his vision. 'Most of the population, with their utter reliance on supermarket food, microwave meals, electricity and all the rest of it, won't have a clue about how to cope. When the great shortages come, they won't know what to do. That's because they've been purposefully turned into soft morons by successive governments who rely on their dependence to keep them – the elite – in power. No one has the ability to do anything but what they're told these days. We are different. We're changing that. We're taking back control.'

I nod. I can see that. Out in the grounds, young men and women are busy, clearing more undergrowth and digging what look like huge pits with the help of a noisy mechanical digger.

'Septic tank,' explains Archer, gesturing to one, 'for when we're off the mains.' He points at another. 'A heat reclamation system, using the earth's stored heat to warm the house. No need for fossil fuels or the grid. Though we will burn wood if we can do so sustainably. And we'll be generating a lot of our own power with a system of solar panels, wind turbines and so on. While the grid is still functioning, we'll use that. But you can expect it to start failing any day now. Our techies are working on keeping all our equipment going with our own power sources.'

'Really?' I can't believe it. It's so hard to imagine a life where the simple act of switching on a light or plugging something in is not possible.

'That's right.' He turns to look at me seriously again. 'I'm telling you, Rachel, we've been closing our eyes to this disaster. The lights are going to start going out. It's no lie; you can read about it in any academic journal on energy security. I've read them all.'

We stop at the border to the woods. 'Is this part of your land?' I ask, pushing my hands deep inside my pockets. Despite the warmth of the day, there's still a chill breeze and my fingers are cold.

'Yes. We won't go in there. It's a bit . . . I guess dangerous isn't the word. Unpredictable.'

I raise my eyebrows at him.

'At any one time, there'll be half a dozen people in there learning survival skills. Not just laying fires and skinning rabbits and purifying water and digging toilets – though they are doing those things – but open-air combat skills too.' He grins at me. 'Don't worry, it's nothing too hard core. But we're going to be ready for whatever happens. This place has been under siege before, you know. It might be again. I've got some top army boys helping me out on that one. They go in at unexpected times to test the guys. It's all great fun.'

'Do you use guns?' I ask, thinking of army commandos with blacked faces and automatic rifles slung over their shoulders.

He shakes his head. 'Knives and hand-to-hand out here. In case ammo runs out. We do gun skills at the local firing range – it's just easier right now. We don't want to draw attention to ourselves.'

I have a feeling that gorgeous girls like Sophia and Agnes turning up at the firing range to practise their gun skills might draw some attention, but I say nothing. We turn and walk along the edge of the woods. I can see that he has it all worked out. He said he had a plan, and he does. He's making this place self-sufficient, and equipping everyone with the ability to face any circumstances. From the sounds of it, the lights going out will be the least of our worries.

'So, imagine,' he goes on, 'a population that has totally lost connection with the earth. It only knows how to exist in convenient, warm houses with plenty of fuel, and food available in abundance. All of that is taken away. What then?'

'Riots?' I guess. 'Marches on Downing Street?'

He gives me a slightly pitying look. 'In the early days, yes. Protests. But it won't stay like that for long. Soon, as the shortages bite, people will start looting, stealing, fighting for what's left. Can't you imagine it? Once your family gets hungry, you'll do anything to feed them. All the morality everyone prides themselves on will go out of the window. Grown men will raid hospital kitchens and take food from the sick for their children. They won't care. It will become the survival of the fittest.'

I see it as he speaks. I think about our densely populated cities and what might happen if there's no food, no sanitation, no order . . . 'But the army and the police,' I say. 'They'll enforce civil behaviour.'

'Yeah, at first. And then a police state will be imposed. All stocks and supplies will go to the authorities to ensure the obedience of the armed forces. The government will turn on its anarchic and rioting people, and when the real violence breaks out, they'll start firing.'

'Oh my God.' I turn to stare at him. 'This is terrible!'

'It's more than terrible, Rachel. It's the truth. It's going to happen. But you don't need to worry. Because you're here with us.'

Our tour continues and I can't help being impressed at everything he's started in such a short time. Lots of land has been put aside for growing vegetables and raising animals. 'We do eat meat,' he says, 'in moderation.' He points out where the solar panels will go. 'But they're incredibly expensive and being handmade in Germany so they won't be here for a bit.'

Wherever we go, we see industrious youngsters hard at work in various ways, all turning to smile and say hello as we pass. Inside, Rocky and Fisher are still toiling away putting up the shutters.

'There's going to be quite a bit of reinforcement,' says Archer. 'Once it becomes known that we have resources, we're going to be inundated with people wanting either to take them or join us. We'll need to be able to go into shutdown if necessary, while we deal with them.'

'How will you deal with them?'

Archer has led me downstairs into the basement. I haven't

been here since Agnes found out I was taking food from the freezer. I go bright red as I remember that I haven't replaced any of it. I haven't been near a shop for weeks. There are now four freezers, and dozens of steel shelving units containing catering-size packets, boxes and cans of all kinds of food.

'There's a lot going on down here,' Archer says. 'Or there will be. Besides being our store cupboard, there's going to be an industrial kitchen too. And come and see this.'

He leads me towards the stainless steel door, the one I became so afraid of when I was here alone. My fear seems ridiculous now. Of course there was no one living behind it. But I'm curious to see what was there.

Newly appeared next to the door is a keypad and a small display. Archer types in a code and puts his eye directly opposite the display. A blue light scans his eyeball, then the door opens.

'There,' he says. 'Our ops room is in here. There are people like us all over the world and we are forming tentative alliances with them, so that we can share information when the time comes. There won't be any air travel by then, though.' He grins at me. 'No aviation fuel.'

I look inside. There's a room full of computers and screens and all manner of high-tech gizmos whose purpose I don't understand. No wonder I could see flashing lights and hear clicks and chirrups. All this was powering away underneath me the whole time and I had no idea.

'This is how we, the faithful, will keep in touch with each other,' he says. 'It's already beginning. We're not alone in our vision of the future.'

'Wow,' I say. 'You really are getting prepared for this.'

'Of course.' Archer smiles. 'We'll go as far as we have to. But this is all you need to see for now. Just remember, whatever happens, we can never be as rotten as the world-governing cabal, who fund terrorists and repressive regimes. Believe me, those guys are the instruments of evil.'

I'm speechless, trying to take it all in. He's so sure of himself. I'm filled with a desire to stay close to him, where I'll be safe and protected, just as he promises. All the bad stuff will happen to other people, the ones who deserve it. The good ones will be okay.

'We'll see you tonight, won't we?' he asks with a smile.

'Tonight?'

'At the church.'

Of course. I'd forgotten about the spiritual element to all of this. 'Yes . . . if you think I should come.'

'I do. It's going to be quite a party.'

Back in my room, I sit on my bed trying to take it all in. Around me, busy preparations are being made for apocalyptic events of the kind I always considered scare-mongering. Maybe it shows a lack of imagination but I've never been able to picture law and order breaking down, people fighting in the streets for food, families starving and freezing in their own homes. Now I can, only too well.

But here is going to be a haven from that. They're getting ready now so when it comes they'll all be safe.

It's a seductive vision: a self-contained, self-sufficient

community, ready to ensure their survival when the worst happens.

Better to be in here than out there.

I think about the church service tonight. I'm curious: what religion can they be practising here? Archer is so keen on forming the world in his own vision, I wouldn't be surprised if it were one he's created himself. I recall the inside of the church and its lack of identifiable denomination, and remember Sissy's vague description of what went on there.

How strange that she used to live here, and so did Archer's family.

I frown. I don't know how old the sisters are, but surely in their late sixties at least. So if they were born here, could they have known Archer's great-aunt? He said his father was getting on when he had him, so it might be unlikely. The years might not work. If I see Matty and Sissy, I will ask them if they know anything about the Kendalls.

I get up and go to the mirror. I haven't looked at myself properly for ages and the word 'party' has made me feel quite anxious. I might not be able to compete with the beautiful girls here but I still want to put on a good show if I can. Still, I can't help gasping as I take in the reality of my appearance. My white hair has grown out so that I have a big stripe of dark roots, giving me the look of a badger, and it's dry and crinkly from lack of proper conditioning. My face is dry too, and I'm gaunter than I've ever been. *Is this really me? I can't go anywhere looking like this.*

*

Sophia knocks on the door and calls, 'Rachel? Are you ready? It's time to go.'

I open the door. She gapes at me.

'Wow. You look great. What have you done to your hair?'

'Just did my roots.' I brought boxes of dye with me to keep up my new disguise, so I've spent the afternoon with plastic gloves on, smearing goo all over my scalp. I feel vaguely guilty about thinking of my appearance, but it's also relaxing and restorative, so I let myself enjoy it too. I even got out some moisturiser and put on some mascara. It's testament to how bad I must have looked if Sophia thinks I look great. I hardly pass muster right now.

She regards my clothes doubtfully. 'You ought to wear white, really. Don't you have something?'

I look down at my jeans and striped jumper. 'There's the stuff that was left in my room. The linen trousers.'

'Yes. Put those on.' Sophia watches unembarrassed as I take off my things and don the soft white trousers and white T-shirt.

'Cool,' she says, when I'm done. 'Goes with the hair.'

'What's the service like?' I ask as we walk through the house towards the front door.

'This Friday is kind of special. Most of us are gathered now, so it's a celebration of that. We'll be reaffirming the group dynamic.' She smiles at me. 'It's fun. Kind of crazy. Don't be surprised.'

'I'll try not to be. No promises.' I smile back. 'Is Archer in charge?'

'Oh yes. Always.' Her expression softens at his name.

'What brought you here, Sophia?' I ask, curious.

'Archer gives my life meaning,' she says simply. 'I was one of those people who seem to have it all, but I was completely hollow inside, yearning for something fundamental, trying to drown my unhappiness in drugs and partying. Then I met Archer. He understood me at once. He really . . . *cared*. You know?' She gives me a sidelong glance from her green eyes. 'He listened. And he showed me the way. This is my path now. He's my – our – Beloved.'

I nod. I've noticed the way Archer seems to connect with everyone he meets, man or woman. At least, he does in here. Perhaps in the outside world he'd put some backs up, with his complete self-confidence and certainty in his vision.

'It seems wacky at times,' Sophia says, as we go out to the drive, lit by torches flaming at regular intervals, 'but if you open your mind and heart to it, you'll receive the message. And once you have . . . it's irresistible.'

I'm apprehensive as we walk along the path to the church, where the stained-glass windows are dazzlingly illuminated by all the candles lit within. Around us are other people making their way to the church, all dressed in white. Some of the women wear snaky long dresses that hang off their shoulders, or tight white shorts and artfully ripped T-shirts. The men are in anything from robes that look like nightshirts to white jeans and shirts. All look in their twenties or early thirties, and they are of many different nationalities. Lots of the men have beards and long hair as Archer does, some with ponytails or plaits or dreadlocks. I envy the way they seem so modern, at ease with their individual choices, happy to find an identity that suits them beyond their cultures.

In the church, I follow Sophia into a row, not quite at the front but near enough to see everything with ease. There's music but not from the organ, which is left untouched. A pair of young men are playing guitars together at the front, a beautiful classical duet that engenders a sense of untrammelled calm.

'What do I do?' I ask. There don't seem to be any prayer books or orders of service.

'Just follow what everyone else does, or go with it. Just do what feels right.'

I'm awkward without clear instruction. I hope I'm not expected to enter transports or speak in tongues, or whatever happens in this kind of place. 'Who are we praying to?' I ask.

'You know . . . the spirit,' Sophia says enigmatically. 'The will. You'll understand soon. Honestly. The Beloved will explain.'

I stop asking questions, as I don't think I'm going to get anything clear from her. It's all so vague and airy-fairy. I wonder how this can possibly tally with Archer's razor-sharp vision of the future and what he needs to do to ensure survival.

Then, without warning, the guitar music stops and the men get up and wander off with their instruments. The buzz of talking gradually subsides. I glance behind me and see that there are about thirty or forty people in the church. I spot Agnes further back, and Kaia and the Chinese girl. There are Rocky and Fisher too.

Then Archer is walking up the aisle towards the altar, where the beautifully embroidered cloth now hangs, and he's dressed in a baggy white robe, open at the neck to show an expanse of chest. As he walks, the congregation burst into noisy applause, whooping and cheering. He acknowledges them with nods, smiles and outstretched arms, turning in every direction as he goes, shaking hands when he can. At the top, he stops and turns and faces the gathering.

'Welcome. Tonight is amazingly special. Here we are. Not all of us, of course. We've got brothers and sisters in our other locations, and they may join us in time. But right now, the core of us is assembled. The heart of us is right here! The unbreakables. We're all together.'

Loud cheers, whistles and whoops greet this announcement.

'Guys, the rules here are no different from anywhere else. We are a community. What we do is for the communal good. We all give freely of our labour and our possessions, into the communal pot from which we are all protected and nourished. Right?'

Calls of agreement and support echo around.

Okay, I get it. It's a new agrarian communism. For those who can afford to buy a huge estate. I remember the room full of up-to-the-minute technology in the cellar and wonder how much all this costs. Surely millions. *But what's the religious aspect?*

Archer begins to talk. It is impossible not to watch him, his magnetically attractive figure walking back and forth at the front of the church, his voice so passionate, so articulate.

Every sentence makes the clearest sense, leading inexorably on to the next, and on, until I cannot help but agree with every conclusion he comes to. He talks of the need for a spiritual life to complement their physical labour and to give meaning to their lives and relationships. He says that there is a second, even greater battle to be won in this world, beyond the struggle for survival in the coming firestorm. It will be the battle of good against evil, the battle of love against hate, and the battle of life over death.

'We will ride into that battle, white-clad, shining, with the power of love and the power of life!' he shouts.

They call their agreement in response.

'We will win this great and final battle because we have the spiritual weapons in our hands. And the greatest weapon of all is love!'

This draws wild shouts of joy from the congregation. Beside me, Sophia applauds and shouts, her eyes shining.

Archer's voice drops to a mesmeric tone, and he says, 'Tonight we affirm our love for each other. We love without favour! We love equally, no matter race, gender, nationality or culture. All are worthy of love and all will be loved. We share, as we share all things, right? No favouritism for us. No shackles of law and state and hidebound, dead churches! We all love each other, and in that we find our strength and our freedom.'

They whoop and cheer again. The atmosphere is now alive, electric with excitement and anticipation.

'So now, we do the ceremony – our own affirmation of our

communal love for each other, and our commitment to complete equality of relationships.'

They roar in agreement and delight. There's a powerful, animal force in the room, which I feel must come from youth whipped up into an emotional and physical frenzy.

What the hell is going to happen now?

I'm standing outside the church, shaky and breathless. I don't know how I feel about it but I have the overwhelming sensation that it's something I shouldn't witness. The people inside the church have no shame, no embarrassment, but I'm not like that. When Fisher came over and took me by the hand, I whipped it away and shook my head. He shrugged, smiled and went to find someone else.

What did I just see?

If it were characterised in a tabloid newspaper, they might say something like 'Toffs go wild at swinging party . . . anything goes in high-class orgy . . .' or similar lurid, attention-grabbing headlines.

But it wasn't like that. Or was it?

'Rachel.'

That voice in my ear. His voice. Archer. I turn and look at him. His face is so bright it's almost shining and he's illuminated behind by the light coming from the church. With his flowing hair, beard and robe, he looks biblical. I can't help feeling awed by him and affected by his presence in a way I've not felt for a long time now.

'Are you all right?'

He's always looking out for me. Checking I'm okay. 'Yes.'

My voice is a bit shaky but not too bad. 'I'm just a bit over-whelmed.'

'I thought so.' He nods. 'I expected that.'

'What did you do in there?'

'Well, it's what you might call the marriage ceremony. This place has a history of them, but in the old days, they were spiritual marriages, between a man and a woman. They denied the physical being because it was supposed to be part of the Devil's realm. But that was how the last dispensation under-stood it, the message he received. I've received a different message, for different times, I guess. What's possible now may not have been possible then.'

'Dispensation?'

'Yeah. There have been manifestations of the Divine throughout time, dispensations given to mankind to help them see the way.' He smiles at me. 'I'll explain it properly sometime. But the main thing to understand is that we affirm our communality by a ceremony in which we are all married to one another – each one person marries all the others. And by this, we share our love completely equally. Do you under-stand?'

'From what's going on in there, I think I get the point.' I'm trying to joke.

'It's the first ceremony for a while, they tend to get fired up. It's beautiful, really. No one is hurt, no one is sad, everyone loves each other with no guilt or recrimination. It's perfect when you think about it.'

It seems so simple. Like everything Archer says, it seems to make perfect sense. And yet, I think, if it's all so good and true, then why, when I left the church, did I see Kaia, the girl who sewed the altar cloth, standing at the back and crying like her heart would break?

Archer takes my hand and lifts it to his mouth, then kisses it gently. 'So, Rachel, don't you think you should share in some of the love too? I promise you won't regret it.'

Chapter Thirty-Two

'You are not to put your hands on me!' declares Letty furiously as the Beloved approaches her.

'I would not sully myself.' He turns back to the door and shouts, 'Come in! Come and take her.'

The gardener and his lad come in, their expression half belligerent and half sheepish.

'I'm sorry, miss. If you come quiet, we won't have to force it,' the gardener says.

Arabella watches, still in her trance-like state, apparently entirely unaffected.

'Where are you taking me?' Letty demands.

'To the church,' snaps the Beloved. 'If your wicked soul can endure the torment of being in a holy place.'

'Of course I can. Very well.' Letty draws herself up tall. 'But I shall walk there myself. I don't want any hands laid upon me.'

The Beloved gestures to the gardener and his boy to let her pass, and Letty walks past them with her head held high, hoping she is concealing her fear. *If only I'd left just a little earlier. But there's no help for it now. And they won't hurt me. They can't.*

The church is empty when she gets there, followed by the gardener and his boy at a short distance, and she paces about inside, wondering what she is supposed to do now. The place feels strangely torpid without anyone in it. It is just a room, she realises. Ornate and decorated and dedicated to lofty ideas, but empty, it has no vitality.

It is not long before the members of the community begin to arrive. Letty sits down in the front row, but no one joins her. They sit a few rows behind or on the other side of the aisle, keeping a safe margin between them as though she were infectious. The Angels come, and the ladies, young and old, and the few men of the community. The Reverend Silas staggers in supported by his walking stick on one side and his wife on the other.

When all are assembled in muttering quiet, no organ playing this time, the Beloved appears, with Arabella at his side. Silence falls as he marches majestically up to the front of the church and stands before them, just as he does for every service, but this time his mouth is set in a grim line and he exudes fury from every pore. Arabella takes her place in a seat at the front.

Everyone waits expectantly as he glares around the congregation. They can all feel his fury. Letty, watching him from her seat alone at the front, finds that the more irate he appears, the more her fear of him subsides.

He's an actor. A pantomime villain. Captain Hook ranting

and foaming but ultimately powerless. What can he do to me, after all? This is a farce.

The thoughts calm her. She thinks of Arthur, laughing at all of it, pointing out the Beloved's habit of puffing out his chest and stalking about like a clockwork soldier. It seemed so impressive once; now it looks ridiculous. Once her world revolved around this man, and now, suddenly, she longs to be free: out in the real world, doing real things, finding out about what matters. She realises that she hasn't seen a newspaper or listened to the wireless since the Beloved arrived, so effectively has he created his own domain controlled entirely by him.

She sees his immense vanity and understands that this little exhibition is in order for him to keep face in front of his flock. She wishes she could puncture it and show him for what he is.

At last he stops striding about and glaring, and stands to face them. 'My brothers and sisters, we have been afflicted by a great unhappiness. The evil one has been busy here! I knew we would draw his fire before too long, but I did not foresee how cruelly. To lose our beloved Sarah is almost too much to bear. But we will bear it, because I am among you.'

He stretches out his hands in blessing, and speaks words of comfort in his deepest, most vibrating voice, and they sigh happily to hear it. They are besieged by the evil one, but they must have faith. Corporeal death means nothing to the spirit. The day is at hand when they will see Sarah in glory again, among the multitude of the faithful. Then he stretches an arm towards Arabella and looks about at his flock.

'And it may well be that Sarah has not left us at all. For a new spirit joins as hers departs. In a miracle, this woman has conceived and she will bear a child.'

There's a murmur, perhaps not the amazement that the Beloved might have expected. Rumours of the pregnancy have been rife for weeks.

Letty knows his tricks by now but she still is taken aback by his brazenness. *Is he really implying that Arabella's is a virgin conception? Surely even he wouldn't be so outrageous! But he's fudging it just a little, tying it into Sarah's death. They needn't be afraid for she's not dead at all. It's a form of re-incarnation. I wonder how he's going to work that into his religious theory! I suppose he simply borrows what he wants from other faiths.*

The Beloved cries, 'Hallelujah! Let us give thanks that we have been granted a miracle!' and Arabella smiles, a little wanly, and accepts the congratulations of the crowd. 'It is,' goes on the Beloved, 'all the more miraculous when you con-sider that there are forces of darkness living and working among us.'

The crowd shifts uneasily, and glances dart Letty's way. She stiffens. There's no doubt of who is he talking about.

'But mark my words, the Day of Judgement will come when all shall be revealed, and the chaff will be taken out and tossed into the fire!'

Letty senses the mood change and harden. The Beloved points at her, and cries, 'Pray, brothers and sisters, for this poor lost soul! Once she was blessed, a true believer, one of the chosen. But she has wilfully turned her back on salvation. She has embraced the Devil. She has fornicated with him.'

There's a shocked intake of breath from the congregation and a murmur of distaste.

The Beloved searches the rows of faces until he sees the Kendalls, and his expression turns to one of abject misery. 'My heart breaks for your pain, the parents of the traitor in our midst. The Judas. The one sent to test us and reveal the truth about what we believe in our hearts. You' – he spreads his arms out over the whole gathering – 'you have remained faithful. Your steadfastness will be remembered in paradise. You will have the best rooms in the great mansion of heaven. You will enjoy the pampered rest of the elect!'

Promising rooms in heaven like it's a holiday camp. He'll be telling them there'll be linen sheets and kippers for breakfast next. She can hear Arthur laughing out loud at it all.

The Beloved has not finished with her. He turns back. 'But evil will out, brothers and sisters. Not all can stay constant. Some fail the test! And this . . . this new Eve . . . could not resist the temptation to take the Devil into her heart.'

An angry muttering starts behind her. The Beloved's oratory is having its usual effect. He knows how to play upon their emotions and how to work them into a frenzy. Letty knows it only too well: how easy it is to give in and believe, because it is simpler than thinking too hard about what is being said. And the strength and conviction of that personality is almost too much to stand up to, so one surrenders and allows it to take control. There's something so reassuring about someone else's absolute certainty that they are right. It's the easiest thing in the world to agree, and the hardest to be the one who stands up and says no.

I know what a scapegoat feels like now. And it's utterly horrible.

Behind her, she can hear the growing murmur of displeasure and resentment. Across the aisle, Arabella turns to look at her, her eyes blank and yet contemptuous. She begins to feel a flicker of uneasiness.

Where will this end?

She has assumed that she will be banished. But the Beloved is working the crowd up to a greater climax than that. She has not been afraid of a congregation of mostly middle-aged women, some men, and domestics. But now she looks behind her and sees that they are regarding her with hatred. They know the stories of wicked women, of Jezebels, thrown to the dogs as punishment for their sins. She is the embodiment of evil now, the one who caused death to visit the community, and she will be blamed and punished in order to cleanse the place and protect the Beloved from the disenchantment of his followers.

'What do we do with those who reject truth and follow the ways of the evil one? What is good for the lustful whores of Babylon who hunger for the spawn of Beelzebub?'

The Beloved has never spoken like this before. Scared, Letty gets to her feet and shouts, 'This is all a lie!'

Her voice startles him into silence. Then he turns to look at her, and she sees triumph in his eyes. He is glad that she has engaged with him, for he believes he is certain to defeat her. He will twist her words until, as he promised, she condemns herself out of her own mouth. She thinks of the way witches were once punished, tossed into a pond or burnt to death, and sees the angry mob grabbing her, hustling her to the lake and forcing her into the water. She begins to shake.

'A lie, is it?' sneers the Beloved. 'You want to defend evil – how can it be otherwise? You will find us united and strong, despite your attempts to defeat us!'

'A lie,' Letty says firmly. 'I intend to leave this place, and none of you may stop me.' She turns to face them all, trying to control her fear and her shaking hands. 'I wish none of you ill, and I reject the claims of the Beloved. It is ludicrous to accuse me of these outrageous untruths, and in your hearts, you all know it. Sarah died because the Beloved cannot promise you immortality. You know this! You can see it with your own eyes! He has fathered a child with my sister! He is the same as the rest of us – human and a sinner.'

She can tell from their faces that they do not believe her for an instant. They do not want to hear it.

'Blasphemy!' roars the Beloved, his eyes flashing. She has played into his hands, but how could she fail to? 'Impious, vile blasphemy, filth spouted by a demon! Seize her!'

Two of the younger Angels, their faces flushed with the passion his words have inspired in them, rush forward and grab her arms.

Will I be beaten? Letty thinks with fright. She would not have believed them capable of it, but now she realises that if the first blow is thrown, they will all rush in a frenzy, like a pack of hounds at the kill. *Where will it stop?*

'A lost sheep who will not be found and brought home!'

411

spits the Beloved. 'A wandering sinner who will not be redeemed!'

At that moment, the door to the church is flung open and young Dickie, the errand boy, comes running in, breathless and red-cheeked. 'They're coming!' he shouts.

Everyone turns to watch him pelting up the aisle, a newspaper under his arm.

'What?' demands the Beloved.

'It's all in the paper – about this house, and about you, your worship! And what you've promised us all, and what you've declared!' Dickie is panting as he comes to a halt in front of the Beloved. He holds out the paper. 'They've had a meeting in the village and they've worked themselves up into a fury all right. That young man what lived here and married the miss, he read it out to them. He wrote it!'

Mrs Kendall shrieks and collapses into her husband's arms, moaning as he tries to hold her steady.

The Beloved snatches the paper from Dickie's hands before anyone can see what is written there. 'Foul lies!' he declares. 'As you would expect. And they are coming here, you say?'

'They're marching here,' Dickie says, his eyes bright with excitement. 'I kept just ahead of them all the way on me bike. They say they want the reckoning, and I've never seen them so het up.'

There's a murmur of disquiet among the faithful. The outside world is about to arrive at the doors and demand an explanation.

'Calm, brothers and sisters, be calm!' The Beloved is at his most serene, his huge hands held out to settle them. 'Do not be afraid. We will meet these villagers, and speak to them, and explain the truth. Be strong in faith! We have nothing to fear.'

'And what about this one?' demands the Angel holding Letty's right arm. Her nails are pinching uncomfortably but Letty dare not complain.

'Bring her with us,' decrees the Beloved. 'We shall decide on her punishment when the villagers have left us in peace.'

He sails forward to lead them out of the church. A procession forms behind him, and the next moment, one of the brass players starts tooting a hymn on his instrument and they begin to sing and clap as they walk behind the Beloved.

He has such complete faith in himself. He's not afraid of what Arthur's written about him in the press, or of what the villagers think. Letty knows that it's the Beloved's claims of divinity that will fill them with loathing and outrage. *Does he guess it?*

'Come on,' mutters the rougher of the Angels, tugging her arm viciously. 'You're coming with us.'

'All right, all right,' says Letty, as they fall into step at the back of the procession, just behind Arabella, who walks slowly, swaying slightly as she goes. 'I'm coming.'

Chapter Thirty-Three

When I wake up in my bed, I can hardly believe what I've done. Archer is beside me, lying on his front, fast asleep, one muscled arm dangling down, the other curled above his head on the white pillow.

I let him bring me here. I let him take me to bed. I curdle inside thinking about it. *I'm old enough to be his mother!*

Maybe not his mother. But there must be a good ten or twelve years between us at least. Why did I do it?

He insisted.

He did insist, in the sweetest, most alluring way, but with a firm refusal to take no for an answer. 'It's written,' he kept saying, holding my hand and stroking my hair. 'It's supposed to be this way. Trust me. I've seen it.'

And in the end, I couldn't resist. He kissed me with soft, tender presses on my lips, again and again, until I could take it no more. My frozen soul unthawed and awoke, filling up with a craving for everything I'd so carefully put to sleep. All I can remember now is the unfamiliarity of his body, his stranger's scent, and the way, most of all, I longed for Rory.

Rory is part of another existence now. One that is far away and that I've given up all rights to. I abandoned it and now I can never go back. I understand that. My experience with Archer has not only made me an unfaithful wife – and an old fool, I suppose – but it has made it clear to me at last that when I left, it was for good. They would never want me back now. I've left them all behind. Rory, Caz, my mother, my sister . . .

'Good morning, Rachel.' A blue eye is fixed on me, a half-smile emerging from under the pillow. 'Fancy seeing you here.' Archer turns over, yawns and stretches. I admire his smooth brown torso with its well-formed muscles, but with a detachment that surprises me, considering what we've done together. He is a good-looking man, there is no doubt about it. But in the end, it's just packaging. And I find myself thinking nostalgically of Rory's soft solidity instead.

Don't. That's all gone. You may as well freeze yourself back up again. Better if you do.

Archer reaches out a hand to me. 'Thank you for that, Rachel. I will really remember it.'

'Oh. Thank you. So will I.'

'It's something that happens with all new recruits. It has to. We have to share the love, don't we? And I was particularly hoping that we'd have an older woman with us. That's why I said to Alison, take that one. She's the one.'

I stare at him, uncomprehending for a moment. Then I remember. Alison, from ARK. The one who recruited me to be a guardian here.

'So,' I say, 'you saw my application?'

'Of course. I saw them all. We thought it would be a good way to get some fresh blood in. And the place wasn't ready for any of us. I wasn't going to send them in here without knowing a bit about it. We had the usual geeks and students applying. But then we had you. Supposedly an artist. So I looked you up. I couldn't find a Rachel Capshaw who matched you. I even sent you to our techie boys to track down and they couldn't. Most unusual.' He grins at me again. 'You tickled my fancy. I guessed you must be on the run from something, looking for a tribe and a new start maybe. And I liked this.' He reaches out a hand and ruffles my white hair. Then he leans over and says seriously, 'You mustn't be offended if I don't sleep with you every night. I couldn't even if I wanted to – and of course I do want to,' he adds hurriedly. 'But I've got a lot of love to share. I need to make sure there are no favourites; it's part of the creed we live by. You understand, right?'

I nod, staring at him. Part of my brain is thinking about boring practicalities like numbers of sexual partners and safe sex and all the rest of it. Another part is listening with an incredulity that is almost amused.

'But the whole point here is that you're not alone. Never. There'll always be someone to love. I saw that Fisher likes you – he was really keen to share with you last night. And Sophia is a big fan of yours. We're fine with sharing between three, four, as many as you like – if you're open to that. It might take a while to get accustomed to the idea if you're not used to it, but honestly, soon it's as natural as breathing.'

'Okay,' I say, feeling as though I'm teetering slightly on the edge of hysteria. 'I understand.'

He puts a hand on my shoulder. 'Honestly, we prize older women here. They have a lot to teach us, and you have less likelihood of getting pregnant. I hope you'll see your way to showing the younger guys how to be mature lovers.'

I start to laugh. I can't help it. It sounds too funny, and besides, it deflates me with an unintended yet perfect precision.

'What's so funny?' he asks, bewildered.

'Oh, nothing. Nothing. I can't explain. Let's talk about it another time. You should get up and get some breakfast. I'll see you later.'

I shower off all traces of the night before, feeling like an adult who has made the mistake of going to a teenage party and getting carried away into believing they are still young, and that the sight of them bopping on the dance floor, pulling some shapes and singing to the music, isn't inherently ridiculous to all who see them. But the comfort is that afterwards, the adult laughs it off and goes back to knowing that at least all the teenage angst and heartbreak lies far in the past.

'I've been so stupid,' I tell myself, but I can't beat myself up. I forgot I wasn't really a part of this crowd. I thought for a moment I was like them: young, gorgeous, carefree; a true believer in a creed that is dubious to say the least. But my illusions have been thoroughly shattered. Now I know I'm the token older woman, with a brief to be a kind of geisha to the inexperienced youth.

Though, going by what I saw last night, it's more probable that they could teach me a few things.

As I get dressed, I feel an emotion I haven't felt for a while: a longing for home. For so long, that yearning has been accompanied by a pain like a knife in the gut, bringing with it the knowledge of what happened to our home and to Heather. Now the pain is still there, but there's a deep hunger for what was inside our home, its true heart. *There is another presence I need to think about. The other person at the table . . . But . . .* I shake my head.

No. I can't go there. It's too much. It's too awful.

Still, the thoughts of home are floating around my head, nagging at me, refusing to let me go. I go to my bag and rummage down until I find the mobile phone that I stuffed inside a sock. I take it out and try to switch it on, but it's completely flat. I plug it in and in a few moments, it's come back to life, the screen bright and packed with missed messages, all from Caz as far as I can see. I go to the messages screen and start to read them. They're all as I expected: asking repeatedly if I'm safe, where I am, could I please get in touch, have I seen the police are searching for me . . .

I'll think about that later.

It's too tiring right now.

I notice that one message is from my email provider and I open it up.

This message is to alert you to unauthorised use of your account. To verify your identity please text the

**verification code you were sent in a previous message.
A temporary reset password will then be sent to you.**

I go further down my texts and there is indeed a verification code. It's all too likely that someone has been trying to break into my account, attempting to find out where I am. Well, a new password will sort that out. I text the verification code back to the number, and leave my phone to carry on charging.

In the kitchen I decide not to drink the fuzz-inducing tea, and get myself a cup of coffee. It's a hive of activity in the house, as usual, and everyone seems very fresh faced after last night. I'm pouring in the milk when I see that one of the other people in the kitchen is Kaia. She turns and sees me, shooting me a look of hatred, and turns her back again.

Okay. So that explains the tears last night. Poor kid. She can't be the only one. They're all in love with him in their different ways.

I take my coffee and go out of the front door, sipping the hot liquid in the coolness of the morning air. I wander round to the rhododendron bushes, admiring their glossy dark green leaves and wondering when they will burst into flower, and what colour they will be when they do.

As I'm staring at them, I hear a noise, a rustling and cracking, and then I see a figure in a big brown coat hiding a little further on in the thicket. It emerges from around the trunk of a tree to look at me and beckon hard with a hiss.

'Matty?' I say.

'Come on!' is the reply and she dashes a little way off before turning to hiss and beckon again. 'Come over here!'

I follow her with my mug still in my hand, curious. She keeps darting off before I can get close enough to ask what she's doing and in this way she leads me out of the thicket and all the way to the path that goes to Nursery Cottage.

When Matty arrives at the gate, she stops and allows me to reach her.

'What are you doing?' I ask. 'Hiding from someone?'

'Hush.' She looks about almost fearfully. 'Come on, you must come inside.' She hurries away down the path.

Inside, the cottage is exactly as I remember it: a mishmash of things, crowded furniture and a fug of cosy warmth. In the old kitchen, the beautiful snow rose bonsai sits in its place of honour, its leaves now out and the petals unfurling. As usual, Sissy is in the rocking chair by the range, knitting a perfect piece of work with an intricate pattern inside it.

Blind, my foot. She can see better than I can.

And yet the eyes are staring somewhere else, blinking slowly as her needles clack.

'She's here!' exclaims Matty. 'I found her. At last.' She sends me a reproachful look. 'We've been worried about you. We haven't seen any trace of you since those people arrived. We had no idea what they'd done with you.'

I'm touched by their concern. I sit down at the table. 'It's nice of you to worry but I'm okay.'

'So . . . they're here then,' Matty says. She sinks down into one of the chairs opposite me, not bothering to take her coat off. 'The owners.'

'Yes, that's right.'

'Who is it? Who's the owner?'

I hesitate. I wanted to ask the sisters about the connection between them and the Kendalls, but now I know what's going on up at the house, I'm not sure how much I should say. But, I reason, they have a right to know. After all, they live right next door, they're going to notice some of the odder things. And the last thing I want is for one of them to get ambushed in the woods by someone practising their combat skills. 'Well, there is something unusual about the people who've arrived.'

'Yes?' Sissy's gone still again, her needles no longer moving. 'What is it?'

'It's not a family or anything like that. It's more like a community of young people, who all share the same beliefs, and want to live in the same way.'

'Ahhh.' The sound comes out of Matty like a sigh. 'As we thought.'

'Is that . . . is it like something that's happened before?' I ask. 'With the church in the grounds, and the things that Sissy said to me about your Beloved? Because that's what they call him.'

'Do they, now?' Sissy starts to rock again. 'And what's the name of this Beloved?'

'Archer. Archer Kendall. He says his great-aunt once owned the house.'

The sisters are visibly shocked. Sissy's mouth drops open,

her hands falling to her lap with the knitting pooling on her skirt, her blank gaze turned to me.

'Kendall!' exclaims Matty.

Sissy turns towards her sister. 'Would we have sold the house to him, if we'd known?'

'Of course not!' replies Matty indignantly. 'To the traitors? Never! But we didn't know.'

'We can't fight the house,' Sissy says almost sadly. 'It seems to draw people to it. There's nothing we can do about it.'

'But how are the Kendalls traitors, if you got the house from them originally?'

'Not from a Kendall,' Matty says. 'From the eldest Evans sister. It was the youngest who married the Kendall, and he's the one who destroyed the Beloved.'

'As good as,' Sissy puts in. 'He was never the same after the siege. He was a broken man, that's what the old ladies told us. He never left the house again. Many left. Only the most faithful remained.'

'The Kendall boy wrote inflammatory lies about the Beloved in the paper and the village marched on us. The night of the fire. They said nothing was the same after that. The Beloved's message began to fall on stony ground.'

'Who was this Beloved you're talking about?'

'A great man,' Matty says gravely. 'No matter what the truth of his claims.'

'Our grandfather,' Sissy says. 'Shall we tell her, Matty?'

Matty glances over at Sissy, then says slowly, 'We find it hard to speak of. We've been so accustomed to keeping it to ourselves. We didn't mix much with outsiders, you see, because of all the scandal. We had everything we needed here. Our mother, the Beloved's daughter, stayed on all her life, and she told us it was our duty to stay too, and look after the old people until the last believer had gone. After that, it was just us.'

'What did they believe?'

'In the Beloved. In the promises he made them. He said the Day of Judgement was at hand, and that they would all be saved, everyone else given over to hellfire. He said there would be no death. But after he died himself, broken, they said, by the ridicule heaped on him by the newspapers and the village, there was no more taking that as gospel. Our mother and grandmother worked to keep the faith alive, and lived in the house, trying to restore its reputation, and stayed true to the memory of those who went before. They didn't dare go to the village, even after the Beloved was gone, but eventually the bad feeling was all forgotten. They forgave us for the way the Beloved had outraged them all. Of course, we weren't there then. We were born later.'

'Here, in Nursery Cottage, where the babies were born,' puts in Sissy, rocking and knitting. 'After the Beloved's second wife died, he married again, and there were three babies from that marriage. Our mother, Glory, was born in 1928. She got married after the war and had our brother David, and then us. The Beloved had passed on by then. She and her husband stayed here to bring us up and look after the believers that remained. Everyone was supposed to stay, and live as one family. Those of us related to the Beloved, we were the holy family.' Sissy laughs. 'Imagine that! The holy family. Better than being the Queen!'

'Yes,' I say. 'In theory.'

Matty says, 'It's all long ago. Far in the past now.'

'And Archer – Lord Kendall – says it was his great-aunt that gave the house to . . . the Beloved?' I ask, getting confused.

'That's right.' Matty nods. 'Miss Arabella Evans. The Beloved's second wife.'

'I see. I think. So he's come back here.' *No wonder he felt a sense of destiny about the place.*

Matty says to me, 'So what are they up to in there? We've seen a lot of work going on. They're certainly busy, aren't they?'

I tell her a little of what is being prepared, though I don't go into details about the group marriage ceremony. I explain that they're getting ready for the near-certain disaster that lies around the corner. Almost excitedly, I tell them the theory that Archer outlined to me: the fertile mixture of climate change, political turmoil, shortages of food and lack of medicine that will lead to the outbreak of chaos and destruction. I explain that Archer is building a shelter for his followers as a sanctuary from the danger, preparing them to face the upheavals of the future.

They listen carefully and when I've finished, Matty sighs and says, 'Nothing changes, does it, Sissy?'

Sissy shakes her head and says, 'No, it doesn't.'

'What do you mean?' I ask, frowning. 'This is entirely a new problem. It's a modern issue.'

'Maybe. But it's no different to what the Beloved preached, is it?' asks Sissy.

Matty says in a booming voice, 'The end of the world is nigh! The apocalypse is just around the corner! Follow me and you shall live!'

'But . . .' I laugh a little. 'It's completely different.'

'Is it?' She stares at me with those almost-black eyes of hers.

'Yes, it's based on fact, not fairy stories.'

'Is it?' Matty asks again.

I falter, suddenly not sure of myself.

'There are strange things in this world,' Sissy says softly. She has stopped knitting now. 'You should know that more than most, shouldn't you?'

'The facts have a way of changing,' Matty adds. 'What one generation believes wholeheartedly, another rejects. It's the way.'

'We grew up being told all the time that any day might bring the end of everything,' says Sissy.

'But it never did,' Matty said. 'And we ended up not really living at all.'

'And as for fairy stories . . . well . . .' Sissy turns her blank – or are they? – eyes to me. 'You know very well that the oddest stories there are can turn out to be true. Can't they? And we can believe quite easily in the impossible.'

I go still. I know she is about to talk to me about the thing, the one thing, I can't discuss.

'So,' she says. 'Your little snow rose. How is she?'

Chapter Thirty-Four

The sky is a pale navy with the first flicker of stars in its depths as the procession makes its way out of the church and back towards the house, then down the driveway to where the high wrought-iron gates are firmly closed. The Beloved marches at its head, his faithful following and singing loudly as they go. Letty is half dragged along at the back by her two hostile Angels, who are clearly of the mind that the Beloved will look kindly on ill treatment.

'Stop pinching, can't you? I can walk perfectly well if you'll only let me,' Letty snaps, and the girls are cowed by her tone, but only for a moment. She realises that it must be after six o'clock. She was supposed to be at the gates to meet Archer, but everything that's happened has driven it from her mind. As they advance upon the gates, Letty cranes her neck and sees that a makeshift barricade has been built by means of driving the old cart against the gates and surrounding it with bits of old furniture, cart wheels and assorted rubbish. Why a pile of old junk should be any more protecting than stout iron gates, Letty can't imagine, but the gardener stands ready for action, a rake in one hand and a shovel in the other, while Dickie the errand boy dances around in a state of high excitement shouting, 'They're nearly here!'

Is Arthur there? she wonders. *Is he waiting for me? How will I get to him?* She longs desperately to see him. If he only spots her, he'll get her away from here in a moment. But how will he, in this crowd?

Now, above the sound of singing and the toot of the Redeemed's trumpets, Letty thinks she can hear another sound, a kind of roar that is getting louder and louder. Another procession is heading to meet them, and Letty can see the flicker of torches held high above a snaking mass of bodies.

'Pray, dear ones!' yells the Beloved. 'Pray and sing! We have divine protection, and no one may harm us!'

The faithful sing with more gusto than ever, though one or two faces betray anxiety when they catch a wisp of sound: ferocious chants and angry yells growing in strength every moment.

Letty tries to shake off one of the Angels, who is singing loudly but tunelessly and is clearly losing interest in her charge. 'Let go, can't you? I won't run off.' Just then, she spots Kitty standing close by, lifting up on tiptoe to gaze anxiously at the gates. 'Kitty, Kitty! Can you see what's happening? Tell me what's going on.'

Kitty turns to look at her with frightened eyes, the trial forgotten for now. 'Oh miss, can you hear them? What can they be wanting with us?'

'Don't be afraid,' Letty reassures her. 'It's the people from the village. We've known them all our lives. They won't hurt us.'

'But they're in a frenzy, can't you hear them? There's been some terrible lies, terrible! They say we have wild beasts in the grounds to eat intruders, and that there's a huge revolving table in the church where the Beloved selects a woman to be his bride for the week. They say we do wicked, immoral things. It's not true! Not a word.'

'You're right, it's not true,' Letty says grimly. 'But there's enough strangeness here to feed rumours like that.'

Kitty shuts her eyes. 'We must pray for protection.'

Letty thinks. It is hard to imagine the local people, most of whom she's known all her life, doing any real harm to the souls here. *When they find it's mostly old ladies, no harem of virgins or public deflowerings to be seen, surely they'll calm down.* But, she realises, it isn't the lurid rumours that have caused this protest. Those have been circulating for a long time without much more than stretched eyes and prurient outrage to show for it. No. It is the Beloved they want. Perhaps they've heard about Emily and the lake. They most certainly have read the report in the paper. It is the blasphemy and hypocrisy they hate. That is what they are here to destroy.

The sound from beyond the gates is getting louder – the shouts and cries of the mob, working itself up into a righteous anger. They are close now, she guesses.

Suddenly she hears the booming voice of the Beloved. 'Come, all ye who have ears! Come and heed the word!'

'It's him!' cries Kitty, her eyes shining. 'He will show them the way!'

Suddenly it is there: a twisting, rolling mass standing at the gates, shaking them so that the bolts rattle and shriek, yelling and shouting in fury. Torches cast an eerie glow over the mob, illuminating faces twisted with rage, mouths open and shouting. There seem to be hundreds of people whistling, calling, howling, deriding the Beloved with open jeers.

'Come out and tell us all about the word!' calls one man. 'We can't wait to hear it! Come on then!'

'Come and do some of your miracles for us!'

'Yes, let's see you walk on the lake, shall we?'

'Or let us break your legs, then you'll see if you can rise up and walk!'

In the darkness, Kitty clutches at Letty. 'They're monsters! They'll tear us limb from limb!'

'Surely not,' she says, but she is frightened. She's never seen a crowd enraged and felt the power of its fury. Some men are trying to climb the gates and Letty sees now that the make-shift barricade is a useful mound to leap for, an easy ladder down on the other side.

We're not prepared for all this! We're only a lot of little old ladies singing! Can't they see?

But just at that moment, the most vicious of the Angels digs hard fingers into her arm. 'Happy now?' she demands. 'Now that your friends are here?'

'They're not my friends.'

'Likely story! You're the viper in the bosom around here. Our Jonah. You're bringing this evil on us!' All their fear and distrust seems to shine out of her angry eyes.

'Now, girls,' Kitty says in a tremulous voice. 'We need to stick together. Let the Beloved deal with her, she's his kin.'

'We ought to do something before they break in and take her,' says the Angel, hardly listening to Kitty.

The Beloved stands near the gates – although not near enough for any missiles to hit him – and lifts his hands high, declaiming about the word and the will and the plan in all his familiar language, the rhetoric that usually serves him so well, but it only enrages those who hear him and sets them jeering harder and louder. More boys are trying to shin up the gates; one is bound to succeed, even with the gardener valiantly pushing them back with the rake. There is noise and tumult and confusion and nothing seems likely to break through it until, suddenly, a loud clanging is heard above the commotion with a voice yelling, 'Stop, stop, I say!'

There is a sudden sinking of the noise and the tones are heard again, strong and clear.

'Stop this madness!'

'It's Arthur!' Letty says with delight. Now she can make him out, standing close against the gates, facing the angry crowd, a dustbin lid in one hand and a hammer in the other which he's been using to make the din.

'Quiet, I say!' he commands, and there is a hush. Even the Beloved stops declaiming, and the hymn singing fades away to one or two reedy voices. 'This has gone too far! You can certainly make known your displeasure, but let's not go so far as to threaten these people. Most mean no harm. And violence is no answer!'

There's an angry murmur but Arthur quietens it down.

430

'Please, be calm. The police will soon be here – I'm told the force has been dispatched from Goreham – and you'll be on the wrong side of them. You are good, law-abiding people! You have made your feelings known. Now, go home.'

There is a pause, a murmur. Calm seems close to being restored.

Then, into the relative peace, a voice rips out, fierce, uncompromising.

'I am the way!' booms the Beloved. 'Only by me shall you see salvation! Only the elect shall be saved, and ye chaff and rubbish shall be cast into the fire!'

It is all it takes. The passion of the mob is reignited, more furious than ever. Men scramble for the gates, Arthur's shouts lost in the melee. The Beloved cries, 'Brothers and sisters, to the church!' and the next moment all of the faithful turn on their heels and run, heading for the safety of the high walls and strong doors of the church. They stream around Letty, as she fights to stand still and not be taken off with them.

'Arthur!' she shouts. 'I'm here! Arthur!'

Her guards have gone. Kitty has disappeared. The gardener cannot hold back the onslaught any longer, and the first intruder drops to the ground inside the gates, then turns to start unbolting them.

Then an iron grip seizes her arm. 'Come with me,' murmurs a steely voice, and Letty looks up into the icy-blue eyes of the Beloved.

'Let me go!' she cries. 'Arthur!'

'You're not going anywhere.' The Beloved yanks her

roughly and drags her after him as he heads in the opposite direction to the church.

'Arthur!' she screams, but no one can hear her against the noise. She cannot prevent herself being dragged away.

A moment later, they are skirting the east wing of the house, and the noise level drops at once.

'Let me go,' Letty pants, her arm painful in the Beloved's grip.

'I've had enough of you and the trouble you make,' snarls the Beloved, pulling her roughly along. 'If you think I'm letting you out to ferment and stir against me out there, and spoil all we have here, you are quite, quite wrong. You will have to learn to accept your place. Your spirit will be broken and you will learn to accept your fate.'

On the last word, he pulls open the door to the old stable, the one used only for storing packing cases and bits of rubbish. Then, with a great shove, he pushes Letty inside. She trips and sprawls on the floor, finding herself in a pile of straw and filth. Before she can speak, he has slammed shut the door and she hears the iron bolt shoot home.

She looks up helplessly at the door, panting, her arm throbbing where it has been gripped hard. 'Let me out!' she shouts, but she knows it's hopeless. All eyes will be on the gates and on the church, where the mob might already be gathering. She scrambles up and shakes at the door but it's firmly locked on the outside, so she looks about instead for a window she might crawl through, or perhaps a loose plank in the wall she can prise out, but it is almost entirely dark now, and she cannot make out much at all.

She yells and shouts for what seems like a long time, but guesses that with the noise and trouble outside, no one will hear her. Then she smells it. Her nose wrinkles and she sniffs. It's unmistakable.

Smoke.

She sniffs again and it is stronger now, getting stronger every second. Then she realises with horror that the stables are on fire.

Is he burning me? Is that his plan?

Surely not. Surely the Beloved is not capable of that! But . . . he wants Letty gone. This way, her money will go to Arabella. She will cause no more trouble for him. Her death will be blamed on the mob.

Panic floods through her. The smoke is growing stronger still, visible now as grey skeins in the gloom. She shakes the door again and shouts. 'Help! Help! Fire!'

The blaze must be catching fast, though she cannot see flames. The stable is filling with the thick black smothering smoke. Letty starts to cough, her eyes sting. 'Help!' she yells again, but her voice comes weak and strained from the smoke in her throat. 'Please!'

She turns to look for another way out, but now the stable is a mass of dense smoke with a bright heart where, she realises, the far wall is now in flames. It's too late to leave by any other way. Her eyes are streaming, she's gasping and choking. Turning back to the door, she bangs again, her fists weak on the wood. She knows now that the smoke will take her long before the flames. The air is almost gone already. She slumps against the door, her eyes screwed shut, gasping. She begins to pray in the way she did so long ago, before the Beloved appeared in their lives. It is all she can think to do.

Then, just as she hardly knows any longer what is happening, she tastes the sweetest thing she has ever known. Fresh cool air is on her face, in her lungs. The door has opened, she has fallen out onto the path, and a soft hand is on her cheek.

'Come, Letty,' says a voice, low and urgent. 'We must go at once. The fire has taken hold.'

Letty looks through swollen lids and reddened eyes. It is Arabella.

Chapter Thirty-Five

Caz cleans her house furiously. It's all she can do to keep her mind off the time ticking away. The trap they laid for Kate hasn't worked. She hasn't looked at her phone, or else she's too clever to fall for the phishing text. Or perhaps Rory is right, and she's dead.

As she works through the kitchen cupboards, emptying each one, cleaning and replacing, even scrubbing the grime from the tops, she can't help picturing ways in which Kate could have died so that no one has found her. Perhaps she jumped from a ferry and has been lost in the waters somewhere, never to be found. There are those presumed dead who've left cars by the sea and vanished.

Then where's the car?

But the car is hired, presumably in whatever name she used for her credit card.

Oh Kate, when you decided to hide, you certainly did it well.

Then something floats into Caz's mind. She remembers going through the post yesterday, and in it was a piece of junk mail with a name on it she didn't recognise. She slung it into the pile for recycling and thought nothing more of it. But now something occurs to her.

What if Kate's pseudonym has been passed on to a marketing list somewhere? What if the circular was for her, and came here because she used this address for the credit card? Maybe it somehow slipped through the redirection order.

She drops the damp cloth and runs to the table in the hall. There's the pile of free newspapers and supermarket leaflets and unsolicited catalogues and all the rest of the stuff destined for the bin. She rifles through it quickly but can't find the envelope, so goes back through again more slowly, and then she sees it: the slim bit of cardboard advertising a new kind of credit card. It's addressed to Ms Rachel Capshaw.

Caz's hands start to shake and her stomach twists in anxious excitement. She picks up the phone and dials Rory's number, which she now knows by heart. His mobile is switched off and goes straight to voicemail, so he must be in the hospital with Ady. 'It's me,' she says. 'I think I might have a lead on Kate. Call me when you can.' Then she hurries to the computer and starts an internet search on the name 'Rachel Capshaw'.

Rory calls half an hour later.

'What is it, Caz? What's the lead?'

'Are you at the hospital?'

'In the cafe there now. Just getting a coffee while Ady's signs are checked and they give him his meds.'

'How is he?'

'Doing well. They're sure the head injury won't cause lasting damage. The internal swelling is down.'

'That's good.'

'So?' He sounds anxious, eager. 'Don't keep me in suspense.'

'It might be nothing. Kate used my address for her credit card application and a piece of junk mail came through addressed to Rachel Capshaw. It suddenly occurred to me that that might be the name she's using.'

'That's a great idea!' Rory says.

'Yeah, that's what I thought. But there are Rachel Capshaws on Twitter, Facebook, LinkedIn, and all the rest of it, scattered all over the world. I can't pin any of them down as being Kate. She wouldn't advertise herself on those places. And of course, the names and addresses in this country would have to be on the electoral roll. She won't be on that either. So I think it's a dead end.' Caz sighs with frustration. 'I'm sorry.'

'I think we should go back to the police,' Rory says. 'They have to listen to us now we've got a name. Maybe they could put out a press release, reinvigorate interest in the case, do something . . . If people just hear the name, it might trigger something.'

Caz takes a deep breath. 'Yes, I think you're right. Let's go to the police and make them listen to us. I'll tell them everything I know.' She's aware that there might be consequences for holding back information earlier, but she's going to have to face that now, if it means they can find Kate faster.

At that moment, her telephone pings with an incoming

text. She sees it illuminate on the table next to her, but she can't read it from the angle she's at.

'But if we don't find her, or it's not even her fake name, then you might be in trouble needlessly,' Rory says.

'I know. But I'm back to work on Monday. The girls are coming home. We haven't got much more time.' She reaches out and turns the phone towards her, frowning as she reads it. It's just five numbers. What can that be? A mis-sent text? She goes to swipe it away, then pauses, her finger hovering over the screen, the delete button glowing red.

Wait. Oh my God. It's worked. It must be Kate's verification code. Lucas has forwarded it without a message.

Her heart starts to race. Rory is talking but she's not listening, instead she stutters out, 'It's here, Rory, it's here . . . the code . . .'

'What?'

Caz can hear his puzzlement down the line. 'The verification code! It's here! We can get into Kate's email. Get here as soon as you can.'

She runs to the computer in the study, goes into Kate's email provider home page and types in the user name and tells it she can't remember the password. A message pops up saying a verification code has been sent and that Caz should type it in below, or request another. She enters the code with a trembling finger, breathing the numbers as she goes, hoping it's still valid. She presses return, the screen goes white for a moment and then boom, the inbox appears before her. There are her last four messages, all unopened. And below, the ones she sent that Kate did read. And along with those, and others from the car rental company, the bank and the marketing junk is a name she doesn't recognise. Alison@ARKHoldings-ltd. There are many from her, going back to before Kate's disappearance.

Surely this is what we're looking for.

Caz goes down to the first message, and starts to read.

When Rory rings on the doorbell thirty minutes later, breathless and inquisitive, Caz opens the door with a triumphant flourish.

'I think I've found her. I think I know where she is. We can leave right now. Do you want to drive, or shall I?'

Chapter Thirty-Six

Letty coughs and coughs, shaking and clutching on to Arabella as they stumble away from the stables, which are now ablaze, the bright orange flames leaping high into the air and showering sparks as they feast on the old dry wood and the straw and rubbish within. In the distance are the shouts of the crowd, now mostly surrounding the church on the other side of the house.

'Come on,' Arabella coaxes her, leading her towards the gates. 'Keep walking, Letty. That's right.'

When at last the coughing has eased a little, Letty says, 'Thank you. Thank you.'

'I couldn't leave you there,' she says simply.

'You saw him throw me in there, didn't you?' Letty clutches at her and they stop walking. 'Did the Beloved set light to the stable, to burn me?'

Arabella looks at her coldly. 'Of course he didn't. I don't know how that started. I'm sure he was keeping you safe from the mob.'

Letty stares helplessly at her sister. Is Arabella telling the truth? Perhaps it wasn't the Beloved who set light to the stable. Perhaps it was an accident. Maybe others saw him throw her there. She remembers the hard-faced Angel with the digging nails. 'But you will come with me, won't you? Don't stay here, Arabella. Come with me.'

Arabella shakes her head. 'Oh no. My life is here, with him. With everything we've built and the child we are going to have.'

'But Arabella!' Letty is amazed, horrified. 'You know what he's like! You don't believe in him, do you?'

'I believe everything,' Arabella says simply. 'And I always will. So don't waste your breath trying to change my mind. But that doesn't mean I want you dead. Go off and live with your Arthur. Be happy, and let me be happy. Leave us in peace, that's all I ask. We won't do harm, you know that.'

They start to walk again and soon reach the driveway. Letty sees that the Goreham police have arrived and calm is being restored. The barrier has been removed to let the black police van in. The sound of singing still comes from the church but the crowd is being sent on its way, only a few men and boys hanging about, hoping for more action. Now a new shout goes up. 'Fire! Fire! The old stable's alight! All hands to the well!' and everyone left goes racing off after the new excitement.

'Letty! Is that you? Thank heavens!'

Someone comes running towards her and the next moment she is engulfed in a strong embrace. She falls gratefully into Arthur's arms, suddenly exhausted.

'What happened?' he asks, concerned. 'I've been looking for you.'

'She was trapped in the stables when the fire broke out,' Arabella says calmly. 'Will you take her away, please, Arthur? See that a doctor looks at her.' She smiles at Letty. 'I'll send your bags on. Go now. Go on.'

'Please, Arabella?' Letty asks.

Her sister shakes her head. 'No. I'm staying here. That's how it has to be.'

'Come on,' Arthur says gently, putting his arm around her. 'It's time to leave, Letty. Let's go.' They turn and begin to walk through the gates.

'Arthur . . . it was awful.' She begins to tremble with the shock. 'I thought I was going to die. That I'd never see you again.'

'I should never have left you here,' he says grimly. 'I knew I should have insisted. I could have guessed it would be dangerous here. I'm sorry, Letty.'

'We're together now,' she says gratefully, as he puts his coat around her shoulders.

'And always will be,' he replies, holding her close as they turn onto the road.

Letty glances back for a moment at her old home. *I should think I'll never go back.* She feels a mixture of regret and excitement. Her gaze lands on the figure of her sister, dark against the house but clearly full-bellied, one hand resting on her stomach. *Goodbye, Arabella. I hope you'll be happy.*

*

Cecily receives Letty at High Hill Farm with the kind of warmth a prodigal daughter might expect. At last, the scales have fallen, and Cecily is all concern and fuss, making sure Letty is put to bed with a cup of beef broth and a big stone hot-water bottle.

'I'm glad you've come to your senses. If only Arabella would see things the same way,' Cecily says soberly as they sit in the chilly farmhouse drawing room the following day. A doctor has looked at Letty and pronounced her unharmed but she is very tired and her chest hurts. They had to walk most of the way to the farm, before they got a lift from a passing motorist, and it was late by the time they finally arrived. Arthur left first thing this morning to report to the police station about last night's events, and then to take the train to London to visit the newspaper he's been writing for.

'She never will,' Letty says. 'She's determined on it.'

Cecily is quiet while a maid brings tea and anchovy toast and sets it out for them. The toast looks cold and unappealing, the anchovy paste thin. The tea, when Letty tries it, tastes watery. She is struck by an unexpected pang of homesickness: for the house, the warmth of the community, the comfort there and the delicious, unending food. Life outside, she realises, is going to be tougher than she is accustomed to. There will be challenges she does not yet understand, harder things to face than bad toast and horrid tea.

That is the price to pay for independence and freedom.

When the maid has gone, Cecily sniffs and says, 'I can't believe she is a lost cause.'

'She is firm,' Letty says. 'We talked about it. I believe that in her heart she knows that the Beloved – sorry, the Reverend Phillips – is pure bunk, but she's come to rely on her faith in him. It gives her life a meaning she's always searched for, in the same way some get obsessed by politics or art or whatever.'

'Politics I could have taken,' Cecily says bitterly. 'At least then we'd have preserved our inheritance.'

'You still have your money,' points out Letty. 'The house was always Arabella's.'

Cecily sighs. 'I suppose so. But she was – is – quite insane, I don't care what the judge said. By rights, Hanthorpe should have been taken away from her before she gave it to that maniac and his ridiculous herd of women.' Cecily takes a sip of tea. She looks over the china rim at Letty and when she puts the cup back on the saucer, she says delicately, 'And was it all true? The scandalous stories of what you all got up to in that house? I know he did some disgusting things, and in public. We all heard about the way he selected girls to be his bride for the week, and married off everyone willy-nilly. Shocking.'

'That's not quite the case,' Letty says. 'Nothing was done in public, and the marriages were supposed to be spiritual only. But I suspect it was a way of keeping people in the flock, and making sure they didn't remove their financial support. It was only the rich ones he married off.'

'Spiritual only!' Cecily says mockingly. 'That's why Arabella's expecting, I suppose!' She sighs primly. 'Such debauchery. I believe we still have a case for proving she's mad if only we could get her out of that place. Edward thinks the same.'

'You mean kidnap her, like you tried to last time?' Letty shakes her head. 'Leave it be, Cecily. Please. If she is insane, it's as well that she lives happily at home than rots in an asylum.'

'But if she's unfit, the house would come to you and me! Wouldn't you want that?'

'You should stop yearning after it. It will only make you unhappy. This house is lovely; you'll fill it with children and make a new home.' Letty puts her teacup down as well. 'Let go of the house. It will only bring you trouble. We both have more than enough to be comfortable.'

Cecily purses her lips and sniffs again. There's a pause and then she gives Letty a look, her eyebrows raised. 'And you . . . weren't you involved in one of these spiritual marriages? I imagine Phillips was keen to keep you in the community with your income.' Her eyebrows rise higher as she sees Letty flush scarlet. 'Ah. I see. You were. And let me guess.' She smiles. 'Arthur?'

Letty blushes even more deeply and nods.

'And not quite as spiritual as it was supposed to be . . .'

'He's always been a perfect gentleman!' bursts out Letty, disliking the insinuation. 'We both knew it wasn't a real marriage.'

Cecily says quickly, 'Of course, quite right. I'm sorry if I implied anything else. But it is quite clear how you feel about each other.'

'Is it?' Letty is filled with a sudden and desperate yearning for Arthur. She hasn't seen him since he kissed her goodnight and promised to see her later today. 'I hope so.'

'I'm pleased. He's a sensible young man. Has he asked you to marry him?'

Letty blushes. 'Yes.'

'Good. And let's hope his writings mean that even if we can't stop the goings-on at the house, we can at least put any more innocent people off the idea of joining in.'

'Yes.' Letty sips her tea. Then she says, 'But you know, despite everything, it was a happy place. I'm going to miss it.'

'Miss it?' Cecily looks outraged. 'How can you?'

'I don't know. But I will.'

Letty is watching the drawing room fire die down to the embers when she hears, at last, the sound of the motor coming up the long drive to the house. Edward is returning and that means he will have Arthur with him. She jumps and runs out of the house, leaving the front door wide open behind her and casting gold light onto the ground. As soon as the car pulls to a stop, Arthur gets out, sees her and opens his arms.

'Come here,' he says simply, and she rushes into his embrace. They stay like that as Edward comes around the car and says:

'Hello, Letty, hope you're feeling better.'

She can't answer, she's too happy to be nestled into Arthur's chest, reunited with him properly and for good at last.

Arthur is staying at the farmhouse but of course there's no question of them sharing a room. They stay up very late, lying together on the drawing room sofa, talking quietly in between their kisses.

'What happened at the police station?' she asks, looking up at him anxiously. 'Did you tell them about the fire?'

He looks down at her, his grey eyes solemn. 'You asked me not to. So I didn't. Much as I wanted to reveal the extent of that man's villainy.'

'We can't be sure. We have no evidence. Arabella would never support me if I accused him, and she's the only witness. It would only be the most awful, terrible scandal. I couldn't face it.'

Arthur sighs. 'I understand. But if he's capable of hurting you and driving Emily to her death, isn't he capable of hurting others?'

'I'm afraid he has a power over others that makes him dangerous. We can't stop that.'

'We could lock him up!' replies Arthur. 'We ought to try.'

'It's my word against his, and Arabella's, and all the rest of them. And I never saw him do it. It could have been someone else. It could have been an accident.'

'Hmm.' Arthur tightens his hold around her for a moment. 'Well, I'll fight him the only way I know – by revealing exactly what he's like in print. The newspaper is interested in my writing a series of eye-witness accounts of what went on in the house. I'll make sure he's turned into a joke. It's the only way you can stop these strutting megalomaniacs getting carried away with their power and causing real harm.' He kisses her again. 'I'm so glad you're away from that man.'

'It's thanks to Arabella I got out of there,' Letty answers. 'She saved me in the end.'

'I never would have thought she'd have it in her.' Arthur thinks for a moment. 'Do you mind very much about what's happened to her?'

'Of course I do. And about the baby. Goodness knows if she'll be able to look after it. You know, in a funny way, I don't think she actually realises she's going to have a child. It doesn't seem to mean anything to her. When the baby finally arrives, she might be in for a shock. I wish I could be there to help her through it.'

'You're a kind soul, Letty. Brave and kind.' He kisses the top of her head tenderly.

'But what about you?' she asks, looking up at him. 'You've lost your parents to the Beloved. I mean, Phillips. And your inheritance.'

Arthur shrugs. 'They're alive and happy enough. It's better that they stay there now. Pa's name is mud in town since the news came out about the place. He's been blackballed from his club, and let go from his firm – not that he's been there in months. The money will be sucked away to Phillips, but all the old ladies will be looked after with it. Worse things could happen than that it keeps a lot of old biddies happy and well stocked with sherry and crumpets while they wait for the great Day.'

'*You're* a kind soul,' Letty says happily.

'Two kind souls together.' He smiles down at her. 'And I rather fancy the idea of being a self-made man. Arthur

Kendall, the great journalist and businessman. And Letty Kendall, the magnificent woman he marries.'

'Yes.' She hugs him tightly. 'Let's get on with living. Right away. We won't waste another moment.'

Chapter Thirty-Seven

The snow rose sits, tiny and exquisite, in its little pot on the windowsill. Its petals are small white trumpets that are beginning to spread out towards full bloom, and its dark green leaves are tiny and almond-shaped. Its gnarly branches twist and bend. It truly is a beautiful little tree.

I don't know what to say to Sissy. I don't understand how she can have known about Heather. It doesn't make any sense.

Matty gets up and goes over to the range to get the kettle, which she fills. 'You look spooked,' she remarks. 'You mustn't be frightened of Sissy. She's got a gift. Some call it intuition, some call it being psychic.' She shoots a look at her sister and says loudly, 'I even call it being nosy. But there's no doubt that she sees things most don't. And it's got stronger since she went blind.'

'How did you go blind, Sissy?' I ask, hoping to divert her away from the thing I most don't want to discuss.

'It was very rum,' Matty says, 'wasn't it, Sis?'

Sissy nods. 'I knocked my head, you see. Bending over to

pick something up, I whacked it on the side of the table. I said at the time, I'm sure I'll go blind. Well, I was fine all that day, but I woke up the next morning and so it was. I couldn't see a thing. And I haven't since.'

'The doctors can't find anything wrong,' puts in Matty. 'That's the strangest part.'

Not wanting to say outright that it looks to me as if she's got perfectly good vision – considering the fact that she can knit, write and all the rest of it – I say, 'But you do so much just as if you can see.'

'That's my gift.' Sissy shrugs. 'That's what helps me do all that.'

I'm not convinced but I don't know what else to say without sounding as if I don't believe her. I manage something inoffensive: 'Well, perhaps you'll wake up one day and you'll be right as rain again. Sometimes it happens like that, doesn't it?'

'It doesn't stop me seeing things that others can't,' Sissy says, turning those blank eyes towards me again. 'That's how I knew about your little girl. I sensed her around you. I felt the weight of your sorrow that she wasn't in this world anymore. She feels it too, very much. She's so sad for your pain. That's why she stayed with you, so you'd have the time you wanted to say goodbye to her.'

I gasp lightly. It's so hard for me to accept the truth. That my little Heather, my angel, my child, really is gone from me, forever. Tears spring to my eyes, blurring my vision. 'I'm sorry,' I say in a broken voice, and the tears rush out of my eyes, pouring down my face as suddenly and fiercely as though an invisible tap has just been turned on. 'I'm so sorry.'

'You need to do it,' Sissy says softly. 'You need to cry. You must mourn her, you must grieve. You haven't yet, have you?'

The sisters look at me with pity. Sissy's kind, quiet voice is too much for me. 'I couldn't bear it,' I say with a sob. 'I couldn't bear for it to have happened.'

'Of course. You must express your sorrow that you'll continue your journey in this physical world without her. But there is comfort. She'll always be with you, walking with you in the spirit world.'

'Will she?'

Sissy nods. 'Oh yes, I can see her now. She's with you. She loves you. She's worried about you.'

'Why can't I see her?' I cry, the tears falling harder. 'I want her so much! I don't want her in the spirit world, I want her here, now. I want her to go to school and parties and play in the park. I want her to grow up, and tell me about the boys she likes and the fashion she wants to wear, and I'll tell her off for piercing her ears and her belly and dying her hair. I want to be at her wedding and hold her hand when she's had her first child. I want all that . . . I want it and it's all been taken away, and it's all my fault because I couldn't save her, and I'm her mother and I couldn't be with her when she needed me and I couldn't save her . . .'

I can't go on. The tears are too strong, the grief too overwhelming. I weep and weep and weep.

*

I don't know how much later it is that the storm subsides, as all storms have to in the end. Matty is beside me, her hand on mine, her other arm around my shoulders. She's pressed tissues into my hand so that I can mop my eyes and stem my streaming nose.

'You need a good blow,' she says comfortingly.

'Yes.' I use the tissue, and sniff. Then I smile weakly. 'I'm sorry.'

'Please don't be,' Sissy says. She's still in the rocking chair but her knitting is on the sideboard and she watches me blindly, rocking gently. 'It needs doing, and why not? It's awful to be left alone in this world, isn't it? Your pain is very great. It won't lessen but it will grow easier to bear, I promise. And you must believe that her essential being – the one that never would have changed no matter how old she got – is with you.'

'I can't stand the pain of losing her.'

'Yes. But you must understand you are not alone in this pain. So many parents have lost their children. So many children have lost their parents. These losses and griefs come to us all at different times. They are part of life, part of our journey.'

I nod, acknowledging the truth of this. Strangely, it helps a little. I think of the photographs and portraits that hang all over this cottage – all people dead and gone. It comes to everyone. I'm not alone. All things pass.

'Is she still here?' I ask, the horrific feeling of loss a little lightened by my outpouring. I want the comfort of knowing that I haven't lost her entirely, as I so feared and dreaded.

'Oh yes. She's very worried about you. She's been trying her best to help you in whatever way she can.' Sissy frowns and seems to be listening to a voice that only she can hear. 'She's been trying to tell you something. It's something you've forgotten.'

I clutch harder to the tissue in my hand. Somewhere, deep down, in the darkness, a knowledge is locked away. Something I've lost and forgotten, something very precious. But . . . I have the mental image of a rusted lock, and a key inserted, about to be turned.

Sissy turns her gaze up to the ceiling, and I feel as though Heather has floated somewhere above her head. 'Ah. She's talking about someone, someone very, very important. What is it . . . who is it, darling? It's . . .' She frowns. 'It's Madam.'

A chill passes over me when I hear that name. I feel something like the sensation of dread I had when Heather said the same word to me. *The invisible friend. The friend from the old home. The one I thought was gone.* I dreaded to hear it because it threatened to break down the imaginary world I'd created with such effort. It could bring everything crashing down, and make Heather disappear. But with the dread is something else: great excitement and wonder as something precious is revealed. The key in the lock starts to turn.

Sissy frowns and shakes her head. 'But Madam isn't a woman. No . . . no . . . it's a little boy. Isn't it, sweetheart? Is that what you're telling me? Yes . . . yes, a little boy. His name is . . .'

'Adam,' I say. 'She called him Madam when she was only little. Adam. My Adam. Madam.' I gasp, a hand flying to my chest. 'Oh my God! Ady!' I get to my feet, giddiness spooling through me but suddenly desperate to move, to leave, to get to the place I'm really supposed to be but had forgotten for all this time. 'I have to go!'

'Yes,' nods Sissy. 'Oh, she's happy now! She's given you her message, and you know what to do now, don't you? There's a good girl, well done!'

I look about, longing so hard to see what Sissy can see. 'Is she here? Is she? How can I leave her?'

'Oh,' says Matty, who's let go of my hand, 'you don't have to worry about her.'

Sissy nods. 'Leave her with us for now. We're a pair of old ghosts ourselves, all that's left of another life. And she'll be with you when you need her. Don't worry about that.'

'Thank you,' I say humbly. 'Thank you for what you've done.'

'You're welcome,' says Sissy. 'You'd better get to that boy of yours. Off you go now. Help is coming.'

Ady. I have to get to him, if there's still time.

I run out of the cottage and down the path, thinking of the car. I'll get the keys and go right now. I'm still shaky but I should be able to drive. I have to get back as fast as I can. If I were too late, I could never forgive myself.

Something else I couldn't forgive.

I run around the side of the house and come out at the front. A large van is there and several of the house members are unloading supplies.

More stuff to fend off the end of the world. And in all the big happenings and the visions of disaster, the less dramatic pains and losses and broken hearts that make up a life get forgotten. That girl, Kaia, crying because she loves someone who can't love her back.

I dash through the front door, flying past the people inside to my room, where I pick up my bag, scrabbling for the car key in the bottom. I pack as quickly as I can, stuffing things in without folding them. I'm more careful with Heather's things, restoring the little suitcase to neatness, her washbag and puffin on the top. When I've finished, I look around at the empty room, with all traces of Heather and me removed. It's strange to think that I haven't left this place since the night I arrived what seems like a lifetime ago. Then, it was silent and deserted. Now, it's full of activity and filled with inhabitants. I don't belong here now, and no matter how seductive Archer's message of safety and protection might be, I have to face the challenges that lie ahead of me.

I gather up the bags and race outside to the car, which looks sadly neglected, a film of gravel dust all over it. Once I've put the bags in the boot and I'm in the driver's seat, I turn the ignition and the engine comes to life. My hands are trembling and I know that I need to calm down if I'm going to make the drive back safely. I start to reverse so that I can turn round to face the entrance, then manoeuvre so that I'm ready to leave this strange and seductive place.

Is Heather going to stay here? I wonder. Sissy's words echo around my head. I find some comfort in the idea that if she is here, there are people to look after her. It was my dread of surrendering her to the darkness and isolation of death that made me cling to her so tightly. I feel that I can, just a little, let her go. *But she'll always be with me. I have to remember that.*

Besides, I have a son who needs me. I remember Heather talking to me about Madam, not letting me forget her brother, telling me outright that he was alive. She wanted me to go to him, that's what Sissy said. I hope I'm making her happy by leaving.

Her words float back into my mind: *Madam says help is coming.*

Maybe help was here all along.

I change into first gear and go to press my foot on the accelerator. Just then, a car roars into the driveway through the wrought-iron gates, sending up a spray of stones. My insides spin as I recognise it.

It's Rory's car.

Chapter Thirty-Eight

My dearest Letty,

It is the hardest thing in the world to accept that, after all this tragedy, we are not to have what is rightfully ours returned to us. It is evident that Arabella was not in her right mind when she died, and hadn't been for years. Her will leaving everything to the community led by that imposter is surely invalid. Edward and I intend to challenge it through the courts. We will not rest until that frightful man has been sent packing, and the house is ours again.

In many ways, I believe it is what Arabella wanted. Surely she intended for her son to have his inheritance. Though I suppose his illegitimate status and unfortunate parentage would have made this difficult. Perhaps that is why she appointed you and Arthur his guardian.

The coroner's court was a miserable place to be, particularly as so few of the people who had benefited from her largesse could be bothered to attend. There was a maid, who testified as to Arabella's extreme depth of depression and her morbid spirits. She said Arabella was afraid she might hurt the child and refused to be left alone with it. It's hardly surprising she felt desperate, with all the madness and preaching of doom and destruction around her. No doubt she needed the love and support of a normal family and that was sadly lacking. That monster of selfishness would have thought only of himself. Indeed, we've heard that he has already married again. Our only comfort is that he is a laughing stock thanks to Arthur's articles. Let us hope that no one else is fooled as Arabella was. The verdict of suicide while of unsound mind was what we expected. I shudder whenever I think of her walking into the lake like that, knowing she would never come back. She must have been suffering very much. Let us hope she is at peace.

How are you getting on with the baby? He did seem a sweet little thing, such a pet. We will try to be generous and forget his father, and think of him only as yours. I'm glad you are giving him your surname and raising him as your own child. With you and Arthur he will have the very best of starts. Any inheritance from the rogue will, I'm sure, be entirely eradicated by your benign influence and we will see an end to any more of this unfortunate eccentricity.

We have seen the photographs of your wedding, which arrived just last week. How beautiful and radiant you looked, and Arthur so happy. You will make a success of your life together, I'm certain.

Things continue well here. I'm uncomfortable with the

baby and now await the arrival with much anticipation if only to be free of the burden. It remains cold.

    With much love,
    Cecily

Chapter Thirty-Nine

Caz navigates and Rory drives as fast as he dares, both eager to reach Kate as quickly as possible, but when they finally arrive, he stops the car just outside and looks anxiously at Caz.

'Are you sure?' he asks. 'This is it?'

Caz doesn't know what they were expecting but an endless stretch of stone wall with thick rhododendron bushes obscuring the view beyond and a pair of high wrought-iron gates was not what she'd imagined. They knew Kate was in a house that needed a caretaker, and Caz had conjured up a rather municipal building, maybe in the middle of a town.

She checks the address she's written down. 'This is the place. I'm certain.'

Rory fires up the engine and takes the turn into the driveway, accelerating along the stretch before the house as if gripped by a strange compulsion to get there even faster. There is the house, a huge and magnificent place, with ornate brickwork, towering chimneys, gables and large bay-fronted windows. Caz stares at it, impressed and also bewildered.

This is where she's been living? It's a mansion. In front is a van with its back doors open for unloading. And then she sees it: a dusty dark blue car, with the registration she noted down from the hire company's emails. And Kate is sitting in the driving seat, her hands on the steering wheel. At least, it must be her. Who else can it be?

'She's there!' Caz says urgently. The car has barely pulled to a halt but she's unbelting and the door is half open before Rory has had time to clock the car. 'Quick! We can't let her drive off!'

She's out like a shot, running across the gravel towards the car, terrified that Kate will rev the engine and be gone, out of the front gate before they can stop her. Caz can see it's her now. She's staring out of the windscreen with huge, frightened eyes, her hair a strange vivid white so intense Caz thinks at first she's wearing a hat. She looks thinner but Caz would know her anywhere. She reaches the car and stands in front of it, flinging her arms across the bonnet, daring Kate to run her down.

'Kate, it's us, we're here! Don't leave, Kate, please! We need to talk to you.'

She stares at Caz dumbly as if unable to believe her eyes and then, just when Caz is afraid that she will try to shake her off by driving forward, she turns off the engine and gets out of the car. Her demeanour is incredibly agitated, her hands shaking. 'Caz, you have to let me go!' she cries out in a high, anxious voice. 'I've got to get home. I've got to get back to Ady before it's too late. Don't stand in my way, I'm warning you!'

Caz runs to her and clutches her arms. 'It's okay. You don't have to rush. He's fine, I promise. Look.' She glances to where Rory is getting slowly out of the car, his race to find Kate suddenly slowed almost to a stop. 'Rory's here,' she says softly. 'He wants to see you.'

Kate gasps, her skin turning even paler. *What's happened to her?* Caz wonders. *She looks awful.* And yet, without that manic intensity she had before she went, she seems, in a vital way, better, even if utterly drained. 'Rory,' she whispers. She closes her eyes with an expression of dread on her face.

'He wants to help you, he always has,' Caz says urgently. 'Please, Kate, let him help you.'

She shakes her head. 'No. He mustn't help me.'

He's walking across the gravel with slow, steady crunching footsteps, his eyes fixed on her, drinking her in. 'Hello, Kate,' he says, stopping a short distance from her as if wary of her reaction to him.

'Rory,' she says faintly. 'How did you find me?'

'Caz managed to trace you.'

She looks at Caz with a hint of reproach but says nothing.

'We've missed you,' he says. 'We want you to come home to us. I've been so worried.'

She drops her eyes and stares at the gravel. Caz can see that whatever is wrong is not yet fixed. Something has changed but not everything.

'Kate wants to get back to Ady,' Caz explains, anxious that Rory understands this breakthrough. 'Isn't that great?'

Rory's eyes fill at once with tears. He manages a smile. 'Oh, yes. That's fantastic news. That's amazing. He really wants to see you, Kate. He's missed you. Come back with us and we'll see him together just as he wants.'

She carries on staring, standing incredibly still. 'No,' she says at last, in a small voice. 'I'll go. But I'll go alone. I'll stay for as long as Ady needs me. Then . . . I don't know. Perhaps I'll come back here.'

'He'll need you for years and years,' Rory says. 'And I need you too.'

She looks so anguished, Caz wants to weep for her. 'No . . . I'm no good, Rory. We need to be apart.'

'But why?' he asks. He takes another step towards her. 'I know I failed you and I know I should have been honest with you. I beat myself up for it every day, because if I hadn't, maybe things would have been different. I am so truly, deeply sorry. I'll never, ever lie to you again, I promise. But I love you, I always have. You're my wife and Ady's mother, and Heather's mother.' His voice trembles on their daughter's name. 'And you and I are the only people in the world who are their parents. Don't let what happened destroy every-thing, Kate, please . . .'

'You don't understand!' Kate says wretchedly. 'You don't know the truth.'

'I know you've been through hell, because I have too. And I know that it's taken you to a dark place where you couldn't deal with Ady's state. I understand it, and I'm not angry.' He spreads out his hands. 'I just want us to be together.'

Caz thinks she should walk discreetly away. This conver-sation is too private and personal for her to listen to. But just then, a loud voice rings out.

'Rachel, are these people bothering you?'

Caz turns to see a young man coming down the steps in front of the grand front door. He's wearing jeans and a zip-up hooded top in soft navy blue brushed cotton and trainers, and he has flowing locks and a beard, looking like a handsome biblical prophet. Behind him are more good-looking young people: a woman with short blonde hair and blazing blue eyes, a Sloaney type with a ski tan and glossy caramel highlights, and three or four others, including a well-built bloke in a vest. They have defiant and hostile looks in their eyes.

Kate watches them approach, a faint stain of red appearing on her cheeks.

'Well?' calls the leader, frowning. He's got the kind of blue eyes it's hard to ignore, the kind that seem to look into your soul. 'Are they annoying you? We can get rid of them if you want.'

'No, no . . .' Kate stammers out a reply, looking awkward. 'They're not exactly bothering me.'

Caz looks at Rory, who is watching the new arrivals with suspicion. 'If you must know, this is my wife.'

'Oh really?' The young man grins, and gives Kate an amused glance that seems to contain some private message. 'Rachel's partner? You're a lucky guy.'

'Why are you calling her Rachel?' demands Rory. He evidently has not taken to this man's cocksure attitude.

'Rachel Capshaw?' Caz asks suddenly.

'Yes,' the young man says. 'Rachel Capshaw. She's a member of our community, aren't you, Rachel?'

To Caz's astonishment, Kate nods and says, 'Yes. That's

465

right. Archer's doing some important work here, about climate change and energy shortages and . . .' – she seems to falter a little –'. . . and war. And stuff like that.'

'Are you some kind of research institute?' Rory asks, frowning.

The man seems amused and turns to look at his followers, one eyebrow raised. 'Yeah, that's right,' he drawls, and Caz notices how very posh his voice is. 'We're an institute. And we're carrying out a lot of important research in utopias and ideal human behaviours. If you're lucky, we might let you stay and join in.'

Kate says suddenly, 'I have to go, Archer. My boy needs me. I just found out.'

'You want to go?' Archer looks dubious. He stuffs his hands into the pockets of his hoody as he thinks. 'Well, we'll have to see about that. I don't usually allow new recruits to leave until their initiation is complete.'

'What are you talking about?' Rory demands. Caz can see his irritation levels rising. 'My wife can go wherever she wants to go.'

'You should stop calling her that,' says the ski-tan girl. 'It's offensive.'

The bloke in the vest says, 'We don't allow terms like "my wife". No one owns anyone here. We all share each other equally.'

'That's right,' Archer says. 'It's all about sharing. And once you're in, you're in. And when you're out . . .'

Caz puts out a hand towards Rory, who has flushed red. 'Stay calm, it's not worth getting upset about.'

He doesn't appear to hear her, but turns his back on Archer and the gang listening to his every word. 'Come on, Kate,' he says. 'Let's get in the car and get on our way. You want to see Ady, don't you?'

She looks over at him. 'Yes. But I must go alone. You can't get used to us being together, because it won't last.'

Caz gasps a little at the sharpness in her words, and glances at Rory. He looks deeply hurt.

'She belongs here now,' says Archer. 'She's one of us.' He reaches out and grabs Kate by the hand. 'I'll take you to the hospital, Rachel, and bring you back afterwards. I can take you every day if you like.'

'Oh, shut the hell up!' cries Rory, unable to stand him anymore. 'What business is it of yours, anyhow? You're nothing to do with us. Nothing.'

'I think you'll find I am. Rachel has listened and accepted and joined with us in body and spirit. This is where she belongs.' He turns back to Kate. 'Your boy can come and live here with us when he's better. He'll be safe here.' He gives her a warning look. 'You know what's coming.'

Kate looks agonised, confused. She says in a small voice, 'He'll be safe here?'

'He'll be *saved*,' Archer says in a tone of utmost confidence.

'Bring him to us,' says the girl, with a happy smile, holding out a hand to Kate.

'This is rubbish!' shouts Rory, his face reddening with anger. 'Don't listen to him, Kate. Just come home with me, right now.'

Caz sees the expression on Kate's face and knows at once

that she is close to her limit. She says, 'Can everyone stop ordering Kate around? The important thing is that she gets to Ady right now!'

'Well,' Archer says, staring at her. 'What is it to be, Rachel? In or out? You're free to leave, but once you go, you're on the outside, with all the other poor fools who didn't heed the call.'

She looks at him, her eyes full of sadness. 'It sounds so good. Like paradise. But you can't make any promises that really mean anything. You can't get rid of pain, and sickness, and sadness and death.'

'You've been happy here,' he says indignantly.

'You gave me lots of attention. You gave me drugs to keep me calm and soothed. You told me that everyone is happy here. But what about Kaia, crying because she loves you? What about the sadness you never let me feel? You never let me grieve. You never even talked to me about Heather. Only Sissy and Matty did that. Your paradise isn't real, because it can't be. You can't save anyone, not in the way you want.'

Archer's face is hardening, the expressions of his followers becoming more wide-eyed and appalled as Kate talks.

'I'm sorry you think this way, Rachel,' he says. 'I thought I saw promise in you. I guess I was wrong. You're just like all the other idiots in the world. Good luck to you. You'll be begging me to take you in one day soon, and I'll take pleasure in watching you grovel and die with your boy in the street while we're safe in here.'

Caz is appalled, anger racing up inside her. She shouts, 'How dare you talk to her like that? I'll have the bloody newspapers here tomorrow, to show you up as the doomsday bloody mongering shit you are! Can't you see she's in pieces?'

Rory yells, 'You've got no control over her, she's free to do what she likes! Stop brainwashing her, you bastard!' He looks like he's going to hit Archer. The bloke in the vest takes a step forward, his expression menacing and his fists clenched.

'Will you all leave me alone?' screams Kate. 'All of you! I need to see Ady!' She screws her eyes shut as if she's about to burst into tears.

Caz puts herself between the heavy and Rory. 'This isn't helping, Rory. I'll drive Kate to the hospital, if that's what she wants.'

Rory turns away from Archer and says urgently to Kate, 'What do you think? Would that work?'

She opens her eyes. 'Yes. I have to see Ady. I'm going now, Archer. That's all there is to it.'

Archer shrugs. 'You've made your choice. Just remember, there's no coming back. No return.'

Kate says clearly, 'I choose life. Not a fantasy.' Then she turns to Caz. 'Shall we go?'

'Yes.' Caz holds her hand out to her friend. 'Let's go right now.'

Caz drives carefully; this is a hire car and she's not a named driver. Kate sits beside her, silent and hunched, watching the road ahead anxiously. Rory follows in his car and Caz keeps him in the rear-view mirror, unobtrusively making sure that he stays with them all the way back. It's a fairly long trip home and, for all of it, Kate barely speaks. She seems exhausted by the confrontation they've just had. Caz asks a few questions but gets no more than grunts in response. They stop at a motorway service station for petrol, drinks and the loo, and Caz gets a sandwich, but Kate doesn't seem hungry. Rory is there at a distance, and Caz signals to him discreetly when they are leaving. The day is drawing on. It's going to be late when they get back but Caz is sure that the hospital will let her in to see Ady.

It's dark when they finally pull into the hospital pay-and-display car park, empty at this time of night. They go up to the ward, with Caz leading the way as she knows it so well. Kate seems dazed by the reality of being in this huge, labyrinthine place and follows her closely like a little child. At the reception desk Caz quietly explains the situation to the nurses. They are delighted to see Kate, knowing how much Ady has longed for his mother. Caz and Kate sign in and sanitise their hands, leaving their outdoor things in the ward entrance. Then a nurse leads them along the corridor to Ady's room. He's on his own because of a risk of infection. A small light glows next to his bed through slatted blinds that cover the glass walls. At the door, the nurse pauses and says quietly, 'He may be asleep. Give him a second to come to.' Then she opens the door.

There he is. Ady is lying on his back in his bed, half propped up on pillows, his head turned towards the electrical equipment he's hooked up to. A drip feeds into his arm via a long snaking tube, and there are the soft beeps and chirps of the machines as they monitor him. His fair hair shines in the dim light, and he looks so peaceful, despite the bandages on his head where they operated.

Kate stares, a strange whimper sounding in the back of her throat when she first sets eyes on him. She draws in a deep breath. Caz wonders what is going through her mind. For a while, she seemed to have erased Adam from her mind completely. But here he is, alive and getting better, still so perfect despite his injuries.

Kate clutches Caz, digging her fingers into her arm. Just as Caz is wondering how they will wake Ady, his blue eyes open and he turns his head slowly to see Kate standing at the door. He blinks and smiles, a huge beam lighting up his face. Then he says, 'Mummy. I knew you'd come.'

Chapter Forty

Caz leaves me at my house and rings for a taxi to take her home. While I sit rather dazed on the sofa, she hurries about, turning on the heating, making me a cup of black coffee – there's no milk in the fridge – and worrying about how I'll cope.

'I'll be fine,' I say.

'You should eat,' she declares. 'What have you had today? You need to get some strength back.' When she sees how little that means to me, she adds cleverly, 'Ady needs you to eat. You have to be strong for him.'

'There's some pasta in the cupboard,' I say, 'and a jar of bolognaise sauce. I'll have that. I can go shopping tomorrow.'

'You won't go back to that weirdy beardy bloke and his gang, will you?' she asks.

'I will go back,' I say firmly. 'I have to. But I won't neces-sarily see Archer. You don't have to worry, I'm not going to join a cult and get brainwashed or anything.'

'What's he doing there anyway?' she asks, looking in the

cupboard under the stairs and pulling out a bottle of red wine from the rack. 'Do you want some of this?'

I shrug.

'I'm having a glass. I need it.' She goes to the small kitchen to rummage for a corkscrew. This place is tiny but it was fine for my needs. I'll need somewhere bigger when Ady comes back. Caz returns with two glasses of wine and puts one in front of me. 'So . . . who was that guy?'

I tell her a bit about Archer and what I discovered about his theories and the group dynamic. Caz listens, half impressed and half amused.

'Polyamorous preppers,' she says, sipping her wine. 'No . . . *posh* polyamorous preppers. How brilliant. I bet the papers would have a field day.'

'He talked a lot of sense,' I say. 'At least, that's what it felt like at the time. It all seemed to fall into place. And when he did his healing on me, it really worked. I felt it – the strength and light going into me and making things better.'

'They can all heal you, if you want them to,' Caz says, more seriously. 'It's the wanting that matters. Maybe you needed someone like him to help you come to terms with everything.'

'Yes, maybe.' I think of how incredibly vivid it had been to live with Heather at the house, how real. And what a desolate gulf of nothingness was left when I was jerked out of my fantasy. I did need someone to pour light and life into it, to bring me back from the brink. And he did. But I knew in my heart that the safety he was offering me was an illusion, just another way for me to escape my pain.

'Shall I make you that pasta?' she asks, getting up.

'No, I can do it. Honestly, you go. I'm so tired. I'll go to bed in a bit as I'm good for nothing. I can't talk.'

'Another time?' she asks, and drains her glass. 'I'm always here for you if you need me.'

I smile at her. 'I know that, Caz. Thanks. Thanks for sticking by me through the bad times.'

'I'll be here as things get better, but no one expects anything. You're under no pressure. You have a lot to deal with, and if you need time, that's fine. It's yours. You don't have to run away again.'

'I know. Thanks.'

Caz's taxi comes and she heads off into the night. The hire car sits on the driveway: my one-time ticket to freedom from all the grief and despair. Now here I am, back again. But I know it's the right thing. I'm about to shut the front door when I see a shadowy figure coming up the path.

'Kate?'

It's Rory, looking tired but intense.

'How long have you been here?' I ask.

'I followed you back from the hospital. I've been waiting till Caz left. I have to talk to you.'

'There's no point. Really.'

'Was it really so bad, what I did, that you can't forgive me, even now? I thought that what we've lost would make all those quarrels and stupid deceptions seem like they didn't matter.' His face is so full of anguish, I can hardly look at it. 'I've been so desperate to see you, and to bring you back to

474

Ady. We can be a family again . . . can't we? Can you really not forgive me?'

'It's not you that needs forgiveness,' I say simply.

'I don't understand.'

I take a deep breath. I've been running from this for so long, hoping that as long as I didn't tell, I didn't have to face it. But I've known in my heart that it will have to come out. I hold the front door open wider. 'You'd better come in.'

'There's a lot I haven't told you,' I say, when we are sitting down together, him on the sofa and me in the armchair. 'I was just so wounded when you kept that huge secret from me. It made me feel like our marriage had been a failure because you'd never really trusted me. I felt that you'd married me because I was bossy and practical and would get things done, and you could sit back and just . . . put up with me. The real bond, the trust, the communication, the sense that we're a team ready to face the world and protect each other . . . I lost all of it. And I stopped being able to tell you things in return. It was all so terrible.'

'I know,' Rory says. His expression shows a yearning to communicate his understanding.

It's taken all this to make him talk to me, openly, honestly. What a price to pay for it.

He's talking intensely now. 'I'm sorry. I've learned so much from it. I've taken a look at myself and I didn't like what I saw. I know I have to take more responsibility for myself and for our relationship and our life together. You're right that I did take you for granted – I took your strength for granted.

When I lost my job, I thought you'd be angry, and I'm not good at dealing with that, as you know, but I never guessed you'd be so hurt. To me, you're confident and capable and fearless. I forgot you're also frightened sometimes, and in need of reassurance and looking after. I'm so sorry I didn't see it. I wish with all my heart I had.'

'But it makes no difference,' I say, moved by his heartfelt words. 'Because it wasn't you, in the end, who did the terrible thing. It was me.'

'What do you mean? What did you do?'

'The fire. I caused it. By accident, of course. But it was me. I killed Heather. I let Ady jump and nearly be killed.' My face contorts when I remember it. 'I was alone and feeling sorry for myself, and I had a bottle of wine when the kids were in bed. I didn't mean to. I just kept refilling the glass. I lit the candles in the snug, and I watched TV with my drink. Then I got up to go to the loo and after that, I turned off the lights and went to bed. But I never went back to blow out the candles.' I stop, trembling with the power of the memory. 'The smoke alarm woke me up, the one by the stairs. I'd . . . I'd taken the battery out of the kitchen one the day before when I was frying bacon, you know how it kept going off, and I hadn't put it back. So it was the stairs one that went off. I could smell the smoke. I ran down and saw . . .' I screw my eyes shut, my voice wavering, but I know I have to go on. 'I saw the whole kitchen in flames, licking the ceiling, attacking it, and I knew Heather's room was just above, so I went running as fast as I could, back to the stairs, past our room and round the corner and there it was, already there, the smoke.

So thick, so hot. I tried to battle it but it was impossible, like banging against a brick wall. I tried to reach her door but I couldn't even touch the handle. I could have gone to Ady, but I kept thinking he'd come out, because I was shouting and the alarm was going, but he didn't come. I didn't go to him. I couldn't. I let him down like no mother should. I think that's why I blanked him out.' I look miserably at Rory. 'It was my fault. The candles. And I left Ady when I could have tried to reach him. All of it, my fault. That's why we lost Heather. I couldn't bear it. I had to shut it all out, all of it, all except Heather, who was gone.'

'Oh Kate. I didn't realise . . . I didn't understand.' Tears run down Rory's cheeks. At last he wipes his eyes, and says, 'You don't know it was the candles. The forensic people said it was probably electrical.'

'No, it was the candles. I know it.'

'You don't know that. Maybe you blew them out before you came upstairs, and forgot. You were woozy but not so out of it you didn't know what you were doing. It's like locking the back door at night or turning on the dishwasher. You don't remember doing it, but you just do it automatically.'

'No,' I say dully. 'It was my fault. That's why we can't be together anymore.'

Rory wipes his eyes and says firmly, 'No. No! That's why we should be together. Whether it was the candles or not. The terrible things in life can bond us as deeply as the good, if we turn them around and take what we can from them. You can't change it, Kate. We can't blame anyone for a horrific accident. All we need is to acknowledge it, share the burden, forgive everything, and move on, taking whatever good we can find from the darkness.' There's a long pause and he says, 'I'm so happy you're back. We have Ady and we have to help him now. There is a difficult road ahead. I'd like to walk it with you, if I can.'

I stare at the floor for a while. The confession I thought would break me has not. Instead, I feel deeply tired but unburdened of something foul that has oppressed me for weeks. He's right. I will never know if I caused the fire. But to admit my terrible guilt and fear that I did, and to remember that moment on the stairs when I had to choose who to go to, is a step towards absolution, and returning to myself.

'Heather helped me,' I say suddenly, looking up at him.

'You've seen her?'

I nod. 'In my mind, I suppose. And in my dreams.'

'Me too.' Rory smiles wanly. 'It's a tricky one, isn't it? It's so lovely to see her again, but it also hurts so much too. Ady told me she'd been with him as well. That's why he was so sure you'd come.'

'She told me to come back,' I say. 'She said Adam needed me.'

'Her gift of love to you and him maybe.' Rory smiles again. 'I know she's dead and gone, but I also know she'll always be with us.'

'Yes.' Tears rise to my eyes and blur my vision. 'We loved her so much, didn't we?'

He gets up and comes over and hugs me tightly. 'Yes,' he says thickly. 'We always will.'

I hug him back, taking comfort from his solidity and presence, and I remember how I longed for him that night with Archer. 'Rory, while I was away—' I begin.

'Shh. You can tell me about it all another time. Let's start again from today and look forward, not back.'

I bury my face in his neck. I've missed him. His touch fills me with peace and his love comforts me. Perhaps, despite the deceptions and the misunderstandings, I can let myself love him again too. 'Yes,' I murmur. 'Forward. Not back.'

'Then . . . you'll give us another chance?'

'It's too soon to know. Give me time.' I pull back and manage a smile. 'But maybe. That's all I can say right now.'

'Maybe is enough for me. I'll wait as long as you need.' And he hugs me tight to his heart.

Epilogue

In Nursery Cottage, Sissy is in her favourite armchair by the range, her needles clacking as usual, the wool beneath growing ever longer.

Matty comes in, sighing and shaking her head. 'More deliveries at the house! What do they want with all that stuff? I don't understand it.'

'He won't let up. He's driven, that one,' says Sissy. 'We know the kind all too well. We wouldn't be here at all, otherwise.'

Matty says, 'I'll make tea.' As she puts the kettle on, there's a sudden rapid knock at the door. Matty jumps. 'Are you expecting company?' she asks.

Sissy shakes her head. 'You'd better answer it,' she says as the knocking comes again.

Matty goes to the door and opens it. On the doorstep stands a handsome young man in jeans and a T-shirt, his muscled arms smooth and tanned.

'Hi!' he says. 'I thought it was time to introduce myself. Can I come in?'

Matty stands back to let him in. 'You're Archer Kendall,' she says as he enters, looking about with interest at the mountain of stuff inside, the remnants of the life that is now long gone.

'That's right.' He shakes his head. 'Wow. Look at all this. It's great.' His eye is caught by a fine oil portrait in an oval frame. It shows a white-haired man with piercing blue eyes and a brown complexion, staring fiercely out of the canvas. He goes up to it and stares. 'Is this him?'

'Who?' asks Matty. Sissy is watching from her chair, her dark gaze fixed on Archer.

'The last dispensation. The Beloved.'

'Yes,' Matty says.

Archer whistles. 'So that's him. My grandfather.'

'Oh no,' Matty says quickly. 'Not your grandfather. Your great-uncle. By marriage.'

Archer looks round, his expression pleasant. 'No. Actually that's not true. I'm not a Kendall by blood. I'm one of you. One of the holy family.'

Matty gapes at him. 'What? How?'

Sissy says slowly, 'But of course. The baby they took away. The one the Beloved said was a miraculous conception and then claimed as his own when Arabella Evans died. Don't you remember, Matty, they talked about the day he was taken away by the Evans family? That was your father?'

Archer nods. 'He was adopted by the Kendalls. It's all in the family papers. They came to me when I inherited. Lettice's account of the house, her sister's letters, all of it. You're welcome to read it sometime, if you're interested. So of course I had to have the house. It's only fitting. I'm sure you can understand that. And I've changed the name back to Paradise as well.'

'A different sort of paradise this time, I'm sure,' Matty says drily, 'if the noise from the church is anything to go by.'

Archer looks serene. He clearly doesn't intend to let the sisters rile him. 'So. This portrait . . . is it for sale?'

'No,' says Sissy firmly. 'It's not.'

'Shame. Let me know if you ever change your mind. I'll buy anything you've got. Well . . . it's been very nice to meet you . . .' Archer raises his eyebrows questioningly. 'I don't think we've been properly introduced.'

'Miss Matty Henson,' says Matty, 'and Miss Sissy Henson. We are the Beloved's grandchildren, by his third wife. His daughter Glory, our mother, married George Henson. That's the connection, if you're wondering.' She gives him a beady look. 'And we hope you're not going to start all those games again. Are you?'

'Games?'

'You want to make people do what you want,' Sissy says. 'You think you're the new Beloved, don't you?'

Archer smiles and says, 'I've got to be going now. But I just wanted to let you know that we're cousins. And if you ever need shelter, you can come to the house. You'll always be welcome there. When the end comes.'

When he's gone, the sisters sit in silence for a while. At last, Matty shakes her head. 'I can't believe we're going to see it start all over again. And he's the Beloved's own grandson!'

'Well, that explains it. It must be in the blood, the desire to be the centre of attention, to make promises that the world takes notice of. Perhaps what happened to our Beloved will happen to this one. He'll run his little kingdom and not trouble the outside too much.'

'I'm not sure, Sissy. It's a different place now, with all the technology and the computers and whatnot. People don't live the way we did, all shut off. There are connections now, all over the world. And what if this one is right, and there is trouble coming?'

Sissy tuts. 'You're starting to fall for it already. You watch, it will be the same thing all over again, just a bit different. The world changes, Matty. And yet it stays the same. War, pain, disease and death, all the fear and hatred. But it's balanced by compassion and love and a search for peace. Even though the Beloved was wrong, the ladies here had a happy life. Maybe it will be the same again. It all goes on, over and over.'

There's another long pause and Matty says, 'Do you think that poor lady has found her peace?'

'Matty, I think she has. She knows that life must go on, and that hiding here is no way to do it. She was tempted, I think. It's easier to shut your mind to things than to face them. We know that. It's the story of our family. It's why we're here, alone, at the end of our lives.'

'Are we alone?' asks Matty, looking about. 'Is the little one here?'

'Not today. She comes and goes. We'll see her less and less, I suspect. That's as it should be.' Sissy knits on, rocking gently back and forth.

'And will we see the poor lady again?'

'Oh yes. She'll be back. And when she comes, I might give her the snow rose. What do you think of that?'

'That's a lovely idea, Sissy. Yes. Let's do that.'

'To remind her she's not alone. The little one is with her.' Sissy nods. 'Yes. That's what we'll do.'

On the sideboard, the snow rose is fully open now, more delicate and more exquisite than ever.

Acknowledgements

Once again, my great thanks to everyone at Pan Macmillan, in particular the marvellous Wayne Brookes, my editor, who is so incredibly supportive and brilliant; and to Alex Saunders, always kind, cheerful and helpful. I'd like to thank Katie James and everyone in the publicity department, and Amy Lines and the fabulous marketing department. Thank you, of course, to the sales force for their amazing championing of their books. I love the warm welcome and great atmosphere at Pan Macmillan whenever I visit.

Huge thanks to Anne O'Brien for a sensitive and clever edit; to Gill Paul for taking time out of her own very busy writing schedule to read the draft and provide valuable input; and to Lorraine Green for her usual excellent and thoughtful copy edit. The encouragement of all of these people really buoys me up when I'm flagging.

Particular thanks to Tina Mitchell, for her very helpful insights into forensic science and protocols in the case of fire.

I also salute the lovely SWANs of the South West, who have provided so much fun, laughter, support and book gossip over the last year. Little did I know that leaving London would open up this rich vein of friendship and new comrades.

Thank you to my wonderful agent Lizzy Kremer, Agent of the Year 2016 – and every year, in my opinion – Harriet Moore, and all at David Higham Associates.

Thank you to my new neighbours and friends who have proved so supportive, in particular to everyone at Winstone's Bookshop (Independent Bookseller of the Year 2016!). Also to the magnificent Marcus, manager of Waterstones in Yeovil. I'm very much enjoying being involved in West Country literary life; there is so much enthusiasm and interest in books and writing.

Thanks to those who contact me via Twitter and Facebook to send their support, it's wonderful to hear when someone has read and enjoyed a book.

And of course, thank you to my family for all their love and encouragement, in particular to James, Barney and Tabby.

Lulu Taylor
Dorset 2016

THE WINTER CHILDREN

Behind a selfless act of kindness lie dark intentions

Olivia and Dan Felbeck's dreams of a family are finally fulfilled on the birth of their twins. The longed-for babies mark a new and happy stage in their lives.

Soon after, Dan's oldest friend, Francesca, offers them the chance to live at Renniston Hall, an Elizabethan house that she is renovating. They can stay rent-free in a small part of the unmodernized house, which was once a girls' boarding school.

The couple accept, and just as they are enjoying the family life that they have craved for so long, Francesca arrives at the Hall and doesn't seem to want to leave. What exactly happened between Dan and Francesca years ago at Cambridge? As Olivia wonders how well she knows her husband, she starts to suspect that her perfect life could be built on a lie.

Meanwhile, Renniston Hall holds dark mysteries of its own, and slowly the old house starts to surrender its long-held secrets . . .

Praise for Lulu Taylor

'Utterly compelling. A really excellent winter's story'
LUCY DIAMOND

extracts reading groups
competitions books new
discounts extracts extracts
competitions discounts
books new extracts
events books
extracts new titles reading groups
interviews events
events extracts
discounts
new books events
events new
discounts extracts discounts
www.panmacmillan.com
extracts events reading groups
competitions books extracts new

reading groups
books

reading groups